ISLAND LOVE:

CORTES CONNECTION

BY VANESSA MATELAND

Cortes Connection

Copyright © 2015 by Vanessa Mateland and
Seapoint Publishing

The Cortes Connection, a passenger/parcel service between
Cortes and Vancouver Island, has graciously agreed to the use of
their name for the title.

ISBN 13: 978-1507888353

Library of Congress Control Number: 2015904192
CreateSpace Independent Publishing Platform,
North Charleston, SC

Seapoint Publishing

2880 Sea Point Dr, B.C. V8N1S8

vanessamateland@gmail.com

Praise for
Cortes Connection and Vanessa Mateland

In Mateland's romance novel, a kayak trip through the Victoria, Canada, region comes alive through the eyes of two lovers.

Dr. Juli Armstrong needs a break from her high-intensity practice, and what better way than a guided ocean kayak tour? Despite the advice of her best friend, who wants Juli to meet a man, Juli is convinced she's there for her own enjoyment...until she gets partnered up with Dr. Richard Thompson, an arrogant, overbearing doctor from rural Cortes Island. She wants peace and quiet, not commands from a man who isn't even her tour guide. However, once others abandon the trip, he actually does become her tour guide. Rich loves his rural island practice, but working constantly for the last several years has taken a toll on his health. He wants a break, and the kayak trip is exactly what he needs . . . Both Juli and Rich are reluctant to trust, but their souls are drawn to each other, pulling them together despite the differences and challenges between them.

The relationship between Juli and Rich is believable, fraught with real-life difficulties. Their emotional growth is complex, with the stops and starts of real life as they try to change and evolve.

. . . The author does a fantastic job bringing the setting to life, providing vivid detail about all aspects of the region . . . an enjoyable romantic adventure with a strong conclusion.

-Kirkus Reviews

Dedication

This book is dedicated to my mother

Gertrude Lydia

who has always enjoyed romance novels.

ISLAND LOVE:

CORTES CONNECTION

BY VANESSA MATELAND

Cortes Connection

PROLOGUE

Wilderness Kayaking in the Discovery Islands
*Come and experience pristine cerulean waters
* Overnight on Read and Cortes Islands
*Slippery seals, soaring eagles
* Kayak paddling instruction
* All equipment supplied
* Gourmet meals
* Expert guide

January twenty-first, after a flu-filled shift at the treatment center and a dangerous ride home on her bike through cold northerly winds and driving rain, Dr. Juliet Armstrong stared at the colorful cover of this brochure promising her wilderness beauty.

Juliet weighed the pros and cons as she always did. On the plus side she would breathe healthy air, learn a new skill - kayaking, and have a firsthand look at ocean wild life. On the negative side, the weather might be rainy or she wouldn't like being cooped up in a small kayak.

Right now she needed something to look forward to and thought this might be it. There was no mention of traffic or sick people. She was sure the other paddlers would be athletic, healthy, and interesting and she could handle gourmet meals and pristine waters and slippery seals. While she read, something began to grow deep inside her, starting as a warm feeling in her abdomen and spreading to her chest followed by a flash of excitement in her brain.

The next day before she registered, she consulted her friend Marigold Thornton, who frequently cruised on a sailing vessel with her husband. "Marigold what do you think of this trip?" asked Juli, showing her the brochure.

Looking at the picture of ocean and forest Marigold burbled, "Ocean kayaking, good! Desolation Sound, perfect!" She smiled, "In fact I'm going to talk Dave into going there this summer on Dream Seeker. Maybe we'll see each other."

Juli watched her friend coming to life and smiled at her. "So Marigold it sounds like you think I should go on this trip?"

Marigold nodded enthusiastically. "Are there birds in the sky? Seals in the ocean?"

"Yes."

"I think it's the most beautiful place in the world. Swimmable crystal clear water, endless forests, ocean birds, and salmon so plentiful anyone can catch them, oysters as big as your hand . . . mountains in the distance. Clean salty air," she drew in a deep breath. "Juli, you have to hear it. See it. Smell it."

"You do make it sound irresistible."

"Juli, you deserve a great time, and for heaven's sake meet a delicious man. There's bound to be at least one gorgeous specimen on the trip."

"You know I'm not interested." Juli stared at her friend and sipped her tea. "A man would complicate my life."

"Nonetheless Juli, I'm going to send that intention into the universe. You need a partner."

"You're a dreamer. Men don't like competent professional women."

Marigold leaned forward, "What are your top three priorities?"

"Zilch. Nada. Forget it." Juli shook her head as she counted on her fingers.

"Be serious."

Juli raised her voice, "I am serious. I'm happy as I am. I don't need a man."

"Of course not," she said in a calm voice. "But just in case someone appears you should have some criteria in mind."

Juli shook her head. "No one will appear. I've given up. My life is full and complete now."

"Just listen," she smiled, "tall and handsome. Color of hair and eyes negotiable."

"Marigold you're crazy. This is a kayak trip not an on-line dating service."

"I know, I know. Nonetheless I'm visualizing a sexy, healthy, rich man for you. A man who will be your soul mate."

"But. . . "

"Shhhh . . . visualize. Trust the universe to send you what you need and want."

"Nope, can't do it."

"But I can," smiled her friend as she closed her eyes. "Universe please send Juli a sexy, healthy man. Rich if possible."

"Hah! I'm going to intention you back." Juli wagged her finger at her friend. "I see you and Dave happy and smiling and supporting one another, like when you first met."

Tears filled her eyes, "Thank you so much Juli. That's what I want too." The two women held hands, shut their eyes and sent their energies into the universe.

Finally Juli opened her eyes and said quietly, "I'm going to register for the trip and my intention is to have the best holiday of my life."

CHAPTER ONE

It's Sunday afternoon July 24th, how did I end up in this mess? I'm stuck in a kayak in the middle of Sutil Channel on the British Columbia coast with a stubborn fool named Richard Thompson controlling the stern steering position.

Like a cougar trapped in a cage, Dr. Juliet Armstrong stared straight ahead, fuming so hard she couldn't think of anything but how much she hated this overbearing man. She knew she should treat him like an angry patient, speaking calmly and agreeing with him, but she couldn't. For some reason the highly controlled Dr. Armstrong was over-reacting. Even Mother Nature was against her as the blue ocean flowed like a river carrying them away from the emerald-forested island ahead of them, their destination.

Suddenly his harsh voice intruded into her thoughts, "Hey, wake up and paddle. Paddle hard. I can't do all the work. The tide's starting to be against us. Do you understand that?"

"I friggin understand," she hissed back. How did she get stuck with all this male testosterone? He sounded like a dictator, probably because he was a dictator. She twisted her head and shoulders around so she could see him; the kayak rocked at her sudden movement. She found herself staring into his eyes: icy blue and hostile. She didn't like that look; he hated her. Maybe he hated all women; maybe his mother was cruel. She didn't know what his problem was, but she was on holiday and she didn't want to be surrounded by his black energy. Ignoring him she stared forward across the bow of the kayak at the beautiful turquoise ocean as they cut a bow wave through the water. To her left a snowy gull sat on a drifting log and clacked its beak at her as if to say, *be quiet and be glad you don't have to fish for a living.*

So she ignored the noisy one in the stern, and the noisy one on the log, and remembered the not-too-perfect conditions of the drive to the Campbell River ferry.

First, she had stopped to fill up her gas tank and faced a twenty cent per liter hike in the price from the day before. She had told herself that, as her car was a brand-new hybrid, gas wasn't really an issue. Next, there had been a slow-down on the Malahat stretch of the highway north of Victoria, as a car was pulled over at the side of the road with its engine steaming. Juli was glad that wasn't her; nonetheless, the heavy traffic moved as slowly as a slug creeping through a forest. Third, on the Nanaimo by-pass she had hit every red light. *Stay calm Juli*, she had crooned, *you will make it*. She was lying to herself and she knew it as she could feel her pulse throbbing at her temples, a sure sign she was under stress, and her blood pressure was creeping up. She continued to reassure herself that this was temporary and all would be calm when she reached the ferry.

After Parksville the traffic had thinned and she had put the cruise control on one hundred and twenty kilometers per hour and watched the highway speed past. She had been confident things were going in her favor now as the road was dry and would remain so because after all it was summer and the sun was shining brightly through her skylight. As well, the terrain opened as the mountains moved back, which she thought was another good sign until she noticed the clear cut: Douglas fir, tall and scraggly, were scattered across the wasteland; lonely sentinels guarding something that had already been stolen. She shook her head forcing herself to bless the small trees sprouting through the debris, a hopeful sign that the forest could renew itself.

Then she had noticed a few hunger pangs and reached for her lunch. The egg-salad sandwich on whole wheat was delicious, unfortunately, several blobs of egg splattered on her shorts. *Damn, now I'm going to be smelly and attract mosquitos*. She dabbed at the spot with a wet-wipe and felt the moisture seep onto her skin. She puffed up her shorts hoping they would dry.

Then when she arrived at the ferry at 11:20 the attendant advised it was almost full and she probably wouldn't get on. Discouraged she pulled into the last slot on line number four behind a battered truck, turned off her engine, stretched and then sank back in her seat. If she missed this ferry she knew the next wasn't for an hour which would make her late for the kayak trip. She didn't want to be late; she hated being late; they might even leave without her.

Much to her surprise the squat ferry had appeared suddenly, pulling into the dock and disgorging its cars immediately. The efficiency amazed her - true it was a small double ended ferry with space on the single deck for only about sixty vehicles. A crew member, identified by an orange safety vest, looked casual with her blond hair in a ponytail, wearing khaki shorts. She barely moved her hands to signal drivers where to go. But based on the speed of events, the crew and probably the drivers had done this many times before.

Finally, when she had given up all hope and was planning her route back to the highway, the attendant waved to her. Juli pressed the start button, the tachometer needle fluttered, she slid into drive and the car jumped eagerly ahead. The attendant pointed at the ground to slow Juli, and then signaled for her to board. Juli smiled and waved her thanks and proceeded down the ramp.

Carefully she followed the directions of the attendant on the deck and squeezed into a space so narrow she couldn't open any of her doors. In spite of being trapped in her car she was elated and grateful as she was the last car on board. Almost immediately the ferry pulled away and the ramp lifted behind her, sealing her future. She was going to Quadra Island. She let out a long slow breath, gave thanks silently, lowered her seat, lay back, and closed her eyes.

The clang of the ramp and the grinding of car starters woke her. She was startled at first, then she remembered she was on a holiday and soon to meet her traveling companions. Juli was the last off the ferry and only had fifteen minutes to find the group waiting at the hotel. She knew to follow the ferry signs for Cortes Island: up the hill, left at the grocery store, right at the school, left again and then follow the narrow country road to the ferry dock. Sure enough when she reached the ferry going to Cortes a sign directed her to the hotel. She made a sharp left on to a narrow steep hard-packed earth driveway which was flanked by Douglas firs on her left side, the ocean on her other.

A rambling, rustic hotel, with cedar siding darkened with age and a faded sign announcing a bar, a gift shop, and a restaurant, caught her attention briefly. *That must be the old hotel.*

The brochure had said *it was established in about 1895 and, after a fire, was rebuilt in 1912.*

Then her eyes swung ninety degrees to examine several bright kayaks lined up like fish in a narrow stream, pointing at the water as if they were eager to be off. Then she spotted a parking spot beside a mud-spattered relatively-new fire-engine-red truck parked off to the side, and slid in to its left. The truck's size seemed comforting and protective. Starting to get excited again she sat clutching her steering wheel, her senses hyper alert. Hurriedly she had turned off the engine.

CHAPTER TWO

She remembered being delighted that she had found her kayaking group. The people milling about three brightly-colored kayaks were obviously her cohorts. She slid out of her car, grabbed her backpack, and locking it automatically, walked quickly toward the group, eager to meet them. The sun continued to beam down and little puffs of dust, kicked up by her shoes, reminded her that it was summer and this was her chance to be in Nature.

The group was small: five adults, all about her age, two women and three men. One of the men looked up, smiled, and came toward her with his hand outstretched in greeting. "You must be Juliet Armstrong."

"Yes," she said smiling back, infected by his broad welcoming grin. *So far so good.*

"I'm Tom Smithers, your guide. We were familiarizing ourselves with the kayaks." His eyes twinkled and glowed when he smiled, making Juli feel at ease. He was tall - about six two - muscular with dark short curly hair. His dark tan and springy step told her he spent a lot of time in the outdoors. Things were looking up, he was a gorgeous male of the species. *Marigold would say, Oh my God: he's sexy, he's healthy, find out if he's wealthy.* And, he definitely looked competent.

Tom took her elbow lightly and guided her toward the group while pointing at a beautiful blond woman. "This is the irreplaceable Sarah who does the organizing for me." Sarah, standing beside a tall blond man in black shorts, smiled. Juli felt the man's eyes examining her so intensely she felt a warm flush rush down her neck and right through to her toes. She had never felt anything like that before and quickly dismissed it, as a sign of her exhaustion. Her thoughts were interrupted as Sarah stepped forward, hand extended, to welcome Juli. She presented a picture of competent efficiency with her short blond hair, cargo shorts, and t-shirt with *Tom's Ocean Yaks* printed on it, but Juli caught the subtle messages of intimacy that passed between her and Tom and was briefly envious. *So there you have it Marigold, your intentions were for naught. Energetic Sarah has Tom and probably the blond tied up.* Juli lowered her eyes being careful to avoid tripping over the kayaks.

"And this is Marybell and her husband Arnold," Tom continued, guiding her toward a friendly pair dressed identically in nylon knee-length shorts, white t-shirts, black water shoes, and Tilley hats who smiled broadly at her. "We're glad you made it," said Marybell as she clutched her husband's hand. "We haven't done this before"

"But of course we've been out in a sailboat," finished Arnold.

So they were friendly and had some boating experience. They seemed okay, Juli thought, a little enmeshed but maybe that was the way it should be.

Tom continued, casually indicating the tall man hovering on the edge of the group, "This is Rich, Richard Thompson. He's an old hand . . . joining us for the first time in years. Right Rich?"

"Yup, and eager to be off before the tide changes." His deep voice seemed to wrap around her; she eased back a step as waves of energy hit her. Startled she looked up into his blue eyes; a momentary flash of curiosity passed through her then disappeared, and she decided to ignore it and him.

Mainly Juli didn't like the look of him. He was one of those lean, tall, wiry types with five o'clock shadow, bleached blond hair and a deep tan as if he spent his whole life relaxing outside. He wore loose black nylon knee length shorts which highlighted his long legs, dusted with golden hairs. The legs disappeared into calf-high yellow sailing boots which were so large she wondered if they would fit into the kayak. In fact he was so tall, nearing 6'5", she wondered if his size would make a kayak tippy. She surely hoped not. She had no desire at all to help fish someone out of that cold ocean. On top he wore a faded-black short-sleeved t-shirt which hugged the muscles of his chest and arms as if they were clinging for dear life at the edge of a dangerous cliff. And, topping it all off he wore a wide-brimmed Tilley hat on his head which was for effect she was sure, as it added another inch or two to his height.

He definitely wasn't the man Marigold had intended. He didn't look like he could hold down a job and wasn't sexy at all, though Sarah did seem to like him; on the plus side he did look healthy. *One out of three Marigold; that's not good enough.*

Juli deliberately turned away from him to concentrate on the bright blue and yellow fiberglass kayaks. Seats for five people. She counted six people. What did that mean?

Tom saw her studying the kayaks and explained, "As you can see we have three kayaks with five seats. There'll be five us on the trip. Sarah stays here." Smiling agreeably, Sarah nodded. Juli raised an eyebrow. Obviously Marybell and Arnold stayed together. She sure wouldn't want to come between them. So that left Tom and Richard and her. Juli shifted from foot to foot, more uncomfortable than she had realized.

Tom continued expansively talking to everyone, "I take the single so I can be more mobile. Marybell and Arnold will be in one double, Rich and Juli in the other."

Juli started to protest, then seeing the logic of the guide being more mobile and realizing the added width of the double would be more stable, stayed quiet as she peered at Rich from under her partially-open eyelids. His arms, folded across his chest, and his feet, planted firmly in his boating boots, gave an air of supreme confidence.

Tom continued, "I'm going to demonstrate how to enter and leave a kayak, then each of you will practice it. Then we'll be off . . . the tide and weather are in our favor right now." Juli had studied an entry and exit on a U-tube video. Tom completed a similar procedure using his paddle as a brace to steady the kayak; that was a good sign. Thankfully she had done the right prep.

"Okay Juli, Arnold, and Marybell here are your paddles," said Tom as he handed them each a slim-bladed light-weight paddle. "Juli in Lemon Yak and Marybell and Arnold in Azure Yak." Awkwardly and with a similar degree of clumsiness the women eased into their respective kayaks. That wasn't very difficult, thought Juli. However, she discovered getting out was a challenge, as gravity colluded with the female body tendency for poor upper body strength and weight storage in the hips; in spite of that, she struggled and succeeded, but she realized that this would be a real test, every time. Marybell fell back three times before she extracted herself. That did not bode well. On the other hand, her husband easily executed the entrance and exit. Rich stood back, arms relaxed, and watched, grinning with amusement at their clumsiness.

She resented his casual, easy-going manner; in fact she was fooled by it. It wasn't until they were packing the kayak that she got the first whiff of his stubbornness as he wanted to stow all their backpacks and equipment. She let him, noting he did seem to know what he was doing and the guide had called him by his first name. She guessed he had done this before. The second hint of his ornery nature came when they were choosing paddling positions: she wanted to flip for steering position in the rear; he refused and announced he would steer. The third hint was the slight sneer on his face. *Supercilious bastard,* if he laughed at her she would demand to leave. She should have walked away, but her fatigue let her down and she gave in. Normally she was very definite about her life and very much in charge of those around her. So here she was, embarking on a trip into the wilderness with four strangers and it was too late to retreat to the safety of her urban life.

Finally the kayaks had been taken to the water. The blond giant had carried theirs with one hand as if it were as light as a feather; Juli had trotted behind him carrying both paddles like an eager puppy, her spray skirt slapping her calves. At the water's edge he grunted and pointed at the floating kayak parallel to the beach, indicating she should climb in. Feeling tentative and very conscious of his critical eyes on her, she closed the ties on her hat, zippered her hoodie, and placing her paddle behind her on the coaming, eased her butt onto her hands, swung her feet on board, and flopped into the kayak with a drop of at least six inches to a hard landing in the seat. Her butt stung and no doubt was bruised. He probably was smirking, but she didn't look. She wanted to scream, *I didn't tip the kayak. Any landing that doesn't tip the kayak is a good landing.* But how was she going to get out of this tippy machine. Sure a canoe was unstable but at least in it she could shift to her knees and use her legs to exit. Between the lifejacket, spray skirt, double-ended paddle and gloves she felt like she was trapped in the confines of a fiberglass tomb. Tom waded in beside her to fasten her spray skirt carefully around the coaming of the cockpit. "Remember, if you tip over, to pull up here on the front of the spray skirt, then you'll be able to exit." Why was she doing this? Putting her life at risk. Why hadn't she taken a course in Victoria?

Marybell had screamed as she crashed into Azure, giving voice to Juli's thoughts, "How the hell will I ever get out of this machine." Her husband soothed her as he eased himself in. Tom and Richard, who had been steadying the kayaks, now effortlessly eased into their seats: Richard behind Juli and Tom in Blue Boy. When she felt Richard's weight as he settled smoothly in the kayak behind her they were off. Juli strained her neck to watch Richard as he pushed away from shore.

Continuing to look back over her shoulder she noted he seemed competent; that is, he hadn't reached his level of incompetence, yet. She hoped it wouldn't be soon. He and the guide seemed confident, and the guide seemed relieved that Richard was her partner. It was obvious to her that the other two kayakers were extreme beginners that he had to keep an even closer eye on them. They made her look good. Now as she settled deep in the kayak she felt the floating feeling through her bottom and legs, way more than in a canoe; sealed in by her spray skirt she felt comfortable; her initial worries were abating.

CHAPTER THREE

She remembered that at first the trip had been idyllic. The kayaks had slipped silently through the calm marina waters as smoothly as if they were blue and yellow seabirds. The soft floating feeling like they were flying through air felt joyful. Keeping her paddle across the deck in front of her she let Richard propel the boat as she examined the sail and power boats secured tightly to the floating dock in the bay. They were a familiar sight: sailboats with names like Whispering Wind and Andiamo, and commercial fishing boats proudly bearing names like Sandra-Elene and WestWind, and small runabouts for day fishermen huddled around the docks as if waiting for something.

As they left Heriot Bay the ocean had been calm, azure, and friendly. Golden sunlight reflected off the glossy surface making Juli glad she had sunglasses. But even now she felt hot under the spray skirt; she wanted a drink from her water bottle but she resisted. The wind was quiet and for that she was grateful.

Paddling seemed easy as they glided out of the bay; to her right and south was a deep narrow bay protected from the open channel by Rebecca Spit, whose white sand beach reminded her of a tropical island paradise. Douglas firs marched down its spine not palm trees; nonetheless it was very inviting. Next she studied the ferry dock and much to her relief the ferry was absent and none was in sight. Richard, reading her mind, said, "The ferry from Cortes is not due till 12:40 so we have time to get out of its way. That's one of the reasons why Tom was in a rush."

"Thanks for telling me." Maybe he was going to be reasonable. She continued to gaze around.

Breaking into her reverie he asked, "What do you know about kayaks?"

Feeling she had to be polite and answer him she called over her shoulder, "I've spent a lot of time on lakes and in boats . . . this is my first kayak trip."

"That's what I thought. You'll learn as we go." The words sounded okay but his tone was sarcastic, reminding Juli of her first impression.

"Hope you're right," muttered Juli as she dipped her paddle, first to the right and then the left, into the water. It was similar to canoeing and soon she had a rhythm going. Rich said nothing. Juli paddled on in silence as she examined the surface for clues as to the direction of the tide. If they were heading north and if Tom was as competent as he appeared then they would be travelling with the tide. Having settled that in her mind she relaxed slightly and watched the sun dance across the wavelets like happy little sparks. Once again, as though he was reading her mind, Richard said "the tide is on the ebb. It ebbs north here. But it's going to turn soon." She paddled on, feeling his strokes moving them through the water, which was good as her shoulders were beginning to ache after an hour of paddling.

Fascinated Juli had watched the bow wave spread in ripples away from her. Was her life like the water, liquid and ever changing but enduring, or was she like the ripple streaming away to oblivion? Pulled out of her reverie by a slap against the hull, she looked sharply at the side of kayak wondering if they had been hit by floating debris. She examined the water. No debris but small wavelets had appeared out of nowhere.

Many, many minutes later Tom had come along side saying, "Good work Juli. Pull a little harder with your left and at the same time push with your right hand." You're doing great, we've been paddling about two hours now and we're about half way. Keep up the good work." Then he dropped back to paddle beside Arnold and Marybell, who were not faring as well as they wandered to and fro not making steady headway.

"Could   you please paddle harder?" And then it came again and louder, "Paddle Harder. Use your whole upper body and dig in."

That was when the man paddling behind her turned into Genghis Kahn, shouting at her. So she had tried to ignore him by slipping into memories, but that wasn't working anymore. So here she was, having missed all the warnings the universe had sent, with no more day dreaming, no more turning back. This was her life.

His sarcastic voice prodded again, "Well then what's your problem?"

She grimaced and dipped her paddle. She wasn't going to show any weakness to this miserable person, "Nothing." She wanted to exercise her body and breathe in Nature and recharge her batteries. The island ahead of them called to her, promising peace and quiet. Juli wished she was in the single, then she could do what she wanted, although deep down she knew she was a novice to kayaking and dependent on him.

"Paddle harder," he roared. "The tide is at the end of the ebb now; it will turn soon and we have to get around the tip of Read Island before nightfall."

"Does it really make a difference?" she challenged. She didn't trust him. He was too surly. Why couldn't he be friendly and nice?

"Of course it does."

"Why?"

"If this wind builds it will be wind against tide with standing waves that will complicate our lives, or worst case, if the tide rips through this channel at six knots, then we would be pushed around like a feather and probably carried down the channel toward Cape Mudge and the vicious water there. Then it would be game over. You want that?"

She could feel him staring at the back of her head. Was he trying to scare her? She was sure he could paddle them to safety by himself even if she never dipped her paddle. Why had she agreed to share a kayak with this stubborn man? She wanted a peaceful holiday away from the demands of people. Then she noticed the wind stirring the wavelets into moderate waves against the side of the kayak. This could become a very cold and unforgiving ocean. "No way. I came on this trip to relax not to drown."

"Well it will be relaxing, maybe later. Not now. Now paddle hard," he shouted. Then soften his order with, "Please."

Juli dug in as she would have in a canoe using the full strength of her arms, shoulders, and back. In a kayak she could brace her thighs against the shell and her feet on the foot blocks. Her arms ached, her shoulders burned. The cold ocean ran down the paddle and soaked her gloves, making her fingers tingle with cold. She could feel blisters developing so she shifted her grip. That helped temporarily, still the salt water relentlessly ate at her hands. Fortunately she was warm and dry inside the spray skirt, but she felt itchy and sticky. Thankfully the shouting had stopped and they were paddling in silence, the other kayaks had dropped back even further.

"Okay, okay, I'll pull harder." What was the use of explaining her hands felt like raw meat? Not only that, and much to her surprise, her bum ached as her nylon panties burned into her skin, and her thighs screamed from pushing against the sides of the kayak. He wouldn't care. So she dug deeply and felt him doing the same; now they were on course and making progress, but it was heavy paddling. Behind them she could hear Tom urging the other couple to paddle and the woman was protesting.

Unfortunately Richard didn't appreciate her effort and his intruding voice became impatient and demanding again, "Stop day dreaming. Paddle harder. The tide has turned but we can still beat it."

Juli wanted to coast and enjoy the wondrous lapis blue ocean. Instead she pulled as hard as she could on the paddle, wincing with pain from her hands and her shoulders. He had ordered her to paddle harder. She couldn't as her arms ached as if she had been lifting weights for two hours, and the dripping saltwater had soaked her gloves causing the forming blisters to sting painfully as if the skin was tearing. She couldn't stand him. She wouldn't be treated like this. He was authoritarian and abusive. She was here for pleasure, not pain. She yanked the brim of her hat lower and gritted her teeth. What an idiot she was. She should have known better than to set off with someone she didn't know. The tyrant was whistling some dumb song, maybe Ravel's Bolero. How irritating and intrusive. Why couldn't he chant native paddling songs, or Row, Row Your Boat; or better yet be silent. She wanted to scream, *I need peace. I came here for quiet.* Tom had assured her *all would be well.* His *well* was different from her *well.* And where was he? Off in his own kayak, tending to his other customers.

The grouchy voice growled, "Paddle harder. We hafta get through this tidal rip."

"Yah, yah," she placated, hoping he would leave her alone. But he didn't.

"This is a kayak trip; you must have expected to paddle." Sarcasm dripped from his mouth like water off a paddle. "We started later than originally planned because of your late arrival and now the tide has turned so that we are losing headway. Our progress is dangerously slow."

"Okay, okay," she shouted but thought, *Marigold where is that healthy, sexy, rich man you intentioned for me?* Marigold had insisted it would be a once in a lifetime trip. She was right. How did she know? So far this was an experience Juli had never had before . . . and never would again.

Suddenly like the fickle ocean he changed his tactics. The voice from the stern of the kayak sounded softer, "If you paddle harder Ms. Armstrong we'll get to that island straight ahead. That means I can build a fire and make us hot tea . . . with sugar and cream . . . and maybe an oatmeal cookie." He coaxed, "You would like that, wouldn't you?"

Juli smiled to herself but didn't let him see it; nor did she verbally acknowledge his words.

Richard broke into her thoughts, "It's called Read Island."

She called back over her shoulder, "I see it."

He shouted back, "It was named around 1864 by Daniel Pender, captain of the Beaver, for Captain William Viner Read, who was a naval assistant."

For some reason he was trying to be friendly. She relaxed, amazed at the blatant transparency. Of course he was trying to motivate her and he was succeeding. As her anger dissipated, redirected energy flooded her arms, enabling her to pull strongly again.

"Ms. Armstrong, we're making progress. Look, Viner point is close. But don't relax," he warned. "We still have to paddle up the coast to that beach." Richard pointed vaguely to the left. "If we have a back eddy that'll help, otherwise we'll be fighting the current all the way."

Juli grunted, not willing to waste any energy on him, cruel task master that he was. *Ms. Armstrong! Humph.* Well one thing she had to say about Mr. Grumpy was that he was a good paddler and seemed to know where he was going. She could feel his presence behind her and the strength of his strokes. As she looked at the towering rocks on their left side, for the first time she was slightly relieved he, and not Marybell, was with her. She didn't know anything about him except his name was Richard Thompson and he came from near-by Cortes Island. She supposed he was a logger or a farmer on a holiday.

Though the pain in her shoulders, as the muscles knotted up, was excruciating, she kept paddling. She had little strength but they kept moving thanks to Mr. Thompson. The round head of a seal popped up to her left and looked at her as if deciding whether she was food or a hunter. Deciding Juli was neither, he slipped silently under the surface. Juli felt strangely lonely as he sank out of sight leaving no sign. Looking across the blue expanse to the dark green island on the other side of the strait she saw gulls gathering. She strained and heard their squawking as they vied for the herrings that must be near the surface

His voice coaxed, "Ms. Armstrong, you're doing great. Keep paddling. We're almost there. We only hafta go a bit farther."

"Thank God. I can't do much more," Juli called over her shoulder. "My hands are going to be a mess." *Now why did I say that? Am I testing to see how sympathetic he can be?*

"I think they'll be minor compared to the ache in your shoulders," he called out.

"I'll be fine," declared Juli deciding she didn't want his sympathy or his opinion after all. She wanted to be alone; she was tired of people and their demands on her. She remembered her last day at work had been a blur of elderly dementing people, streaming in with relatives; probably because their relatives were on holidays, and finally noticing how mom or dad had deteriorated since their last visit.

For example, Mr. Tobins, seventy-six, was brought in by his daughter. She had found him on the floor where he had fallen the night before. He was confused: he didn't know the day of the week, or where he was. But he did know his home address. And, knew who his daughter was. Luckily he had no broken bones, particularly a hip. He had a fever and needed to urinate twice during the short exam. Juli tested his urine and found he had a bladder infection. As the daughter was able to stay with him and would administer the medication Juli agreed to let him go home, but asked for a follow up visit in three days. She made sure she saw him for that visit. When he returned he was markedly improved so Juli didn't admit him to hospital for further tests. The next biggest group were accidents, mainly with bikes. And then, there were a few crying babies with otitis media, a woman with a wart in her ear, a carpenter who had tangled with a power saw, a young boy with possible meningitis, a woman with migraine headaches, and one chest pain. She was exhausted. That's how she allowed herself to be in this situation, in this kayak, with this strange man. She decided to ignore him.

CHAPTER FOUR

Finally they eased into Lake Bay. As the summer sun beat down on them she longed to hide in the dense dark green conifers crowding around the quiet little bay. Obviously Tom had been there the day before and set up camp as two double tents and one single perched well above the beach and the storm tossed driftwood. Juli stared at the tents, her mouth open.

As if he read her thoughts her stern paddler announced, "You're going to have to share. This was set up double kayak, double tent."

Juli jerked her head round demanding, "The single. I want it." She pointed at the tent as she sat in the kayak, bow on the beach. She was exhausted and needed sleep. The men would have to share.

"That's Tom's," said Richard his voice placating. "He's the guide and gets the privilege of being alone." She felt his eyes boring into her back as if to say, he puts up with us all day. He deserves peace and quiet at night.

"Okay," she responded, sounding reasonable. "But I don't know Marybell . . ."

"Ahh." He hesitated. "Not Marybell. She's part of a couple." The silence dragged on. Juli stared at the tents. He didn't say anything. The tension built until it seemed sheet lightning might leap from the ends of their paddles. She didn't care. No matter what, she was not sharing with him. "I'll sleep outside," said Juli back pedaling. Anything would be better than sharing with this ornery person. She looked around at the pile of driftwood above the high water line and thought that the beach looked safe enough.

"Not a good idea. It might rain." He sounded curt.

"No problem. I can handle rain." She would settle between two logs and drape plastic over herself.

"The seals come out of the water at night and might mistake you for food."

Surely he was kidding. But maybe he wasn't, she thought.

Sounding more reasonable he added, "Besides you paid for half a tent and you should have half a tent."

She was too tired to argue with him. "Okay but you stay on your side of the tent." He wouldn't bother her with Tom close by.

"Of course," he purred quietly as he carefully held the kayak, bow in, to the stony beach.

That settled, Juli shifted her weight to get out of the kayak. She lifted her hips several inches off the seat. Her hands screamed with pain. Her butt smacked back. *Whoa what happened to my upper body strength? My bum feels like it's made of lead.*

"Wait," ordered Richard as if he was talking to a helpless child. "I'll bring us parallel to the beach and get out first. Then I can help you."

"I don't need your help," huffed Juli. She watched him back the bow off the beach and skillfully maneuver the boat parallel to the beach and somehow deftly removed himself. Standing beside her, all she could see were his yellow boat boots which ended at golden-haired muscular calves.

She cleared her throat and declared, "I can do this."

"Fine. I'll steady Yak." It wasn't an offer, more of a command.

"No need. Give me room." Juli placed her paddle behind her, steadying it against the coaming. "I've done this before."

"Yah, on solid ground. This is quite different." He stayed close to the stern but he didn't touch the kayak.

"No sweat," she bragged as she transferred her weight to her hands, holding the slippery handle of the paddle tightly across the coaming behind the seat back. She pressed down; her hips didn't move. Then she wiggled, bent her knees, and put her feet on the floor of the kayak as close to her bum as possible, and pushed. Suddenly she shot upward and bumped her bum onto the back of the seat crushing her hands into the paddle. As excruciating pain shot through her hands, she bit her lower lip to keep from screaming. Simultaneously the kayak shifted under her. Instantly Richard grabbed the shore side of the kayak deftly stopping it from tipping. She grunted her begrudging thanks and prayed her next move would be successful. She eased her right leg out of the kayak and placed her foot on the beach. Now she was stuck like a butterfly on a pin board, touching at three points: one, her bum on her painful hands; two, her left foot on the floor of the shifting kayak; and three, the heel of her right foot on the beach. Could she shift her weight to that right foot? She had to. Richard grinned but didn't move to help her. Suddenly it was over. Her weight was on her right foot and leg, on the cold sand, her left foot was on the gunwale of a tipping kayak, her right arm smashed into a grey rock; sharp pain shot through her. Rich reached her, grabbed her paddle and the kayak with his left hand and swung his right hand and arm around her waist and lifted her to her feet as though she was as light as a feather.

Juli sucked in her breath and shouted, "Let go of me you, you ape. I can manage." She was shocked that had come out of her mouth. He had kept her from smashing onto her face.

Rich eased his arm away from Juli, set her on the cold rocky beach, and pulled the kayak safely above the row of wave-tossed silver logs. A small smile teased his lips for the first time today.

Juli glimpsed the smile out of the corner of her eye. So he didn't take offence; that was a good sign. Probably that was the very first time anyone had called him that. In a way it was better than 'Hey you'. Juli rubbed her arm, chagrinned that she had been so inept. Slowly she followed the kayak up the beach and perched on a log warmed by the sun. Silently she reviewed how she had ended up in this mess.

Why am I here? Because this is where I want to be? If that's true I better look around. Juli's posture straightened as she gazed turning her head and body 180 degrees. Diamonds glinted on the wavelets in the strait; sapphires glowed overhead; jade dripped off the trees. A light wind rustled the cedar and fir needles like a murmuring brook, and small pine siskins chirped and flittered in a flock so tightly they were like one being. She sniffed as the tang of salt mixed with the iodine smell of sun-warmed kelp surrounded her. Her body relaxed; she did want to be here. She would ignore Richard, the despot; she had as much right to be here as he did.

Richard had started the fire and was heating the tea water when the last two kayaks finally arrived. The other beginners were even more miserable than Juli, groaning with discomfort and clinging together after it took both Tom and Richard to lift Marybell out of the kayak. Marybell, leaning heavily on her husband's arm, limped to the fire. Tears streamed down her face as she huddled close to it. As all the men were fussing over Marybell, Juli didn't move. Instead she gently peeled off her paddling gloves to see what her own damage was. Her finger tips were white with cold, and her palms and fingers where she had gripped the paddle were red and swollen. First she tried easing them into her arm pits thinking the warmth would be healing. Instead it increased the pain so much she slipped off to the edge of the ocean and soaked her hands in the cool healing salt water. Rich looked past Marybell and saw her crouching by the water.

Tom tried unsuccessfully to bring the four of them together as he served them steaming soup. Arnold and Marybell continued to huddle together, while Richard sat aloof and thinking. Juli sagged on a log, so exhausted she didn't care to talk.

Once she was full of warm potato-leek soup she bid them good night and, too tired to even question the sleeping arrangements, decided to turn in for the night. She crawled into the first double tent and was instantly asleep. She turned over several hours later and cried out with pain as her left trapezius muscle knotted up. Sweat beaded on her forehead; waves of nausea wracked her body.

"Hey tough girl." Richard, breaking in to her misery, hovered over her saying, "I've got some analgesic. Here take two."

"Thanks." Juli took them and swallowed with the water he offered. It wasn't until they hit her stomach that she realized she hadn't asked what they were. She'd never done that before. "What were they?" she gasped. "Did you poison me?"

"Not likely. Ibuprofen." He shone his light on the bottle and then shut it off again. "It'll help with the pain and inflammation."

"Thank God." She could feel his warm breath on her neck. The heat from his body engulfed her, helping her to relax. Clearly it wasn't Marybell sharing with her.

"Here let me put a thumb on that muscle. Even an ape knows what to do for a muscle spasm."

"I didn't mean that." She protested feebly. Actually she did mean it at the time but now, in the dark, with pain shooting through her shoulders, she welcomed his help. "If you could press here," she pointed at her left shoulder right above the scapula.

He shifted his weight edging his warm body behind her. Juli felt his fingers slide confidently down her neck and under her shirt. Then the pressure as his thumbs dug into the muscles on either side of her neck made her bite back a gasp of pain. Two hot pokers stabbed into her back.

"Hang in there," he breathed into her ear and pressed until the muscle relaxed. Juli sighed and then froze, this tent was too dark, too intimate, too isolated from the normal world. She felt him reflexively tightening his muscles, jerking away from her as though he had touched a hot coal while his husky voice declared, "The muscle will relax soon."

She knew it would. She had done this many times for friends and patients. "Ahh," she breathed out as the muscle stayed soft. Exhausted she relaxed back and found herself leaning against his bare chest. Now that the pain had eased she sensed his overwhelmingly masculine body. Skin sensors all over her body tingled; her hearing tuned to his breathing. Even in the dark she could feel his strength; it was very comforting. Who was she kidding? It was electrifying. She was surprisingly and totally in a sexual sensory state. She sucked in his scent driving her pulse rate up as though she was on the downhill side of a racing rollercoaster. Her lips swelled: she wanted to feel his soft lips pressed against hers, his tongue licking and prodding. She ached for his powerful hands to move to more intimate areas. With great effort she pulled away. What was she thinking? He was a stranger. He could be married with five kids for all she knew.

He patted her arm as if she was a child and said, "Good night" as though he hadn't been affected at all. She wondered if his pulse was racing as hard as hers and if he was as celibate as she. She had no answers and he wasn't talking as he turned quickly away and climbed into his sleeping bag.

Cold air hit her skin when he withdrew. Juli heard rustling then quiet snoring. She, on the other hand, couldn't sleep. She laughed at herself: in spite of the pain she had been turned on; obviously he wasn't attracted to her. She kept thinking about his touch and how he knew exactly how to give her pain relief. He was a healer. That was a good thing; however, he disturbed her thoughts in other ways. She hated it when she couldn't have her own way. At the treatment center she had seniority; the other doctors deferred to her. She hadn't known they would, it just seemed to happen as she was an excellent diagnostician. But here she was depending on a stranger to diagnose and treat her paddling injuries. Probably he had taken a first aid course. Her last thoughts were to dread the morning and having to face the paddle again.

CHAPTER FIVE

Juli woke with a start. Her first thought was that she had to get to work. She lifted her head and saw that; there was no comforter; a blue, fluffy sleeping bag covered her legs. There wasn't even a bed, or a bedroom; she was on the ground, in a tent. The sunlight, diffusing warm and orange on the nylon material, reminded her that she was on holiday. It was sticky hot already. She shrank from the heat; her cheeks still tingled from yesterday's sun. The odors of sweat and earth mixed to make her shift uncomfortably. Lying back inside her sleeping bag she tried to relax in the softness, but couldn't, as now her shoulders burned as though she had been whipped.

Next she tried to wiggle out of her sleeping bag and discovered to her horror that her hands were paralyzed. Focusing all her energy she bent each finger on each hand and they moved. But when she tried to squeeze them around the edge of her sleeping bag they screamed with pain. *I'm going to be a cripple if*

I keep on at this rate. This couldn't be happening to her. She was helpless; she wished she had never come on this trip. What a contrast to yesterday's morning when she had been healthy and full of joyful expectations.

She had awakened at 0700 precisely, with the thought that today was going to be the best day of her life. She felt confident and certain. Still lying in bed, she examined her surroundings. The air coming in her window smelled of the ocean; she sucked it into her lungs. Sunbeams danced off her crystal balls hanging from the light fixture; her eyes danced with the sparks of color.

So she had hopped out of bed, flinging the duvet with its joyful sunrise colors back, and stood by the bed listening. The duvet crackled, air in the vents hissed, a happy thump on the ceiling reminded her of her condo neighbors. All normal. She shrugged, thinking she was being an optimist, and pulled on her luminous orange-sherbet silk kimono as she bounced into the kitchen to start her morning before-work routine. First she filled a cup with day-old tea, and popped it in the microwave to heat. So far there were no surprises; it was a normal day.

Next she had pressed on her smart phone. The digital calendar showed Saturday, July twenty-fourth, Quadra Island. She read it again. Saturday was still there. Her eyes blinked rapidly to clear her vision; Quadra Island was still there. Incredulous, then delighted, she smiled. Air burst from her lungs as she shouted, "I'm on holiday," and twirled, still clutching her phone, like a child let out of school. A vision of long and lazy days at her grandparent's summer cabin on the lake: no shoes, no underwear, nude swimming, nightly wiener roasts, watching sunsets, and listening to the buzz of insects, added to her pleasure and anticipation.

When she had examined the calendar on her phone again, the second message was Jack W's hemochromatosis. She had ordered blood work yesterday afternoon and hadn't seen the results. He was counting on her to let him know if his iron levels were dangerously high and he needed to have a phlebotomy. She phoned the lab, giving her physician number and the patient's details. The test showed his blood within normal levels. Following through on her phone she emailed him the results.

That done, she turned her mind back to her personal life. Details flew through her brain like a pulsing strobe light: four hour drive, 11:30 am ferry, and 12:00 noon rendezvous. She swiftly did the time calculation and realized she had to be out the door by 07:10. It was 07:05.

With a glad whoop she sailed back into the bedroom, flinging her kimono on the bed. In her dressing room she slipped into her light nylon bikini panty, which was good for travelling as it would rinse out and dry quickly, and started to pull on her yoga pants. *What was she doing?* She needed to wear nylon shorts as she would be in a kayak and the forecast was sunny and hot. In fact the long range forecast was for sunshine for at least a month. She quickly pulled on the shorts over her long slim legs. Reaching into another wire basket, she selected a sports bra and then, thinking *holiday,* gleefully flung it back and pulled on a stretchy short-sleeved soft blue t-shirt which would brighten the beige of her shorts.

On the floor by the door her bulging backpack waited for her; she stuffed in the yoga pants. For the millionth time she checked her list. She already had her clothing in hand. As it was high summer she was counting on being in quick-dry shorts most of the time; however, on the advice of the staff at a local kayak shop she had added a sun-proof hat which shaded her face and neck and fastened securely, plus a bright orange hoodie for cool evenings. She had included basic medical supplies (a suture kit, gloves, antibiotic and hydrocortisone cream, a rubber tourniquet, several syringes, adrenalin, Demerol, antihistamines and oral analgesics) plus sunscreen and a few personal items. She efficiently finished packing everything and checked the bathroom.

07:10! She was on schedule. She laughed with delight and triumph. Her heart pounded in her chest as she grabbed her lunch out of the fridge and raced to her car, snatching up her backpack as she passed it.

Right then a scratch at the tent flap brought her back to the present and her painful predicament. "Who is it?" asked Juli.

"Me. Tom. I want to see how you're doing." He sounded worried.

"Okay," groaned Juli struggling to sit up and failed, still hurting and feeling drugged.

Tom entered slowly and knelt by her. He winced as he examined each of her hands, saying, "tut, tut." The blisters were raw and weeping. "Well you're better off than the other beginners. But it was a rough night for everyone. We're probably staying put today to let you all heal, but there is a chance Marybell is too injured to continue on the trip. We're assessing that now. We might have to leave."

"Fine, fine," she mumbled barely aware of what he was saying. "I need to sleep today. Do what you think is best."

"Thanks for being so cooperative. Snuggle back under cover and relax." He tucked her hands gently inside the sleeping bag.

"That's me 'old cooperative,'" she mumbled even though she wanted to say, *Could I please have the hydrocortisone cream out of my bag,* but Tom disappeared as fast and silently as he had come.

Suddenly Richard appeared in the opening of the tent flap. "I heard about the hands. Why didn't you tell me last night? I thought it was your shoulders" His blue eyes blazed.

"Are you blaming me?" she retorted hiding her hands like a child caught doing something wrong.

"No of course not." His voice softened. "Tom and I shouldn't have chosen such a difficult paddle."

Juli sniffed her agreement.

"Maybe I can make amends. Here, I have some ointment that works like a miracle." He held a small white jar in his large hands. She couldn't help but notice how sturdy and capable they were. And, his male scent of smoke and salt surrounded her, making her feel dizzy and vulnerable in her sleeping bag.

She leaned away from him. "So do I," she snapped.

"Mine's better," he insisted as he cradled her right hand in his large one and gently massaged cream into her delicate skin.

She caught a look at the label 'Calendula with Boric acid'. That seemed pretty harmless. Her mind wandered: if he's into old remedies maybe he studied *The Red Book* of Hergest from 1382. It contained a collection of herbal remedies that lasted 500 years; some must have worked. Or, maybe Bohme's *The Signature of all Things* which was based on the Christian belief that herbs which

50

resemble body parts can be used to treat that part like the seeds of skull cap can treat headaches. Probably the latter, as even Galen in 200AD had endorsed this theory. She would go along with him on Calendula, but if he chose anything else she would refuse.

Richard seemed to have read her mind again as he offered gently, "There're more powerful ointments but I'd rather use the most natural treatments possible. This's what we need." He smiled down at her, the burnished glow of the sun on the tent forming a golden halo around his head. She blinked, knowing it was an optical illusion, knowing he wasn't special. He was a man, capable but pushy.

Juli still could feel the warmth of his hands. She shook herself, this man was practicing medicine without a license. She should report him. Then she noticed her hands weren't stinging any more. The cream was starting to heal them. And, when he offered her another analgesic, first showing her the name on the label, she accepted, swallowed it with most of the glass of water, thanked him quietly, lay down, and was instantly asleep. She didn't know Richard stayed by her side until she was deeply asleep, watching her face as though he was mesmerized.

Much later she awakened to the sound of clinking metal. She lay still wondering what time it was. The rosy tan on the side of the tent was her first clue; afternoon. The dull ache in her shoulder her second; the analgesic was wearing off; three or four hours must have passed. She was on an ill-fated kayak trip with a strange man who seemed to be taking care of her . . . and Tom, she added as an afterthought. She struggled to sit up and noted a twinge in her left shoulder; it wasn't a stabbing pain any more but it definitely was not back to normal. She was relieved she didn't have to paddle today. Then she checked her hands. The redness and swelling were gone and all her fingers flexed almost normally. And the skin where it had been blistered was healing over. She knew how resilient the human body was, but its healing powers still amazed her, and, in her case, seemed to have been aided by the Calendula cream. She would try it again, if he offered.

Now she could smell bacon. She was in the middle of nowhere, how could there be bacon? She struggled out of her sleeping bag and into her stretch pants which she had chosen deliberately for comfort but now realized they clung to her body, revealing every curve and muscle. The doctor in her came forward saying, *it's only a body. Settle down.*

Juli lifted the tent flap and peered out. Richard huddled around a small fire tending a pan. No one else was visible. She stood up outside the tent and looked around. The sun shone brightly, another golden day. A light wind ruffled her hair. Two ravens cawed at each other across the tents. One kayak was on the shore – a double. Two tents were visible, the double behind

52

her and the single. Richard didn't look at her but was concentrating on the bacon as if it was a volcano about to explode. Her heart lurched. Where were the others? She staggered to the beach searching the clear sapphire water for answers.

CHAPTER SIX

"Where's everybody?" she asked as she swiveled toward him looking like a cougar about to pounce. "Did they go on ahead?" She advanced slowly toward him and the bacon.

"Not exactly," he paused as though grappling for words, still averting his eyes like a guilty person. She continued to glare at him and after a few moments he blurted, "They went back." Her eyes widened with surprise and shock. Presumably to soften the news he added, "Marybell was crying that she hated kayaking and wanted to go home. Her hands were bleeding. Nothing we said would convince her to stay."

"They went back?" Juli couldn't compute what that meant. "Already?"

"Yes. It was the tide. They had to leave fast to catch the tide." Richard stirred the bacon recklessly as he explained.

"Tom didn't talk to me."

"Sure he did. I saw him go in your tent. And he told me about your hands. He said you said, 'he should do what he thought best.'" Rich shrugged.

"I did not." *Maybe I did.*

"You were sleeping."

"I was drugged," she screeched. Then smiled apologetically, "Yah I know. . . I needed to be drugged. My body sure was screaming." As she talked she moved closer to Richard. "When does he get back?"

Richard swallowed and fed another piece of driftwood to the fire. He still didn't look at her.

Juli peered at the ocean as if Tom would appear any minute. "Tom? Do we wait here for him?"

"Ah no." He fussed over the bacon, staring intently at it as if it might hop out of the frying pan.

She turned toward him with a jerk. "No! What?" Her voice was loud and directed like a javelin right at Richard. The crows were silent. This couldn't be happening to her. Marigold was wrong about this trip; it was nothing but unrelenting pain. Juli should have brought a morphine drip, which she could have set up and totally blissed out in the tent and not moved for a week.

"No we don't wait." His eyes pleaded for mercy. "He's not coming back. He urged us to go on and enjoy ourselves. He has caches of food set up along our route." He shrugged as if to say it didn't matter.

"Not coming back?" Juli couldn't believe it. "He should have asked me." Tom was the guide. Guides didn't leave their people on a deserted island. "I don't want to go on. I demand to be taken back. I don't know you." Her heart was racing, her blood pressure sky high. No one ever treated her this way, making decisions without consulting her.

He stirred the very crisp bacon avoiding eye contact with her, exactly as if she was an angry bear, and repeated calmly, "Tom said you wanted to sleep and he should do what he thought best. He thought it best to take Marybell back." Finally Richard looked at her, eyes pleading, "Please don't be unreasonable."

"I'm not unreasonable. No one has ever called me unreasonable before. Who do you think you are?" She heard her voice attacking him as enraged emotions boiled through her body. Here she was in pain and helpless and depending on this stranger. Ever since her dad left when she was six, and she took charge of her younger siblings with her mother, she had always been in charge or consulted about anything that affected her.

His voice was defensive, almost begging, "This is my first holiday in two years. Maybe I shouldn't have stuck my neck out and offered to continue. But I know the waters well and the timing is right for me."

"So what's that to me?" Arrogant bastard, she wanted to shout. Pain spasms shot through her shoulders, making her wince. She had never seen him before and would never see him again once she got back to Vancouver Island. A mosquito buzzed around her legs unnoticed.

"Probably nothing, but I'm pretty burned out. I'm a solo physician on Cortes Island, on call 24/7. I haven't been able to find a locum until now. I really need this holiday." He raised his eyes to hers, beseeching.

He was a doctor - that was why he seemed to be a healer. And using Calendula fit with an island lifestyle. He did have a job; she was wrong about that. Her mind rapidly cycled through data: he didn't know she was a doctor, she was as burned out as he was, he seemed harmless as a man as he hadn't even flirted with her, he seemed to know how to handle a kayak, and as he lived in these islands and as Tom treated him as a peer, he must be a good guide. So she thought she would be safe on a number of fronts. She never took risks and here she was thirty-four with nothing exciting to report about her life so far. She decided to take a chance. She blurted, "I see Tom left the single tent. Can I use it?" *I'm negotiating terms. That means I'm considering continuing.* For the moment the pain eased and she was calming; even the rage was disappearing as she felt her normal in-control-self coming to life.

"Certainly, we have room for it . . . just." He explained, "Yak will be a little harder to paddle but we'll be more comfortable at camp."

"Okay I'll go on. But this is strictly with you as a guide. I need a holiday badly as well." *I must or I wouldn't agree to this. He must be desperate too, why else would he continue with a reluctant woman he didn't know?*

"It's a deal," he smiled tentatively, seemingly happy to have the trip continue.

She liked the way his eyes lighted when he smiled. *Stop it Juli*. He was too much of an authoritarian to be a candidate, she chided herself. Besides there was no candidate, as there was no position. He didn't even fit Marigold's intention: he was burned out, not sexy, and with unknown finances - zero out of three. *Well, he's a doctor with a job. So maybe one out of three. Sorry Marigold, not good enough.*

"How are the hands today?"

She thrust them out for his inspection, knowing he would be interested in her ability to paddle, turned them over and flexed her fingers. He reached out to touch them, but she put them behind her back. "Quite a bit better. I heal fast." She didn't want his sympathy. She could take care of herself. "Something smells good," sniffed Juli as she moved toward the fire and warmed her back, being careful not to let the heat irritate her hands.

Rich watched her silently then commented, "Probably best not to warm those hands. They'll start to swell again." He stared at the bacon as if it was the most important thing in the world.

I wasn't warming them. Why did he say that? Probably to stop thinking about my shapely gluts. Out loud Juli muttered, "I know that," and crossed her arms over her chest, protecting her hands from the heat and elevating them to reduce the swelling.

"We're having toasted bacon sandwiches for brunch. C'mon and sit over here." He indicated a spot on a log near him. Juli nodded agreement but chose her own spot on a rock, asserting her independence. But her hunger and the aroma of bacon made her greedily reach for the sandwich. She carefully grasped the sandwich with her tender hands and, as there was nothing the matter with her teeth, she bit into it. *Crunch, chew, crunch, chew*, the crisp salty bacon stimulated her salivary glands and taste buds. She couldn't remember food ever tasting this good, mainly she ate on the go: sandwiches or a hardboiled egg, and an apple; things she could transport easily and gulp down.

"I made lattes. Hope that's okay as I thought you needed the extra protein." He held the mug, handle forward, out to her. He shrugged apologetically, "It's canned milk. Not up to Starbuck standards for sure."

"I've never tried canned milk." Her eyes widened with appreciation as she carefully clasped the handle with her tender fingers and balanced the bottom of the warm cup on her arm. The smoky aroma of coffee called to her. "Right on. I love lattes." *That's what I call class. Maybe this trip won't be a nightmare.*

He smiled, seemingly relieved with her response.

She noted that when he smiled his whole face lit up. Juli get a grip, whispered a small voice in her head. He's not your type, much too casual. Be careful. Don't encourage him. He's a country GP; you're aiming for a lucrative specialist's practice in Vancouver.

"We've chicken kabobs for supper. Then to bed, and up and pack early. By my calculations it'll be slack at seven am. Best to cross Sutil Channel then." He pointed across the water, "Over to Cortes Island."

"Hope my body's up for it." She looked at her palms. The redness and stiffness had eased enough to allow her to hold the latte to her lips and sip the strange-tasting liquid.

He reassured her as though she was a patient, "Don't worry. I can do most of it."

"Is this route all planned?" She sniffed the remaining bacon and leaned closer to the fire.

"Yes, Tom laid it on so we have a cache at each places. Makes life more luxurious."

"I don't care about luxury." If she wanted luxury she would have gone to the newly rebuilt Oak Bay Hotel to sun bathe and swim in their heated salt water pool on the edge of the ocean, and been pampered and coddled like a very precious person. Instead she had chosen a wilderness kayak trip with strangers to refresh her spirit and reunite her with nature. "I mainly want to be safe and comfortable."

"I'm into safe and comfortable. So we agree." More bacon sizzled in front of him; tiny bubbles of fat formed and broke gently.

So he thinks I'm agreeing with him. No use arguing. I want peace and quiet. I don't have to talk with him. I won't even have to look at him as I'll be at the front of the kayak. She could see he was absorbed with the fire, so she turned away to gaze over the dark blue water to the distant emerald island beckoning to her from across the strait. It didn't look very far; she felt confident she would be able to make the paddle tomorrow. Next she examined the beach, but could see no trace of Tom or his unhappy clients; it was as though they had never existed. She swung back, her eyes made a one hundred and eighty degree sweep to rest on Richard still bent in great concentration over the fire. She couldn't resist disturbing him. "Do I call you Richard or Ric or doctor?"

He looked at her with a boyish smile. "I like Rich. It makes me feel wealthy."

"Okay Rich, let's do it. I'll be ready at six am for pack up, especially if I sleep on and off all day today." *Rich? Marigold would say that was a qualifier; she said he had to be rich. She meant money, but maybe the universe doesn't differentiate between Rich and rich. Okay Marigold, a definite one out of three.* Juli shook her head muttering inaudibly, "no way Marigold: not till an eagle descends and speaks to me."

"Good idea, that's my plan. The tide'll be at slack and won't pull us north or south. Piece of cake." Rich started the clean up taking the pan to the ocean to scrub it with sand. "I've been wanting to explore this side of Cortes from the water since I came to the island four years ago," his voice sounded excited. "But if you hadn't agreed we could have gone back. Thanks for agreeing. I want to keep going. Who knows when I'll get this opportunity again? For safety reasons I wouldn't do it alone, that's another reason why I had signed up with Tom." He stood up, clean pan in hand, turned toward her and asked, "What should I call you? Juliet?"

"Not Juliet. Try Juli. That's what my fr . . ." She stopped herself. He wasn't a friend. "That's what people call me."

"Sounds good Juli. Tomorrow we're heading across to Carrington Bay. As I said we'll go at slack tide. It'll be an easy paddle."

He didn't look at her, probably for fear she would get her hackles up again. "My hands are still pretty sore," complained Juli. "Not to mention my shoulders, which could use a Cortisone shot." *I sound like a wimp; my injuries are minor.*

He soothed, "This will be a gentle paddle. You won't have to do much. I can handle most of it, especially if we time this right." He plunged the BBQ fork into a piece of bread and held it near the coals.

She moved close to him saying, "I don't know anything about tides. I'm depending on you." *Did I say that? I never depend on anyone. And, I do know something about tides.* "Don't look so stricken. As soon as these hands are better I'll do my share." The crease on his brow smoothed out but he was still deep in thought, probably wondering if he should have encouraged Tom to come back for her. "Hey watch the toast," shouted Juli grabbing the fork from him. She slid it off the fork onto a tin plate and efficiently drizzled honey on top.

Rich raised his eyes and stared at her intensely as if he was trying to decide if he should trust her. "If our positions were reversed I'd be asking a lot of questions too. Let's try one more day. Once we're on Cortes if you want to leave I can take you to the ferry and go to my home."

Juli heard him and realized he was not one hundred percent committed to the trip either. He might dump her on

Cortes. Then, based on the smile tugging at the corners of his mouth she decided he was relaxing, now that he had thought of a way to get rid of her.

After the late breakfast they each cleaned their own plate and stored it for the next meal. Rich tended the fire and then disappeared into the double tent which Juli assumed meant she would have the single. She would move her gear later, for now she needed a walk on the beach. At the far edge, well away from their tents, she lay down on a dry silvery log, relaxing. The warm sun heated her well-fed body, the ocean murmured, squirrels trilled, and insects buzzed. She would stay one more night and one more paddle.

When she opened her eyes the first thing she saw high in the Douglas fir was an immature eagle eyeing her as if she were a potential piece of meat. "Sorry eagle, not today," she said as she carefully sat up and eased off the log. There was still no sign of Rich, and as she walked back toward the tents she saw her sleeping bag opened to the sun. Rich must have done it - that was thoughtful. She gathered the sleeping bag on her way past and carried it to the single tent. When she poked her head inside, she saw that her backpack was there. Gratefully she dragged her sleeping bag inside, and laid it on the slim air mattress. Rich had placed the calendula cream and analgesics by the entrance. Chugging from her water bottle she downed two pills and then carefully smoothed cream over her tender palms. She liked this cream so much that she would recommend it in the future. Then she carefully eased out of her boots, and pulled the bag around her and settled back into a very deep sleep.

She was struggling to climb a rock face and was being dive bombed by two adult eagles protecting their nest at the pinnacle. She moaned. A voice intruded to save her, "Juli, Juli wake up. You've been sleeping all afternoon."

"I hear you," she called from inside the tent. "I dreamed there were eagles; they hated me. I slept but I'm not refreshed; I'm still tired." She noted the confusion and whining in her own voice.

"I can't help you with the eagles but supper will be ready in twenty minutes. Baked potatoes, baked beans, and garlic marinated chicken breast on a skewer."

The dream faded from her memory as the urgency of hunger became a priority. "Now you're talking. That's worth getting up for." Her stomach rumbled reminding her the bacon was long gone. Quickly she tossed back the sleeping bag, flexed her fingers to find they were almost completely healed and slipped on her beach jellies. She massaged more Calendula into the sore spots. Took a deep breath, threw back the tent flap, and squared her shoulders, ready for the next adventure. Rich huddled over the fire, faithfully cooking, waiting on her as if he was a paid guide. In fact he was another tired doctor on a holiday trying to rejuvenate.

She sat close to the fire, allowing its warmth to further relax her. As she waited for the food to finish cooking she watched Rich. His yellow rubber boots covered his legs to mid-calf, attractive strong calves, and his black neoprene shorts covered his bulky muscled thighs. He obviously was fit. The bit of skin that was showing intrigued her so much she wanted to see more. Unable to resist, her gaze shifted upward to note the bulge in his groin. *Juli stop it, you have no right to assess this man like he's on your examining table.* However if he was on her table she would be completely clinical and not feel the stirrings inside her body that were leading to sexual excitement. She must be getting rested. She had to control this. She was on this trip to recuperate not to complicate her life. Marigold would say, *healthy, rich and sexy, three of three criteria have been met. Pay attention Juli.*

Rich, under her intense inspection, shifted uncomfortably, took a gulp of his beer, and turned away to tend the food. Juli forced her heart to return to a normal slow rhythm and moved to organize their plates and cutlery. "There's another beer in the cooler. Help yourself," he called over his shoulder.

"A cold beer. Great." Juli dashed to the cache and selected a can of lager. She popped the tab and sipped the cool bubbly fluid. She realized how thirsty she was as she had very little to drink today; she scolded herself and sat down to enjoy the beer.

"This looks done to me," called Rich. "Come and check it. I don't want to cook the chicken until it's leather . . . I don't want us to eat raw meat either."

"I'm coming, I'm coming," cried Juli as she navigated the stony beach. When she reached Rich she slipped, his hand shot out to grab her arm to steady her. Like a tsunami, warmth and energy flowed from his fingers through her body. Their equally startled eyes met, time stood still as they stayed locked in contact as if they had both touched a live electric wire. Rich regained control first and released her arm and stepped back. "Sorry, I thought you were going to fall into the fire."

I think I did fall into the fire. As Juli turned away, thoughts raced like the tide through a narrow channel, swift and unstoppable. This was crazy; they were alone on a remote beach. This was not a reality show on TV, this was real life. The truth was she knew nothing about this man. Her intellect warned her to stay away from him. Out loud Juli said, "No problem. I'll get the plates."

Rich gazed thoughtfully into the fire.

The baked potatoes with sour cream and chives, beans in sweet molasses, and garlicky tender chicken were the best she had ever had. As she licked her fingers she thanked him, "Thanks

Rich, I'm enjoying your cooking. But I can do more. My hands actually . . . much to my surprise . . . feel almost normal. That Calendula really works." She held her hands up, fingers spread wide for him to see; smudges of grease on her cheeks made her look like an eager young child.

"Good about the hands. I knew the cream would work." He smiled a small sympathetic smile as he inquired, "Now what about your shoulders; I bet they're still sore."

She shrugged her shoulders back and winced.

"Here let me fix that," he offered as he carefully placed his hands on her shoulders. She bent forward giving him access to her neck and back. She had hesitated at first not wanting to take advantage of his skills, but then she reasoned that the success of the trip depended on both of them being healthy and it was to his benefit to have her in paddling form. *Wow*, the last time hadn't been her imagination: his fingers almost sparked when they touched her flesh. She wondered if that happened with all his patients or was this peculiar to the two of them. For sure this had never happened before to her. His hands seemed so large and strong compared to her body that she suddenly felt fragile. She could barely breathe as his fingers massaged her neck and then moved to her shoulder blades, finding and pressing the knots.

"Ouch, that's it. That's it. Don't stop. I hate it; I love it. Ahh, you did it," she sighed as the muscle relaxed. Then Rich carefully massaged the skin over and around her shoulders. The searing pain followed by deep relaxation of the muscle was almost orgasmic. She shook her head: Juli get it together that was pain and relief from same; sex is pleasant, leading, hopefully, to nirvana. She had never reached that peak with her first boyfriend as they were both too inexperienced. She wanted Rich's hands to run down her spine, then his soft lips to nibble each vertebrae; the roughness of his palms would be a sensory contrast to his soft lips. She ached for his touch; she had never felt this before, never wanted anything so much. *Juli get a grip*, shouted the voice of reality in her head. *This is a combination of the isolation and that you are rested and full of energy. Even Dave, your boss, would look good to you now* – no way, she would never be that desperate. Besides he was Marigold's.

Finally Rich pulled, seemingly reluctantly, away from her. Then safely on the other side of the fire he grinned at her much like the cat who had swallowed the bird.

She absorbed the smile and knew it was friendly and found herself involuntarily smiling back. Their eyes met blue to blue, violet to cobalt. A flash of energy seared the air between them. Juli backed up startled and looked into the fire which seemed pale in comparison. Every time she relaxed with him something happened to jolt her awareness of him as a powerful human being, a desirable exciting male of the species. He must have felt it too, as he turned away saying in a colorless voice, "There's not much to do but yes we can share the cooking and clean up. I still will pack Yak."

"Of course you pack Yak. I know the limits of my abilities." Did she? Did she really? She hoped so. But for sure she was letting him touch her again. He seemed to be full of electricity. She was not interested in his electricity. She was not interested in anyone's electricity. She only wanted to get healthy again and get back to work.

The air was still warm after supper was cleaned up so she drifted down to the beach where she could glimpse the sunset. A rhythmic dance of colors - fiery cherry, tangerine, and opalescent gold entranced her. She wondered if Marigold was on Dream seeker looking at this same sky. *I wish she was here so we could talk.* Finally, as the sky darkened, she headed for her tent cradling her hands which felt tender again.

CHAPTER SEVEN

The clank, clank of the hull hitting a buoy woke Marigold. Adrenalin flowed; she was on Dream Seeker with Dave.

Yesterday! She wanted to put that out of her mind. Dave had been careless even to the point of endangering them. First there was the crash into the fuel dock which startled the attendant enough so that he warned Dave not to do that again, and next, when they approached a buoy at Sidney Spit he had gunned the boat after she had hooked the buoy and almost lost her overboard.

This whole year, especially the last two months, had been strange. He had worked long hours, was forgetful at home, was checking and rechecking everything on the boat, but making clumsy mistakes anyway. Now, worst of all, he was sleeping only a few hours at night or passing out with alcohol and sleeping almost in a coma. None of it was fun for her or good for their relationship. She couldn't remember the last time they had a quiet supper together or for that matter any sex: good, bad or indifferent. Didn't he love her anymore?

So here she was the morning of a new day. She rubbed her forehead, then realizing Dave was not in the berth with her, she scrambled to the cockpit. He was on the foredeck letting the lines off the buoy. "Dave," she called as she left the cabin, "How about a life jacket?"

"Later, I'll get it later."

The rule was always wear your life vest or jacket when cruising. What was going on with him? A puzzled expression crossed her face as she quickly slipped into her shorts and t-shirt and headed on deck again. He was winding the lines in a tight pile on top of the cabin, completely unaware of the tide drifting them away from the buoy and toward another tethered boat. Marigold raced to the stern to start the engine. It fired up on the first try. Dave crashed into her and took over the helm, steering straight across the bar toward Sidney.

It was low tide. The bar was going to be close, Marigold thought as she watched the water grow lighter in color, then she could see the sand rushing past. The boat, heavy now with way, pushed across the bar, hesitating slightly mid-bar, then breaking through. When the ocean became darker in color Marigold heaved a sigh of relief. Maybe he did know what he was doing. She was being over-anxious.

She stood beside him at the wheel. He ignored her as he put it on auto then sprinted to the foredeck again. The sail covers were still off and stowed below, so quickly he removed the sail ties and dashed back to the helm and flipped the electric winch to 'on.' The mainsail rose slowly and steadily and filled partly. As the wind was light it didn't really make much difference but it did steady Dream Seeker. Marigold could easily have done the ties but he seemed to want to do it all. She hoped he wouldn't run out of energy half way through Sansum Narrows.

They made steady progress toward Sidney. One of the Spirit series of ferries appeared, heading for Swartz Bay. Marigold pointed it out to Dave as she knew it was travelling fast. It was best to stand off till she passed and then cut across her stern. At least that's what Dave used to say. Today apparently he planned to cut across her bow. "Dave it'll be too close," warned Marigold.

"No, no, it'll be fine. We've got lots of time," said Dave not looking up as he fiddled with the GPS.

Marigold handed him his life jacket, "Put this on."

He pulled it on and fastened it loosely muttering, "Don't know how I forgot that."

Marigold prodded, "Dave, c'mon. Let's rethink this race with the ferry. We're in no rush. They are. They have a schedule to keep."

"We have a schedule. We have to be at Dodd Narrows by seven." He looked up and saw the ferry bearing down on them. His eyes widened in surprise. "But the GPS says we're okay."

"Dave, we have to be there alive. Please stand down. She'll be past in minutes." Marigold put her hand on his arm.

He shrugged it away and growled, "Well okay. Just to make you happy." Dave turned a hard right, still facing the oncoming ferry, but on a path to miss it. The ferry honked five times, warning them they were sailing into danger. Passengers peered expectantly out the windows. Dave frowned as he steered along the side of the speeding ferry and as soon as she passed he turned into the wake which made the bow rise out of the water and slam down hard. Marigold hung on to the lifeline. Dave frowned with worry but veered west leaving Saanich peninsula to port and Salt Spring Island to starboard, bouncing almost out of control over the far side of the wake.

Marigold felt weak in the knees. She sat down hard on the cockpit bench. She was too old for this ride'em cowboy stuff. Why was he looking so worried and making such bad judgment calls? What was going on? He wouldn't have done this last year.

They crossed north of the Saanich peninsula without tangling with any other ferries. That was sheer luck, not great planning on Dave's part. He gripped the wheel smiling, life jacket flapping, sun and wind burning his skin. The tide held and carried them past Cowichan Bay and into cliff-lined Sansum Narrows, past Burgoyne Bay on Salt Spring, which she knew as an emergency anchorage only, as the bottom wasn't very good for anchoring. As Mill Bay floated past off the port side she knew they weren't going to stop until Dave's goal for the day was reached. Resigned she went below and prepared ham (which had been intended for breakfast) and lettuce sandwiches and coffee. For a few minutes she thought she would cancel the coffee but then she knew Dave would complain. He liked at least four cups before noon.

She took over the helm while he ate, pacing on the foredeck. Finally after a quick trip to the head he returned. "Dave please put on sun screen," she suggested. He took the tube from her and slathered great quantities on himself. Stepping behind her he hugged her with his left hand and eased her hand off the wheel and casually put his on. They travelled thus for ten minutes, Marigold loved the feel of him as the muscles of his arm held her close, and his chest heaved as he breathed. He smelled of coffee and sun lotion. She could stay in the comfort of his arm all day. But it wasn't to be.

Dave put Dream Seeker on auto and went forward to untie the jib. Racing back he activated the furling gear and the sail unfurled, filling as it went. Dream Seeker picked up speed as they passed Chemainus, then Ladysmith, and eased between Ruxton and Thetis Islands.

They arrived at Dodd Narrows at seven thirty. The ebb had started. Dave furled both sails and plunged into the passage. The current, probably at two to three knots against them, slowed Dream Seeker to three knots headway so they inched though the channel. The boat was large enough not to be bothered by the back eddies; Marigold knew a smaller boat would be buffeted about and even dashed toward the steep rock faces. However, the main danger they faced was from the boats whipping past them almost out of control as they proceeded south with the ebb. She hated to think of the damage that they might cause to Dream Seeker. Dave's face was in a permanent frown.

Marigold breathed a sigh of relief as they left the unfriendly waters of Dodd Narrows. The wind freshened so that Dream Seeker, with the jib unfurled, picked up speed. They slipped past Duke Point while the ferry was unloading, and into Nanaimo Harbor, straight to the Yacht Club where they were expected, and greeted, and assisted to tie up. Dave, sipping on yet another coffee, tied up the sails while Marigold went below to remove her warm cruising clothes to put on shore attire. "Well babe I'm starved. Let's head over to the water front restaurant. If I remember correctly the food is good. Hope they have the same cook as last year." He flung off his life vest and still in his shorts and t-shirt and boat shoes, no socks, took her hand and headed for the dock. They climbed the steep wooden steps, through the locking gates, registered in the office, and headed down the waterfront walkway.

At the restaurant they sat right in the window with the best view of boats and float planes. Dave ordered a bottle of champagne, "We have to celebrate a great day on the water." As he smiled at her, warmth and love bathed her in a golden glow, almost back to normal. Then as quickly as it had appeared it disappeared as he stared out the window, tapping the side of his wine glass restlessly. It had been a nerve wracking day but she smiled, trying to encourage his attention on her. She sipped the champagne to steady her nerves. Dave polished off the bottle, and then two glasses of Shiraz with his steak and lobster, and then cognac.

He leaned on Marigold heavily when they left. He had done it again, drunk way too much. That was two nights in a row. Now he would pass out. She had thought this would be a trip for the two of them to have time together. That wasn't happening. She helped him stumble back to Dream Seeker and into bed. He started snoring immediately. Marigold settled down to read. As she picked up the book she noticed something had fallen out of Dave's pocket. She picked up the bottle, tranquillizers. Her eyes blurred. Why would he have that? She felt mystified, puzzled. She put the bottle back in his pocket and returned to the cockpit.

The air was still warm. Above the dark silhouette of the Nanaimo Yacht Club the sunset, with strands of fire-engine red, orange, and gold, promised wind for the next day. "Red sky at night, sailors' delight; red sky in the morning, sailors' warning," she muttered to herself. *I wonder if Juli is looking at this same sky. I so wish I could talk with her.* She sat on the foredeck until the darkening sky and chilling air drove her in. Dave was still snoring.

CHAPTER EIGHT

Juli woke early and snuggled into her sleeping bag, watching the sun dance across the roof of her tent. She had been dreaming about a cool bubbling stream; the one at the south end of the lake where they used to wade and play on hot lazy summer days. She opened her eyes wide and sniffed for moisture that would herald a rain storm. *No moisture. No rain. That's a good omen.* She had had a great sleep after Richard massaged her shoulders

As she lay there she could hear Rich moving silently, packing up camping gear. She let him, as he liked to pack Yak. How easily she had fallen into the familiar way to refer to her kayak and to letting him take care of her. Finally she slid out of the warm sleeping bag and shrugged into her quick-dry shorts. Her fingers protested at first but gradually they loosened up, movement was good for them. Then, rolling the bag expertly into a small packet and letting the air out of her mattress, she carried them out of the tent. While Rich was busy tending the fire and breakfast she slipped down to the kayak with her things. On one hand he was a slave driver, and on the other he really was a nurturing male looking after her and giving her lots of space. *My, my, how my opinion has changed,* she observed. Fleetingly she wondered if he was gay. *He must be gay, all men flirt with me. He hasn't even made a pass. Sure there's been a spark of energy between us but it never seems sexual . . . on his side at least.* That had made her feel a little disappointed, and then relieved as if a huge burden had been lifted from her shoulders. *So there Marigold, he's gay; we're back to a maybe rich, not sexy, and probably healthy; one and a half out of three.*

This was the ideal holiday for her. He was a competent guide and cook and a strong paddler; what more could she want? This was perfect. She would enjoy this holiday, then when she got back to Victoria she could start a serious search for a partner. Marigold was probably right; Juli should consider finding a partner and building a family. It was time to have a baby; that is, if she wanted a healthy one. Her eggs were starting to get old. She hadn't figured out how she was going to do her specialist training and have a baby . . . yet. She stared at the cobalt water looking for an answer. She wondered if she should freeze her eggs, then she could relax and get back to her peaceful life.

She picked a dry spot on the beach and, adjusting for her tender hands, did her morning yoga sun salutations to stretch her body. She was very pleased to feel her muscles responding normally. At the top of her salutation, arms and hands stretched to the heavens she gazed out across the ocean. The dry summer air was so clear it was as if she had brand-new eyes; the blue mountains on the Vancouver-mainland side stood out so clearly and distinctly it was as if they had moved closer in the night. Attempting 'downward dog' her hands screamed, forcing her onto her forearms and elbows. Comfortable again she raised herself into a half plank. Thus she continued modifying her poses to avoid pain but get the maximum benefit. Once she was limbered up Juli looked for Rich. He was huddled over the camp fire and as she moved toward him he looked up and greeted her with, "Hi. Perfect timing. The oatmeal and raisins are ready."

"Yum, thanks," purred Juli as she sat on a rock close to the fire.

"How are your hands today?" His eyes riveted on them as though he was sending a blast of healing energy.

"Getting better." She held them up for inspection, holding them away from her breasts which heated up from the intensity of his gaze even though he was focused on her hands. Right then a trill cut through the air, Juli turned her head to search the near-by cedar tree. The call came again, from deeper in the tall trees and then from her right. "What kind of a bird makes that sound?" she asked, distracting him from her hands.

"Not a bird. Squirrels. That's our local squirrels, they communicate with that trill. It's a way to keep track of one another in our dense forests." He didn't even look up as he talked as if he was determined to keep distance between them. "Red Squirrels and Douglas Squirrels are our native tree squirrels and are approximately the same size. The Red Squirrel is just that, rusty-red in color with white underparts, whereas its cousin the Douglas Squirrel is reddish-brown with yellow underparts. Both are adapted to a life in coniferous forests, but the Douglas Squirrel is found only on B.C.'s southern coast, whereas the Red Squirrel is absent here but found virtually everywhere else in B.C."

"Our local squirrel is reddish brown with yellow underparts," stated Juli. Why couldn't he say that? Why was he so convoluted?

"That's what I said."

Sure, she thought. "They're so beautiful. I'm going to leave them some of my raisins." She swiveled on the rock, noting its hardness cutting into her butt.

"Don't . . . don't feed the wildlife." He lifted his head to frown at her. "There's a balance here. People disturb it enough as is without deliberately doing things." He carried her share of the oatmeal over to her in a metal bowl. "Besides they eat pine cones.

If you watch the forest floor you can often see a small pile of scales that's left over from their feast. They have lots of natural food."

"I'm going to leave some anyway," she said as she turned away.

"Stubborn, stubborn," he muttered under his breath.

"Likely the crows will get it first and the squirrels'll never see it," declared Juli. *So take that Mister know-it-all.* Juli raised the spoon to her lips. The oatmeal warmed her mouth, the sweetness of raisins and honey danced across her tongue. "Yum, this's good." She smiled her thanks into his watchful eyes, realizing for the first time that her opinion might be important to him.

"Glad you like it." He smiled back tentatively. "This is going to be our regular breakfast."

"That's good for me," said Juli offering him a warm smile.

"Another reason for not encouraging them is that we have a cache of food and we want it to be here when we get back." He sat down holding his own bowl and scooped large spoonfuls into his mouth.

"Oh I see what you mean," said Juli thoughtfully. Then she continued, "If I can't leave food I think I'll go off for a few minutes and talk with the squirrels."

"Don't take too long." He started to clean the bowls.

She watched him for a moment and then offered, "As soon as my hands heal I'll do the cleanup. You and Tom make meal prep look easy. I can't compete with that." Compete, why did she use that word?

He smiled a full broad smile that reached his eyes, "Now you're talking. But let's be sure those hands are up for it. Paddling is our first priority."

She liked basking in the warmth of his approval and concern.

He continued, "We have to scoot across Sutil Channel. We leave in the next half hour."

She stopped with a playful smile on her lips saying, "I bet you know how Sutil Channel was named."

"Sure do." he smiled, delighted to recite facts. "Around 1864 Captain George Henry Richards named it in honor of the ship Sutil used by Galiano in exploring the region. We'll go past a group of small islands today called the Subtle Islands which are named for his ship as well but translated to English."

Too much information, thought Juli. Was he trying to impress her? "Where are we going again?" Juli actually had her own chart along and knew exactly where they were going. But she liked to test his patience and she did like the sound of his voice, even if he was gay.

He pulled out a chart, sealed in plastic to protect it from the salt water, and pointed, "To Carrington Bay on this side of Cortes." He moved closer holding the chart for her to see and pointed at a bay. "We're approaching from the west." The heat from his body danced across her skin like the sun dancing across wavelets, making her sway toward him. He backed away clutching the chart as though he was trying to protect himself. "Right. We'll enter the bay going past Jane Islet . . . staying in the north channel. There're some unmarked rocks due south. I know, I saw them last time I was here." It was a good sign that he was explaining where they were going. The more they both knew the safer the trip would be.

"I'm counting on you to remember where those rocks are. I'll help as much as I can, but basically I'm depending on you." There, she had said it again, depending on you. She could navigate through that north channel, easy peasy. Why had that come out of her mouth?

"No problem, I know these waters well." He didn't look at her, it was as though she didn't exist.

She determined to keep him talking to see if she could get him to show some interest. "What makes this a good stop over?" As she sat back on the log letting the cool ocean air bathe her in calmness she could feel his body heat making her hormones happy, *what a pity he was gay.*

His head came up but his eyes were veiled behind heavy lids. "On the plus side, it's got good protection from a southeaster; on the negative side, it's relatively open to the prevailing northwesterly winds that spring up in late afternoon or evening. But, in fact, the winds from any direction are not going to be a major problem. It's a very protected bay."

His five o'clock shadow was like a magnet for her eyes. "Sound's good." She stood up, rubbed her neck as though to erase his hold on her, and stretched. Her shoulders were still sore but exercise, mild exercise, would be good for them. And, a way to get some space from this man to stop her body alternating like a pulsar between indifference and intense awareness. As if he was aware of her attraction he held up the chart like a shield as he cleared his throat and continued, "And, there's our camp site . . . behind Lucy and Ronnie Islets. Plus, the whole bay is surrounded by a provincial recreational reserve. There's even a lagoon which we could get to if we wanted to portage over piled-up driftwood." He seemed to be rattling on like a teacher trying to fill her head with information.

As she turned away she thought his eyes followed every movement of her slender body especially the curve of her butt under her tight pants. "No thanks, not for me. Piled up driftwood sounds fraught with danger." And too much of a challenge for her tired body. How thoughtless of him to even suggest it. Did he want her to break a leg?

"I suppose so but it would definitely give us a workout."

She couldn't just sit around camp staring at his facial hair. Maybe exercise would help their relationship. "Let's deal with today's paddle, then consider your outdoor gym idea." As she talked she pulled on her spray skirt which made her look like an escapee from the Swan Lake ballet, the comic version. However once she was in the kayak it would protect her from drips off the paddle, and rogue waves. Was she looking for trouble? Rogue or monster waves occurred far out at sea where physical factors such as high winds and strong currents caused waves to merge to create a single exceptionally large wave. And that was not going to happen in these protected waters. What was the matter with her?

"If we don't go to the lagoon for sure we could enjoy the glorious sunset from the reversing waterfall."

"Hum," replied Juli trying to discourage his monologue as his voice had become irritating. She didn't even want to see the lagoon. He droned on, "When the tide is flooding the waterfall drops to the land side and of course on the ebb it drops to the ocean side. It's quite remarkable to observe. But if you don't see this one, we have another one in Von Donop Inlet."

He was so persistent she decided to egg him on as she would have done with her brother. "Now that I can get on side with - a sunset and a reversing waterfall. Sounds exotic. Maybe I do want to see it." He was spewing information like a tour guide, maybe he was a wannabe travel agent. While they talked Juli watched Rich efficiently extinguish the flames and finish packing the kayak. Ordinarily she would be right in there pulling her weight, but her hands were still tender.

Her whole life was taking care of others and had been for as long as she could remember. As a doctor it was constantly worrying about others. As a child her mom always said, 'look after Mikey, he's your little brother. He needs your help.'

Now her mom and stepdad were in their sixties and her stepdad's diabetes was a concern, as he wasn't good about taking his meds regularly or checking his blood sugars. His last hemoglobin test, which measures the average blood sugar over the previous two to three months, was too high, so she was concerned he was at risk for vascular disease. Then there was her mom's arthritis and she wondered if she had inherited that weakness. If yes, would she pass it on to her child? What child? She still didn't even have a man in her life. *Stop worrying Juli, you'll probably never know.*

While she thought she wandered toward the trees. Standing under a thirty-foot cedar she squinted up through the branches thrilling softly as her tongue vibrated in a satisfying manner. Then a small squeak caught her attention, small bright black eyes stared at her. A small red-brown furry animal chirped at her flipping his fluffy tail as he talked. She chirped back, "Mr. Squirrel you're so beautiful. I'm glad to meet you. I'll call you Raisin because your eyes are like them. You have lots of cedar cones to eat so I won't leave you any food. Remember to stay in the protective cover of your tree. You would be a tasty morsel for a hawk or an eagle. Yes, stay deep in your tree; it feeds you and protects you." A trill called from higher in the tree, the squirrel flipped his tail and scooted easily upward until Juli lost sight of him. The trills sounded from deeper and deeper in the forest as Raisin and his mate travelled, leaping from branch to branch, through the high canopy. Even squirrels could find a mate in a forest miles and miles deep. What was the matter with her?

"Juli," called Rich tentatively as though not sure of her reaction. "Yak is loaded." He was standing beside the kayak in his high yellow boating boots, his spray skirt draped around him like a party dress. His boney knees protruded tanned and bare.

Juli glanced at his knees and wanted to giggle, instead she said, "Coming." After thanking the birds and animals for sharing their territory, she loped down to the kayak, her spray skirt slapping against her legs.

Rich held the kayak parallel to the shore while she climbed in. Careful to balance her weight on her hands and equally on both sides of the kayak, she slid gracefully into her seat. *There take that! I learn fast.* Using her paddle to help steady the kayak she felt Rich easing into the steering seat. Today she didn't resent it that he held the power. Her hands were far too tender to do anything but assist. However, as she gained her strength and her experience in Yak, she would want to steer. But not today. Today she was going to continue healing. She turned back to check on Rich, who was looking across the channel to Cortes Island with an eager look on his face. Then she focused on the job in front of her.

The sun reflected off the mirror-like surface almost convincing her that the ocean was friendly to humans. She knew otherwise from living in Vancouver and Victoria. She had great respect for the strength of nature. Without turning she called back to Rich, "Sorry I can't put much power into my strokes."

"Relax, I can handle it," boasted Rich.

So for today with her private guide and paddler at the helm she would take the opportunity to relax and enjoy their travels. A sleek round-headed pup seal surfaced close-by and seemed to be pacing them. "Look there's a Harbor seal," whispered Rich as he rested his paddle on the gunwale. "He can dive to depths of ninety meters and stay submerged for fifteen to twenty-eight minutes. His ear openings close for the dive and he can slow his heart rate to only four to six beats per minute, which slows his metabolic rate and drops his body temperature. As well he can tolerate high carbon dioxide levels, and as he has a greater volume of blood than a land mammal of the same size he has more oxygen."

"Enough information. Let me enjoy him," she ordered turning her head and body so she could watch the seal. Then, peering into the seal's liquid brown eyes she felt like she was touching his soul. Her own heart rate slowed; she sighed with satisfaction; this was why she was on this trip. Languidly she turned back to Rich and glimpsed similar emotions flitting across his face and knew he cared deeply for the wild life.

After a few minutes Rich continued as if it was a way to stay in touch with her. "He has ten times more than humans of myoglobin in his muscles which binds oxygen." As he talked he checked the line he had dropped over the side as traversing this channel was an excellent opportunity to catch a fish.

Juli turned her head and in a hushed voice said, "I suppose that's important, but I don't care right now." She pointed, "What I see is a glistening round head with large prominent eyes - as cute as a baby's. The wet spots around his eyes are tears but not because he's crying but because he doesn't have lacrimal ducts like humans, I know this somehow from anatomy class." *Oops I shouldn't have said that.* "And look at that dear little snout with a V-shape."

"Anatomy class? Hey I hope that means you're a lab tech or a nurse."

"Something like that," she muttered.

Sea gulls cried and squawked over a herring ball. Far over head a jet vapor trail reminded her of the busy outside world which she was trying to forget. Ahead of the kayak dark green conifers beckoned to her from the shore. It was as though a giant had thrown a handful of jade in the air and it clung to the trees, sparking and shining. Her eyes scanned the dense green for the telltale-white dots of eagle heads, and saw none. As they came closer to Cortes she could make out individual trees but she couldn't see the entrance to the bay. Maybe he had made a mistake. She hoped not as she was lethargic with fatigue and her hands burned.

As if he had read her thoughts Rich assured her, "The entrance is to the left of that rock out cropping. It's hard to see. We'll be inside soon."

She twisted to look over her shoulder at him. "I'll have to take your word for it. I can't see any break in the forest." She felt vulnerable all of a sudden, not sure if she should trust him.

"It's there; I've been here before. Besides I have my GPS and it says we're right on course." His voice was strong and convincing.

"A GPS seems like cheating," she called back over her shoulder, challenging him again. He was being responsible. Why couldn't she leave him alone?

"I could use a compass." He back pedaled. "I have one for back up, but why bother when the GPS is so accurate and so easy. It's enough being in a kayak without making it harder."

"I'm not complaining but for a man-against-nature trip, it seems to make it too easy."

"This is a man-WITH-nature trip," he corrected her.

"I like to give Mother Nature a chance," continued Juli ignoring him.

"I do too, but electronic navigating doesn't bother Her. And if it means we'll arrive safely and in good time, I say go for it." At that moment his line tugged. "Oh ho, I think Mother Nature is providing our supper. You paddle slowly, I'll pull it in." Juli looked back in time to see a torpedo-like silvery fish surface beside Yak, which Rich grabbed before it escaped, creating a dangerous rocking motion. "Yahoo," he hollered as yak's rocking settled. "It's a salmon, a Spring, about eight pounds. I've always wanted to catch one of these. They have always eluded me. Look at that." He laughed like a boy. "This'll feed us and the crabs: salmon tonight, crabs tomorrow." His voice was as speedy as a teenager's at his first driving lesson.

Juli forgot to paddle as she twisted to watch Rich struggling with the agile salmon. "Rich, I thought salmon were hard to catch." She laughed with glee, caught up in the excitement as the salmon flipped on Rich's spray skirt, rocking the kayak again.

"They are. We lucked out. Must be a stream of them passing through. This isn't even The Salmon Highway."

His happy face radiated warmth, adding to her heightened pulse rate. "The Salmon Highway? You're joking," she called over her shoulder.

"No." Rich shouted as he bent to examine the fish.

"There's no such thing," she challenged in a soft laughing voice.

"Sure, the passage between Quadra and Campbell River is called that because the salmon are forced through there on their way south. However, and lucky for us, some come across the top of Quadra and head south through these waters." He was babbling as if he wanted to please her.

Juli twisted her body again to look at Rich. She grinned. Rich looked funny, holding a flipping salmon on his spray skirt, smiling like a little boy looking at his favorite toy. "Okay I agree you were lucky to catch him. I'll paddle; you enjoy." She kept paddling toward the bay even though her hands protested. The fish slipped around so much he finally put a rope through its mouth and gills and towed it behind. "I'm going to tow it. Sure hope nothing eats it. If you see that seal again shout and I'll drag him in." Juli thought he was rather clever and at supper time she would be grateful for the delicious meal it would provide.

Finally after about an hour and a half paddle they came to the mouth of the bay. "There's a camp site behind those two Islets and the whole bay is surrounded by a provincial recreational reserve."

He's repeating himself. I guess he thinks I'm a dumb twit. It looked peaceful and safe. Juli felt her blood pressure drop another notch. This was good for her. She had no worries here, especially now she was in a safe harbor for the night. She would be even happier once she had her tent set up.

"Over to the left . . . we'll tuck in there," he said nodding toward a small beach, which was a typical West Coast beach with grey barnacled rocks. He steered them parallel to the beach and steadied the kayak with his paddle. "You'll have to get out first. I have this fish to cope with."

"Yup," answered Juli as she carefully eased her spray skirt off the coaming and placed her tender hands on the paddle behind her back. The pain was excruciating as she eased her weight on them. Luckily the rest of her body cooperated and her weight shifted smoothly to her left foot on the shore and she did an airborne roll out of the kayak, holding her hands protectively in the air. The back lash pushed Rich and the kayak back into the bay. Rich yelled, "Whoa, steady," as if he was riding a horse and used his paddle to push the kayak back on the beach.

"Sorry," shouted Juli as she stood rubbing her scraped knees with her forearms. She had to perfect that exit or she would be maimed by the end of the trip. *Damn.* Now she had sore knees.

"There's a camping area up that rise," called Rich as he struggled with the slippery fish while trying to climb out of the kayak.

Sure enough, when Juli climbed the bank there was a flat grassy area with picnic tables and outdoor toilets. *Absolute luxury.* She looked back in time to see Rich struggling out of the kayak. Unbalanced by the slippery salmon, he tipped over and splashed into the ocean. He stood dripping water, clutching the fish to his chest. Juli laughed so hard she had to hold her abdomen, "Don't let it go," she sobbed. "That's our food. I can't stand it. You look so funny." She slipped on the bank and landed hard on her seat. Slightly stunned she sat there as Rich squished over to her and laughing dropped the slimy salmon into her lap.

"Yuk, he's slippery," screamed Juli, tossing him back.

"Be careful, that's lunch." Rich grabbed the rope from her and, dangling the fish, started to march up the beach, water dripping off his sleeve. "In fact I'm going to gut it now while I'm a wet mess."

"Do you know what you are doing?" Now why did she say that? He had been nothing but competent so far. Why was she prodding at him?

Stopping to look back at her he challenged, "If I say no, will you do it?"

Oh ho, I got to him. "I could, but you caught it, so you clean it. That was what my stepdad would say." *Oops* she had given another clue about her life. This morning she woke resolved to treat him as the guide and keep herself totally separate. She didn't need a new friend; what she needed was to rest and heal and have time to commune with nature.

"Fine by me. I caught it, I can clean it. What can you do?" He persisted, "Can you get the fire going? Can you do that?"

Maybe I should say no. No doubt he'll do it. Juli nodded her head. She had always pulled her weight. "I think so. At least I passed my fire lighting at girl guides." *Oops*, she let down her guard again; she must be exhausted. "That was a long time ago."

"Starting it's easy; not burning down the forest is hard," he warned very much the responsible guide again.

"You prep the fish. Leave the rest to me." *I want to help so I better find out what equipment we have.*

"Juli here's the dry bag. You'll find stuff for the fire in it." He tossed her the bag. Being careful not to damage her hands, she caught it with her forearms like a seal clapping its flippers.

"Best make it close to the water," he cautioned. "The forest is pretty much dry tinder waiting for a spark."

"Yes, sir." *Untrusting man.* He knew nothing about her and she wasn't telling him that she had camped for years with her mom as well as her summer holidays at her grandparent's cottage. Juli hummed, enjoying the midday sun beaming on her as she set about gathering some of the dry tinder from the edge of the forest and larger pieces of driftwood from the beach. Once she was organized she started the fire easily. Standing back to admire her handiwork she noticed Rich's smile of relief. Maybe he wasn't the total controller that she thought he was.

After cleaning the fish and tying it First-Nations style to a plank of driftwood, he planted it in the sand near the fire. "Juli, please keep an eye on that." He gestured at the fish. "I'm going to find out what Tom has done about a shower." She watched Rich as he went to the cache hidden under driftwood and pulled out a metal box and a bucket. "I'm fetching fresh water from the stream." Then he bounced away like a fleeing deer toward the forest. Juli felt suddenly alone as he disappeared. At first she imagined that the crystal-clear water was so inviting that he stripped and plunged in, ridding his skin of salt crystals which would become very itchy. Then maybe after he rinsed his outer light nylon clothes and hung them to dry on a blackberry bush in the full sunlight, he probably laid back in his damp underwear at least until they were partially dry. She was tempted to creep up on him and feast her eyes on his body. She shook herself and turned back to the cooking salmon, thinking *I wish he would return*. She felt uneasy, being alone on the beach, and was beginning to realize he was important to her, and not just for guiding. When he returned to the camp site he was clean and damp so her imagination had been accurate. He moved close to the fire, first conscientiously checking on the salmon and then he stood close and turned slowly, enjoying the heat and allowing his clothes to finish drying. She hated that her unease came out as irritation, "You took long enough. Did you use all our shower water?"

Rich justified, "I took a dip in the stream to get the salt and stink of salmon off me." The questioning look in her eyes urged him on. "But it was cold. You wouldn't like it."

She glared at him, suddenly more annoyed. *How dare he?* How could he know what she would like? Why was she reacting so strongly?

"I set up the sun shower for tomorrow, so for today there's fresh water in the bucket up there and towels. Tomorrow, with luck, we'll have warm water." As he talked he added a few dry sticks to the fire. His voice sounded normal, "While you're splashing around I'll make some biscuits. Good old Tom also left flour and baking powder and a pan."

Maybe he was right. She didn't want to jump into an icy stream and she wasn't very salty. Mainly she was worried about her hands, so she would try to be reasonable. He did haul water for her. "Thanks for the fresh water and yum to the biscuits," said Juli as she left the fire. She found the bucket and soaped herself down and rinsed off, shivering under the cold water. Suddenly realizing that she had stripped in the open, ocean on one side, forest on the other, she glanced at Rich. He had shifted around the fire so his back was to her and was sitting with his head in his hands. Finally Juli dried off in the sun, pulled on her clothes and skipped back to the fire

Much later they sat around the fire, relaxed from devouring roasted salmon and biscuits and chardonnay from the food cache. A squirrel trilled in the giant fir trees crowding the shore. The pink blush of the evening sky bathed them in softness. "How thoughtful of Tom to leave us flour and wine and a water bucket," grinned Juli.

"Good thing, otherwise we would be hungry, sober, and covered with fish scales." He laughed a full throated laugh that encompassed his whole body. Juli laughed, too, enjoying his deep masculine vibrations.

"Right! I am the antithesis - full and relaxed and clean." Juli stretched and then realized she had bumped against Rich. He felt warm. She looked at him. He was stretched out on his side, face rosy from the fire light, his fair hair tousled, very relaxed and exceedingly attractive and sensual.

Their eyes caught and held for an intense second, his body tensed slightly. That felt good, she thought. Maybe his pheromones liked her pheromones. What happened to her assessment that he was gay? Maybe she was wrong; maybe he was world-weary and exhausted, just like he said. Just like she was.

He cleared his throat, "We better turn in. Daylight comes soon. We can stay here two nights, so tomorrow we hike up to the reversing waterfall and around the lagoon."

"Right," agreed Juli. She didn't remind him that she had said that it was too dangerous.

As if he read her mind he said, "That's if it's okay with you. It'll be good exercise and we'll avoid the dangerous driftwood piles."

Maybe he did want her opinion. "If you can do it, so can I." Her voice was strong and she was so comfortable she decided not to mention their discussion about putting her on the ferry back to Quadra. Deep in thought she wondered why he never asked about her life. Wasn't he interested or was he so egocentric he didn't care about her. Probably the latter, one of those male doctors who requires constant stroking by a bevy of handmaidens. With that thought she stiffened and leaned away from him. Going for a hike was a good idea as it was much too dangerous to hang around camp with him. He was looking more and more attractive every day; she knew it was a version of cabin fever. She should never have agreed to stay; she should have insisted that they return to Heriot Bay. They sat in silence on opposite sides of the fire, each absorbed with their own thoughts. Unnoticed the sensual orange and fuchsia sunset surrounded them and seeped deep into their bodies. Finally a chill in the air woke her to cool limbs and she decided to retire for the night. When she stood to go to her tent he said, "By the way there's a bit of a wolf problem on this island." He paused dramatically, "So don't wander about alone at night."

"Did you manufacture that to make me nervous?"

He snorted, "Whatever."

She didn't believe him, however she kept her flashlight on when she went to the outhouse and back to her tent. In the night she thought she heard the faint howl of a wolf in the distance, in response she pulled the sleeping bag over her head and went back to sleep.

CHAPTER NINE

Juli woke and sniffed. *That smells like frying bacon, again. It can't be.* Her stomach growled. She sniffed again, pushing against the inside of the tent flap she stuck her nose out, confirming the bacon was not a dream. Then she settled back in her warm sleeping bag, waiting for him to announce breakfast. Her hands felt almost normal; spots of redness warned her where the tender areas were. That calendula cream country-doctor Rich had given her did work. She smiled languidly and stretched like a satisfied cat. Then she curled up in her sleeping bag knowing she didn't have to rise and tend to the sick and lame. For a brief moment a feeling of guilt flashed through her mind, guilt that she was here in comfort and there were people suffering. She shrugged, others would have to step up, for now she was free of all responsibility save what she chose. She was on holiday, in the wilderness, away from the demands of humans. Only Mother Nature could force her into a response.

"Come and get it, egg muffins." A deep persistent male voice hollered over the clanging of a metal tin. "C'mon sleepyhead. Rise and shine."

She smiled. That man knew a way to her heart. He fed her and she came running like a starving puppy. And yes she chose to let him feed her. She found it very nurturing and healing and he seemed willing. Yesterday he had asked her to start the fire. That was the first time he had asked for help, other, of course, than that horrible first day of paddling. It was the first time she had been able to help as she knew about fire lighting and she was rested enough finally, and starting to feel glad to be alive, glad to be human.

Dressing was quick, as she was sleeping in her t-shirt and panties, even her socks. So slipping into her shorts and black hoodie and bright blue jellies, which she had brought for land use, she opened the tent flap to bright sunlight dancing on a stream of wavelets ruffled by the wind. The golden summer continued, all was well. She breathed deeply, noting the rush of oxygen into her body, a body that was coming alive again. She could get used to this. She stretched, while walking eagerly toward the fire with a spring in her step. Once again Rich was taking care of her. She was beginning to like this too much. "How did you produce this meal? No way is there a chicken laying eggs out here."

He responded with a welcoming tone, "It's Tom again. He's made a fridge of sorts with a solar powered cooler. That's where I keep the left-over cooked salmon."

She stopped, faced the East, and bowed from the waist saying, "Thank you Tom" then she skipped toward Rich and perched on a log close to the fire. "He must have come out here a few days before we left and brought all this stuff."

"Sure, he did all the prep for us. He's got a runabout so it didn't take him very long to set this up. You've got to get something for your money," he waved his arm, fork pointing at the azure sky, "besides all this beautiful wilderness." Her intelligent eyes swept the panorama of ocean and forest; she loved the wilderness and could see he appreciated it, too: he listened to the squirrels, was quiet and thoughtful, and was careful with garbage. As a bonus he could sit for long periods without talking; good thing, as she couldn't stand people who talked incessantly; although yesterday on the beach, he had come close to incessant.

Juli barely heard him as she was hungry and focused on the spattering ham pieces. They called to her via her scent neurons which were hard wired to her stomach. Totally driven by her senses she edged close to Rich watching him intently as he prepared the food. He fumbled the English muffin, almost dropping it in the fire. He retrieved it and completed the assembly and handed it to her. As she took it their fingers touched. An electrical spark jumped, causing her to lurch back, and his hand to jerk. Just as quickly the moment disappeared as she turned away and quickly devoured the egg muffin, savoring the runny yolk, the salty ham, and the toasted bun. "It's heavenly I need another." She paused, flushed, "Sorry I'm not usually so greedy and out of control. Hunger has pushed me over the edge."

Rich shrugged, "Hardly out of control," and smiled, not a flirty smile but a steady friendly one. "Coming right up. You're hungry, that's a good sign. Your hands must be getting better." He held his hands out, palms up, beckoning her.

"Only a few tender spots." She held out her hands for his inspection. She was surprised that she wanted his opinion. She was beginning to trust this man. She qualified that as for his medical opinion and his outdoor skills. Nothing else. She placed her hands, palms up on his large weather darkened hands, heat radiated upward cradling her hands with care.

His voice rumbled, "They look almost healed to me. Glad we didn't have to use something stronger."

Juli noted his pupils dilate slightly as he stared at her hands; intuitively she knew it was a sexual response, the first she had seen in him, but what was more surprising was that she felt moisture between her legs. *Get a hold Juli*, warned a small voice in her head. *You don't need to roll on your back for the first hunk that smiles at you. Of course not, but he is handsome . . . and strong . . . and smart. Marigold said healthy, sexy and rich; he seemed healthy, was sometimes sexy, and was Rich. So was that a three out of three?* She quickly withdrew her hands and plunged them out of sight in her pockets. His body tightened as he changed from a pussy cat to a tiger in an instant. She had never experienced that with a male before; nor ever felt her own response change from playful kitten to tail wagging panting Labrador wanting attention. It was nothing. She was totally isolated from the world of humans and she was dependent on him for her survival. This was not normal life. She would keep her distance from him, and when he found out she was a doctor, he would turn tail and gallop full speed in the other direction.

She ate the second egg muffin slowly, savoring every bite and chewing thoroughly. It didn't get better than this: good food, sapphire ocean, golden sunshine, chirping birds, trilling squirrels. Work seemed far away. She hadn't turned on her smart phone for twenty-four hours now and she decided to leave it off. Who would call her? Marigold? Maybe. Work? Unlikely. Mom? She was busy taking care of Pete.

Rich moved jerkily around putting out the fire while describing the day to come, "We can leave our camp here. The meadow is at the foot of the bay beyond the lagoon; unfortunately we can't take the kayak there because of the log jam and reversing waterfall. We'll follow the deer trails through the forest and skirt around the bay to the east end where there's a beautiful meadow. Should be peaceful. There's no one around and only one house at the foot of the bay . . . it's abandoned. It's only us and the animals and not many of them."

Did he have to point out how isolated they were? It was just the two of them. Like Adam and Eve. *Stop it Juli, this is nothing like Adam and Eve*, she argued with herself. *Well yes there are some similarities: I'm a woman, he's a man, and we are in a type of primeval garden. Yes, and that's it. Nothing more. This is a garden, lush and wild, and I'm a burned-out physician needing a stress-free holiday.*

Rich turned away to sort through the supplies that Tom had left, but Juli could see his hands were shaking. Maybe he was as affected by her as she him. That was something to think about. She felt like she was peeking in Pandora's Box and in danger of having the lid stay open, at least partially. She didn't need a complication in her life right now; she needed to think and heal and decide about her future.

Julie watched Rich cleaning up, a smile tugged at the corners of his mouth, and she moved to help him. They were going on a hike; it would be good for her; she needed exercise. Juli drank in the intoxicating atmosphere of this wilderness paradise. The ocean lapped gently against the small rocky beach, the cedars stood tall and graceful rimming the bay with green and absorbing noise so that other than the murmur of water and the faint whisper of wind, and the occasion trill of the squirrels, all was quiet. A deep stillness, deeper than she had ever felt before, settled over her.

Rich's deep voice drew her attention. "I've got bottled water and some snacks from the cache and Tom even put a backpack in it. So supplies'll be easy to carry. Do you think that'll be enough?" He held up the items for her inspection.

Why was he asking her opinion? Was he seeing her as more competent, even part of a team? "Sounds like you have what we need." She was being totally agreeable; she felt so relaxed she didn't want to argue about anything. "Tom really is making this trip trouble-free." Well only trouble-free in regard to food and showers; there was still the human element to deal with, as Rich and she were doing some kind of boy-girl dance. Hopefully they would get through that today and settle down to become friends. Maybe she should reveal more about herself, which would dispel his fantasies of her as a desirable female. If, indeed, that was what he was thinking.

Rich bundled the supplies into the knapsack talking amiably. "Tom's been guiding a lot of years. He and I went to school together on Cortes. I went off island to UBC, he to U Vic, and we met again on the island recently."

He was sharing personal stuff; that was interesting. She couldn't decide if she should encourage him or not so she decided to be friendly but cool. "So he's an old school chum. That explains why he trusts you so much." Rich nodded. She stood up wiping her hands. She knew she was just a client of Tom's, Rich was doing him a favor while having a holiday for himself. He had made it clear he was exhausted and didn't need a woman in his life. Nonetheless she would tie her tent closed tonight.

"I guess so," said Rich. "We were friends before. . ." His voice trailed off.

Juli noticed the sudden pain in his eyes and wanted to ask him about it but she felt she didn't know him well enough and they weren't friends and she wasn't his doctor.

Rich rubbed his chin, the stubble of a beard was beginning; suddenly she couldn't take her eyes off him; she felt something hot in her abdomen. He was not the man for her. He was a doctor. Two doctors in a family would be hell. He didn't even live in Victoria. She needed to forget it. It was only physical attraction. She knew it took a lot more than that to keep a relationship together.

He moved away from her saying, "When I was packing Yak I noticed that you had hiking boots so I hauled them out." He pointed and walked to the other side of the fire near the kayak, picked them up, and deposited them at her feet.

"Thanks, these jellies would be hard to walk in." She picked up the boots, muttering over her shoulder, "Then I could have blisters on my feet as well as my hands."

He smiled, "Speaking of blisters, your hands look pretty good to me?"

"Pretty good? That doesn't sound very medical." Her voice was playful and light.

"Ha! I'm not a doctor here - just a fellow kayaker." He had the backpack slung over one shoulder and stood staring at her like . . . like an absent minded stag in rut. She couldn't believe she thought that. He was only being friendly.

"Whatever . . . that calendula cream is amazing." She looked up and clapped her hands to acknowledge him and to demonstrate her freedom from pain. He was standing so close to her that her finger tips brushed his bare leg causing a ripple of hot energy to flash through her arms into her chest making her breath hesitate. Time stood still and as if she was in a slow motion dream, she watched him cradle her slender hand in his. Caught in a slow-motion dream she noted how tiny she seemed compared to him. *He's six foot four, everyone seems tiny next to him.*

His voice, surprisingly gently and hushed said, "Good. After today you should be ready for the paddle to Von Donop."

She imagined his eyes said, *I love your hands. I want to kiss them. I want them to touch me."* She turned quickly away and bent over to ease into one boot, "I'm looking forward to it." *My God, I'm like a teenage girl. I better not make eye contact.*

"First let's enjoy today. It's slightly overcast so it shouldn't be too hot for hiking." As he talked Rich bent over, eased her foot into the last boot and helped her tighten the laces. She steadied herself by putting a hand on his shoulder. That was a mistake as she felt the rippled response of his muscles.

He must have felt it too, as he stood up and backed away, adjusting the back pack, saying in a husky voice, "Let's go" and started off along the edge of the rocky beach, the forest on his left, and the restless ocean on his right. He didn't look back.

Juli scrambled after him not wanting to be left behind. The simplicity of nature surrounded her and calmed her. The terrain was rough and rocky even when they found the deer path through the forest. She stayed close, which was a challenge as he had a long confident stride, almost as if he was running away from her. But the thought of the wolf pack spiked her adrenalin, keeping her close to him.

Suddenly he stopped. She banged into him. He steadied her, placing his strong hand on her upper arm. "We're going to double back and find another path. We're close to a road and I definitely don't want to be seen by any of my patients. This is my holiday." Her breathing hesitated when he touched her and to her surprise her eyelids fluttered seductively as though they had a mind of their own and she heard her voice say casually, "Fine by me." Though she thought he was dreaming as there was no one out here but the squirrels. They were alone.

"We'll head back for a few minutes and then turn south sooner that's another way to the meadow . . . a pleasant spot for a snack." So saying he eased past her and started marching.

She couldn't believe how hungry she was again. Totally alert, her senses - hearing, sight, and smell - were vibrating and so super-keen that she wondered if there had been magic mushroom in their breakfast. Mesmerized she watched Rich's back as he moved along the path like a sure-footed deer, confident and courageous. His broad shoulders were easy to follow and if she slowed he would whistle and slow as well. At least for a bit, then he would pick up the pace again. The tall Douglas fir canopy towered over them providing shade for the forest floor which was dry and bare except for scattered Oregon grape and spindly salal. No wonder she hadn't seen any deer; there was nothing for them to eat. Nor did she hear the squirrels anymore; neither did she see any piles of fir-scale debris as evidence of their presence. She stumbled over a giant tree root; even the trees were searching for nourishment. The stumble made her realize she was not in her best form, though she had thought she was in good shape. Obviously she still needed rest.

Finally they arrived at a lush meadow enclosed by forest on three sides and open to the lagoon on the fourth. The grass brushed her thighs; an apple tree, left by an early settler, was dotted with small green apples struggling to grow and mature before the wildlife devoured them. Juli caught up to Rich when he slung the backpack onto a log on a slight rise providing full sun and a peaceful lagoon view. Juli hoped he was magically going to pull tomato and cucumber sandwiches out of the backpack even though she knew what the snacks were. He offered her a water bottle and a granola bar. She longed for a crisp juicy apple.

They sat side by side on top of a dry log as silently as deer resting; each lost in his thoughts. Abundant wildlife ignored them: a woodpecker drilled a tree for unsuspecting insects, a flock of pine siskins moving as one flitted past chirping, a frog croaked signaling his mate, a mosquito buzzed looking for a sustaining meal. Rich dropped his hat over his face and slid off the log to total relaxation on the moss. Following his lead Juli slipped lower to sit on the summer-dry moss and rest her back on the rough log. As her chin dropped to her chest she began to snore gently.

Juli woke first. A small black insect with wings tickled her arm, carefully she flicked it off and watched it take flight and lazily circle her head, and then gently land on Rich's hat. *Rich!* She jerked to full awareness as she realized he was stretched out right beside her, so close she could feel the heat of his body. Calming herself, she rolled up on her left arm, facing him, so she could study him. Strong limbs. Golden hairs. A male of the species in full testosterone splendor. Even asleep he exuded confident masculine strength.

Then cautiously, like an animal coming to life in a potentially dangerous place, his left arm moved, bent at the elbow, and fingers grasped the rim of the hat. He tipped it back carefully. His eyes opened slowly, like a lynx sensing prey was close, and she found herself staring into deep blue pools full of questions . . . and something else . . . enticement? Caught unaware she answered the invitation with a coy smile, then realizing she was encouraging him she rolled on her back so she couldn't see those provocative eyes. She sensed him withdrawing and heard the crackle of dry moss as he, too, leaned back. The charged air dissipated without a lightning bolt.

"We better head back," he said very casually as though he had felt nothing. "You'll feel hungry soon and we don't have any more food with us."

She ignored the huskiness in his voice saying, "Thanks for showing me this spot. I would never have found it myself. You're a good guide." Nonetheless she could feel the tension building between them again, so she stood up saying meekly, "I'm ready to go. You lead, I'll follow."

Much later, after they had hiked back to base camp and shared supper, she walked along the beach to a peaceful spot where she had a view west over the top of the small islet at the mouth of the bay. Soft pink and blazing orange and glittering gold, swirling as though stirred by a magic wand, greeted her eye. How could there be sickness in this world where there was beauty like this? The fading rays bathed her in softness. Juli smiled with contentment as she slumped against a log watching the magnificent display and digesting her delicious dinner of baked potato and salmon. After tomorrow's lunch sandwiches, which would finish the salmon, Rich had promised that they would have oysters off the beach. She looked forward to that as she was starving at every meal.

That night after supper she had been ready to babble about her day's experience, but Rich seemed distant and needing solitude. He had retired to his tent, muttering, "See you in the morning." That was probably for the best, she thought. Now she could fully concentrate on her sunset. The rhythm of living outside with nature, the ebb and flow of the ocean determining their paddling, and the sun bringing life each morning and bathing them in warmth throughout the day was awakening a primal newly discovered part of her body; layer by silken layer peeled from her psyche, leaving her feeling fresh and as vulnerable as a newborn baby. And yet she felt strong, stronger and more real than she had for years. She definitely was rested and becoming a sensory hog. All her neurons were tuned to observe and remember every sensation.

Rich lay in his tent staring at the muted light dancing above him. He had made a mistake coming with this unknown woman. But he liked her. He liked her soft skin, the way she smelled, the casual curl of her blond hair, her sapphire eyes. "I've been celibate since long before Sylvia died, and now I'm acting like a love-sick schoolboy," he muttered. "She fits with me physically: tall for a woman, probably 5'10", which works with my height; blond and fair like me; energetic and a good hiker like me, and she's brave to come on the first kayak trip of her life alone. I like independent women. She says what she likes, she's clear. I like that. I know she's from Victoria. Tom told me that. Maybe she's a fabulously rich heiress who will marry me and take care of me. Maybe she's a shop clerk who is penniless. Actually I don't care how much money she has. I care if she is healthy, has goals, is sane, likes sex, and definitely wants children. My next relationship will be permanent. I want a family. I have to find the right woman. Maybe it's Juli. Maybe it isn't." He turned over and bunched his pillow under his head. "I'll forget it for now. I'll see how the trip goes. So far it's been the best holiday I've ever been on." And drowsed off.

Juli watched the burnished sun slowly sink over Read and Quadra Islands. Then as the air chilled she reluctantly retired to her own tent and was soon deep in REM sleep. Neither of them knew a doe and her twins wandered past, seeking the relative safety of humans over the wolves which could be heard howling as they ran through the distant forest.

CHAPTER TEN

Morning dawned hot under a clear cobalt sky. Another day in paradise, thought Juli as she stretched through her yoga sun salutations like a flower opening to the sun. The ocean murmured its greeting: 'come paddle on me, I'm friendly today.' The golden summer high was holding and the ocean was at its most obedient. She knew winter with gale force winds would be a totally different story, and one to be avoided at all costs in her kayak.

Later as they sat by the fire and munched their egg muffins, no ham today, Rich described his plan for their day, "We're heading for Von Donop Inlet. And we'll stay there four nights. That will give us lots of time to rest and explore." A distant squirrel trilled as it called his mate. Rich sounded calm and back in control; back in his guiding, protector persona.

In an excited tone Juli said, "Four nights in one place, that'll be like a permanent camp." A tingle of excitement started in her toes and rapidly spread through her body.

Rich elaborated, "We'll do day trips. The inlet is five kilometers in length and almost cuts right through the upper part of Cortes."

"That long?" Juli looked up from the cooking fire to stare into his sky-blue eyes. Blue eyes like her stepdad's when he was happy.

"Yes, it's that long. Really." He glanced at her, exasperation showing.

"That would make it quite a unique stretch of water." She couldn't seem to let it go; she wanted to hear his voice and wanted to test his patience.

His voice was calm and low, "There are other spectacular inlets around here: Toba, Princess Louisa, and there're lots more. What's unusual with Von Don is that it's long and narrow with exceptionally well protected waters. We can really relax there. And Tom has left us some goodies I'm sure." As he talked they cleared up and cleaned the breakfast dishes and packed everything except for Tom's metal food chest, which Rich buried as before and placed a large rock on top to protect it from curious animals.

"Tell me a little more about it," encouraged Juli liking the sound of his voice. He wasn't on the make today, she was sure of that. He avoided eye contact with her and wasn't doing any male posturing, so she could relax and enjoy his masculinity. Yesterday was different. Maybe they could be friends . . . for today.

"It was named after Edward John Breton Von Donop, RN. He was a midshipman who arrived in Esquimalt in 1862, where he joined Captain Pender who was in charge of a hydrographic survey. Why exactly Pender named this inlet Von Donop I don't know, but maybe Von Donop was the first to realize how extensive it was."

"It looked like a small indent to me. If you hadn't suggested it and if I didn't have a chart, I would have missed it." He looked at her sharply and she realized she had revealed she had been keeping a secret. She couldn't explain why she had done it, other than to keep some knowledge and power for herself in case he turned out to be incompetent.

"It's pretty special," he shrugged, as if to say if I was on a trip with a stranger I would have brought my own chart too, and continued, "and rather narrow in spots with twists and turns, nooks and crannies, a peaceful lagoon and surrounded by forest hiking trails."

"Sounds wonderful." And so was his voice.

"BC Parks, in partnership with the Klahoose First Nations, declared the five-kilometer long inlet and surrounding three thousand acres a marine park in 1994." She knew she was admiring him openly and making lingering eye contact and wanting to prolong the conversation. His eyes were clear. And oh so curious.

Why was he starting to make eye contact again? Was their relationship changing? Suddenly she couldn't stand the intensity of his gaze. "I can hardly wait. Let's get going," she said jumping to her feet and picking up the backpack and heading to the kayak to stow it.

He lurched to his feet. "Sure. It's a magical spot. Hathayim Marine Park here we come." They worked as a team to get ready to leave, with Rich packing the kayak and Juli bringing their supplies to him. Juli had come to admire his work and see the art and skill involved to balance the kayak while stowing all the supplies. Then Juli made a final trip to the outhouse. Following the golden-buttercup-edged trail led her through juicy yellow salmon berries hanging plump and inviting like the sirens of Ulysses. She plucked one, her mouth puckered. It wasn't as sweet as the wild strawberries hidden in shady places; she searched in vain for one of those to sweeten her mouth. A demanding voice prodded her on, "Hurry up Juli, we have to flow with the tide."

"Coming," she called as she stopped to thank the spirits of the forest and tiny white wild flowers for sharing their gifts. Giving thanks always was a good thing. Love flooded her body and soul as her eyes drank in the beauty. On her way back to the kayak she stood on a ledge of rock, looking at the swaying ocean constantly moving, carrying life-giving nutrients with it. A blue heron, stood ankle deep, alert with hunger, searching for her breakfast which surely would swim by soon. Canada geese honked and waddled on the beach. Man was their greatest enemy: would pollution end it all? Juli breathed deeply and shook her bad thoughts away. This golden day with golden weather required golden thoughts.

"C'mon Juli. The tide waits for no man . . . or woman. I want to catch the ride north," called Rich already seated in the kayak picking salmon scales off the gunnels. Then he shook his head as if to clear his thoughts and studied the narrow exit ahead of them.

"Here I am," said Juli as she skipped blithely toward him like the forest sprite she was, stopping only to pull on her spray skirt. She eased into the kayak as if she had been born to it, secured her spray shirt, and raised her right arm pointing to the mouth of the bay, "Wagon train ho! Or maybe I should say thar she blows!"

Obediently Rich dug his paddle deep, giving them a burst of speed across the calm water. "You're right. We might see a whale . . . grey humpbacks are known to cut through the channel."

"That would be exciting," said Juli as she stared eagerly and hopefully about her. The ocean was as smooth as a pool of molten gold, reflecting the warm sun into their faces, and the paddling was easy. Juli couldn't help but compare her life with the ocean: sometimes it flowed smoothly, other times it was rough and dangerous. So where was she now? In a calm or in a dangerous place? She was very quiet as she pondered this deep question, and forced her heart to beat at a regular rate and rhythm. She wanted to turn and look at Rich, but she dared not reveal what she was feeling. Instead she allowed the energy rays pulsing from his body into her back to spread warmth and passion through her aching muscles.

As Rich had predicted the tide, combined with his vigorous paddling and Juli's light paddling to conserve her hands, propelled them after a six hour paddle into Von Donop Inlet. A lonely park sign on the north shore confirmed their location for Juli. The entrance was a generous hundred meters wide and four or more meters deep. "We'll stay to the south. There's a rock that might bother us over there." He pointed at the rocks on the north side of the narrow inlet. "Though I doubt it, as we draw so little water."

Juli stared unbelievingly at a corridor of rocks and trees that were so rough and 3-D that it felt like she was in Disneyland and the rocks were foam.

Rich echoed her thoughts. "It looks fake but those rocks are sharp. Stay alert. There's no one to rescue us if we hit one and sink."

"There must be a few boats anchored in the inlet. They would help us."

"Sure. Juli . . . if they knew help was needed. Remember emergency communications don't reach this spot. There's no calling the coast guard for help."

He sounded nervous for the first time. She stared at the still surface and then looked deeper to see fine pieces of kelp flowing into the inlet and realized she would have to watch out for danger as a lot was happening under the surface. That would be easy, her whole life had been fraught with hidden dangers in the masculine profession of medicine. "You mean there's no pizza delivery?"

"Exactly," smiled Rich. "I hope you've got some first aid training in case I slip on an oyster shell."

"Relax, I can handle that, but no brain surgery please." She did it again; she didn't tell him.

"That's a relief. Knowing your limit is half the battle. And I, too, prefer it if you don't do brain surgery, at least on my brain, in the wilderness."

"Okay," smiled Juli noting the hesitation in his voice. For the first time she thought about it from his point of view - in the wilderness and responsible for a novice, an unknown quantity. She decided to tell him when they were out of the kayak that she was a doctor and reasonably competent.

"Look at the white flecks in the trees," said Rich as he rested his paddle on the gunwale and the kayak floated with the current deeper into the bay.

Juli examined the trees closely, "It looks like someone has shaken a feather pillow into a dark emerald comforter. Look a fleck is moving." She heard her incredulous voice saying, "It's flying. Soaring into the sapphire sky." Sapphire sky? Emerald comforter? Where did they come from? Was she a closet poet?

"They're bald eagles."

She squinted making her eyesight as keen as possible. "Wow! They are . . . eagles." Her voice rose in excitement, "Look that one is coming this way. He's checking us out. Look out." Jill ducked as though she thought the bird might mistake her for a salmon and plunge his claws into her.

"It's a female. They're larger than the males. Did you hear the air being pushed out of the way by those giant wings?" As he talked he started paddling again very gently, steering them carefully through the channel, keeping them in midstream.

"Yes," cooed Juli in a hushed tone full of awe. She had seen an eagle before, of course, but never this many or this close. Even the aching of her hands didn't take her attention from the magnificent scene. Automatically she rested her paddle in front of her.

"The average lifespan of Bald Eagles in the wild is around twenty years, with the oldest confirmed one twenty-eight years of age."

"Mmmm." Her hormones were responding again to his deep baritone voice.

"The Bald Eagle was officially removed from the U.S. federal government's list of endangered species in 1995."

"Mmmm." She felt vibrantly alive.

He continued as though trying to entertain her, "Bald Eagles are sexually mature at four or five years of age. When they are old enough to breed, they often return to the area where they were born. It is thought that Bald Eagles mate for life. However, if one member of a pair dies or disappears, the other will choose a new mate. A pair which has repeatedly failed in breeding attempts may split and look for new mates."

"That sounds very human." She wondered what else he knew about their sexual habits. Somehow she was sure he was going to tell her.

"Bald Eagle courtship involves elaborate, spectacular calls and flight displays. The flight includes swoops, chases, and cartwheels, in which they fly high, lock talons, and free fall, separating hopefully before hitting the ground."

Why was he emphasizing their mating? Juli tried to shut out his voice as she squinted into the clear water to see the occasional silver flash of a fish framed by brilliant orange and violet starfish clinging to the rocks like a bouquet of flowers. Her body betrayed her as her ears couldn't hear the screech of the eagle or the splash of water on the rocks since they were tuned selectively to the man's voice.

The voice sounded again. "Bald eagles are early breeders: nest building commences by mid-February, egg laying is often late February, and incubation is usually mid-March . . . hatching from mid-April to early May, and fledging late June to early July."

Juli,noted that even though his voice was like a musical instrument resonating with her, and she definitely was resonating, he was taking care of them by steering the kayak carefully in the center of the channel which now was starting to open up.

"They are dedicated parents with both the male and female taking turns incubating the eggs, but the female does most of the sitting. The parent not incubating will hunt for food or look for more nesting material. For the first two to three weeks of the nestling period at least one adult is at the nest almost one hundred percent of the time. After five to six weeks, the attendance of parents usually drops off considerably." he chuckled, "But they don't go very far, often perching in nearby trees watching to keep their baby safe."

She liked his chuckle and she liked that he had observed the good parenting of these birds. "Humans could learn something about parenting from them." She forced her voice to be calm as she didn't want to reveal the excitement she was feeling which was, she was sure, only due to a combination of the pristine wilderness and her release from day-to-day responsibilities.

"That's for sure, they even build and maintain their nest together. Which is saying something as the nest is the largest of any bird in North America; it is used repeatedly over many years and with the new material added each year may eventually make it as large as thirteen feet deep and eight feet across. Usually nests are viable for five years or so, as they either collapse in storms or break the branches supporting them by their sheer weight."

"So they cooperate to make a home, and look after their offspring."

"Yah but it's not all lovey-dovey. Like people it can go sour. In my office I've seen the ugly side of relationships."

Now he was warning her off. Her interpretation was that he was attracted to her but scared of closeness. Well so was she. If that was the case they should be able to keep this very platonic. "So what's the bad news?"

"The oldest chick often bears the advantage of larger size and louder voice, which tends to draw the parents attention towards them and it sometimes attacks and kills its younger siblings, especially early in the nesting period when their sizes are most different."

"They are meat-eating raptors. If the parents don't bring enough food I can see how that would happen. I don't think evil or malice enters into the equation."

"I didn't say it did. Basically it's survival of the fittest. We can see it plainly when we're so close to nature."

"Hopefully a few humans can rise above their animal instincts." She sounded jaded.

"Some do. In my rural practice most do." He pointed to a tall fir, "Keep watching; we should see some of the immature fledglings as they remain close to the nest."

"If they haven't eaten each other." Why did she say that? Was she becoming a sour old female?

"They're surviving as a species so they must be doing something right." Rich paddled steadily and they smoothly slid deeper and deeper into the wilderness, each lost in their own thoughts.

"Juli we have some choices here, we'll make camp near the reversing waterfall at the entrance to the lagoon. We're here three full days. Day one we can go through the reversing waterfall into the lagoon, day two we can hike into the lakes, and day three we can paddle to the south end and hike in to Squirrel cove. By then we might appreciate the great cooking at The Cove restaurant."

"I thought you didn't want to be seen," she peered over her shoulder challenging him.

He grinned like an eager boy, "I think my need for a steak will overcome my need for anonymity."

Juli laughed, "So you can be bought."

"Looks like it." He shrugged while he skillfully guided Yak.

"The hike into the lakes sounds great, so long as the wolves and cougars don't get me."

His smile shone with a sudden wolf-like leer, "You better stay close to me. There's bear, too."

"I will. You're a larger target. You know what they say: I don't have to run faster than a bear . . . I only have to be able to run faster than you." There, take that, she thought.

He laughed again, a full belly roar that startled some small black water birds into flight. "I better stay in good shape." While they talked they floated placidly deeper into nature.

Juli liked him relaxed. His eyes crinkled at the corners when he laughed. She smiled looking back over her shoulder, "If we hike to the lakes on day one, then the next day, if we're still alive, and while we're still clean from the lakes, I'd like to hike to that restaurant."

"That would leave day three for the lagoon."

"Sure that's fine by me," said Juli mesmerized by the beauty unfolding around her.

"I'm easy."

Who did he think he was kidding? He was intent on having his way. But she didn't care enough to fight. She was in a drifting mood.

After a few minutes of silence he continued, "I'm going to pull rank, I think we should do the lagoon tomorrow on day one as the tides make sense. We need a high tide at slack to get through comfortably: tomorrow that's at ten am going and the next day at eleven am, which is day two. Then we would still have time to hike into the lake before darkness, and do the Cove on day three. Hopefully we would still be clean."

He didn't say it, but as she analyzed his plan, she realized they would overnight behind the waterfall and she briefly wondered how that would work. "Okay, if that's what Mother Nature dictates. That's what we do. Go with the flow, I always say." If he believed that, he was not a very good judge of character. She had to have iron will and determination to get through med school. So she left the schedule as he first suggested it and he would maintain his male dominance needs. She wouldn't sweat the small stuff. It really didn't matter to her.

As they proceeded deeper into the seemingly innocent waterway a seal appeared and disappeared, and seagulls cried in the distance behind them. Talking in hushed tones they continued to paddle down the center of the inlet, more cedars and firs and hemlock towered above them, more flecks of white revealed perched eagles. The golden day had morphed to emerald as the trees reflected in the still surface of the protected inlet. Now they talked in hushed voices, both aware of the sacred nature as they penetrated deeper inland. One lone sailboat motored far ahead of them going toward the head of the inlet; Juli saw no other sign of human life. She breathed deeply, finally she was completely relaxed. Rich was a good guide and companion, not prying into her life with questions. At first she had thought this was disinterest but now saw it as respect for her space. He was very calm to be with, his movements had purpose and were fluid and paced. She sensed a deep well of strength within him. *What am I thinking? I don't know him. He might be an inadequate person and a terrible doctor.* She shook her head; she didn't believe that.

When they arrived at a small beach Rich announced, "Here we are. There'll be another cache over that rise." Juli looked where he pointed. The small cliff and giant trees looked the same as everywhere else.

She shrugged, "if you say so."

"I do."

They beached the kayak and set up camp together. Juli knew the routine now, and as she was feeling stronger and rested, in fact stronger than she had for years, she pitched in just as she had when she was a girl when they camped on a lake near their home. Her mother, a very practical woman, had insisted on family holidays, and as Juli was the oldest of three children and as her father left them when she was six years old, she also helped her mother load the car and set up camp. She was used to being in charge and being responsible.

Once the tents were up Juli sat on a rock. The more she examined this forest the more detail she saw. She could distinguish different shades of green. At first it had been an emerald-green forest, but now the subtle greens, lime to dark blue called to her and seemed as rich and colorful as any tapestry.

"Yahoo," came Rich's call. He stood on the cliff waving something. "Cold beer," he called. "Cold beer."

She grinned, realizing the shift in appreciation that was transforming them both, so that now they were grateful for things they normally would have taken for granted. *Yes, a cold beer would taste good.* She smiled and waved back, encouraging him.

Rich climbed down to the beach and brought his find triumphantly to her like a caveman of old bringing home his hunting prize. He laughed gleefully, "Can you believe it? There's almost a dozen cans still on the ice. Tom I love you," he shouted to the sky, arms wide, one hand clutching a can of beer.

Juli grabbed the can from him. Flipped open the tab. As foam bubbled out, she licked it off and gulped some, making cold fizzy liquid bubbles burst in her mouth and slide down her throat. She splashed some on Rich. He grabbed her and took the can away saying, "If you're going to waste it you can't have it." Then he poured some down her neck. She tore off her top and flung it at him, shouting, "Give back my beer. I'm a paying customer. That's my beer. Tom left it for me. You're the guide. You have to stay sober." She grabbed the can from him and started running, laughing down the beach and then scrambling up the hill.

"Come back here. You have to share," he chased her. Laughing he tackled her on the rise so they rolled in the sand and dirt, juggling the can of beer to keep from losing the golden liquid. He lay on top of her his full weight pinning her down. She still held the can high over her head. He reached for it, their heads came together, nose to nose. She could feel the tickle of his three-day beard. The heat of his body. Their eyes locked as energy flowed between them; she couldn't look away. She was shaken and electrified and so aware it felt painful. It was as though she had tapped into a deep reservoir of love. This man was not gay, flashed through her thoughts. Her heart jerked to double time then started to race almost out of control as the next wave was passion, sweeping through her body setting her sexual neurons to action, making her nipples harden and her breasts swell, and heat spread through her pelvis right to her toes. *Juli, Juli,* called her common sense, *get out from under this man.* She started to wiggle and shove while waves of confused and tumultuous feeling washed over her like a storm surge. Thinking back she remembered she had watched the curve of his arms when he was paddling, listened for his dream-mumbling voice at night, enjoyed watching him eat. All warning signs her libido might be engaging, but it wasn't until he was full out on top of her, and she in a minimal undershirt, that she realized she wanted him badly. Did she love him? That wasn't possible; she didn't know him. Did she want a relationship with him? Probably not, they were ships passing in the night. Would he be interested in a casual affair, one that would end with this trip? She didn't know. Most lovers pledged fidelity for life and hopefully accompanied it with a guaranteed income; she couldn't promise either right now. She didn't know who she was any more or even where she would be working in a year.

He clamped down harder as if instinctively clutching his prey. Then suddenly he became very still and rolled off her saying, "Sorry, you can have the beer there's plenty more." His breath came in gulps as though he had run up a hill.

Juli abandoned the beer on the beach and staggered back to her tent. She lay on her air mattress breathing hard. *What a reaction!* They had to be together for another week. If they went on like this they would be in bed together. Would that be so bad? She didn't know him. Sure she did, he was a doctor; he would be healthy.

He lay at the top of the rise, sand in his hair, watching the azure of the sky beginning to shift to the reddish hue of the weakening sun settling nearing the horizon. His work life had been messed up by local politics. Of course he hoped to still be on Cortes, and still be their doctor, but that would be the board's decision and though he knew all the members, the board and its sympathies had changed. He wasn't sure they would offer him a contract to continue. That was democracy and that was how the health care system was run now. Of course he had a billing number and could practice elsewhere, maybe Campbell River if he had to move, but he would never sell his land, two hectares near Manson's Landing, waterfront completely forested with views of Marina Island. He had needed time to think; thus when Tom had called him and asked him to join this trip because he had so many beginners and because he wanted to spend time with his buddy, Rich had decided the kayak trip was exactly what he needed to get some distance from his everyday life and here he was.

He was not husband material, thought Juli, her thoughts whirling as fast as her hormones. Was she really looking for a husband? No, her life was full and complicated enough. Well not quite complicated enough as since she talked with Marigold she had been thinking about a child. Freezing her eggs was crazy. She was still at an age to have a healthy baby but she needed to do it soon. Maybe Rich was sent by the universe. He was intelligent and strong, and her period had just ended, so for the next week she would be fertile. And, as she could support herself and a nanny, she could manage a child. Could she be that cold blooded?

She didn't know this man. He would have rights. Did she want to share a child with him . . . forever? No. He didn't need to know. That was deceitful. Sure, but she didn't know that she would become pregnant. And it would be fun. She was sure he would be a great lover. His shoulders were broad and he had hair, golden hair on his chest. She wanted to run her fingers through it. Maybe he would turn her down. Maybe he really was gay. She would be disappointed. But she had taken a risk to go on this trip; maybe she should go with the flow and keep taking risks. Juli stared at the roof of her tent, smiling with excitement like a teenager before a prom.

Much later she lifted the tent flap to see Rich bent over the fire. She quietly joined him and sat on the log beside him. The blush pink sky hovered above the dark trees. He looked at her sideways as if searching to understand how she was feeling. Juli decided to break the silence, "Richard I overreacted, sorry."

"Don't be sorry. I was way out of line. I shouldn't have touched you." His face was turned away from her as though he was ashamed to look her in the eye.

She liked that, so she continued, "We were having a little fun, it turned serious. That happens sometimes. The real question is what do we do now?"

He turned to face her, his blue eyes exploring her face as if looking for answers, "Well there are a limited number of choices. As you know we are in the middle of nowhere. We have to stay here tonight, but we could go back tomorrow."

"Rich I don't want to leave, unless you do." She stared at the fire avoiding his eyes now for fear he might suspect her plan, which she was still debating rather vigorously in her brain. Wild color flooded her cheeks.

"I'm not sure." His voice seemed calm and under control.

"This is your first holiday in years, and certainly my first in a year. We both need a holiday. I think we can make this platonic and enjoyable." There, she had decided, no baby, she could relax. She smiled, "So long as we don't wrestle over beer."

He smiled back a blazingly guileless friendly grin as though he sensed her change, "That beer did over excite me. I'll blame it on the beer. Seriously I do need this holiday and I'm not ready for civilization yet. If you could stand to stay out the rest of

139

our time, I promise to be the best hands-off guide you will ever have."

"Richard I believe you." Their eyes met and they shared a close moment. "Let's try again." She sniffed the salt air, heard the trill of a squirrel in the trees following the inlet as it progressed inland. She felt calm. Then her paddling sore bum signaled for assistance as she felt the rough driftwood under her butt and shifted to find a more comfortable spot. "What's that pile of shells?" On closer inspection she recognized the large thick oblong shells which were roughly sculpted like ocean waves. In spite of their unattractive grey and the barnacles and clumps of sea moss she suspected that inside was a soft, slippery delight.

"Oysters. That's our supper. I gathered them off the beach. We're going to have them cooked over the fire."

"Yum, sounds good. I know if you cook them until the shells open that they are ready, but I like them cooked a bit longer."

"Me, too. As you can imagine, I'm not much on raw meat since medical school and all the parasites."

Juli laughed and started to say, *me too* and changed it to, "m . . . murdering parasites is the way to go." She nodded and asked, "Is there any PSP in this area?" Bivalves like oysters accumulate toxins as they filter feed. She knew about red tides and how fertilizer dumped into the ocean fed the algae, which when heated by the summer sun produced neuro toxins. Yet another example of human destruction.

"Paralytic Shellfish Poison? Not right now. I checked the Fisheries line before we left. We're in a safe area." He smiled, a benign grin, "Friends?"

"Friends. Let's enjoy ourselves." She thought she could do this as it was simple to just be friends. Maybe she would even confess she was a doctor.

"Ready for an oyster Juli?" His voice was steady.

"Anytime. I'll go up and find two beers so that we don't have to fight over them." Juli struggled up the incline, saw the flag marking the cache, and rooted out two beers. She returned waving her prize.

They ate in silence each lost in their own thoughts. Using the cold and effervescent beer as a palate cleanser Juli devoured an oyster. She took her time with the second, letting it sit on the half shell, the lining smooth as a pearl. Juli held back the top shell trying to be careful not to burn her fingers. The shell which was hot from the fire presented a problem until she saw that Rich used a hand towel to protect his hands and had left one for her. Protecting her hands, she nibbled on the oyster enjoying the flavors of the ocean. Then realizing the briny smoky flavor and the soft meat were delicious and she was starving she bit deeper into the flesh. Juice dripped down her chin as she chewed the warm satisfying treat. After a sip of beer she reached for another oyster, this one smaller, and quickly grasped the slightly open shell and forced it completely open. Quiet, broken only by the crack of a shell opening and slurping of liquor from a half shell, they sat close to the fire: their fronts hot, their backs cool, their stomachs warm from the heat produced by the steaming oysters. After mopping up the juices with tea biscuits that Rich had baked in a pan Juli lay back on the beach, head on a log, sated. It was a warm summer evening and she was still in her shorts. Rich tended the fire then he, too, rested back. Together they watched the sky turn dusky. Finally Juli rose to her feet, "I'm off. Have a good sleep. Tomorrow's the lagoon."

"Right . . . We'll leave the tents set up here. The nights are warm enough for sleeping under the stars. There's no light showing from Campbell River and there'll be no moon tomorrow night so the stars'll crowd down on us. I need that reminder of how man and his petty conflicts are so small as to be unnoticed by the rest of the universe."

"She yawned, "Sounds good. See you then."

She didn't know he watched to be sure she made it safely to her tent and then, riveted on her silhouette dancing against the tent wall as she slowly removed her t-shirt and then stepped out of her shorts. Slim long legs, the curve of a breast, he couldn't stop staring; it was as though they were connected by threads of energy and his eyes couldn't move. But his heart could; it jerked and thumped wildly in his chest. He reminded himself that he had agreed to platonic. Platonic means no sex. Trying to stay true to that he wrenched his eyes away from the delectable scene. He picked up a stick and poked at the fire muttering, "Rich old boy, she's not for you. You're on R & R. You need to get yourself in order." Nonetheless he smiled a wide satisfied smile. The coals had burned down to a light glow and the evening stars were beginning to reveal themselves.

CHAPTER ELEVEN

Juli woke remembering they were heading across the waterfall and had to time it right. Then she poked her head out the tent flap to check the weather which, as it had been from the beginning of their trip, was sunny and warm. The Golden Weather as she now called it. Rich was tending the fire and making breakfast, but she couldn't tell what that was: Oatmeal? Bacon? Eggs? Oysters? Whatever it was, it would be good. Smiling she retreated inside to climb into her shorts and t-shirt.

Rich who must have caught the movement of the tent flap and glimpsed her tousled head called, "Hey right on time. I have a ham and vegetable quiche coming out of the pan."

Juli stepped out of her tent laughing with delight. "How do you do that? I can't even manage it in the city with grocery stores and full equipment." She jumped quickly down the small slope to the fire on the beach almost stumbling into Rich but she caught herself. He reached out as if to steady her but instead turned and poked at the fire. "With Tom assisting it's easy. He left the dry ingredients for pancakes or biscuits. I used it as a crust for my quiche, the ham was in a can, and he's left us lots of drinking water. I'm heating some for tea. Do you need coffee?"

Why does he keep giving Tom so much credit? This man needs to realize how great he is. "I prefer tea most mornings, and coffee in lattes. So yes, the tea will be great." Why was she talking so fast? She stretched and then crouched down beside him, watching him cook. She realized she was close to him, and told herself it was because he was feeding her such good food and she was starving. She pushed thoughts out of her mind that it could be anything else, and rationalized that friends stay close.

"We'll have to pack lunch, supper, and breakfast. You okay with pancakes? And more oysters? And some canned chili?" He deftly slid half the quiche on to her plate and the rest on to his.

"So long as they're not mixed in the same pot, sure, sounds good." She picked up her plate and walked toward the beach. "Out here I could eat a bear. Oops, are there bears here?"

He shook his head, "Maybe one occasionally. They tend not to swim over from the Mainland. The stretch of water surrounding Cortes discourages animals and people."

"Good. I don't want to be mauled by a bear." She lifted the hot quiche to her mouth. The egg almost melted on her tongue and the crust crunched between her teeth in a very satisfying manner. "Yummmm, that's good."

His smile shone with pleasure as he scraped the pan; he had accepted that compliment. *Good, she thought.*

Out loud he said, "Wolves are the problem recently. If we run into any of them remember to back away slowly: keep your eyes on them, raise your arms over your head to look taller, make noise, and throw things."

"Right, boss." She sounded much braver than she felt.

He nodded, "Above all we'll follow the 'leave no trace' camping rule. Tom makes that easy with his metal lock boxes which he maintains and removes."

"He's an asset for sure." Full of hot quiche she slumped against a log. Her energy coping with digestion left her feeling weak. She breathed deeply, infusing her body with fresh cool ocean air, allowing Mother Nature to heal her. Every cell in her body perked up.

Sensing her return to alertness Rich stated, "We should leave here at around ten. That's soon."

"I'll take your word for it. I have no sense of hours any more, only sunrise, high noon, and sunset." Eager for the next adventure Juli announced, "I'm ready after I brush my teeth."

They set off with the kayak lighter without the tents. The high pressure system was holding; the golden sun shone so warmly that Juli needed her brimmed hat. They had left their spray skirts in their tents as they knew it would be a hot day; air circulating around their legs would be a good thing.

The tidal waterfall was calm. Under the gentle clear river of water she could easily see rocks and boulders lurking below the surface; that was a relief, as yesterday on the ebb, tumbling water had bubbled white against the rocks exciting the molecules as they raced to join their buddies in the inlet and then into Sutil channel and beyond. Thankfully that ferocious lion was now a pussycat letting them paddle sedately through the passage. The power of the moon to move all the water in the world was awesome and yet another reminder of her vulnerability as a human.

The lagoon was still, too. "The water's so clear the bottom seems near enough to touch," whispered Rich so quietly she could barely hear him. Water birds dipped and caught small silvery fish; conifers crowded close like eager children waiting for a party to begin. Juli sighed, the beauty and peace reached right into her soul. She could hardly remember her life in the city; all the sick people were gone.

"Don't let it fool you," he warned. "This lagoon is like a pond right now; it won't go dry on the ebb but rocks and snags will appear. We have to avoid them . . . so let's reconnoiter by paddling the whole lagoon and then pick our camp for tonight."

Ever the guide, he was responsible and careful as they could die out here. Juli appreciated that but all she wanted to see was the beauty, as nature was seeping deeply into her cells, relaxing her, freeing her energy. "Good idea," whispered Juli, feeling the sacredness of this place. It was like the Tales of Narnia when the children entered another world. She felt it deeply: it had started when they entered Von Donop Inlet and now crossing the waterfall brought her to a new and deeper place of peace and wholeness. She had felt this once before when she stayed in an ashram in Virginia.

Without speaking they paddled the perimeter of the lagoon leaving the island in the middle to their right, exploring nooks and crannies, and floating, and watching deer grazing and red-winged black birds feeding in the grass. Finally, when the sun beat down and it was becoming hot and sticky in the kayak Rich spoke, "I saw a spot on the island I like."

"Okay," agreed Juli extremely mellow and glad to trust his judgment. Rich seemed to be more relaxed, too, maybe her cooperativeness was helping their friendship develop.

They unpacked the kayak together. "We have to be above high tide," warned Rich.

"I see the tide line . . . Let's go above that rise." She lugged the tarp and sleeping bags to a flat area a few yards beyond the crest of the small hill. An Arbutus tree with its lipstick red bark offered low branches to hold their bag of food.

"Fine by me. I'll make the cooking fire down by the water again . . . it's easier to control. Summer on the island is dangerous for forest fires; the smallest spark can set the tinder off."

She was relieved that he was so careful. She felt safe. "How big's this island Rich?" asked Juli as she stood on the rise looking around: grey stony beach to the south, green towering forest north, east, and west.

"About a hectare, two and a half acres, I think."

"That's a good size."

"Big enough for our purposes for sure," he said as he secured the kayak.

What are our purposes? This is a very isolated spot with no way out 'till high tide tomorrow. Stop it Juli, you've agreed to be friends, just friends. Juli estimated it was around noon. She retrieved her book and lounged on the grassy slope while Rich prepared lunch. She felt a little guilty as this was the sixth day of Rich preparing all the meals. She was finally feeling rested and doing her share in other areas. Still she hesitated; it was not characteristic of her to languish, but she actually wanted him to take care of her. She wanted to see if he would continue to nurture her. *Am I testing him? What for? This trip will be over soon and I'll never see him again.* The words on the page blurred as Juli examined her motives. But it was a hot July day with the temperature rising like emotions out of control, so in order to counteract and enjoy the heat she stretched out on the grassy slope and closed her eyes. The sun glared down warming the skin of her face so she rolled over on her belly seeking shade for it and that was as much as she could manage as her whole body heated and her will 'to do' dropped correspondingly. The ocean murmured a slow, soft, sultry song which lulled her into sleep with her head on her arm and her fingers dug into the sandy soil hiding from the hot sun.

Rich heard her breathing gear down into sleep mode and knew she would burn in the sun. He had to wake her, but he hesitated as his gaze moved over her body with CT scan intensity: curved butt, slim waist, curling golden hair. Initially an exquisite tenderness flooded his body; then as his eyes paused on her buttocks, suddenly he was lost in a haze of sexuality: tenderness and lust melded together until he mentally chided himself. Gathering up her portion of food he called, "Here's lunch," as he walked over to her and knelt next to her, holding out a small brown bag. Languidly she rolled over. His eyes met hers, instantly the intensity was there, as though a magnetic beam held them locked together. Juli shook her head slowly as if trying to clear it, her lips curled at the edges into a broad welcome as she smiled her thanks, slowly sat up, and forced herself to peek inside the offered bag. A shiny red apple and a small container of almonds and raisins greeted her. Perfect, she thought, that's what she would have packed for herself. Rich eased himself onto the slope near her. Side by side bathed in sunshine and cooled by the light breeze, they slowly ate their lunch. As she crunched on the apple, flecks of juice splattered on her face; her tongue licked off her lips and the back of her hand took care of the rest. Then one by one she savored the raisins' sweetness and the almonds' crunch.

He watched her like a baby seal watching its mother, waiting for a signal to close in. Finally he said, "Juli, here's some sun screen." He took a tube out of his pocket and flipped it casually toward her as if he didn't dare take a chance on their fingers touching.

"Thanks, I need that." Quickly she lathered her narrow arched feet, slim long legs and arms and face. As if he was unable to look away, Rich watched her slender fingers massaging her legs. Dulled by the hot sun and food Juli noted his attention and didn't turn away; instead she prolonged the sensual contact with her skin, teasing him playfully. After she screwed the cap on the sunscreen Rich relaxed back, covering his face with his hat. Soon Juli could hear gentle snores. Soporific, but restless, she quietly rose and slowly walked the perimeter of the island along the rocky shore, being careful not to twist her ankle. The quiet was so deep that the slightest sound seemed magnified: ducks quacked softly as they talked with their mates, gulls floated quietly on the calm surface waiting, small silvery fish slipped quietly past under the surface, and a float plane buzzed past probably on its way to Squirrel Cove. Eventually she perched on a shiny silver log, preserved by the salt water, and thought about her life. Mainly, she concluded, she was content with her choices so far. But she recognized she was at a turning point and the decisions she made now would determine the course of the rest of her life. However for the present, time stood still as if she had entered a parallel universe of tranquility.

Thirst finally forced her back to their temporary camp; Rich and the kayak were gone. For an instant she felt abandoned. Had he left her here? Was she supposed to swim back to civilization? That was unlikely. At the very worst Tom would come and retrieve her. Feeling calmer she wandered down to the waterline being careful not to step on the oysters helpless in the intertidal zone. What a strange life they led, lying on the beach like a rock, waiting for the returning tide to bring them food. Now that was trust; trust that was tested twice a day, every day. Maybe she should relax and be more like an oyster. With that thought she went to their supplies and selected Canadian astronaut Hatfield's new book and settled down on a warm rock face to read. Again her eyes closed and she slipped into a deep sleep. The sound of rustling pierced her dream of swimming through space. She lurched to her feet, adrenalin pumping.

"Whoa . . . I'm checking supplies for supper. It's getting late."

Juli staggered back relieved a bear hadn't found her and sat down again. "Rich where have you been?"

"Meditating."

"Oh, I was worried. Please let me know if you're going off again." She sounded huffy and angry and she didn't care. He was the guide; he was in charge; he shouldn't abandon her like . . . like her father had all those years ago. But she knew that was ridiculous as she wasn't six years old anymore and she was in no danger and perfectly able to take care of herself.

"Did you think I had left?" he asked puzzled.

"Not really? Although the kayak was gone." She sounded like a tearful child.

"I paddled over to the forest for shade. You're right. I should have told you. But you looked occupied with your thoughts and I desperately needed to be alone."

Why did he reveal that? He was the guide. He was supposed to be in charge of himself, and everything. "I know you didn't sign on this trip to be a baby sitter."

He nodded.

"I know you're on holiday too."

He nodded again.

"From now on count on me to cook some of the meals." Damn! Was she really able to do that? She felt rested but . . . If it was too much she would have to tell him. For right now he was so close to her she could feel male power and she liked it.

"Thanks Juli but we can take it easy." He was calm and centered from meditating. "Neither of us needs to be stressed. We'll do whatever works for both of us."

"Sounds do-able." He seemed reasonable. She should relax. Juli sat up, clutched her book protectively to her chest and stood up. Rich glanced up at her and it happened again, their eyes met and electricity sparked, not a harsh lightning but a slow sensual exchange of energy that set her senses humming. Juli turned away first and said, "I'll finish my rest on my mattress." What was the matter with her? She felt so vulnerable. She had to get hold of herself. Meditating was probably a good way to spend some time.

Rich watched her retreat and shrugged, a puzzled caring look on his face.

Supper was successful. After a satisfying meal of oysters followed by chili with pan bread she had gratefully crawled into her soft puffy sleeping bag, which she had set up near the top of the gentle slope, and watched the blush and azure sky gradually fade to grey as her heavy lids closed. Much later Juli woke suddenly, sat up and stared around. The howl of a wolf was so close she thought he must be on the island. At first the sound froze her immobile, like a deer surprised by a hunter. Then thoughts of fangs dripping saliva filled her with quaking fear making adrenalin flash through her body. Panting, sweating, she wanted to scream at the top of her lungs. She would fight the monster to the death. In the moonless dark she could see nothing. Rich was snoring gently near-by. That was comforting, but it was she who was on guard. She looked around for weapons and remembered a piece of driftwood. She eased out of the sleeping bag. Her bare feet crunched on cold pebbly sand. She found the stick, clutched it close, and retreated to a log close to the glowing coals, carefully she added small pieces of driftwood until it was blazing. Wolves were afraid of fire. Still clutching her weapon her eyes squinted as she peered into the night, expecting a grey flash to leap at her. Nothing moved. Her breathing calmed. The howls became more distant. The hunting wolves were moving off. She relaxed and eased carefully back to her sleeping bag.

Stars called to her from the velvet-black sky. So many stars, layer upon layer, millions and millions, surely there was life in one of those galaxies. Her own troubles forgotten, and like early humans she relaxed, puzzling over constellations and making up names. To add to the wonder shooting stars streaked the heavens like a fleet of spaceships arriving from Mars.

Suddenly she jerked to alert as a husky voice beside her whispered, "What are you doing?"

Startled she turned saying, "You did it again. Don't sneak up on me."

"I didn't sneak; I'm lying here in my sleeping bag. I was concerned."

Did he have to sound so calm? "I was looking at the night sky."

"Me too. I bet you haven't seen this before. It happens every year when the Earth passes through the stream of debris behind Comet Swift–Tuttle." His voice was matter-of-fact; obviously he was trying to distance himself and calm her.

"Is this the Perseids meteor shower?" asked Juli taking her cue from him as another burst of pin-point sparks spread across the sky.

"Yup, ain't it pretty?"

She hardly knew this man. Maybe it was because she didn't know him, whatever it was, she was comfortable with him. "I've always wanted to see it."

"If we could stand to be awake right before dawn it'll be at its peak for the night. It's got something to do with the side of the Earth nearest to turning into the sun. Somehow it scoops up more meteors as Earth moves through space. That aside, I always think it's like a millionaire's fireworks display on New Year's Eve."

"Shh Rich, don't talk; enjoy the heavens with me." She stretched out in her sleeping bag, pulling it up to her chin and they waited for meteors together. Watching the heavens perform she felt a deep shift as she became one with the cosmos. Their combined energy cushioned them in a glowing bubble that lifted and transported them through space and time. Never before had she felt this oneness. This interesting man was worth getting to know. Once she had made the decision she dropped into a light sleep.

Much later a single howl announced a wolf close at hand. Juli woke with a start, heart racing. "Rich, Rich," she hissed as she shook him. "There's a wolf."

He sat up, sleeping bag sliding to his waist, and listened. "It's okay. They don't come on the island at night." He reached over and patted her as if to reassure her. "The natives say they don't like to swim in the dark."

"You sure?" she asked putting her arm out of her sleeping bag. He grasped her hand and leaned toward her so closely a soft wiggly puppy, let alone an adult wolf, couldn't squeeze between them.

"Sure," came his confident voice.

How could he know that? "I don't believe you. We're stuck here on an island, trapped by a waterfall." Her heart raced as her anxiety increased. She sat up, senses hyper-alert. "Maybe you can sleep if we're going to be eaten alive by a hungry pack of wolves. I can't. You brought me here. Now you've got to get me out of here . . . alive."

He soothed her, "C'mon let's get some sleep," as he eased back into his sleeping bag he kept his hand protectively around hers and flicked on his flashlight.

She pushed his hand away, "You dreamer. I can't sleep. That wolf was too close."

"Juli you sound angry." He swung the beam 360 degrees around them.

"I am. I'm mad that you put me in this position."

"Juli I think you're really scared," his voice was calm as though trying to talk down an excited animal.

"Aren't you?" As he talked she felt her anger melt away and she could see clearly that it was covering fear, no, terror.

"No, we're fine. But I'll stay on guard and build the fire up if that will make you feel safer."

She liked that he was willing to protect her. "Yes, that would help." Her voice sounded calmer as her terror reduced to fear.

"Let's try." He climbed out of his sleeping bag. "I'm going down to the fire. I'll move my sleeping bag a little closer to yours."

Clutching her driftwood weapon Juli shrugged out of her sleeping bag. Another howl, higher pitched and close, cemented her plan to stay really close. "Are you kidding? A little closer? I'm not going to be eaten alone. I'm staying with you." She picked up her sleeping bag and air mattress. "Closer is good," she said as she dragged her bag on top of his. "I'm going to zip them together."

His voice seemed surprised, "It'll be crowded. "

"I don't care. I don't want to be wolf meat. You have the hunting knife. I'm staying close." Working quickly in the dancing light from Rich's flashlight she laid her weapon by his bag, then zippered their sleeping bags together as Rich protested, "I don't think this is necessary. What are you doing? I can't do this."

"I'm scared. I'm not spending one second alone," panic sounded in her voice.

"You sure are determined," he said as he shut off the flashlight. "This isn't a good idea."

"Yes it is."

"Well I don't agree . . . you do what you have to do to feel safe. I'm going to build the fire up with some drift wood." So saying Rich left her for the small beach and the hot coals. Juli climbed into the sleeping bag and was soon asleep.

Hours later in the grey before sunrise she woke and realized he was sleeping with his arms protectively around her. She liked the feeling; she didn't move just lay there letting her breathing come in unison with his. *How pleasant,* she thought. She could handle this, maybe forever. His body heat seemed to surround her and penetrate her body, triggering a tingling sensation in her lower abdomen. Suddenly, like the sun bursting over the horizon, he opened his eyes and his azure sleep-filled eyes peered into her blue ones. Nose to nose. He didn't speak, his breathing increased in rate. Her breathing followed. He didn't move; she knew it was up to her, her choice to encourage him or to run for the hills. Once again she thought of her barren lonely life: *Juli, you're thirty-four, he's a good man, give him a chance.* She closed her eyes and snuggled into him whispering huskily, "I need you to protect me from the wolves."

"Juli the wolves are long gone. Turn over and go to sleep." When she didn't move he rolled over so that his back was facing her.

She could hear his breathing as it settled into a steady rhythm. She snuggled closer, turning her head so her cheek was against his back and imagined her hot breath sending prickles of delight through his chest and through his body. His voice caught, "Juli, I'm not comfortable . . . This is crazy."

"Hmmm," she hummed as she kissed his vertebrae. Her body pressed against his, hot and delicious, her hormones responding as eagerly as a teenager's, over reacting because of long disuse. She couldn't control her desire with him so close. He cleared his throat to rid it of huskiness, "I don't have a condom. That settles it. Thank God." He pushed her away from him but the sleeping bag held them close.

He turned toward her and she felt his gaze burning with an intensity that caused her heart to flutter. She gasped a deep breath like a diver preparing for a crucial dive and blurted "It's okay. I do." She giggled as she felt him shudder with surprise, "They make good protection for finger injuries. They're part of my first aid kit. I can reach it if I stretch." That was one for him, she thought. No condom, thus he wasn't planning a seduction. She hoped he didn't think she had planned one, because she definitely hadn't. She had come here to regain her health and be in tune with nature.

She felt him melt; his resistance shattered. "Good for you," muttered Rich, kissing her shoulder as she reached, encouraging her.

Juli felt his lips burning through her t-shirt as she stretched for the condom. Hormones streaked through her body stimulating individual cells and whole organs to prepare for sexual intercourse. As a doctor she knew exactly what was happening, but as a woman her brain was gradually turning off as pleasant sensations washed like gentle waves through her body.

Rich groaned, "Juli, you do something to my body. I have never had such strong desire ever before." Silence and expectance filled the minute space between them. "Did I say that out loud? Yes, and it's true. I can't turn back now."

"So there's something special about me," she teased as she gently pushed his chest away.

"Mmmm, I love your smell," he said as pulled her close and sniffed her neck. "I love your taste." He nibbled and licked her ear. Huskily he murmured into her ear, "Juli . . . you okay with this? Are you sure? We can just hide out from the wolves."

"My name is Juliet and yours starts with R. That must mean something." *Did she say that? Did she imply he was Romeo?* She tried to lighten it with a giggle, but found her lips were trembling.

He could barely compute what she was saying. His brain was shutting down. This was what was meant by a mindless haze of sexuality. He struggled against his raging hormones to give her an out. *"Juliet say 'no' if you want to. I need you to be sure."*

"My hormone levels are too high. For god's sake even my lips are swelling. If you want to back out, you can. I'll understand." Juli breathed in the sweet smell of his skin, forcing herself not to nibble on his neck.

"I'm not backing out. Juli you have the greatest body, my hormones are crazy." So saying he pulled her tightly to his chest, and began to gently kiss her eyelids, nose and lips, and chin. His lips were as soft and gentle as a rose petal, not demanding, simply offering her a taste of and a promise of what was to come.

Her breathing matched his as he ran his hands down her back and then up under the edge of her t-shirt, carefully pulling her t-shirt off. Cool air slipped between them waking her briefly from her mesmerized state. His t-shirt was next. As he pulled it over his head with his arms outside the sleeping bags she started kissing his chest and sucking on his nipples. His breath caught as waves of sensation washed over him. He wanted her with an intensity that precluded stopping. Quickly he discarded his t-shirt and wrapped his arms behind her, pulling her body even more tightly against his. Their warmth and energy fields fused, paralyzing them until, reawakened by soft skin against rough, their seeking lips connected. The roughness of his whiskers increased the exquisite swelling of her lips. Her teeth gently nibbled his tongue. Her breasts swelled and pressed against his chest, nipples taut. He groaned as if he was in pain. There was no going back, even if a pack of wolves appeared, and she knew it. He wanted her desperately. She had never felt passion this strong ever before. Every atom in her body was focused on one thing, receiving his half of the essence of life.

Strong arms pulled her on top and she opened to him, feeling him slide inside. His hardness felt exquisitely right for her body. Panting she joined his rhythmic motion, faster and faster until she exploded in pleasure. Somewhere in her sexual delirium she noted he waited for her before his orgasm. Total bliss and a bonus of an unselfish man. Exhausted and content, her head on his arm, they lay side by side watching the heavens. The humming hormones couldn't hide the stars diming gradually. Maybe this was a dream. Her body was floating in bliss. This man was so perfect he couldn't be real. As if the universe was agreeing the heavens flashed to life with a final burst of light. "Look! Another star shower," gulped Juli as the spark seemed to run through her, re-igniting ecstasy in every neuron and cell in her body.

"And another and another," added Rich, his deep voice vibrating against her ear.

"Wow! She gasped. "That was a great orgasm, enough to make me see shooting stars."

"Juli you're funny," he chuckled turning to kiss her soft neck.

She felt like she had come home; home to a man she could enjoy but not be devoured by. Mating, yes mating with him had been comfortable and . . . and delicious; it was as though they

164

were old souls being reunited. Maybe they had been together in another life. Her feelings were too tender, too new to her to talk about.

CHAPTER TWELVE

Golden sunshine warmed her face. Hard earth poked into her back. Without opening her eyes she felt around the sleeping bag, she was alone. She listened, a squirrel called its mate, and metal scraped letting her know that Rich was fussing over the morning fire. As she ran her hands languidly down her arms and breasts and abdomen she felt alive and beautiful. She licked her lips noting that they were swollen and abraded from Rich's whiskers. She liked what she felt, her body ripe and full and satisfied. Juli wondered if he would regret last night's hot passion. He truly was a considerate lover. She decided to act as if nothing had happened.

He seemed to have made the same decision as he greeted her appearance casually, saying, "We best get out of here at slack high tide." He crouched down by the fire his back to her, "After breakfast of course."

"Good idea, those wolves were a little too close for me."
Wild color flooded her cheeks.

"So I noticed," his glance glinted with mischief,
transforming his serious-guide look to that of a warm close friend,
and something more.

"Rich I'm sorry. I took advantage of you last night." She
had leaped right into his arms.

He laughed almost with relief, "Any time. I didn't feel
taken advantage of, au contraire, I felt blessed." His large moist
eyes spoke volumes about the depth of feeling he was
experiencing.

The phrase, *a man with feeling*, flitted through her mind
making her hesitate, but sticking with her resolve she replied, "It
was pretty good but let's not do that again." She thought, *I told
Marigold I didn't want to change my life . . . I didn't want a man.*

"I agree. I'm trying to sort out my health and my job."
That was the most he had revealed of himself and she wondered
what the problems were with his health and job. "Don't get me
wrong, last night was bliss. But I also know it was a function of
fear and proximity."

He looked down as he stirred the coals and carefully
placed the metal pot on top of them. "Juli I have to agree with
you. I'm sorry but I'm in no position to commit to anything. I was
comforting you."

"Fine by me. I think that's the best way to go, after all we really don't know one another." She sat on a large rock and stared at the sparkling ocean. "What's for breakfast?" asked Juli, glad to change the subject. She was amazed at herself, climbing into Rich's sleeping bag. She had never done anything like that before. She was your staid, hard-working, spinster lady, nose to the grindstone, little time for fun or the opposite sex. Suddenly she was risking all. She wondered if this was 'having a nervous breakdown'. No. She was perfectly functioning, at least her intellect was intact. Her emotions couldn't seem to stay on track; in fact there wasn't a track to stay on. Marigold was right Juli was ready for a family, ready to meet her life partner. There hadn't been anyone since she broke up with Ted when she was twenty-one because he wanted babies right away, but she had her career in front of her. He hitched up with a nineteen-year-old and had three kids in four years. She was glad that wasn't her. She was glad she trained as a doctor. But now . . . now she was ready for more.

"Oatmeal and raisins. They were light and easy to bring along." Rich poured some on her plate and handed it to her, carefully avoiding touching her hand or looking into her eyes.

She shifted uncomfortably. She desperately wanted them to be friends and have a great holiday, but like attending the birth of a new baby she never knew what direction things were going until the babe drew its first breath; in this case, until he could relax near her. "Yum, golden raisins, my favorite." She ate slowly savoring every bite.

"Another reason we have to leave is we're out of food."

"I haven't missed a meal since we started; I sure don't want to start now." She smiled. "Truly I have appreciated your planning and cooking." Juli hadn't been so well taken care of since she was a preschooler, as once her father left her mom had to go to work to support them, leaving Juli to help babysitters feed and take care of her two younger siblings. Then by the time she was twelve she had what felt like almost the full responsibility for them.

"We have four bottles of water left," added Rich thinking and planning out loud.

"I'll have a bottle now please and then I'll be ready to head back and keep with our original schedule."

"Right, the tide is friendly now." He stood up, "While the fire is cooling I'll pack the sleeping bags."

"I'll help," called Juli scampering ahead of him to the sleeping bags. Rich followed close on her heels. The radar between them was so strong she could feel him closing the distance so that they reached the bags together; kneeling beside him she started the zipper on one side, he the other. Their fingers met at the bottom. Again, as if for the first time, a fresh flash of electricity joined their bodies, suspending them in time. Juli, shaken and aware, gasped and leaned toward him as though she was being pushed from behind. Automatically and as naturally as if he had practiced catching her in a past life time he grabbed her, steadying her. She tilted her face up like a flower toward the life giving sun, his lips covered hers and he groaned. Their bodies pressed together. Rich eased her t-shirt off and gently, sensuously kissed her nipples, sucking them to hardness. "Juli," he gasped, "I can't help myself."

"Neither can I," she heard her reply from a great distance as he swiftly slid his t-shirt over his head and holding her close collapsed on the open sleeping bag. Like a swimmer struggling to the surface Juli sucked in a gigantic breath, "Wait, we need a condom." He loosened his hold as she reached for her first aid kit and retrieved her jury-rigged finger cots. "I'll keep these close. We may need more than one," she giggled.

He murmured into her hair, "Whatever you say. You're the boss here." Nevertheless his hips began to move against hers driven by the same heedless compulsion that drove all living things to procreate. Golden morning sun caressed their bare skin. The water of the lagoon stirred gently; squirrels trilled, but were soon drowned out by heavy breathing and soft moans emanating from the young couple locked in a mating ritual familiar to the animals.

The sensations swirling through her body had taken over. Swelling breasts made the nipples exquisitely painful, burning and tingling pulsed between her legs. She wasn't a doctor any more, just a woman, a woman with an urgent need to couple with this hard man, hard just for her, causing her to feel special. She wanted him, moving her hips rhythmically against his powerful thighs. His harsh groan let her know he was equally as affected.

He gently but single mindedly eased on top of her effectively pinning her to the ground. He was going to thrust into her, she wanted it, was ready for him. The smell of female secretions drove him into a frenzy, his breathing was rapid. He wanted inside her immediately; that smell meant she was ready, but he wouldn't rush. He had to be sure she was as aroused as he. Her breathing was as rapid as his and her eyes were closed, sensation seeking. Red suffused her neck; taut nipples pressed into his chest. Legs open in welcome, she moaned as he slipped his hand up the tender inside of her thigh. His fingers caused her to arch and pull him toward her. He responded by sliding inside of her, climbing as high as he could. She hung on, pressing toward him. Tension built in her body and her head thrashing back and forth. Suddenly, involuntarily, she screamed her release. He clung to her and jerked. Gasping for air they collapsed side by side, nose to nose, eyes open she smiled her satisfaction, then blurted, "Where did that come from?"

"I'm not sure. You're like super-charged petro to me."

"Whatever, it's wonderful," she stretched feeling sticky and loved.

"I thought we agreed we wouldn't do this anymore. That wasn't planned, but thank god you had the condoms handy."

"You know what Rich?" Juli lay back rejoicing in the happiness coursing through her body.

"What?"

"I think we should do it one more time and get it out of our systems. Then we'll wash and head out of here back to relative civilization." Did she say that?

He laughed with surprise and pleasure. "No way, not physically possible," he drawled, as he lounged back, letting the warm sun and gentle breeze revive him.

Juli grinned a wicked little grin in response and planted her lips on his. Lovingly she licked his soft full lips. Rich responded with a gentle tonguing and totally to his surprise, as it had never happened before like this, his body started to respond. The corners of Juli's mouth curled in a happy knowing smile. Rich pulled her on top of him stretching her body full length along his; its warmth and soft curves sustained his erection. Her breath was hot against his neck and her breasts were pressing into his chest. She felt giddy and relaxed and mildly aroused. She had challenged him and he had responded, now she didn't know if she could meet his response as she too was in a satiated mode. He turned his head, stubble of his new beard ticking the top of her head as he bent forward to kiss her forehead and lift her gently by the armpits to bring her swollen lips to his. Then he proceeded to shower her with kisses, soft and gentle as a summer rain, gradually increasing the intensity to open mouth stimulation. Waves of sensation swept through her body in response. Warmth spread from her burning cheeks, down her rosy throat, to her bursting breasts as he slid her further up and sucked on each breast, until the hormonal response caused them to swell double. Now her whole being was alert to his minutest movement as her senses opened to him like a newborn to its mother. Sparked to life, suddenly she straddled him and engaged him by sliding him inside her swollen parts until she felt the fullness, the connection. Then spasms from her coming orgasm melded together, rushing like a swollen spring stream to a crescendo. She screamed as he pumped into her simultaneously, totally in tune. Sobbing and laughing she collapsed on his chest. Languid and loving their bodies melded together as time stood still for them as it did for all lovers.

Much later, rolling over on to her belly Juli croaked, "Oh my god I didn't really think we could do it again."

"Life is full of surprises," said Rich playfully tousling her hair. "Much as we'd like to lay here and relax into our bliss we can't. The tides wait for no one; we have to get through while it's slack."

He didn't remind her of their agreement not to do this again. She stayed quiet thinking the sex was sensational. He was a patient lover but that was it, they had no future. She wouldn't encourage him again. Out loud she said, "Base camp here we come. Then we won't be at the mercy of a tidal waterfall if we want to leave." While she talked she washed herself off in the ocean knowing the salt would need to be washed off at base camp, and then gathered her scattered clothes and slipped them on, wishing they were by a fresh water lake.

"Speaking of our tidal waterfall, tidal is the operative word. We better get a move on." Rich shrugged into his clothes and helped Juli roll up the sleeping bags. Then together they carried all their supplies to the kayak. "I'm estimating it's close to high tide. I'm not positive because I don't want to check tides with my satellite phone any more often than absolutely necessary."

"Of course, we have no way to charge the batteries."

"Exactly. We need to save it for an emergency, heaven forbid that there is one." As they talked they finished loading the kayak. Juli noted that she was allowed to pack some of the equipment now, she took that as a sign that her expertise was growing . . . and his trust.

As they approached the reversing waterfall Juli called over her shoulder, "I can hear it. It's not at slack tide. Will we be able to handle it?"

"It must be pretty close. I vote for going ahead. We could portage around . . . it's easier to paddle through. That's my first choice."

"We'll be paddling against it, right?" Juli turned her head to look back at Rich, wanting to be sure she heard him correctly.

"Yes, it's flooding and trying to refill the lagoon."

"Let's do it Rich. It'll be a good workout and I can spot for rocks." Juli felt excited, anticipating the challenge. She was on hyper-alert, smiling and feeling free for the first time in years.

As they approached the inlet, paddling became different. Juli pulled on her paddle, the double ended kayak paddle dipped right then left, but its effectiveness was poor because the paddle and the water were flowing the same direction. She could count on Rich to steer the kayak and keep it pointing into the streaming water. The danger was that they would be carried back into the lagoon, or worse yet, if they turned sideways to the swift flood they might tip or be stuck in the banks and rocks of the narrow channel. Then one of them would have to get out and push. Juli smiled, that surely came under the job description for the guide. So with light heart and healed hands she paddled as hard as she could through the sunshine and flowing water.

A silver fish slithered past, a few ragged strands of seaweed gracefully slid over the rocks. "Paddle hard," shouted Rich over the roar of rushing water as they approached the entrance to the lagoon. It was worse than he expected: the ocean was pouring through the narrow passage with a vengeance. Turbulent water rushed at them jostling the kayak. "Dig, dig," shouted Rich as both of them dug deeply to propel the kayak forward through the white frothing water. Cold water dripped on her arms, her paddle was ineffective in the foam. They seemed to be standing still no matter how hard she paddled. With no turning space they had to go forward. She dug deeper. Her paddle blade hit a stone with a crack. "Keep going Juli," urged Rich. "A few more strokes." A black vulture perched on a bare tree watching for failure. "Together now, pull," called Rich. "We're making progress." She dipped right, he left; they gained. "Again," shouted Rich. "Again."

Just as the muscle cramps in her shoulders became unbearable they burst into the calm water of the inlet. Her shoulders sagged with relief. Rich laughed in triumph, calling out, "Good paddling Juli."

Juli called back, "And I didn't tear open my blisters." Her breath came in ragged gulps, blood pounded in her arteries, euphoria filled her every cell. This was living. Laughter bubbled out of her like frothy bubbles they had come through.

"Great! That's enough paddling for today. We have to. . ." He gasped, "Rest your hands. Back to camp, unload and prepare for tonight." He sucked in a deep breath, "Then we can hike into Robertson or Wiley Lake. Robertson is larger. I think that's where we should go."

"Have you been there before?" Juli rested her paddle on the coaming in front of her.

Rich skillfully and powerfully propelled the kayak toward camp. "About three years ago. There's a trail . . . about an hour's walk."

"Sounds good I could use the exercise . . . and a fresh water bath. Let's take soap." She laughed gleefully, "I'm so sticky I'll have to wash my clothes." She smelled like smoke . . . and sex.

"My thoughts exactly."

She rested in her seat; she liked that he was taking care of her. She felt his eyes caressing her shoulders. She wanted him to help her with her burdens.

Once they were back at camp and with the day organized they became quiet, each focusing on their own thoughts. A sailboat passed them as it heading toward Sutil Channel. Juli noted they weren't alone. However this was only the second sign of humans since they had entered the inlet. In a way it was comforting to know competent sailors with their usual electronic communication devices were somewhere close-by. On the other hand, after three days of solitary boating, it felt like an intrusion. It was all relative and it was unlikely they would see them again.

They set off for the lake shortly after a lunch of oyster stew, carrying snacks as they planned to be back for supper and an early night. Juli followed Rich who set a steady and brisk pace over the surface roots of cedars and fir trees, following a trail that she couldn't discern most of the time. She had total confidence in Rich to lead her to the lake and back out. She hadn't heard the wolves since last night, or of course during their heavy breathing, and she hoped the pack had moved to another part of the island. So fearlessly they plunged deeper and deeper into the forest. Even the warm summer weather couldn't reach here and the shade of the high, green canopy sheltered them from direct rays.

After a steady forty-five minute hike they paused and sat on a rock outcropping. Rich told her that they were in a forest consisting of twenty-seven hundred acres that bisected the island from east to west. He passionately extolled their significance: "These lands hold the deepest soils, the biggest trees, and the island's central water recharge area. It's very precious as the pockets of old growth are part of the one percent of old growth that remains in British Columbia."

"I didn't realize that." Her eyes opened wide in appreciation of the elderly trees surrounding her.

Now that he had started he couldn't stop. "Yup. The forests and wetlands are home to ten species and ten ecological communities that are threatened or endangered. The northern goshawk is one. Others of concern are the common nighthawk, red-legged frog, great blue heron and northern pygmy owl." His breath caught, "plus the pacific sideband snail."

"Wow." He was really into this island. She was reminded he was a country man at heart. They stood close together staring at the cedars crowding closely like sentinels.

He felt so deeply that once he started he couldn't stop, "The Cortes Island community has worked for over two decades to oppose industrial scale logging and bring ecosystem-based forestry to these lands."

She leaned closer to him, wanting to support this thoughtful man. "You must be proud to be part of such a community."

"I am. We're trying to protect the plants, which, in turn, give the animals a home."

"Like what," she encouraged looking for more information and to listen to his voice and his concerns.

"On the provincial list of endangered or threatened are western red cedar . . . like that one over there," he pointed and then rose to his feet, shouldering the backpack. As he walked he continued, "Others are the three-leaved foam flower, western hemlock, Oregon-beaked moss, deer fern, sweet gale, and Sitka sedge. We've seen arbutus, hairy Manzanita, shore pine, common juniper, Lodgepole pine, reindeer mosses, and grey rock-moss. They're threatened too."

"And I thought everything looked healthy and perfect." Juli stood up and looked around, studying each tree as though it was a patient in emergency, which in a way all the plants were. Then she followed him.

His voice called back to her, "There's more. On the list of ecological communities and indigenous species and subspecies of special concern here are Douglas-fir, western hemlock, and salal, Sitka sedge, Pacific water-parsley. . . " He drew a deep breath, "So you can see this forest is not just a forest, but a home for some of the most endangered species on Earth."

"It's a privilege to be here." She felt the sacredness of the forest and breathed deeply as she stepped carefully to follow in Rich's footsteps to cause as little damage as possible to the precious undergrowth. In the cool shade of the giant conifers she was glad she had worn her hoodie.

After about an hour's hike, as predicted, the pristine lake appeared. Quiet water and a soft sand beach enticed her closer. "Rich it's breathtaking." Deep green cedars, hungry for nourishing water, crowded the shore, while small Siskins flitted through the branches. A squirrel trilled and the return trill came from close by: forest life liked this fresh water source. Juli noted the pile of scales at the base of a near-by tree. She peered up the tree but couldn't see the squirrel that must have sat in the high branches nibbling the cones, carelessly allowing the inedible scales to drift downward. Juli approached some boulders on the edge of the lake, which had been warmed by the sun and she sat down, mesmerized by the mirror surface of the water. An itchy feeling on her calf attracted her attention. She scratched her leg and then looked at it. A tiny black insect was burrowing into the skin of her calf.

"Rich, I think I have a tick." *Damn it*, she wanted to avoid this.

"Let me see," he said as he came to her side, bent over, and peered at it. "Sure enough. No problem I have a tick removal system."

Relief flooded her body as she felt cared for again and knew he was competent. "I hoped you would."

"Hold still. I don't want to crush it. I have to pull slowly upward." Rich swiftly dealt with the tick using his tweezers to grasp it close to her skin.

She held her leg very still. "I thought you were supposed to twist it counter clockwise."

"No, now it's recommended to do it this way, very gently." As he talked Rich carefully held it up for her to examine.

"That's a relief," smiled Juli. She peered at the tiny tick, "My, my, he is ugly."

"I'll put the little devil in this envelope and when we get back I'll send him off to the provincial lab for analysis. Now wash that bite with soap and water." He fumbled in his pack as though he was nervous and pulled out a small squirt bottle of liquid soap. Juli washed the spot with the soap and rinsed it in the lake.

"Now come here. I have an alcohol swab" With shaky fingers he swabbed the bite. "There, that's taken care of any Borrelia burgdorferi bacteria that may be lurking around."

Juli noticed his shaking fingers. This was a minor event, and he was a doctor. Obviously he was beginning to be emotionally connected to her' just as she was to him. It felt scary and blissful, all at the same time. Still she was glad he was so well prepared though she knew it would be unlikely that she was infected.

"Lyme disease can be ugly, with fever and chills and headache," said Rich, carefully placing the swab in their sealed garbage. "I sure wouldn't want that to happen to you."

Not to mention, Juli thought, second stage Central Nervous System damage or arthritis from the spirochete, which acts much like the spirochete of Syphilis. She remained standing close to him as she liked being in his energy field.

"If you get any of those symptoms we can do a blood test for the disease."

He sounded reassuring. However she knew that test wasn't very accurate for antibodies early in the disease. "Yuk, I sure don't want to get Lyme's disease."

"No cases reported around here that I know of." He looked up at her careful to avoid her eyes.

"As the doctor on Cortes you would know."

"Yes sure, but the symptoms are pretty vague."

You can say that again. They're a doctor's nightmare.

"Still we'll take every precaution. I don't want anything to happen to you."

Out loud she said, "I'd better check you for ticks as well." She knew he could check himself, but she wanted a reason to stay close to him and touch him.

He smiled a curious little smile, as if he was intrigued that she wanted to check him out. Nonetheless Rich sat on the boulder and examined his exposed skin with her.

She noted his muscular legs and the golden hairs as she ran her fingers gently over his skin. "Looks okay to me." Her fingers lingered lovingly on his warm skin.

With as much clinical detachment as he could muster he forced himself to ignore her feather-like touch and said, "Check my scalp, too. Then I'd better check yours. Sometimes they jump

183

on board when you duck under a branch." They both were standing now; Rich bent over as Juli checked his scalp; then Rich looked down on her scalp, running his fingers through her down soft silky hair, she wanted his fingers to stay there forever. Her hormones didn't remember that they had agreed to be platonic friends; they were still raging. She wanted to pull away and dive into the cold lake, but she couldn't move. "Better check my neck too," said Juli pulling off her hoodie and exposing her neck.

"Looks clear," he said leaning away from her. "To be sure, you better go for a swim and I'll shake your clothes out. Take the liquid soap." He picked it up off the rock and tossed it to her.

She caught it and turned away, intent on disrobing for a swim to cool her hot, sticky body. "Good idea, you turn around and I'll go in."

Rich turned slowly, reluctantly as though he wanted to watch her slender body being kissed by the clear water.

Juli slid efficiently out of her shorts and t-shirt, leaving them in a pile on the dry bank, and walked toward the water. The sharp sand prickled under her city-tender soles making her prance. Often as a child she had swum nude in the lake near her grandparents' cabin. And, being a doctor, she was used to examining people in all states of undress. So it was totally unselfconsciously that she waded enthusiastically into the water, soothing water. Her sweaty skin welcomed the coolness. Finally chest deep, she turned around, "Rich I'm in. It's great."

He turned to her voice like a plant to the sun. "Sure looks good on you." He smiled at her vulnerable shoulders, beaded with silvery drops like a mermaid's, as she rose from the sea, "Enjoy! I have a job here . . . to shake your clothes." His fingers closed tightly on the soft fabric; the seductive perfume of her body stimulated his olfactory glands, which made his heart race even faster. He was seduced by the smell of her, and mystified that he was once again an awkward teenager, crazy in love.

She could see how careful he was being with her clothes. No one had helped her with personal things like that since she left home years ago. It felt good, not invasive, loving in fact. "Thanks," she called. "Why don't you come in too? You can bring the soap out. I forgot it, sorry." Why not? They were friends, weren't they?

He hesitated, "I don't know. It looks great." Carefully he draped her clothes over a rock in the sun. "I'm beyond sticky with salt and sweat." He needed a dunk in the lake so he gave in. "Okay, I'll bring the soap."

Juli watched him strip down to his shorts, boxers with fish all over them. She wanted to giggle but knew she better not. So he wasn't a black bikini type, just a good old, outdoorsy guy. She thought about that and realized that was exactly what he was. She

185

liked him being conservative and maybe shy. But she didn't kid herself, he was a very virile man and she was toying with a lion, albeit a lion that didn't seem hungry, at least not now. She started to swim deeper.

"Wait Juli. There're a lot of snags in the water, you could . . ." At that moment she hit her leg against something sharp. Pain ripped through her calf. She screamed. A short piercing sound that echoed around the still lake. All was quiet except for the sound of splashing as Rich churned through the water toward her. Juli saw him coming recklessly toward her, "Watch out!" she warned. "There's a snag. I found it." Blood clouded the water.

"Juli, we've got to get you to shore." Rich was treading water beside her, his eyes riveted on her as though he was afraid she would die instantly.

"I'm okay. It's not much blood," said Juli trying to reassure him. "The water makes it look worse than it is." *Damn it*. Why had she been so careless? They were miles from civilization and modern medical care.

"You're probably right. We have to get you out of here. Blood won't coagulate under water." His voice sounded in staccato as his mind jerked through solutions.

"I know that," she said irritably. "Anyone who reads detective novels knows that."

"Not now Juli," he said patiently. "No arguments. Let me help you." He pulled her into his arms, his feet sinking into the mushy bottom of the lake, the water lapped at his chin.

He was right. She needed his help. She should be more grateful.

With Rich partly pulling her they swam slowly to avoid any more accidents, and flopped in the shallows together. Juli was lying in the water aware of her nakedness and wondering why she hadn't at least kept her bra and panties on. He scooped her up in his arms as though she was a feather and carried her up the bank into the sunshine and set her down gently on a towel. Bright blood trickled down the outer side of her left calf. "It's nothing," she protested, but her breathing was rapid.

"We have to treat it with disinfectant. Hold still." He fetched his knapsack and knelt beside her. Pushing his muscular thigh against her foot he expertly applied pressure to the wound, then antiseptic which stung, and finally a water-proof dressing. His hand shook as if to say he was sorry he hadn't protected her.

"Thanks Rich," Juli said, the intensity of his eyes caused her to inhale sharply. Suddenly they both became aware of their nakedness, neither was embarrassed; both gazed and allowed their senses to reel, pulses to race, breath to shorten. Then he leaned forward, bearing his weight on his hands, and kissed her with fresh-water cold lips. Opening her lips eagerly she welcomed him.

Carefully cantilevering his body over hers while maintaining lip contact, he slowly eased on top of her, continuing to support most of his weight. Juli felt his care and concern. The soft exploration of his lips launched a cascade of excitement and anticipation through her body, alerting her hormones to prepare her body to receive him. Intellectually they had agreed to stay platonic, but their bodies were like raging forest fires, unstoppable.

"Juli, it's happening again," whispered Rich into her ear.

"SShh Rich. It's okay. Lay beside me." He rolled off her on to his back, shoulder and hip still gently touching her. The heat from their bodies comingled, forming a cocoon of glowing energy that pulsed waves of gold and violet, enveloping them in a private universe. "Rich," she whispered. That was all the encouragement he needed, so in the sunshine with the trees and squirrels watching they clung together. "Juliet," he cooed into her ear and as his tongue licked gently behind her ear, sensations of delight cascaded through her, while his hot breath sent sensual sparks to her pelvis. Her whole being was focused on this spot; if a squirrel had run across her foot she wouldn't have noticed. Warmth. Heat. Total concentration. They were as one, joined in spirit as well as body.

She laughed her orgasm so loudly she thought the boaters on the inlet might hear. Rich, as last night, was considerate and persistent and passionate. He knew professionally and instinctively what would please her, and she, him. Exhausted and energized Juli lay in his arms, grass on her back, sand on her legs, happier than she had ever been before in her life. She wanted to drift in this bliss forever.

His muscles rippled as he rolled away, then lifting his body off the grass he struggled to his feet; cold air rolled down that side of her body. Rich shook his head as though trying to wake up. Then turning into the conscientious guide again said, "Juli it's getting late. We have to get back through the forest." Rich paused and checked her wound and finding no fresh bleeding, he took her hand and gently pulled her to her feet. She leaned against him, more affected than she had thought possible.

She felt shaken to her very core. She was always the competent one, always in control; or rather she used to be. Since Sunday, only six days ago, she had depended on Rich to cure her blistered hands, paddle their kayak, feed her, protect her from wolves, and now, today, to treat a tick bite and a bleeding wound, and through it all he had been compassionate and loving. She had never experienced such caring and support. Never felt so vulnerable. Never filled with such bliss. Never before experienced such sexual joy. She wanted to be near him, wanted his support. Could Marigold's wish for a . . . soul mate . . . be coming true?

Using the lake water they cleaned one another off as if it was a ritual to bring them back to the real world. As they stood calf deep in the cold clear water Rich gently brushed twigs and grass off Juli's back, then cupped water in his hand and gently washed her skin starting at her shoulders, down her slender back and over her strong buttocks, down the back of her thighs. Then he did the same to her front adding nibbling kisses to the clean flesh and gentle massage to her swollen breasts. Then he crouched before her cleaning the sand from her slender legs, being careful to avoid the bandage. Then he stood before her not moving, not wanting to break the spell woven around them. As though in a trance Juli walked round him copying his behavior, brushing his broad shoulders and strong back free of loose dirt. Then cupping water in her hands she rinsed him clean. Her hands memorized each intimate detail of his body from the golden hairs on his broad chest to his tight abdomen to his generous private parts and his sturdy legs.

Once they were in their clothes, Rich held her tenderly saying, "Juli you're like no other woman I have ever met. Tonight at campfire I want to hear your story. I want to know about your life." He held her hand as they started the hike back to base camp he continued, "I resisted . . . I thought if I didn't know you I could stay aloof. I know about pheromones and hormones, so that was stupid thinking." As the path narrowed he took the lead.

"Rich," she panted as she tried to keep up to his long strides, "no one could ever call you stupid . . . maybe sexy . . . sensual. . ."

"Sweetheart save your breath you can tell me tonight." His voice was husky with concern and he stopped briefly, to assess her progress. "Are you hurting?"

Sweetheart? That sounded wonderful. "A bit but not enough to worry about. I'll take an analgesic when we get back. Keep going, I'll follow." She realized she would follow him almost anywhere for more of today's bliss.

"Sorry, we have to keep up our pace," he called over his shoulder as he started to walk again. "No way do we want to be travelling through here after sunset."

She agreed, remembering about the wolves and cougars; but in addition there was something human with a greater potential for disturbing her. She blushed, *after sunset?* More joy tonight. She hoped she had brought more condoms, no sense being unprotected like today, when she hadn't brought one as she foolishly thought she could resist him. Now that it was clear she couldn't, she would be prepared.

"Can you do it?" concern showed in his husky voice.

"Certainly," came the reply as Juli stumbled on, faithfully following her fearless leader.

When they reached the camp site she crashed into her tent and lay on top of her sleeping bag. Her calf had swollen slightly and now it ached like a deep annoying toothache. Tears squeezed from her eyes; she hated being helpless. "Knock, knock," came Rich's quiet voice. "Can I come in? I have analgesic and ice."

"Welcome, so you're not just a pretty face." Juli struggled to a sitting position not aware of how young and vulnerable she looked with her flushed face and mussed hair. She wanted Rich to take her in his arms and croon to her saying she was safe, instead he knelt beside her and offered her the cup of water which she drank thirstily and downed the capsule. Rich had cold water in a plastic bag which he arranged on her wound. Do you think I should put some stitches in it?" He pointed his head toward the covered wound on her leg, never losing contact with her eyes. "Rich, it bled a lot but it's pretty superficial. We can leave it." Juli sank back and shut her eyes as she let out a sigh of relief. Relief that what she had said was true, and relief to hear him ask her opinion.

"You have a nap; I'll organize supper and give you a call when it's ready." Juli was already snoring gently. He smiled down at her, soaking in her beauty. Then slowly and quietly he backed out of her tent. He was surprised at how tender he felt, and protective. He wanted her safe, always. He shook his head, he needed to find out more about this woman; sure the pheromones were right, and that was good for sex, but he knew everyday living required more. Could they be compatible on other levels? He didn't know anything about her except she lived in Victoria, was independent thinking and acting, and had a wonderful healthy strong body. The last was of major importance to him after Sylvia's protracted battle with cancer and his desire for children. Certainly he wanted a healthy happy partner with similar goals. Tonight he would find some answers.

After supper they sat by their small fire on the secluded beach, watching the changing drama in the over-head screen. Once again the fiery sunset shot with fuchsia and tangerine and lemon exploded as the first act for the dramatic night sky to follow. With his binoculars in his lap Rich relaxed beside her on the blanket he had spread to protect them from the damp sand. The clear still evening, the pure kind following a dry hot summer day, cradled them in warmth and, as a last gasp, the sky glowed magenta. Then as the heavens became greyer and greyer, dusk settled in and the last rays of color faded; they waited patiently, side by side, for the second act. This was a good life. Juli could hear his quiet steady breathing, and the warmth radiating from his body made her want to touch him. She focused her hearing behind them toward the forest, just a gentle stirring of fir needles in the light breeze, no danger there right now. She peered around, her eyes sweeping across the inlet and up to their tents, no danger there either. So she settled back on the blanket enjoying the feel of her body humming in tune with Rich's and nature. She wanted this moment to go on forever.

Just as dusk was ending Rich stirred, smiled at Juli, and slowly raised his binoculars toward the sparks of light winking into sight. And said in a hushed voice, "Look Juli there's Jupiter." He paused holding his breath as if the sight was so powerful he needed time to absorb it. His hushed voice continued, "Rising in the east. It's one of the giant companions to earth on our journey through space and time." His voice resonated with awe while his finger pointed at a speck of light. "Wow. This is the closest it's been in fifty years. Try the binoculars."

Juli took the binoculars, which were still warm from his hands. The heat spread like the flash of a photon through her hand right to her heart, which stepped up its throb to a steady rapid beat. She raised the glasses to her eyes and smiled, "I see it. Oh I see it . . . how incredible." She sighed with delight. "Jupiter attracts most of the space debris that's heading our way. Without mighty Jupiter life would be very different."

"That's right," Rich replied, delighted that she was as interested as he was. "Look, you can see one of its moons on the right hand side. It could be Io, or Europa. . . . or maybe Ganymede, or Callisto. I like to think that it's Io which is the most volcanically active surface in the Solar System. It spouts plumes of sulfurous gases."

She knew most of the facts, but didn't say anything. She liked him being the tour guide, taking care of her. What harm was there in that? Rich eased his arm around her and pulled her close. She snuggled into his chest savoring the warmth, letting her heart rate pace his until they were as one, waiting, waiting for the celestial dream to unfold. And unfold it did.

"This was worth waiting for," declared Juli, meaning both the panorama and her developing relationship with Rich as she moved to lay on her back, head thrown back, left hand in Rich's right one while he lay beside her. "Black velvet."

"Soft space," responded Rich softly.

"Glittering diamonds." Diamonds, as in engagement rings, thought Juli, very surprised by her jump in context. That's crazy thinking. Diamond engagement rings are a sign of ownership, a signal to other males to stay away. On the other hand, she argued with herself, they show a couple is committed and that's a good thing and an easy signal to others. Besides, diamonds sparkle like the night sky and that would be a reminder of this wonderful night.

Rich interrupted her thoughts, "Each is a star like the sun."

"They seem so close," she whispered as she continued her train of thought. She had never considered marriage before, never even thought it would be a possibility. But now with this man, this wonderful competent, considerate and very sexy man, she was contemplating a permanent union, a union to make babies and establish a family.

"One day we will star travel."

Focusing on Rich's fantasy she added, "One day humans will live on Mars. But for now we are star travelers bound to Earth."

"Right, Earth is our spaceship carrying us safely through mysterious space."

Juli shivered. "That sounds so comforting."

"It could be if we stop polluting."

"Let's not go there. We can't do anything about humans tonight."

"Right," he squeezed her hand gently. "But," he said getting the last word, "Makes me realize how insignificant my daily problems are."

Juli sighed and leaned back into him, wondering what his daily problems were. He slid his arm around her and they shared their body warmth in total silence, each lost in thought. Gradually their breathing harmonized. Juli loved that he smelled of smoke and wood. Her senses went on hyper-alert; she should move away from him and get a safe distance between them. Her body was so tuned to his she wondered if he had bewitched her. No, not him, it was this place, this magnificent ocean and forest, full of peace and love. There were no cell phones or Wi-Fi. Here what was important was being in tune with her body and with the rhythms of nature - the day and night cycles, the ebb and flood of the ocean. These were the things that were vital; things that would determine her survival. Rich had tuned into nature, much faster than she, so that she felt safe with him and wanted this time to last forever. But of course it couldn't, as she would return to Victoria, and he to Cortes. She would provide care for people, and sleep and eat alone. Could Rich survive in Victoria? Would she like what he would become there? No, he was a man suited for the rural life; she for the urban life. They were worlds apart. This trip was an anomaly, a freak event that should never have happened. One part of her said the sooner it was over the better. Another part said she wanted it to go on forever. This relationship was a risk, but also a chance for her to have an even better life. Rich was wonderful and they had a lot in common. At that moment Rich tightened his arm and pointed at the heavens. "Did you see that?"

They snuggled together on the blanket and stared upward. "Shooting stars?"

"Yes, that's the Perseid shower again."

"There goes more." Streaks of light flashed past like sparks from a fire being propelled by an invisible wind. They silently watched together, gradually syncing their breathing and heart rates.

"Juli tell me about yourself," he said nuzzling her neck.

She had to respond, maybe he wouldn't like what he heard; she had to take that risk. "Sure. I was born thirty-four years ago in Saskatoon, Saskatchewan. Got A's all through school, went to U of S and then moved to Victoria."

"MMM sounds wonderful. You smell good." He sniffed her neck. "What was your major?"

"Science." There she went again, hiding her medical degree. Was she so insecure?

That was pretty vague, she was covering something. Maybe she didn't finish her degree. He decided to give her more time to come to trust him in that area and switched the subject. "Tell me about your family."

She watched the flashes, feeling like she was in a surreal dream. "I'm the oldest of three kids. Shirley and Mikey are two and four years younger than me. Shirley's a teacher in Saskatoon and Mikey's a pharmacist like our stepdad."

"Stepdad?" He heard her sharp intake of air as though she needed strength to continue.

"Yah, my dad left when I was six." She paused for many seconds, "He acquired a new wife with two kids . . . moved to Calgary . . . I rarely saw him. After that mom found a job as an office manager, supporting us as best she could."

He felt the subtle tightening of her muscles letting him know she was way more affected than she wanted him to know but he prodded again. "That must have been tough."

"Yah, I had a lot of responsibility for Shirley and Mikey." They both were quiet: he waiting for more information; she reluctant to tell him about the after school sports she had to give up or the shame she felt with her cheap clothes. "I managed to get a scholarship to university. When I started undergrad Shirley was sixteen and Mikey fourteen so they didn't need me as much." Her voice brightened, "Right about then Mom met Pete and fell in love. They got married two years later when Shirley had started university . . . so only Mikey was at home. Pete was good for him; now he's a pharmacist like Pete. When I was thirty Pete sold his drugstore and he and mom moved to North Vancouver and bought a condo there, and one at Whistler. By then Shirley was teaching and Mikey was working for a Vancouver pharmacy."

He prodded a little about her father. "So your mom managed to form another relationship. Did your dad stay married?"

"Yes he's still with Maria. They seem happy together." Why was he asking all these questions? No one had ever asked her so much about her family. She didn't want to tell him anymore; it wasn't any of his business.

"Aren't you mad at him for messing up your childhood?"

She chuckled, thinking she knew what he was doing. He was trying to see if she had resolved these issues or if she had buried them. "I was . . . very angry. Now I see him as a very weak person. That's after years of therapy. I bet you think I'm in denial."

"Yah."

"Sometimes I am. Other times I'm grateful I had the chance to get to know my siblings so well. And glad mom found someone she could be happy with. Unfortunately I'm not as mature and resolved as I'm saying. I don't have a permanent relationship. Just one serious attempt . . . when I was twenty-one. We broke up because he wanted kids. That wasn't my plan. I had just finished raising my brother and sister. Since then there's been no one; work keeps me occupied."

"Work?"

That was as much as she wanted to say so she turned to ask him, "So it's your turn. What's your family like?"

He shrugged, "I'm an only child. I was raised in Port Alberni and went to UBC." He cleared his throat. "My dad died when I was twenty. From a massive myocardial infarction, on the golf course. He was a doctor; you would think he would look after himself."

"Your father died. I'm so sorry. You were older than I was when my dad left, but your dad's departure was more permanent. I'm so sorry."

"I'll never get to talk with him again."

"I guess I should be more grateful that I can talk to my dad, though I don't want to." She felt a great compassion for Rich, wanted to nurture him as she had her brother Mikey. A shudder ran through his body as she hugged him. Quiet tears oozed from his eyes, mixing with the wetness on her cheeks. They both had lost their fathers and could support one another.

After many quiet comforting minutes Juli looked up at the heavens again. Another bright display of shooting stars flashed across the dark sky. "When I look at the heavens I see my own struggles as minute."

"Minute in the full scheme of things, but heart breaking as you live it." His voice was ragged with emotion and his arm pulled her closer.

"So true," she sighed. "I visited mom and Pete in Whistler recently and noticed they weren't coping very well. I need to go and see them again, soon."

"They must be quite a concern for you."

"Of course, thankfully Shirley and Mikey are very involved too. What about your mom?"

"Dead, from a stroke six months after dad died. I wished I'd spent more time with my parents instead of running around with friends."

"How old were they when they died?" He was not as good father material as she had thought, family medical history not good. Plus it really must have shaken him up losing both parents in six months. On top of that he must have been in med school, surrounded by death in the hospital. "Dad was sixty-five, Mom sixty."

"Wow, your Mom must have been forty when you were born?"

"I was a menopausal surprise. Dad had a low sperm count and they had long ago accepted they wouldn't have children," he sighed. "That's enough of childhood traumas." He pulled her close nipping at her neck. His hot breath heated the side of her neck and radiated like warm sunshine through her body, making her feel soft and pliable.

She gently pushed him away. "Rich I love you close and I have been encouraging you but . . . we weren't going to do this."

"I can't help myself. My whole body goes into spasm when you're close." He tugged her close again; his hot breath on her bare neck zinged happiness and desire through her body. She laughed, "That doesn't sound very medical."

"Nope, very basic. That's how I am with you."

"Rich," she said hands on his chest, "the chemistry sure seems right with us but it might be our isolation. We need to take this slowly." Her nurturing feelings seemed to be moderating her sex drive, which was good, she thought.

"Right," he said and placed his lips gently on hers. Zap! A gentle flow of electricity hummed on her lips, spreading warmth through her body, making her nipples harden and tingle. As the kiss deepened he rolled on top of her.

Oh my god, it was happening again. She couldn't stop him, didn't want to stop him. She whispered, "Rich you need a condom."

"It's okay, I won't go that far. I want to nuzzle your body."

Juli giggled. "Nuzzle away but that's all. Taste but don't eat."

He gently pulled up her hoodie to expose one of her breasts. Warm lips brushed across, prickling her with his light growth of whiskers. Warm flashes sparked her pelvic area. She knew her uterus was contracting in mild orgasms. She still felt in control and able to say no. Then he fumbled for her zipper again. *Oh, oh,* she thought. She liked it but how would she recognize the

203

point of no return? She put her hand over his, slowing the relentless journey down her abdomen. As waves of sensation flooded her pelvis, she twitched her orgasm and he muttered, "go girl go." Wave after wave of sensation had her panting. His breathing was rapid now. She knew he was stimulated, and could feel the hardness of him on her thigh. Suddenly he jerked away. Cold air hit her abdomen and she lurched up as he rose hurriedly and left, opening a hole in the circle of sensual energy she hadn't realized they were creating. She was disappointed that he had stopped. He really could control himself, obviously better than she could.

He came back to the fire, warmed his hands, and said rather briskly, "You better go to your tent. We have a big day tomorrow. We'll hike to Squirrel Cove."

She wanted to shout, *I feel cold and abandoned. Hold me.*

He continued, his back to her as he fetched water, "I'll put out the fire."

I'm such a fool. He's doesn't need me. Reluctantly she stood, protecting her injured leg, stumbled up the low bank, and then entered her cold and lonely tent. She felt more alone than she had ever before. She had expected to sleep with him again tonight; she was mistaken. Fully dressed she crawled into her sleeping bag, pulled it over her head and sobbed quietly. She was never going to find her soul mate. She was going to travel through this life alone like Earth through space. No, worse; at least the Earth had the moon, cold and pock marked and airless as it was. How sad. She heard him rustling around tending to the camp and then all was quiet.

She heard the wolves howling very faintly in the distance as she fell asleep.

CHAPTER THIRTEEN

Juli was curled in fetal position when she woke, partly to keep warm, partly to protect her soft abdomen from the wolves. She had had a restless sleep: no shooting stars to watch, no lover to hold her. On the plus side this morning, her leg felt cool and healthy; probably the hike back to camp yesterday had stimulated the healing process, or perhaps the healthy sex. As she stretched her hand hit the side of the tent. She examined her bare arm closely, definitely stronger from all the paddling. That wasn't the only part of her body that was changing as her breasts tingled at the thought of Rich's warm breath on them, which was crazy. She had to stop thinking of him that way. He wasn't interested in a committed relationship. He was a loner. Anyone with half a brain could see that. Nonetheless she caressed her abdomen, fluttering her fingers lightly as butterfly wings, while an undeniable yearning built within her.

Then she heard Rich rattling pans. As the stand-in guide he seemed to think he was responsible for every meal. She would ask him if he wanted her to do more, but he was doing such a great job she would encourage him. Today they were going to Squirrel Cove and the restaurant there. She wondered about the wisdom of this, as Rich might find himself inundated with his patients. However, she was ready for fresh bread and a salad and maybe a chicken pot pie. *Food's on the way*, she thought as she scrambled out of her sleeping bag. Carefully she smoothed her clothes. She had slept in them as she didn't have the strength to undress.

As she stepped out of her tent she glanced toward the inlet. Pink and orange and purple starfish flowers, scattered among barnacled rocks, brightened the grey beach garden. The summer sun pierced wisps of mist that were floating gently above the inlet while the stars, bowing to the golden sun, had disappeared.

"Oh, hi," said Rich looking up as though he had forgotten she existed.

He had withdrawn from her as if he had to think and organize his life. Couldn't he see she was a wonderful sexy woman who could make him feel strong and wise and sexually attractive? Could he really afford to push her away? When would he ever meet a woman like her again? This was kismet. "Hi, what's for grub?" She couldn't believe that's all she had to say to this gorgeous man as she sauntered down to the beach toward him, pushing her hair into some kind of order. Then she sensed his turmoil and stood quietly next to him.

"Secret," Rich teased, indicating a rock close by for her to sit on. "You sleep okay?"

He was trying to be casual; she would respect that. "Sure." He nodded, staying focused on the fire.

She was silent for a few minutes and then added, "Not as well as the night before." *Oops*. Now why did she say that? Was she trying to provoke him?

He raised his eyebrows, but said nothing.

"I heard the wolves last night." Juli ignored the rock and pulled up a piece of driftwood to sit on.

"I heard them too. They were a long way off. No problem."

"I guess you're right. I'm still here." Juli smoothed her hair again, unconsciously preening. The ocean breaking restlessly on the surface of a rock reminded her of the dangers lurking below the seductive, gentle-looking surface.

"They're after raccoons and squirrels . . . small stuff . . . and the occasional deer. *"*

"I hope you're right about that. I don't really want to face a hungry pack of wolves."

He smiled mischievously and added, "I suppose they compete with the cougars for prey."

"Cougars?" Juli paused, thinking, "We don't really have to worry about them." Suddenly Juli started spouting facts, "According to what I read on the internet conflict between cougars and humans is extremely rare as they're very secretive and elusive. In the past one hundred years, a total of five people have been killed by cougar attacks in B.C. The bad news is four of these fatal cougar attacks occurred on Vancouver Island . . . and twenty of the twenty-nine non-fatal attacks in B.C. occurred on Vancouver Island."

"I'm glad you checked that out, but remember we are in the wilderness, with emphasis on wilderness." He swept his arm expansively. "So if we meet a cougar stay calm, talk confidently, never run, never turn your back, try to look as big as possible cause you're trying to convince him you're not prey, but if he attacks . . . heaven forbid . . . fight back with stones or your camp knife."

"I have a camp knife in my backpack. When we're hiking I'll put it on my waist. But don't worry I'll fight to the death." Life was full of risks. She was probably in more danger from Mr. Doctor here than the cougar, or for that matter the wolves. Or, she thought, every day at work from exposure to lethal pathogens.

His eyes riveted on her as if to say, 'I know you would fight to the death if you were attacked.'

She shrugged trying to lighten the mood, "Maybe the wolves and cougars will be so busy chasing each other they'll never notice us puny humans."

"I like that thought. We, on the other hand, are going after beef this afternoon . . . if your leg is up for it." He stared at her leg intently, then shook his head as if to say *don't go there* and said, "After we eat I'll change the dressing."

"Thanks. Right now it feels great. Walking will improve the circulation and healing. Let's do it."

"Atta girl! He smiled. "Right now I gathered our bountiful breakfast," he waved his arm toward the tidal flats.

He said our. That was encouraging. He was not an I, I, me, me man. Juli sat by the fire watching Rich heat oysters in their shells. He put several on the hot rocks. After a few minutes he announced proudly, "That's it. The shells are open."

"I don't know if I can do this for breakfast." She thought back to her city breakfast of a latte and an apple. This seemed like too much food.

"Try one," he encouraged. "They're fresh."

"Thanks but I'll stick with granola this morning. We'll be having a large lunch."

"It's up to you. I'm doing oysters," he said as he retrieved one from the coals. "This trip's our chance to be in sync with nature. Come, move over here," he indicated the log across from him. "Oh yah, I heated some pan bread and we have fresh jam and a new small jar of peanut butter courtesy of Tom. Maybe that'll work for you. Remember we've quite a paddle and hike ahead of us today. You need sustenance."

"You're right. A few calories will be a good thing." So saying Juli smeared a generous helping of soft peanut butter and sticky raspberry jam on her bread. "Yum," gasped Juli as she bit into the hot crisp pan bread, licking her tongue over her lips she cleaned off the jam. "MMM that's heavenly."

Rich bit into another oyster and squirted liquor down his chin. "MMMM now this is a breakfast for royalty." His eyes moved over her and jerked away. She watched him staring across the inlet as a flock of eight cormorants stretched their wings and preened. The tide stirred softly.

They finished with canned-milk lattes. Juli grimaced, "I'm going to get fresh-milk for tomorrow's latte."

"And I'm having a large juicy New-York-cut steak with a baked potato," smiled Rich as he turned toward her.

"Sounds good. Do you know how to find this restaurant?" She wanted to keep the conversation going. She liked the sound of his voice and liked that he wasn't shutting her out any more.

211

"Are there trees in a forest? Birds in the sky?"

"Yes," she giggled. "But what's that to do with us not getting lost."

He smiled as if to say, I love teasing you. "I've hiked in here twice from the Squirrel Cove end, so I think so."

"Think so? Could you please be more reassuring? I'm not planning to do a reenactment of Hansel and Gretel."

He laughed, "You're about as far from little lost Gretel as possible. No worries. However there are no guarantees in life so I'll take the compass and my sat-com phone, which I can recharge at The Cove."

"Good idea." He was right again. There weren't any guarantees in life. She might get hurt; so what? Was it better to be a frozen, unhappy old maid? What was the worst thing that could happen? Once she admitted she was smitten he could laugh at her. That would hurt. But it wouldn't be the end of the world. Her life would go on. It would be his great loss. Or, even scarier, he could say he, too, was interested; then what would she do? She drew a blank, couldn't think past wanting him.

"Juli," he called. "It's a bit of a hike, so we'd better clean up and get going." He stared at the sky, "The weather looks great. The summer high is holding. . . I was hoping it would."

Juli went to the outhouse and then washed up, tidying her unruly hair as best she could. It was close to needing a cut. She

212

thought she must look terrible, but it didn't matter as she was in the middle of nowhere, and for sure Rich wouldn't judge her based on her hair; his priorities, she was sure, were different.

Rich was sitting in the kayak when she returned. "Wow you look clean. Everyone will think you've been at a spa."

She laughed, "Is there one around here? If there is I want to see it."

"Sorry no spa."

"I don't really need it. All this wilderness is soothing me."

"Good answer. Right now we'll paddle as far as we can, right to the east end of the inlet. That'll put us at the head of the trail . . . The sailboat we saw yesterday likely will be there."

"Sounds like a plan." Juli stood bare-foot in the ocean with her hiking boots and dry socks slung over her shoulder. She peered around inside the kayak. "I'm not ready. Can't find my backpack."

"I stowed it already. Your water is on your seat."

"Thanks, I see it," said Juli as she eased herself skillfully into Yak. She was amazed at her professional entry; "Practice makes perfect," she hummed. Tucked her boots between her legs, fastened her spray skirt, and pulled on her gloves. When she picked up her paddle she realized her hands didn't hurt. Maybe that was because of the analgesic she took for her leg this morning. Prudently she decided not to over-paddle.

The glassy surface of the inlet mirrored the blue from above. The few puffy clouds reflected so perfectly she didn't have to look up. Suddenly the surface was broken by a small flock of diving birds, and a seal's small round head popped up in the channel to the west, water dripping off its whiskers, proudly surveying his realm.

Juli relived her perfect entry, pleased she had been careful not to bump her wound, which Rich had carefully cleaned and redressed. It was as she expected, almost healed. And, the tick bite had healed without infection. She dipped her paddle creating a whirlpool as she forced the bow of the heavy kayak away from the beach and closer to the curious seal. "Let's go," said Juli. Rich grunted and added his strength, digging his paddle deeply into the still ocean, and they slipped easily through the water. Smoothly. Quietly.

The narrow inlet was about a block wide where they were camped to the west of the reversing waterfall, but as they continued deeper it closed in to about half a block wide, lined with giant first-growth cedar trees. They silently passed a cove sheltering a sailboat quietly anchored like a ghost ship. No one was visible so they kept on their silent, effortless journey. The flooding tide assisted their passage and soon they had covered the two kilometers and reached the foot of the inlet. Rich held the kayak parallel to the shore as Juli, bracing her paddle behind her, shifted her bum from the seat to her hands on the coaming, eased her bare foot onto the cold sand, and shifted her weight shoreward onto her left foot, pulling her right leg out as she rolled toward the beach. Not graceful, but safe, and she didn't tip the kayak.

"You okay?"

"Yup, didn't reinjure my leg." She pushed up to standing and leaned forward to retrieve her hiking boots.

"Stand back," ordered Rich as he steadied the kayak. "I'm coming out." Gracefully, with years of practice behind him, he eased out of the kayak as though he was rising from a chair on dry land.

Then after drying their feet and easing them into hiking boots, they stood, two healthy eager adults, looking expectantly at the beginning of a rough trail. Without talking, like a well-oiled team, they pulled the kayak right into the forest to be sure the tide wouldn't suck it out to sea and leave them stranded. Then hoisting their light backpacks they started out, Rich in the lead as usual. Juli trotted behind, happy to follow him. She liked the way his blond hair curled down his neck, and the broadness of his shoulders made her feel safe.

Maybe she should have told him she was a doctor too. She had a chance last night but she avoided the whole truth.

Tonight she would tell him. He had been straight with her. It was the least she could do. Why, she wondered, hadn't she told him? It was fear. She was starting to like him, well more than like as she was attracted to him almost as strongly as a satellite to Earth. And like the satellite, she had to stay at a certain distance or she might crash and burn. It was fear he wouldn't like her if he knew she was competent. Men liked their woman dependent, at least the men she had known till now.

She bet Rich's mom had always agreed with her husband, at least to his face. She also bet his mother didn't drive and didn't have her own credit card. Her husband probably liked her taking care of the home and making his life smooth. Who wouldn't? Maybe Juli was being unfair; maybe she was wrong; she would have to check with Rich. Right then Juli stumbled over a large brown root crawling across the surface of the path searching for nutrients for its sixty foot Douglas fir, and decided she better pay attention or she might add another injury.

The path had been wide and well-marked for the first few yards then it narrowed to a single-file trail through what seemed to be dead straight soldiers of bark. The rustle of wind in the high canopy, which blocked the sun and made it cool and shady for walking, was the only sound other than the crackle of twigs as they marched along. An occasional scraggly salal plant grew among the sprinkling of dry needles.

The narrow trail was so strewn with blow downs and roots of the giant trees that she had to watch closely or she would stumble again. "Where are the deciduous trees? I thought we would see an occasional large-leaf maple, or more likely red alder."

"No, as you can see," he said expansively waving his arms, "conifers . . . cedar, fir, and pine dominate and control the forest."

Dominate and control? Where did that come from? Queer little prickles ran up and down her spine. Suddenly she remembered her parent's almost nightly argument, her dad screaming 'do as I say, you never do what I want.' And her mother's sobbing reply. This was the second time this trip that memories about her father had surfaced. She knew not to fight them, knew to let the emotion roll through her body and be neutralized. Oblivious to her reaction Rich marched on calling back over his shoulder, "Huge Western Red Cedars sixty feet tall and even taller Douglas fir and Hemlock and the occasional Sitka Spruce and Lodge-pole pine reign supreme."

Before she could reply a flick of yellow caught her eyes as a flock of Pine Siskins swept by and were absorbed into a pine tree. From such small living things there was much to be learned. They were monogamous and the male faithfully fed the female when she was sitting on their eggs, then they worked

217

cooperatively to feed the babies. Very similar to the Bald Eagle. How was it that the birds got it right?

Rich talked as they walked. "Cortes is right at the northern end of the Salish Sea between Vancouver Island and the British Columbia mainland."

"Didn't the Salish Sea used to be the Strait of Georgia?"

"Right. It was the territory of the Coast Salish First Nations." He waved his hand toward north. "The Klahoose tribe moved here permanently to Squirrel Cove in the 1800's after their Toba Inlet village was flooded. We're hiking through Ha'thayim Provincial Park which they dedicated with to the province."

"That was generous. Now I need to stop for a rest." Juli eased herself to a fallen log, gently rubbing her wound from yesterday. Rough bark scratched her legs. On the log beside her a telltale pile of discarded scales from fir cones alerted her to look around for a pine squirrel but she couldn't see one. Then the familiar trill sounded overhead in the canopy of fir branches; a second trill sounded from deep in the forest, no doubt warning the inhabitants of the forest of the humans progressing through their territory.

Rich stopped, turned and came back. Stopping several feet away and avoiding eye contact as if he was trying to establish a relationship with more distance. "Your leg still okay?"

"It aches a bit . . . but yes it's basically okay."

"Good let's have some water and a short rest then we'll continue," said Rich as he shucked off his pack and sat on the log with his back to her.

For the second time that was a message, loud and clear: he didn't want to be entangled with her. She almost giggled at her thoughts using the word entangled because that's exactly what they had been at least three times: the first beyond the reversing waterfall because of the wolves, later that same night by mutual desire, and completely and explosively at the lake. Good sex was one thing to bind a couple together, but sex alone did not make for a happy marriage as she had seen with her parents. She remembered again how they argued and then each sunk into silent isolation. After years of therapy she realized they never could resolve their power struggle. Juli didn't want to be in a relationship like that. She and Rich didn't argue, nor did they chat comfortably without fear of offending the other. She still was getting to know him; so far he had been competent and considerate, if a little distant. She blushed. Except for sex, she thought. Once she regained her breath Juli bounced up, saying, "Let's go get you that red meat."

Rich smiled and hopped up, "Now you're talking." His smile lit his whole face like a kid who had been told it was hot dogs and marshmallows for supper. "C'mon Juli. I'm eager for that steak," called Rich as he hoisted his backpack.

"Coming," called Juli struggling with her backpack. "Don't leave me here for the wolves."

Rich laughed, his full rich booming roar filled the forest. Juli laughed too, just for the joy of it and to celebrate their freedom.

The trail widened and they were able to walk side by side. Rich continued his information download. Juli knew it had another purpose than informing her, which was to warn wild animals they were coming and give them time to scurry or slink away. "Cortes was mapped by Spanish explorers in the late 1700's. Notably Juan Francisco de la Bodega y Quadra."

"Guess that's who Quadra Island was named after."

"Of course. He was a contemporary of good old Captain George Vancouver who first circumnavigated Vancouver Island."

"So George and Quadra were sailing around here at the same time. The English versus the Spanish." She kept her eyes down watching for dangerous roots.

"Right. And Cortes Island was named after Hernan Cortes de Monroy y Pizarro, who was the first Marquis of the Valley of Oaxaca, the infamous conquistador of Mexico."

"You know any personal stories about them? Like falling in love with First Nation Princesses?" Why had she said that? Couldn't she even be subtle?

"I'm sure that happened. I don't know the stories, but what I do know is . . . this group of islands including Quadra are called the Discovery Islands." As he talked he helped her over a large fallen fir, the complex of roots looking like a saucer on end, small considering the length of the tree. Juli wondered how a tree with a diameter of five feet and a height of over forty feet could have a root ball of only ten or fifteen feet in diameter. A*mazing, both the root ball and . . . his gentle touch.* Her skin felt hot where he had touched her, as if the energy from his body had penetrated her skin.

Juli shrugged, trying to pull herself together. She had to stop acting like a hormone-driven teenager. She decided to follow his lead and distance herself, too. She could hold her own talking facts. "I know that and that Cortes is twenty-five km long by thirteen km wide." She yawned and rubbed her leg which was beginning to ache. "How much further do we have to walk? I'm hungry. Breakfast was a long time ago."

"A long, long way." He teased and then smiled at her as if she was a little girl.

She didn't like that, didn't like being patronized. No one, but no one, had treated her like that since she was a first-year intern. Indignation stirred her body, and she held her head high and marched ahead following the narrow path. She was startled by her reaction: what was the matter with her? Was this man's opinion so important to her that she couldn't stand a little teasing? He had crept under her skin and she wasn't sure she wanted that. The dilemma sapped her strength making her footsteps slow.

Rich brought up the rear, shaking his head, as if he was wondering why he had teased her. He didn't understand women very well; their moods and hormones were so different. That wasn't right; as a doctor he was very helpful to his female patients; it was this specific female he didn't understand, wasn't sure if he wanted to understand. She had huge traumas with her father leaving when she was so young, she would not trust a man easily, and when she did, he better be committed deeply and for life. That wasn't him; he liked being single and selfish. Well most of the time. She sure brought him pleasure. Even now walking behind her, watching her butt moving, made his shorts tighten. He was on holidays, he decided to enjoy the feeling, to hell with the consequences.

Finally they broke through the forest onto a gravel road and sunshine. *Wow!* A road through a forest. What a miracle, thought Juli. As if reading her thoughts Rich pointed out, "This is the road, really the only road, which passes from Whaletown on the west side of the island to Squirrel cove on the east side of the island, and then swings back to Manson's . . . and south to Smelt Bay."

"Well since we're going to Squirrel Cove that works out." *Was that my sarcastic voice?* Walking was easier so they picked up their pace, Juli still in the lead, limping slightly. Tall grass, seed heads bobbing, lined the road. White daisies with sun-yellow centers competed with leggy dandelions to offer color and a friendly greeting. She paused to enjoy the white of the daisies. A daisy symbolized innocence and purity and also new beginnings. Was she experiencing a new beginning? She remembered the flower meaning of daisy was loyal love. Could she experience loyal love? Would she let loyal love in? Thoughtfully she continued down the road. After a few minutes she was sweating. She wanted a drink. Her adrenalin rush had passed, she felt calmer. She crossed the shallow ditch and, sat on a log. "Slow down Rich. I need a break. We're not trying to set a world record."

Rich had passed her, then came back when she called and joined her. Encouraging her to take care of herself he said, "Good Idea. Drink all you want. We can refill our water bottles at the restaurant."

Juli watched the tall purple flowers nodding gently and knew they were digitalis purpurea and a source of digoxin. This extract was first mentioned in medical literature by William Withering in 1785. It was often prescribed for patients with atrial fibrillation, especially if there was concomitant congestive heart failure. Most people called it Foxglove. She took a deep drink from her water bottle and asked, "You sure there's a world-class restaurant here somewhere? We're definitely in the middle of nowhere."

He laughed. "Trust me. Trust me," as his green eyes swept over her.

That was the heart of it. Could she trust him?

"If you're tired we could hitch a ride," offered Rich.

"In the back of a truck? Without a seat belt? No way Dr. Yak." Juli had started calling Rich this nickname yesterday. She wanted to tease him. She remembered she didn't like it when he teased her. So now she was doing it. She was very quiet as she analyzed her behavior and decided she had been testing him, testing to see if he would snap at her. Somehow in the quiet of this wilderness, she was able to look at herself. She saw that she was trying to provoke him and wondered why. She plunged deep into her memories and saw her father's angry face, heard his angry words: 'Juliet you can't do that; Juliet you behave right now or I'll lock you in your room.' He did lock her in her room, though not very often. Her mother had come to her rescue.

Rich smiled calmly as usual, "Well c'mon then, we better get hoofing. By the time we eat and hike back it'll be getting late . . . and I'm sure you don't want to be in the forest when the wolves are looking for supper."

There was that stupid smile again but this time it looked cute. What was the matter with her? She was incredibly ambivalent about him, hot one minute, cold the next. "Right," said Juli making up her mind. He was darn right. She was not going to be wolf bait.

As they walked they passed the sign for the Klahoose First Nations. Rich pointed at it saying, "We have a thriving community of First Nations."

"Do you provide their health care too?"

"Yes, they're pretty healthy."

"So you've got one thousand permanent residents, a First Nations community, and thousands of summer people. That's a busy practice."

"Yes a little busier than I want to be. And for the past two years I haven't been able to find a locum to cover for me."

The sun beat down on her back so she took off her hoodie and tied it around her waist. Her light colored t-shirt with Times-Colonist Ten KM Race printed on the front felt comfortable. "You've been two years without a break!" She was incredulous. He was worse off than she. He was on duty 24/7.

"Don't say it like that." He threw up his hands. "I didn't have a choice."

"Sure you did. You had a choice. You chose to work unreasonable hours." Juli was striding beside him now, keeping

225

up easily with his moderate pace. "You always have a choice, even when you are the only doctor. Besides that's impossible. How long do you think you can go on like that and stay healthy?"

"You're right. Let's talk about something else."

As they trudged down the road, a RAV4, a Mercedes, and a rusty old Nissan truck passed them, the last slowing to see if they were okay. The driver recognized Rich, in spite of his new beard, and smiled and said, "Hi doc. What you doin' wanderin' around on this dangerous road?"

"Hi Sam, we're off for a meal at the Cove." Rich smiled and leaned on the edge of the open window.

The driver laughed, "There's easier ways to get there than back packing."

"Go away Sam. I'm on holidays." Juli noticed Sam's approving at her.

"Okay, okay, I get the message. See you later." Rich backed away and the truck took off slowly.

"He was friendly. One of your patients?"

"Yup, they're all my patients," said Rich as he started down the road again.

"Where's the Mercedes going? It sure looked out of place." Jill felt so hot and sweaty that she wanted to go back into the cool forest and lie down in the shade.

"Probably the restaurant but maybe the recycling center. Now there's something I can't understand. These summer people have million dollar homes but they love to come to the free store at the recycling center."

"People can't resist something for nothing," smiled Juli.

"There's a sign that says 'shop lifting encouraged.'"

"Wow! That's funny."

"So they take stuff they probably don't need. Fortunately they bring interesting stuff to drop off. Generally it's very good." Suddenly he pointed, "There's the restaurant." As he guided her down a steep gravel drive, the ocean came into view - cobalt blue mixed with navy where the wind rippled it. Several yachts danced at anchor close to the large government dock, presumably so their crew members could get provisions from the general store. The grey pebbly beach, exposed by the high tide, hosted darting sea birds feasting on tiny crabs.

Rich's arm swept over the view, "That's Squirrel cove. It's a huge harbor with an island and a reversing waterfall at the far end. It stretches inland almost to Von Donop Inlet. It can hold a hundred anchored boats, no problem." Rich stepped more quickly now he was near to excellent food.

Juli drank in the view as she trotted behind him, "What a great harbor. I bet the boaters love it. And it's only a short way to Desolation Sound. I'd like to kayak there next summer."

"Sounds great." He turned to her smiling, "If you're looking for a guide, I know that area well too."

"I'll consider it. Depending on how this trip goes," frowned Juli sensing his eagerness. That was a change that surprised her, and suddenly she didn't want to encourage him. She would leave soon going back to her solitary life, which she reminded herself was very satisfying.

As they approached the restaurant Juli could see it was a small one story wooden structure with a fresh coat of white paint, windows on three sides to catch the spectacular view of the bay and the distant blue tinged mountains, and a wooden deck on the ocean side. "Let's sit out on the deck," suggested Rich.

"Good idea," said Juli shrugging off her backpack. She looked around, "Looks like there is a general store over there. I'd like to buy a few supplies."

"Me too, but we can't add too much to Yak." He started eagerly up the stairs.

She nodded agreement, "Some fresh fruit and milk and a baguette would suit me."

"Fresh eggs too," he added as he moved through the restaurant as if he owned it. Obviously very confident he would be received well. Just then the staff spotted him and three women surrounded him like a flock of Siskins, giggling and hugging him. "Dr. Rich where you been?"

228

"Dr. Rich I'm so glad to see you."

"Anne . . . Mary . . . Jane . . . I'm so glad to see you. We're really hungry." Rich smiled broadly.

Juli held back, watching like a seagull wondering if its supper had been stolen. No one noticed her.

"You look like you've been in a cave," gushed Anne.

"No, on a kayak trip. We walked in from Von Don."

"That's impressive!" said Mary. "Come sit down you must be hungry and tired." Two of the women pulled him to a chair still fussing over him. "Let us take care of you."

"Please do. This is Juli," the women swung their eyes to Juli and appraised her as if they wanted to be sure she was good enough for their dear doctor.

Juli smiled and shook each of their hands warmly, saying, "I'm escaping from the city. And I have to admit Von Donop really does seem to be pretty much the end of the road."

They giggled and said in unison, like the Rhine Maidens in Wagner's Ring, "We don't go there. We try to get to the city. We're tired of oysters and sea gulls."

"Never mind them. C'mon you two, sit down," said Mary. "Let us take care of you."

"We have a delicious seafood chowder and fresh baked bread," gushed Jane.

"I don't want to hurt your feelings, but we need land-based food. Beef for me." Rich smiled his wide friendly smile at the women.

"Chicken for me," added Juli as she sat down across from him on the deck and looked around. The breeze off the ocean was welcome and cool. The high tide lapped at the grey rocky beach. The smell of salt was strong in her nostrils, reminding her of their birth in the ocean and the salinity of her blood. She once again remembered that she was an animal affected by nature, not the superior insulated human she thought she was in the city. The purple and orange petunias in hanging baskets surrounded them with swirling, sensual perfume, breaking her reverie. Juli relaxed back closing her eyes, wanting this life to go on forever. Could she make a go of it on a remote island like this? She couldn't believe she even thought that. It was holiday fever. It would pass.

"How about steak and chips? Or a baked potato for you Doc?" asked Jane.

"And a Caesar salad with a chicken breast for your friend?" added Mary

"Great," Juli and Rich nodded in unison. Rich added, "And bring us two cold beers as well, and lots of water."

Juli smiled and gazed at the ocean. She didn't mind him ordering for her, in fact she liked that he sensed what she would like, and if she didn't want the beer she knew he could drink both bottles.

Rich glanced around the restaurant as he sipped his beer. She sensed his unease building as he identified one patron after another in a whisper to her: "there's John who had the heart attack last summer and had to be helicoptered off island, and the commercial fisherman who had appendicitis and drove himself to Campbell River, crossing on two ferries, and was whipped into the operating room as soon as he arrived, and in the corner is Peter who has cholesterol and high blood pressure problems but refuses all my advice."

"Stop it Rich, you're on holidays," whispered Juli when she noticed the tension around his eyes.

As soon as he heard her, he let go and slumped back in his chair. His eyes stopped scanning. "Thanks." He smiled at her weakly. "My contract with the local health board is up in December. I have to think about my reaction before I sign up again. Maybe I can only handle this part time. He forced himself to look casual, relaxing back in his chair sipping his icy beer.

Pleased Rich was confiding in her, Juli relaxed back with her cold beer, feeling the bubbles tickle her palate and her throat, and the cold liquid hitting her stomach,. The beer was wonderful but she better be sensible as the alcohol would hit her hot dehydrated brain like a forest fire. To mitigate it, she picked up a glass of water and chugged it all down; then she leaned over and nudged Rich's glass toward him. "Rich you need this," she muttered.

He looked at her, startled, then said, "You're right," he grinned sheepishly and followed her advice. Just then their food arrived. Juli was famished, but she didn't want to think as hungry as a bear or wolf as that might tempt the fates. So she thought, *I'm as hungry as a pussy cat after a long sleep*.

The friendly trio delivered their food with a flourish and hovered like humming birds at a feeder waiting for more requests. Rich smiled broadly and reassured them all was fine and they fluttered away like colorful butterflies. She could feel him watching her and smiling approvingly as she devoured her food. Once they both were finished she stated, "We're going to treat ourselves to Blackberry pie and ice cream."

"I'll be too full to walk back to camp," groaned Rich.

"Stop your complaining. I'll carry your pack."

"Possibly," he smiled and signaled the waitress. "Annie could we please have a piece of your home made Blackberry pie and ice cream for my friend, none for me."

"We'll share," said Juli looking deeply into his eyes. *Wow* thought Rich, *That's an invitation if I ever heard one.*

Anne, who obviously doted on Rich and could hardly refuse him anything, smiled her willingness and rushed to do his bidding. Juli didn't know if she could take their treating him like a king. She certainly didn't.

After lunch they headed for the general store, a rickety looking two story wooden structure. Inside was tidy and clean and organized. Juli was fascinated with all the choice; had she only been out of civilization for eight days? Even the selection of canned beans fascinated her - BBQ, tomato, or honey. The fresh fruits and vegetables were irresistible: she chose two bananas, two oranges, three apples and some salted almonds, a quart of milk, a head of lettuce, and two tomatoes. As she walked up to pay for her purchases she heard her name.

"Juli, Juli . . . is that you? It is. Isn't it?" called a loud voice. "It's me. We're here at the dock." The women embraced warmly, Juli's surprise was momentary as she clutched her friend. "What a coincidence. I knew you were here somewhere but I never thought we would connect. Dave will be glad to see you . . . though I don't know what Victoria will be doing with two of its best doctors hiding on Cortes. Lucky Cortes."

Doctor? thought Rich as he ducked back down the stairs toward the fishing supplies, surprise and hurt flicking across his face.

"Marigold, of course," she blushed, startled to find her Victoria friend here. She had to keep her away from Rich. Intent on removing Marigold from the store Juli quickly placed her items on the counter and offered her credit card.

Marigold chatted on, "You've got to come to the boat. We're at the dock right here." She pointed out the window behind the counter. "We were in Lund last night and came down Thulin Passage and across the Strait to Squirrel Cove, and here we are. We're anchoring out tonight but I needed milk."

Why was Marigold babbling like an idiot? Juli pulled back, Marigold's unconscious response was to move closer. Marigold asked, "What are you doing here?" Then she took Juli's arm as though she was going to pull her to the boat. "Pay for your stuff and then I'll take you down to the boat. I thought you were on the west side of Cortes."

Juli paid for her purchases and stuffed them quickly into her pack. Then grabbing her pack with one hand she steered Marigold to the door with the other. "Nope, I'm here." Juli didn't want to give her too much information and for sure she didn't want her to see Rich. Their relationship was too new to share with anyone. Besides, she had not told him about her working life.

"Dave'll be delighted." Marigold waved vaguely toward the boats tied to the government dock as she carefully navigated the rickety wooden stairs. "C'mon."

"I'm not sure," said Juli, stalling as she considered her options. "I have to hike back to my kayak today."

"Hike?" Marigold, still surprised from meeting her friend so unexpectedly and just when she needed to talk about Dave so desperately, peered at her, "You're going to Desolation, aren't you?"

"Well no, I'm going to Von Donop," said Juli vaguely, while peering around nervously for Rich.

"Von Donop? That's on the West side. A long way from here." Marigold looked puzzled and then stared intently at her friend seeking an answer.

"It is . . . by boat . . . but we walked from the end of the inlet." Vague again. She would let Marigold think she was with a group. While they talked they continued their downward journey to the dock on the driveway and then through a sparse hedge to a dirt path to the dock.

"We?" Marigold remembered their conversation and wishing for Juli's sexy, healthy, rich man. "That reminds me, is the guide delicious?"

"Not sure." Well that was a non-answer. Should she have described Tom, the real guide, even though he wasn't here? For sure she wasn't describing Rich . . . yet.

"No worries. If he appears you can introduce us. In the meantime . . . can we slow down a bit?" Marigold started to drag her feet to slow their pace.

"He's not here right now," Juli lied. She couldn't believe she was being deceitful with her friend. What was she thinking? Not only did she not want to share Rich, she didn't want to declare a relationship with him. She wasn't committed; if anything she was fearful the suddenness of their attraction might wane as quickly as it had flared up if it was examined too closely. It probably was an artifact of the isolation and beauty of the holiday, but she wasn't ready to find that out. "Which is Dream Seeker?"

"That one, straight ahead." Marigold pointed to the right. "I wanted a chance for a chat. Juli I'm so glad I ran into you. I'm worried about Dave. He's been anxious and not sleeping well." Marigold tried to stop so she could talk, but Juli didn't take the hint and kept walking toward the dock

"Not today Marigold. I'm so sorry but I have a long hike ahead of me. I'll say hi to Dave and be on my way."

Marigold opened her mouth, then closed it; she had wanted to hear Juli's opinion about Dave. She desperately needed advice; now it was too late. Nothing she could do. She wanted her husband back; how she longed for his touch, his lips on hers, the melding of their bodies. But more than that she wanted him to focus on her, and her alone. When they were courting and until about a year ago he made loving eye contact and remembered things that were important to her, tried to please her. She loved him more than life itself. She would be patient: maybe this trip would relax him and get them back to normal.

Marigold looked so hurt that Juli eased her declaration saying, "I'll be back in Victoria next week. You're due back too. Why don't we do lunch and then you can tell me all about it."

Marigold's face brightened as though someone had given her a gift and she said, "Yes, definitely lunch is on as soon as you're back. I'm counting on it." She hugged Juli, a hug of desperation and relief saying, "Dave would be disappointed if I didn't bring you." As she talked she quickened her pace and pulled gently on Juli's arm.

Juli looked around and was thankful she couldn't see Rich. Her eagerness to draw Juli to the boat seemed to have thrown Marigold off her hunt for Rich, so Juli started to relax. "Marigold I'll have to be quick. As I said I have a long hike back to camp." She let Marigold's hand pull hers and walked companionably toward the ocean, praying that Rich wouldn't appear.

Dave, pacing on the deck, spotted them and waved frantically. Juli wondered what was going on as she watched Marigold square her shoulders and smile broadly as they approached Dream Seeker.

Dave, offering his hand to steady Juli, smiled and welcomed her on board. He seemed surprised and delighted to see her, but seemed relieved that she couldn't stay. In fact he had refueled, had the engine running, and was ready to depart.

Marigold protested, "Dave, I want a visit with Juli. I've been cooped up on this boat for six days now."

Dave laughed a little too loudly, "In Victoria you complain you never see me. Now you're complaining you're seeing too much of me."

Marigold blushed in embarrassment. Juli said, "Dave and Marigold we'll have to have supper in Victoria. I'm off to base camp before it's dark." She was relieved he had the engine running; it gave her an excuse to leave. With luck Rich wouldn't have seen her with Marigold.

Dave's face became serious, "Juli, you be careful. The gas attendant warned me that there's a pack of wild wolves cruising this area."

Juli hugged him thanking him for his concern and hopped off the yacht. "I'll untie your lines and see you off."

"Great," said Dave. "We're staying here tonight and then heading around to Gorge Harbor on the west side for a few nights. We hear there's a good restaurant there too."

"Have a great trip," called Juli as she tossed them their lines. She stepped back on the dock and watched their sleek white sailboat pull away.

She turned around and headed back to the store to discover Rich was standing on the wooden steps, watching her. When she got closer, he asked, "Who was that?"

"Someone I know from Victoria. Dave and Marigold Thornton; Marigold's my best friend. They were in a hurry to leave." Why hadn't she told him the whole truth? She still didn't trust that he would like her work-day self.

"Too bad. We could have had a beer together," he said giving her another chance to come clean.

Juli laughed, "No more beer for me. You would have to carry me and my pack back through the forest."

"I couldn't do that. You're no feather weight." He looked away.

"So you noticed I'm robust." She smiled broadly encouraging him but he didn't notice.

He tightened his pack and shuffled his feet, still avoiding looking at her. "You are robust," he nodded.

Juli laughed again. She was laughing too much, she thought. "I'm for sure not a dainty princess."

"Good thing." He started walking away, "I bought some bottled water for us. Did you get what you needed?"

"Yes." She looked up at his retreating back a bit disappointed.

CHAPTER FOURTEEN

Marigold watched her friend as they slowly pulled away from the dock. Her heart was sinking from the lost opportunity to get Juli's advice. Then she saw Juli walk up to a tall young blond man who could have been straight out of a man's health magazine. They looked like a devoted couple, smiling at one another; Marigold felt a momentary flash of joy for her friend. *Good*, she thought, *Juli has met someone. I'll hear about it in Victoria. No wonder she was glowing.* And then, an aching yearning filled her heart.

Sitting on the bow she stared at the water rushing past the hull, puzzling over Dave's behavior. In Victoria, though he seemed exhausted when she saw him, she rarely saw him. The company, Doctors Unlimited, was getting too big. That was it. He had three treatment centers that he managed: Oak Bay, Gordon Head, and at the new foods center. This meant employing doctors and other staff. That wasn't so bad as a lot of doctors these days wanted to be in a clinic, work a shift and go home. Being a family doctor was too stressful, with long hours and few holidays. Today's young doctors, like Juli, wanted their freedom; Dave had seen the trend and invested in it. He bought one of the buildings and leased space for the others. He was currently negotiating on a fourth in a new shopping center. She had discouraged him from increasing his empire, but he hadn't listened. Sadly he didn't seek her advice anymore; they used to make all the decisions together. She virtually hadn't seen him for the last three weeks except for brief meals and sleep, which was only a few hours a night. Basically she was alone, running the house, paying the bills, hiring cleaners and gardeners.

As an only child she was used to taking charge of her own life. Her parents had acted as guides, at least until she was thirty. They were killed on the twisty highway to Tofino where they had planned to watch surfers and walk on the endless beaches. They had prepared her well: she handled the funeral and settled the estate. Briefly she had toyed with the idea of managing her parents company but quickly she realized Dave would never move to Port Alberni, and for sure she would not leave him; they had been happily married for two years. Unstintingly she invested the considerable capital she realized from the sale of her parents' waterfront home and the commercial fishing boats, the fish freeze packing and canning plants, and the refrigerator trucks, in the treatment centers. Dave had been delighted.

Dave was her love, her reason for breathing. His voice, his smell, they comforted her. At least they used to. This new obsessive Dave had little time to support or cuddle or talk. The word, edgy, buzzed her brain. Would he? No. He knew better than to get involved with drugs. But did he? When they met he was a smoker and it was huge struggle for him to stop. Plus he had a tendency to overdrink, almost as if he couldn't stop, but that was mainly beer and on the weekend. So that wasn't really a problem, or was it? She was watching him carefully on this holiday, trying to learn the truth. Deep down she wanted the best for him, and knew she would stick by his side no matter what she found.

They had no children. That was an aching sadness for her. They had tried through their thirties, with no luck. It seemed the mumps that Dave had when he was a teen had left him sterile. They had considered a sperm donor. Marigold could have lived with that, at least the baby would have her genes, and they could have picked a donor with similar physical and mental traits to Dave. But he wasn't interested. Finally they decided if they couldn't have their own child, they would have none. For a long time she had yearned for a baby. Now at forty-eight she wasn't interested for herself.

But dear Juli was still young, still able to have a child. That's why Marigold had urged Juli to find a partner, and based on her glow and secretiveness when they met, the gorgeous blond man might be the one. Marigold wished she had not been so wrapped up in her own problems and had questioned Juli more thoroughly. She sighed. That would have to wait till they met in Victoria.

Maybe Juli would have some answers for Marigold's problems with Dave. This trip had been one potentially-dangerous incident after another. Something terrible was wrong with Dave; Marigold desperately needed Juli's help to get him and their marriage back on track.

CHAPTER FIFTEEN

Rich turned back and waved her on and pointed toward the road. "We better start back." As he talked he started out with a brisk walk heading down the road which paralleled the beach before turning west and toward Von Donop.

"I think you're right." Juli followed close on his heels. No way was she falling back.

Rich pointed to the east over the water, "There's that pretty yacht again."

"Mmm," responded Juli. "It's called Dream Seeker. Dave and Marigold cruise on her every summer. But this year Marigold is worried about Dave. He's been anxious and not sleeping well. That's partly why I didn't introduce you. The timing was bad for them." Juli sighed, she was gradually letting him into her life.

She was diving deeper and deeper into this relationship; where would it lead?

Rich nodded a vague response and then pointed across the bay, "Look at the smoky sky over there. That must be from Princess Louisa Inlet."

"Is that close?"

"Not really . . . on the mainland . . . south of Desolation." His speech was clipped as though he didn't want to talk.

"Let's think sunshine." She said brightly trying to ignore Rich's coolness. Maybe going to the restaurant where he saw his patients wasn't such a good idea. Maybe not introducing him to Dave and Marigold was a mistake. Maybe he was a moody person and she was just finding that out. "That's what we need."

Their hike through the forest went quickly, probably because they were both fully fueled with great food. Juli couldn't help but notice how dry fallen needles crackled under her hiking boots. *Tinder, tinder*, kept echoing through her thoughts as she puffed along, trying to keep up with Rich.

Their kayak was patiently waiting. They stowed their packs efficiently, and silently carried the kayak down to the water which had receded at least ten feet. Their feet crunched on the grey rocks and Juli tried to avoid the oysters lying about.

Each lost in thought, they paddled, with the help of the ebb, swiftly down the forest-crowded inlet. The moored sailboat was bobbing silently, no doubt with the exhausted crew still sound asleep, so they paddled quietly past and headed straight down the middle of the inlet.

At base camp Juli climbed out of the kayak first, and as she steadied it for Rich she said, "If it's okay with you Rich I think I only want some canned soup for supper tonight." She stretched and yawned, "Then straight to bed."

Rich answered, "Suits me fine. I have a new pocketbook to read."

"Good," grunted Juli, helping to carry the kayak to safety and unloading their backpacks.

Rich scanned the western sky and said, "It's got to be seven. We had a long day. Dusk's early . . . probably the smoke."

Juli was too tired for conversation so she sat on a rock with her aching left leg elevated on another rock, and watched Rich start a small fire below the tide line. He was very careful with fire; she liked that. He methodically opened the cans and heated the soup. When it was steaming he carried a bowlful to her. Too tired even to stand to receive it, she thanked him and slowly sipped the fragrant blend of tomato and carrot and spices. She cradled the warm bowl in both hands. Rich fared slightly better as he stood to eat and walked a short distance to lean against a boulder and gaze at the inlet water. He took her empty bowl and washed it in the ocean while Juli stumbled off to her tent, where she fell into a deep sleep.

Waking hours later, Juli rolled off her sleeping bag, slipped on her jellies and pushed aside the tent flap. It was after sunset, fortunately some light still lingered. She headed for the outhouse, wishing she had done this right after supper as it was over the crest of the rocks on the edge of the forest. The path was easy to follow as it was edged with silver driftwood.

When she left the outhouse she suddenly felt a cold chill along her spine. She smelled something rotten, heard panting. She looked up and there between her and the forest were three lean wolves. She froze. Her heart stopped. Time stood still. Nothing moved. The closest wolf was black with piercing eyes. Two smaller grey ones hung back slightly, their hungry eyes riveted on Juli. She remembered that she shouldn't turn her back on them. As she tried to look confident and big, she prayed they weren't starving.

Then time began again. She stood up as straight as she could and screamed at the top of her lungs, "Go away. Go away. Scat. Get." Her heart raced. Her breathing started high and shallow. She stepped back one pace. Eyes glared. The black wolf stepped forward, a low growl rumbled in his throat. She didn't think that was a good sign. She kept edging back, one cautious step at a time. She dared not look over her shoulder to see if the path was right behind her. If she could get to the tent she would have a chance as she could call Rich. The black one signaled the greys and they moved so each was on a side of her and they were the same distance from her. Her hands were clammy. *What am I going to do?* If she threw a rock at one of them the other two would get her. She decided to continue her careful retreat, another step back. This time Blackie didn't follow. Encouraged she took two steps back. Blackie growled and bared his teeth. His tail was straight up. Juli knew he was ready to jump her. She grabbed a piece of driftwood from the edge of the path. "I will club you to death if you come closer," she shouted. "Get out of here." She bared her teeth. The black wolf didn't move, the greys growled. Juli took another step back. *Where's the tent. I should be there.*

Suddenly a hand reached over her shoulder and grabbed her driftwood. Rich screamed, "Get out of here," and hurled the wood at the leader, hitting Blackie on the ear. He yelped and retreated three feet. Then he turned, snarling. Undaunted the greys circled looking for an opening. Rich hurled two more pieces of driftwood, both aimed at Blackie, both finding their mark. Juli shouted and hurled wood as well. Blackie retreated to the edge of the forest, the grey wolves approached him whining, licking his wounds. He nipped them and drove them off, then he came at Juli and Rich again for another try. He leaped at them. Rich pushed Juli behind him, stabbing at Blackie with his hunting knife. Juli stepped to his side and bashed the wolf with a driftwood club. Blackie yelped, rolled on the ground, and slunk back to the forest. The greys, tails between their legs, slunk silently after him.

Breathing hard Rich wrapped his arm protectively around her saying, "Juli, let's get out of here."

"Right. I don't need encouragement," panted Juli, grabbing Rich's hand, as they raced side-by-side back to camp.

Rich's ragged voice whispered, "My god that was close." His heart raced. Sweat showed on his forehead. She heard him, but she was so deep in an adrenalin rush she couldn't compute what he was saying.

They huddled together. "Juli I'm so sorry," Rich panted. "They usually avoid humans."

"I'm okay," gasped Juli, "a little winded." In truth her heart was speeding like a run-away train. Her head pounding, her mouth dry. She tried futilely to swallow. She had been scared, more afraid than she had ever been before in her life.

He wrapped his arms around her. "They're gone now." He cradled her in his arms, then freed a hand to caress her back. Gradually her shaking eased. Then she noticed Rich was trembling and realized he had been as affected as she. He had lost his mother and his wife and, now that he was beginning to open up again, his new lover had been in mortal danger. Juli crooned,

"Rich I'm okay. I wasn't expecting them. Blackie wasn't even close to having me for dinner."

"Juli," he sobbed. "I want you to be safe." He clung to her so tightly she could hardly breathe. Finally he relaxed a bit as they struggled to calm their bodies.

"Me, too." She wrapped her arms around his chest. She liked that they were mutually comforting one another. Finally feeling calmer, she tipped her head back, "Hey Rich why'd you come?"

"I was almost asleep in my tent when I heard you heading to the biffy. Because it was dark I was waiting for your return. I heard your shout and dashed out. I was sure surprised to find Blackie and his harem sizing you up for a feast." His voice was hoarse with emotion as he gently kissed her forehead.

"You arrived in time." She gave him a gentle squeeze of reassurance. "It's okay. They're gone now."

"I hope so," he caressed her hair. "Nonetheless I'll build the fire up and stand watch until I'm sure they're hunting somewhere else."

She gave him an extra hug, "Thanks Rich. I appreciate that. Wake me and I'll take a turn." She crawled into her tent and snuggled into her sleeping bag. The last thing she remembered was straining to hear a howl.

Several hours later Juli woke to Rich's quiet but insistent voice, "Wake up! Wake up, we've got to get out of here." His cold nose hit her cheek as he coaxed, "Juli. Wake up."

Dazed from sleep Juli couldn't understand what was going on. "Rich stop kidding around. I'm sorry I didn't tell you everything. Now let me go back to sleep." She snuggled back into her sleeping bag.

"Juli," he persisted. "Juli listen to me."

Remembering the wolves she shot up to sitting. Her heart raced like it had earlier when she faced the vicious wolves. "Are they back?"

"The howls are closer." He tugged on her arm helping to get her out of the sleeping bag. Then they scrambled together to get out of the tent.

Juli listened intently, noticing the faint growls for the first time. "What's happening?"

"I saw shadows at the edge of the forest?"

"They're back." Fully awake now, pulse racing out of control, Juli grabbed Rich's arm. "This can't be happening."

Rich darted in and out of the tent, pulling its contents out and stuffing them in a bag, like a squirrel trying to get her babies to safety. "They're close."

"No," she said as she noticed the other tent was gone.

"They're hungry," he warned.

251

"Damn, it's a nightmare." Juli's heart raced. She felt confused. She was always prepared, always the calm one in emergencies. She crawled around the ground looking for her shoes and stomped into them.

His voice struggled to be calm but she could hear the urgency he was trying to disguise. "They think we're weak. They've been watching us."

"If it's a pack, we're dead meat."

His staccato voice continued, "Not quite. I packed Yak. Leave your tent. We don't have time to fool around."

"Right." Her eyes probed the darkness, expecting to see the glow of hungry eyes, followed by snapping teeth and dripping fangs. Holding her backpack like a shield, she grabbed her paddle and backed to the beach. She could hear Rich ahead of her stumbling over rough rocks and swearing softly. Together they hauled the loaded kayak over the rough beach like fugitives fleeing a torturous death.

Juli slipped and slid on the barnacled rocks in her haste to reach safety. She stumbled at the edge of the water and crashed into the side of the kayak. Grabbing the coaming near the bow she slid her backpack in. With adrenalin driving her muscles she balanced her paddle and slipped into her seat with a clunk. Yanking her life jacket from where it was jammed by her feet she dragged it into her lap, intending to put it on as soon as she could.

She hoped her sudden weight hadn't impaled them on a rock. She peered up the rise to her lonely tent to see three dark shadows slinking along like assassins in the night. She guessed more were lurking behind them. Rich clunked into the stern seat and pushed out with his paddle. She helped him push away from shore, digging her paddle mercilessly into the rough sand and rocks. The kayak floated free and rocketed into the inlet. Juli dug her paddle deeply into the cold water to drive the bow toward the entrance of the inlet; wind whistled past her ears. "That's it Juli, we're doing it," encouraged Rich. Adding breathlessly, "Not safe yet. They can swim."

Cold sweat ran between her shoulder blades. A low growl. A splash. "Blackie's in the water," shouted Rich. "He leaped all the way from the tent." The hair on the back of her neck twitched. She drug her paddle into the ocean, straining her muscles. Grabbing the light from her pack she flicked on the flashlight, fixing it like a miner on her head, and peered into the darkness. Rich grunted behind her, "We have a chance. Stay calm and paddle as hard as you can. The tide is ebbing out of the inlet, that'll make it easier for us to escape. On the other hand, the wind is on our beam and will want to push us into the north side of the inlet. Toward the grey wolves."

"I'm paddling . . . as hard . . . as I can."

"Turn out that damn light. Ruining my night vision."

She flicked the light off and was temporarily blinded, but then shapes formed enough so she could see the center of the channel. "The wolf . . . swimming," he grunted. Her hands were starting to blister and burn. She ignored them; better to lose a hand than to die.

"We have to get through to the open," he panted. "Paddle harder. These wolves will follow us. They have the strength."

"And hunger," shouted Juli as she pulled on her paddle, forcing her muscles. Pulse racing. Sweat beading on her forehead. *Don't panic.* Hungry wolves were way out of her comfort zone. She trusted Rich to make good decisions, if he said they should be in the open ocean, then that's where they would go. She focused her energy on paddling, every cell in her body strained to propel the kayak forward.

Behind her she felt Rich digging his paddle deeply, engaging every muscle in his body. Again. And again. And again. Forcing the kayak to speed through the ebbing water away from the inlet and a painful death.

Juli's heart pounded in her chest. She was sweating. Adrenalin pumped. A splash behind them made her hiss, "Blackie's closer."

They bent low, grunting, paddling hard. The current strengthened as they neared the mouth of the inlet. "We're doing it Juli. Just a little further." Juli pulled, taxing her muscles to their

254

limit, each stroke as hard as she could, knowing Rich was doing the same. The kayak slid forward seeking safety. They squeezed through the narrow entrance as a grey wolf raced from the beach on to the rocky entrance, growling. Intending to leap on them. The sight of open water ahead gave impetus to their paddles as they dug even deeper. Suddenly they burst free like a molten rock from an erupting volcano, shooting forward into the calmer water of the open channel. Black wolf splashed frantically behind them. Grey wolf on the rocky cliff howled in frustration. Juli rested her paddle on the gunwale, her aching shoulders jerked with relief. They had escaped.

Once in Sutil channel Rich turned the kayak so they could watch the entrance. Two shadows jockeyed for position on the rocks as Blackie swam toward them; the greys howled like furious devils. Finally Blackie, unable to scramble up the slippery rocks, turned back, flowing with the tide into the inlet, and disappeared in the dark. Juli sighed with relief; he was giving up, his harem would follow him.

Juli started to cry, tears ran in a torrent down her cheeks. "That was close," she sobbed. As she peered forward she could vaguely see the dark edge of the shoreline. What was she doing out here in the dark, on an equally dark slithering ocean in a tiny kayak while wolves howled on the shore? This was so far from her normal comfortable city life it seemed surreal; nonetheless, at some level she knew it was real, and as fear settled deep into her bones she felt her hands tremble. "Don't worry," reassured Rich hearing her sobs, "Sutil channel is hundreds of feet deep. We'll stay in the center where the current is the strongest and it will carry us south to safety. If it was midwinter with a southeaster howling and building waves, I would be concerned, but this ocean is a piece of cake. Don't worry."

"It's not the ocean. I'm having a delayed reaction to the wolves." Juli shuddered, "It's the wolf. I called him Blackie. He could be suffering, drowning." She sobbed, "My Blackie suffered, too. He was a big friendly black lab . . . still a puppy with big feet. I was on a bike trip with someone, maybe the girl guides. Mom was supposed to keep him in the house. He escaped and followed me. We were a line of young girls on bikes. He came galloping along, tongue hanging out, tail wagging, bounding along in the lane next to us as if he had done something great. I saw him as a car came round the corner coming toward us. If it had swerved to avoid Blackie it would have hit us. The splat when Blackie hit the bumper will always reverberate in my head." Juli put her face in her arm and sobbed great heaves as if the pain was tearing through her.

Rich's voice came from behind her, warm and loving, "Juli that must have been horrible."

"He was a friendly, gentle dog. He loved me. That's why he came trotting after us. He didn't know about cars. I should have kept him safe." Juli sobbed as if her heart would break. She had never told anyone about it before. The pain felt worse than the numbness.

She wanted Rich to hold her and smooth her hair; he couldn't reach her from the stern, but his voice could. "Juli, the driver had no choice and neither did you. You were a kid."

"I know but he suffered so, squealing in pain. I was so helpless. I couldn't help him." The pain churned her gut and made her heart ache. With Rich listening to her it was safe, so she let the waves of pain roar through her body like water breaking through a dam. Finally as the pain became a dull ache Juli lifted her head and looked around at Rich. "Rich, Wolf Blackie could suffer a painful death, too."

"Maybe, but he's adapted to island life. He knows how to survive." His voice sounded confident.

"I'm thankful for that," came her muffled voice as she wiped her nose, reassured by his strength and calmness. "Rich thanks for listening to me. I haven't thought about my Blackie for years. I thought I was all over it. But obviously I wasn't." Juli blew her nose and sniffed. "I don't feel so guilty now, but I still ache down deep. I loved him a lot."

"Juli you're so thoughtful." Rich carefully paddled the kayak down the middle of the channel. Juli, feeling comforted, felt the pain and moved through it.

Finally she began to paddle again, telling her hands to relax. She liked the calm sound of his voice, liked that he listened to her. Scanning the ocean she noted that Rich had been guiding Yak, taking care of her. As her pulse slowed to normal she was able to see he was right that they were smoothly proceeding down the center of the channel; she didn't even have to paddle hard; the ocean was doing the work. "The wind is getting lighter," she commented to make contact with him.

"I noticed," said Rich. "Let's hope it stays light until we get there."

"Nature sure is an experience of extremes, exquisite beauty to deadly danger."

"We handled that well. You grasped the danger instantly and followed my directions without question. I appreciated that."

"I trusted your judgment." Her voice was sounding stronger.

"I know you're competent too. Next time you can be in charge."

"So you trust me?"

"Sure," he replied but she wasn't totally convinced.

Laughing Juli asked, "What I want to know right now is: Where exactly is THERE?"

"My cabin."

Oh ho, thought Juli. *He's taking me home.*

He continued, "It's near Manson's Landing. There's only water access."

"Sounds isolated." So he had a waterfront cabin. That was sweet. Maybe it was a cave.

"Not really. Just inexpensive water front. I have a dock and a few boats."

Oh my, thought Juli, *yet another adventure*. How could this be? She used to have such a dull, routine, predictable life. Then she smiled, "Sounds wonderful." Definitely this man was good for her.

Just then the moon peeked above the island and lit the water. Mother Nature was taking care of them, thought Juli. That was a sign, a good sign.

And the wind was calm. Juli could feel the current now as it caught their kayak. *How incredible*, here she was bobbing along on the cold unforgiving ocean, guided by silvery moonlight, sliding down the side of a remote island at the north end of Georgia strait in the early, early morning. Why wasn't she afraid? They could hit a deadhead and hole their craft. In spite of the danger she had complete confidence in Rich. She had known him

259

nine days now and she trusted him more than anyone else she knew. But it was more than that. She was solidly attracted to him, sexually attracted. She wanted to spend her life with him. She might even move to this island to be with him. Before the wolves he had seemed distant. That was right after Squirrel Cove! Was he disappointed she didn't introduce him to her friends? Did he sense her deceit? She couldn't stand it; she had to tell him she was a doctor, soon.

They left Sutil Channel and turned southeast, keeping Marina Island on their right and Cortes on their left. After the fifteen-kilometer paddle from Von Don the red and green buoy markers for Whaletown harbor were very welcome as they glided silently past. Snug in the harbor for the night the ferry Tanaka glowed with safety lights.

As they passed Shark Spit and entered Uganda passage dawn lit the sky to a calm powder blue. Juli wiped her eyes, blinking back tears of relief. She would never forget this peaceful quiet, broken only by the splash of their paddles. Rich, misinterpreting her sniffs, leaned forward to whisper reassurances, "It's not much further. Hang in there Juli. It's going to be okay." She liked his concern. Near the entrance to Gorge Harbor they coasted, paddles balanced across the kayak's coaming, quietly refueling with snack bars and water. Juli's shoulders ached. Her eyes were so heavy she had to force them to stay open. They had been steadily paddling for at least six hours. That, on top of yesterday's hike and little sleep, made her feel lethargic.

"Juli we're at the entrance to Gorge Harbor, we could stop here. There's a small lodge," said Rich. "The tide is right for going through the gorge into the harbor. If you're tired we can head in there."

"Can we get to your place from in there?"

"Not really. Tomorrow we'd have to paddle back out. This tide's gone slack so right now we have a bit of a paddle ahead of us." She sensed that he didn't want to go into the marina, but he wouldn't force her to go on. Juli stared at the dark entrance, where ragged rock cliffs rose steeply on each side. It didn't look safe or inviting. "Forget it then. Let's keep going."

"You're a good sport," his voice sounded relieved.

"Not really, I'm afraid if I stop paddling I'll fall asleep." Juli sat straighter, forcing her eyes to stay open.

"Well, keep paddling then . . . I'll do the heavy pulling."

Tears filled her eyes again. She felt supported by Rich. Here was a man who would be a good friend and partner. "Thanks Rich."

"Before the wolves the wind was out of the south," said Rich thoughtfully. "Now I don't feel any wind, so that's in our favor."

"That's good." Juli felt very relieved. She wanted to put her head down as it was so heavy.

"Look." Rich pointed ahead at dark shapes clustered together, "There's the public wharf at Manson's. We're almost home." The excitement in his voice fed energy to her adrenals.

We're almost home. We're almost home, Juli liked the sound of that. Over the glassy ocean Juli could see the public dock twinkling with fairy lights, lights on the odd assortment of boats and above them the eastern sky was gradually lightening. As they glided silently toward the boats, Rich veered to the left, steering them toward a small private dock on the north side of the bay. Juli noted it was tucked deep in a crevasse in a rock outcropping. Small boats rocked gently with the floating dock, waiting for his return. Rich skillfully maneuvered them to the uncluttered side of the dock into a narrow space between the dock and the rock out cropping. As the kayak rubbed against the wooden dock Juli grabbed it. The rough wood tore at her hand but she didn't care. Soon she would be safe on land. Senses alert she heard the ocean splashing against the rock face to her left. She breathed deeply.

"We're here. I'll steady Yak while you climb out."

"I don't know if I have the upper body strength to hoist myself that high," said Juli eyeing the floating dock as it was at shoulder height.

"Get your upper body up . . . then roll across the wood."

"You make it sound easy." Juli sighed. *Come on body, there must be a bit of adrenalin left to get me out of this boat.*

"Worst case I'll get out first and haul you up onto the dock," he promised.

She chuckled, "Let me give it a try."

Rich whispered seductively, "Juli, there's a hot shower in the cabin."

"Okay, now that's incentive. Here I go." Juli pushed hard on the kayak coaming, raised up, and plopped back, rocking the kayak violently. "Sorry. Sorry."

Rich grunted as he grasped the dock trying to hold the kayak steady. "Try again, you almost made it," he encouraged.

"Here goes," Juli declared as she grasped the dock and bent her knees, getting her weight on her feet, then pulling with her hands and pushing with her thighs she burst onto the dock, scraping her chin. The front of the kayak crashed into the rock wall as she rolled away to safety on the rough wooden dock, breathing as hard as if she had sprinted one hundred meters.

"Good girl. When you get your breath, take this line and tie it to that cleat."

Juli crawled on her hands and knees and tied the kayak securely.

"Good. Now move away," ordered Rich waving his hands toward the cabin. "I'm coming out."

Juli scrambled away on all fours, then sat at the land end of the dock and waited, and watched Rich smoothly in one fluid movement ease himself out of the kayak and onto the dock. She enjoyed watching him and an undeniable yearning filled her heart.

He crawled over to her and whispered huskily, "Welcome to my dock." Before she could answer his lips were on hers, warm and demanding. She could feel a throbbing pulse through her body. Her heart jerked and started to beat more rapidly sending oxygen and hormones careening through her body. She lay back on the narrow dock with dry wood pressing into her back with the ocean swaying underneath and lapping incessantly, restlessly against the rock face. Slowly, gently he lower himself on top of her pressing his full length down her body as if he wanted to keep her there. The heat of his body caressed her skin as though neither was wearing clothes. Both were breathing heavily, "Rich we're going to fall in the ocean." She pushed him gently. "Don't you have a bed in your cabin?"

He drew back and looked at her, once again she was struck by the passionate intensity in his eyes "You've got good ideas. Yes," he whispered in her ear, "I have a bed in my cabin. A wonderful bed. Do you want to see it? It's been waiting for you." His warm breath caressed her ear sending shivers of delight through her body.

"Mm."

He helped her up and together, in single file, his left hand behind his back clutching her right hand, they inched off the narrow wooden dock toward the cabin with its greying cedar siding and shake roof blending into the rock face. On solid ground they scrambled along the exposed rock path, his arm against her back helping to propel her forward. He pushed open the rough cedar door and took her in his arms and kissed her. His soft lips gently brushed hers, sending waves of warmth washing through her body, until she slumped back against the door unable to support herself. Hands on his shoulders she clung as though her life depended on it while he continued his relentless pursuit of her body, kissing her cheek and then her ear. Her brain ceased to function; her whole world became his lips and hot breath as they stimulated and soothed her nerve endings. Juli had heard about legs going weak but she hadn't believed it. Now, in fact, her whole body had turned to into jelly that she wanted him to coax into any shape he wished. She didn't notice how securely the cabin was fastened into the rock cliff, or the windows revealing a panoramic view of the ocean, or the comfortable sofa, as he steered her into the bedroom which was dominated by a king-sized platform with a soft foam mattress. The latter she saw, and appreciated.

He pulled off her hoodie and nuzzled her neck. His hot breath awakened her to act and she pushed his jacket off and pulled his sweater over his head. She was giggling now, giggling with excitement and anticipation as she ran her fingers through the golden hairs on his chest. He bent over shucking off his stretch pants and at the same time pulling hers down to her knees. Juli flopped on to the bed and kicked them off onto the floor while pulling her t-shirt over her head. He pounced on her and held her hands over her head on the bed. Their nude bodies caressed each other like the softest silk. Juli loved what was happening, she had never enjoyed another human as much as she enjoyed Rich. But it wasn't only sex, even though it was passionate and caring; she wanted to share her whole self with him. Suddenly, plunged out of bliss, she felt cold air on her breasts.

"Wait a minute. Wait a minute. I have to protect you," he mumbled as he disappeared into another room, presumably the bathroom where she could hear him rummaging around like a bear in a garbage can. "Voila there's that little devil. Now hopefully it's not too old to do its job."

"Hurry up Rich, I'm freezing."

"I'll warm you up. Are you ready?" he asked as he eased himself on top of her.

"Yes, oh yes. I'm swollen in all the right places and dripping with lubrication." *Oops*, she was talking like a doctor not a helpless female. If that turned him off, better she find out early in this relationship. "Hot and heavy please." Why did she say that? That was what the nurses said about the enemas for women in labor. Then her thoughts focused on her pelvis, crowding out everything else. If she swelled any more she was sure she would burst. She groaned. *Was that her voice?* She was out of control with desire. She tilted her pelvis to encourage him, though he didn't need any help or encouragement as he skillfully slid inside her moving slowly at first and then more rapidly as she joined his rhythm. As she thought, *I want this man*, her orgasm released sending waves of convulsive pleasure through her body. "Rich you too," she screamed.

"Oh no, not yet. You have another of those in you." He was amazed at how comfortable he felt with her. It was as though he had the key to unlock her body. He eased back while smothering her breasts with kisses, smelling her skin until they both were burning for more. Then he nudged her thighs apart and slid back and forth bring them both to a shouting climax.

Juli lay back panting, sated for the time being, but she knew as surely as she knew the human body that she would want to experience more orgasms. Small aftershocks titillated her pelvis as Rich collapsed beside her and pulled her into his arms, her butt tucked into his abdomen. Juli sighed, "Oh god that was good." Then she was instantly asleep.

When she woke she was warmly covered and burnished light glowed in the windows. She peered out to see a gull landing with a splash on the blue ocean. She suddenly remembered this was not a dream, not a beautiful fairy land, but Rich's waterfront cabin, and Rich's very generous warm bed.

Rich must have heard her stir as he appeared in the doorway, "Hi beautiful," he smiled at her tousled appearance as she ran the tips of her fingers over her swollen lips. "I've been busy. I turned on the well pump and opened the water for the house and turned on the hot-water heater. I laid a fire laid for later when it is cooler."

"A hot shower is all I need." She stretched like a satisfied cat. "Looks like it's going to be another hot day."

"Could be. I'm going to listen to the marine weather."

"I'm looking out," she said clutching the covers to stay warm, she slid over the bed to the window on the water side of the house so that she could look a distance. The other bedroom window faced a giant granite rock that must have been there since the glaciers retreated. "We have a blue sky and golden sun," she announced.

"Juli you're right. It's beautiful summer weather," he called from the kitchen.

She flung back the covers, stretched, and waltzed humming into the bathroom. First she took off the neglected bandage from her calf; the slight gash was healed so she didn't cover it again. Over the drumming of the shower she called, "This is great hot water." She stood eyes tightly closed as she shampooed her hair.

"I think so, too," said a husky voice in her ear as Rich joined her.

"Rich don't." Juli playfully pushed him away. He grabbed her arms and pulled her to him with a barbaric growl; crystal clear water spilled on their heads running down their bodies like liquid sensations. He bent down to suck gently on her ear.

"Stop it you cougar. I don't want to be eaten." She playfully punched him.

His voice, husky with desire, asked "What is it you desire then my sweet?"

Her brain was fogging like the glass sides of the shower and she could barely whisper, "I desire a gentle rub."

"Like this?" he asked as his fingertips massaged more shampoo into her hair, running his fingers along her scalp and down the curve of her neck. Juli felt the amazing force that his gentle touch imparted; so that, wherever he contacted her body immediately an electric connection opened, allowing electrons to flow between them like a dam had released. His probing hands slid lower; her spine tingled. Soapy hands caressed her firm buttocks; sensation built; the throbbing between her legs called insistently, wanting release. "Rich you're driving me mad."

"Just wait sweetheart; more is to come." Warm water flowed down his head and face as their lips met and parted as they became one throbbing mass of energy. Time stood still, the primal urges took over: man and woman, mating for all eternity. "Juli you're so beautiful . . . I can't wait." She giggled her response, giddy with passion as he backed her against the wall and entered carefully but determinedly. Suddenly he pulled away, the warm water cascaded between them, "Rich?"

"Sorry no condom . . . can't take a chance."

She sighed and turned away. "You're right but I need you."

"C'mon, I must have one left in the bedroom. Lord knows I never use them." He opened his arms and she slid against him as if this was the most natural thing in the world. He wrapped a soft fluffy towel around her and swiftly wiped the drips off himself and off her. She waited for his touch as if mesmerized. While he worked he kept a hand or arm on her, never breaking contact. Gently he guided her toward the bed. Once again she liked him looking after her. Passing the dresser he reached in and found what he was looking for, positioning it as he nibbled on her ear, and backed her toward the bed, dropping the towel so that they were bare skin to bare skin. They eased on to the bed laying side by side, face to face, eyes closed. They breathed in each other's essence as though completing the ritual of becoming one.

"Rich," she begged in a strangled tone, coming from the deepest part of her body. Her voice played on his hormones and, as if he couldn't stand any separateness, he pulled her to him roughly, flipped her over like the willing rag doll she was and thrust into her. Coming alive she backed into him encouraging the deep thrusting as warmth filled her belly and she screamed her delight, over and over. Her muscles clasped him, encouraging and sucking his essence into her until, exhausted, he slid beside her clutching her tightly to his body as though he would never let her go. For the moment they were one being, perfectly in tune, drifting together through space and time.

From a great distance Rich's mobile phone vibrated on the top of the dresser. He reached out and scanned the message. Jerking to a sitting position on the side of the bed he reread the message, punched a reply and sent it. "Juli. . . bad news." His eyes looked very serious.

Her heart skipped a beat. "Oh, what's that?" She tried to sound casual as she pulled the blanket over her chest and swung her legs over the side of the bed to sit beside him.

"The health center just texted . . . car accident. Right near Hague Lake. That's a bad spot. The teens were making a left turn into the parking lot. A truck loaded with firewood coming from Whaletown couldn't stop. The ambulance is there now bringing the injured to the health center: five teens plus two adults in the truck."

Coming to life Juli shot rapid fire questions at him, "Seven injured? Any bystanders? Who's at the clinic?"

"The locum . . . the nurse."

"Is the locum any good?"

"Good question." Rich ran his hands through his hair. "His credentials and references were great, unfortunately I didn't actually work with him as I wanted to escape on holiday too badly."

"Of course."

Rich shrugged. "I texted that I'd come in to help." As he talked he bent on the side of the bed, head in his hands, looking at her as if he wanted it all to go away.

Juli felt a cold chill, *I better fess up.* Suddenly she realized she was making a good decision as calmness settled over her; it was the right thing to do. She would accept the consequences. "Rich we need to talk for a minute. I have something to tell you," she said as she moved slightly away from him. Undaunted Rich leaned toward her, sniffed in her fragrance and waited.

"I didn't tell you everything about myself. I don't know why . . . I hope it doesn't make you angry." She couldn't look at him.

His eyes examined her closely then he whispered, "Juli, please don't tell me you're really a lesbian. I can't stand the disappointment. And, I won't believe it." His eyes held an earnestness that encouraged her.

Relieved and reassured by his reaction Juli giggled, "No. No, that's not it. Listen."

"Okay Juli spill the beans. Just remember, nothing you say can drive me away."

She took a deep breath and plunged in. "Rich I'm a doctor, a GP practicing at a drop-in clinic in Victoria." She held her breath waiting for his burst of anger.

"So, what's the problem?" he asked calmly.

Juli let her breath out slowly, pleasantly surprised by his non-reaction. "So I don't want it to make a difference." She watched his face as if her life depended on it and in some ways it did.

"Well sure it makes a difference," he hesitated, the silence grew longer. Juli shifted, expecting the worst, then he laughed, "It's great. Someone who can understand my problems, someone who can work with me." He grabbed her and wrestled her flat on to the bed.

"I thought you wouldn't like me if I was a professional woman with a career. Men like women who need them."

273

"Not me. I like you as a competent person. A practicing physician . . . that's an added bonus."

Juli expelled her breath in a small explosion of relief, "I'm glad you're not upset." He turned so they were facing one another. Their eyes met; it was as though their souls opened up allowing love and caring to flow freely between them. Then he lowered his eyes as if he was ashamed, "Look Juli there's something I didn't tell you either."

"Oh, what's that?" She pressed back into the pillows moving slightly away from him, terrified his secret might destroy them. *Don't let him be married.* She couldn't stand that.

"Take it easy. I can tell by the horror in your eyes you think it's something awful. Relax, I'm not gay and I'm not dying of some dread disease."

That still left married. Juli swallowed, "Then what is it?"

"The reason I'm on holidays is that I'm really on medical leave. My blood pressure has been acting up." There he had said it. He stared at his hands waiting for her response.

"More detail, please." She thought of ugly diseases resulting from hypertension: myocardial infarction, CVAs, kidney failure. And, his family history of both parents dying young.

"I'm sure I can control it," his voice sounded dubious. "I'm working on it."

Now she placed her hands gently on his face turning him toward her, studying him intently. "How bad?"

"Bout 175 over 105 . . . on and off for the past six months."

"Rich that's unacceptable." She raised her voice like a scolding parent.

His eyes lowered again. "I know. I know. I'm aiming for 110 over 75."

"Meds?" She felt like she was taking a medical history and couldn't help herself.

"Hydrochlorothiazide and ACE inhibitor. But I've been feeling so good I stopped them." There, he had told her everything.

She flopped back on the bed saying, "Rich, you can't tinker with your health like this."

"It's been normal lately without meds."

She didn't like it. He was so stubborn she decided to take another tack. "What about lifestyle changes?"

"Interesting you should mention that. The second day on the trip with you my blood pressure settled right down to 115 over 78. I stayed on the ACE inhibitor and cut the hydrochlorothiazide to every other day. My vascular system is pretty much functioning normally."

"Rich I'm glad. I didn't realize I was having such a great effect on you . . . I did know my own body has been very happy on this trip. Nothing like good sex and a holiday to cure one's ills."

"Well, let's see how it goes. For now I have to help out at the clinic."

"Whoa, you're not going without me. I'm a practicing doctor." Her voice rushed on as if a dam had burst. "I can bill through MSP." He was watching her; his eyes inscrutable. "But even if I couldn't I would volunteer. So let me get dressed and I'll go with you." Not waiting for his response Juli slid off the end of the bed like a fireman down a pole on his way to a rescue.

Calmly he said, "Great, I was hoping you would say that."

She stopped in mid track, wondering how he could be so calm. She looked at him eyes narrowed and probing, "Why are you taking this so well?"

"I, I," he stuttered.

She leaped on him forcing him on his back on the bed. "Rich I know you well enough now to know you're not telling me everything."

"Okay, okay," his hands were raised in surrender. "I heard Marigold when we were at Squirrel cove."

She punched him lightly. "You dirty rat. Here I've been scared stiff to tell you."

He laughed and picked her up and whirled around the room. "Why would I be upset that you are a professional with everything in common with me? It couldn't be better. I was upset because you were holding back. That made me wonder if I could trust you."

"Rich I'm sorry. I did hold back for fear you wouldn't like me."

"Juli you misjudged me."

"I can see that now."

"Juli I love you. Nothing you can do can shock me or drive me away. I'll never abandon you."

Relief flooded her body. Juli hugged him close, tears of joy in her eyes, and tipped her head back so he could kiss her lips. He lowered his head and gently caressed her lips. "I've got oatmeal porridge on the stove so we can go well fortified. It's after one pm so we should go soon." Juli hesitated, one foot in her yoga pants, "You sure you're ready for work? Your blood pressure is still fragile."

He shrugged, "What else can I do? They need my skills."

"I hear you. Maybe with both of us helping we'll be able to clear out in a few hours."

Galvanized into action, they dressed quickly and eased themselves into the metal runabout and motored over to Manson's Landing, which was a long wooden dock providing land access for a large commercial fishing boat, several sailboats and a number of small runabouts. "Rich, there's Dream Seeker," Juli pointed at a sleek yacht tied at the far end. "We could use Dave's help." Rich nodded as he maneuvered the boat to the dock. As they approached, a boater raced to meet them, saying, "Hi doc. What's up?" Juli liked the casual respect.

"Car accident . . . We're off to the Health Center. We'll let you know when we get back," promised Rich as he tossed a line on to the dock. "While I secure the boat and get the truck started you go see if Dave's willing. Meet me at the top of the ramp."

Marigold and Dave were on deck, curious about the chatter. When they saw Juli coming toward them they smiled and waved. Juli, being careful not to trip on the rough dock, hurried toward them. "I'm so glad to see you. We're on our way to the clinic . . . an accident . . . car accident." She felt the concerned eyes of all the boat people on her as she appealed to Dave.

"How many injured?" asked Dave immediately.

"Probably seven."

"Staff."

"Rich and me and a nurse . . . and a locum."

"That's a lot."

"Can you come?" asked Juli.

Dave looked away from her and swallowed, "Not today. I'm not up for it. Sorry."

"But Dave I . . . ," sputtered Marigold as he hushed her by pressing on her arm.

"Oh too bad," said Juli. "But we can handle it." *Odd*, she thought. "Rich is at the truck. I've got to hurry." She pointed up the hill.

Rich had the engine running and the passenger door open. She raced down the rough dock past the assorted boats, up the steep ramp, and breathing heavily jumped in and slammed the door. The truck lurched on its way as if shot from a cannon. "No Dave?"

"He said he couldn't do it. I didn't have time to find out what was going on."

"Doesn't matter, we can handle it." Juli nodded agreement. Rich added, "The Health Center is close. Hang on."

The narrow tracks joined a wider paved road as they continued to climb away from the ocean. "It's a few miles to the Health Center," he repeated. His hands gripping the steering wheel were pale, bloodless. Juli could see the tension building in his body. The whine of an ambulance ahead of them stirred her blood. This is what they were trained for; they would save lives.

"Rich, what are the facilities?" Juli asked trying to prepare.

"We have a fifteen hundred square foot building with four examining rooms, and four stretcher beds at the rear."

"I hear a siren ahead of us."

"Yup, we have an ambulance . . . and a helicopter pad. We only use the chopper in daylight and good weather and in extreme cases. But when we need it, it's very efficient. Otherwise the ambulance, during ferry hours, can take people over to Quadra Island and transfer to their ambulance to finish the trip to Campbell River or Comox hospital. That way our ambulance can come back on the same ferry and we are not left without it." As he described the facilities his fingers relaxed and his voice slowed.

"What happens at night?" Juli hated to ask that question as it might make him tense again. Night time was always a problem for health care workers as their bodies wanted to sleep and their patients' bodies were at their lowest ebb and closer to the enemy, death.

"It gets pretty dark."

"Guess I shouldn't have asked."

"I was teasing. Actually if we can't handle it then the Coast Guard zodiac comes from Campbell River in about forty minutes and takes the patient off island."

"Rich, I'm impressed that there are so many choices." The truck sped along the narrow road between the ever present conifers lining the road, sounds of urgency sweeping through their tops.

"The people of this island have worked hard to make it happen." His voice sounded proud.

"Who will be at the Center?" Juli's thoughts were racing ahead to what they might find at the center. The equipment sounded modern, perhaps not up to city standards, but the patients would be the same. A quiet confidence grew from deep inside her; she knew what to do.

"Jennie is front desk, Mary is the nurse practitioner who does the initial triage and some treatment. The locum . . . Andy Wiseman."

"It's better than I expected. Will they be okay if I help?" Her mind raced. The work would be similar to the treatment center. She would need a careful history because although everything would be accident related there were almost always underlying problems that would affect her decisions about treatment. The ambulance staff would have IVs started and initial assessments.

"Is there salt in the ocean?"

"I guess that's a yes."

"They will be delighted to have help." As they drove past a cluster of buildings he pointed, "That's Manson's town center with a general store and library and the co-op grocery store. We turn right down here," he said turning off the main road. On the left was a skate board park and next to it, a low flat building. "That's the Health Center," said Rich proudly.

So far so good, thought Juli. The parking lot was full of assorted vehicles from rusty trucks to a shiny silver convertible. As soon as the truck stopped Rich jumped out and headed for the door. Juli strode after him feeling her confidence growing. This is what she was trained for, this was something she knew. Rich stopped briefly to introduce her to the receptionist Jennie, who raised her eyebrows and smiled as if the cavalry had arrived, as indeed it had. The waiting room was full of summer patients, sitting and standing quietly, watching everything. She was familiar with that look as well; it was the same in the city, fear mixed with hope.

Rich progressed deeper into the center as a woman came out of an examining room. She was casually dressed in blue jeans but the stethoscope around her neck announced she meant business. She stopped abruptly when she saw Rich. "Rich you're a gift from heaven. We really need you."

Rich smiled, "We were kayaking in Von Don. Some wolves were stalking us; fortunately we escaped. It was close." The words rushed out of him like water racing down a mountain stream.

"Did they bite you? Need a tetanus shot?" asked the woman.

"No, we're okay."

"They're probably coming from over from Princess Louisa Inlet where the summer fire is ongoing."

Remembering why they were there Rich cleared his throat and introduced her, "This is Dr. Juli Armstrong. She's volunteered to help us sort this out today. She normally practices in a treatment center in Victoria." Then he turned to Juli, "Juli this is Mary Jones, nurse practitioner."

Juli noticed that Mary hesitated and glanced at Rich before she offered her hand in welcome. *Oh, oh,* thought Juli. *This young woman has her sights set on Rich.* Juli hoped that wouldn't make things awkward today. Mary shook Juli's hand and very businesslike said, "Welcome. Can you bill your work?"

"Yes, no problem."

Then Mary gave report. "The ambulance just arrived with Johnnie R and Ocean R. Head injuries. Andy Wiseman is with them. The helicopter is on its way here and the ferry turned back and will stay in Whaletown to take people to Campbell River.

"Good." Rich nodded his approval.

Mary looked at him, "You can't imagine how happy I am to see you. I thought Andy, Jenny, and I were on our own and I was sweating blood. I was about to send everyone in the waiting room home."

He patted her shoulder, "No worries." Ever efficient he added, "Since we'll now have three doctors it would be best for you to keep up the triage function. If necessary Andy can go back to the accident site with the ambulance." They nodded agreement. Mary added, "I'll also help keep an eye on the patients in the waiting room, then we'll have all bases covered."

"Rich and I could each take one of the kids on the stretchers at the back. Can Mary and Jenifer notify families?" Mary nodded.

Juli's attempt to buffer him didn't go unnoticed as Rich smiled and said, "Sounds okay." Then he took Mary aside and drew a small packet out of his pocket. Juli nodded gratefully as she recognized the tick that had bitten her and heard Rich say, "Get this off to the lab as soon as you can. We need to know if it's infected." Mary nodded and efficiently disappeared to carry out his request. Turning back to Juli, Rich said, "Okay, let's get going." He rubbed his hands together and began to assume his role as country doctor to all of Cortes.

The next three hours flew by as they provided excellent care for all the patients. The copter took the two with head injuries to Victoria, and the ambulance transported two others, one with a fractured pelvis to Comox and one with fractured fibula to Campbell River. When the last patient left they finished their dictation and gathered in the coffee room. Rich was tired and he was flushed. Juli knew he was hypertensive. She handed him a glass of water, "Drink."

Mary flopped in a chair, "I doubt we could have made it without you two. Thanks. It'll calm down now . . . Andy and I can the waiting room."

Rich leaned against the door jam, "Good, I prefer to finish my leave. And, Juli has to be back on Quadra four days from now. "

Sure, thought Juli, *let them all know* we're *spending the next four nights together.* She blushed as she looked forward to that. But she was also concerned to get Rich out of this environment that was stressing his body. Only four hours of work and his BP was up. That was not a good sign.

Jennie, ever the good administrator, who had caught the tail end of the conversation said, "Juli and Rich could you please come in and sign your notes. I'll have them printed and in their files any time after noon tomorrow."

"Of course," agreed Juli. Rich nodded.

As they left Juli asked for the truck keys and said she was driving. Rich nodded agreement and handed over the keys. He seemed to like that she took care of him. Some men might see it as a challenge to their masculinity. Not Rich, he seemed to relax and appreciate. "What's this?" he asked as he moved packages aside.

"I slipped out and picked up a few groceries at the store: eggs, bacon, bread, butter, you know . . . staples." The truck was heavy and sluggish, Juli had to concentrate to keep it moving.

"Thanks," he muttered overwhelmed by her thoughtfulness.

At the dock they were greeted by worried faces. "What's the news doc?"

"We were able to see everyone and only referred four people off island."

"That's good," murmured several people leaning out of their ragtag boats. Juli looked over the little band of bearded men who were dressed in baggy mismatched clothing; men who lived close to an unforgiving ocean; men who did not judge on appearances. The concern and thanks in their eyes made tears come to her eyes. They loved and appreciated their doctor; no wonder Rich gave them his all. "We sure appreciate you looking after our youngsters."

"Glad to be of service," said Rich as he headed for his runabout holding on to Juli's hand.

"We'll help you," offered the man following along behind them like a puppy; he steadied the boat as Juli and Rich hopped aboard. Juli noted Dream Seeker wasn't at the dock.

"I'm beat," said Rich as Juli eased into the bow seat.

"Sure doc. We'll shove you off." Two of the men untied the boat and pointed them toward home and pushed.

"Thanks," called Rich as he started the motor, too tired to row. The men nodded as they waved them off. The engine caught and soon they were speeding toward Rich's. The protected ocean from Manson's Landing to Rich's small cove was so calm the boat seemed to fly on top of the crystal water.

Once they had docked the boat and entered the cabin Juli continued her plan to take care of Rich. "I bought some beer. You sit and have one. It's my turn to cook and I'll start the fire you laid this morning." That seemed long ago. Had it only been nine days since she had left on this trip?

Rich sat heavily in a kitchen chair and put his feet up. "I didn't realize I was so tired. I think I will let you take care of me."

"Good decision, doctor to the world." After Juli checked cupboards and sorted through supplies she announced, "We'll have bacon and eggs. That won't test my cooking skills too much."

"Sounds wonderful," smiled Rich. He stood up and pulled her close, his lips drifting over the delicate skin at her

287

temple. He tightened his arm around her waist as if he never wanted to let her go. She could feel him relaxing and returning to normal.

Juli hummed as she cooked and sipped on a bottle of beer. She noticed the frilly curtains and wondered who had chosen them - probably the woman in the picture with Rich, both in wetsuits and holding boards. She must have been important to him. Juli wondered what happened to her. Maybe she couldn't stand being married to or living with or maybe dating a doctor.

After supper Juli announced it was shower time and that she was going to soap him and when he was in bed give him a foot rub and that there would be absolutely no sex. "Great," said Rich sounding relieved. As promised she massaged his body lovingly, not demanding anything in return. Here was a man who gave everything. Hopefully she could help him learn to look after himself.

Once he was in bed and completely relaxed she used the lotion she had found at the store and massaged his feet, carefully pulling on and massaging each toe, then the acupressure spots, and then more gentle massage. Rich was like putty in her hands and soon he was snoring, deeply asleep. Juli pulled on one of Rich's t-shirts and crawled quietly into bed. She too was instantly and deeply asleep. Water lapped quietly against the rock as the tide flooded the bay.

CHAPTER SIXTEEN

In the early predawn hours Juli woke to warm breath on her neck and a warm hand caressing her thigh. She giggled, "So you've recovered." Her heart gave a little jerk and then began to pound in double time.

"MMMm," came the answer.

She turned toward him wrapping her arms around his head as his body heat pulsed through her causing a tingling, then a throbbing sensation in her breasts.

He nuzzled each nipple.

"Yikes. My hormones are raging." She had never experienced this before she met Rich. She was so tuned to him that it only took the slightest touch to make her 'ping' like a harp. Another way to think of this was that she was like a pump that had been primed, so that now she responded quickly; however, instead of gushing water, she gushed hormones.

"Mine too . . . isn't it great?" His breath came in short gasps as he kissed her seductive flesh.

289

"MMM . . . I took a handful of the clinic's condoms . . . just in case. They're in the drawer."

"You wanton woman. Now you're in for it." His fingertips rubbed her sensitive skin in a wildly exciting circular motion.

"I hope so." Juli could see the drumming pulse in his strong tanned throat and touched it with her lips as a promise before reaching in the drawer for a condom. His kisses continued to burn into her, sending spurts of fire through her veins. She arched toward him, urging him on. And he responded, filling her with pleasure. Then they moved in a slow loving rhythm until simultaneous orgasms, not the wild animal ones of before, but gentle satisfactory ones building to climax, shuddered through their bodies. As she calmed Juli slid under the covers, pressing the full length of her body against his. This was so good. Could they keep it up? Or would the stress of day to day life pull them apart?

"Go to sleep Juli. We can stay in bed." Rich looked out the window saying, "The sun's not up yet. We can languish in bed and maybe have a hot shower later.

Juli didn't need any encouragement; she was quickly asleep again. About ten am, after a hot shower, Juli announced, "Rich we have only three condoms left. We have to stop this continuous sex or else we have to replenish our supply."

"Let's practice celibacy for a few hours. I want to check and see how those two kids we referred to Vic General are doing." He reached for the phone.

"Good idea."

"Then we have to talk about returning to Quadra."

"I thought about that already. We have four more nights then you can put me on the ferry Saturday morning . . . I'll talk with Tom at the hotel, so he knows we're safe. I'll pick up my car and I'll drive down; then I'll have all day Sunday to organize myself and get extra sleep. I have a shift on Monday."

Rich was very quiet, his eyes filled with tears.

"Rich how are we going to stay in touch?" He was as quiet as death. She didn't like it.

Then his voice, calm and thoughtful offered, "Let's stay calm. We're only two ferries and a four-hour car ride apart. That's nothing."

"It's something. Let's not kid ourselves." Why did she say that? He was trying to reason himself out of doom and gloom.

"Juli, you are the best thing that has ever happened to me." His eyes pleaded and his voice was husky with emotion, "I want you in my life." He kissed her and held her gently. "It's like we have been together always. I want to wake up to your head on my pillow every morning. I want to share my life with you."

"Well then, come to Victoria," she said abruptly.

"Hey no ultimatums. Let's keep looking for the win-win. For now I have a home here and you have a home in Victoria. I'm on leave so I'm free to move around. What about this? I'll come and stay with you for a while, and then you'll get a leave and try living up here with me?"

"Sounds reasonable." She paused, thinking. "The treatment center might allow that. However, I'm not sure." She paused, her eyes fixed on his hands a she was afraid of his reaction. "I'm planning to specialize in internal medicine and I'm registered for January." She held her breath, worried about his answer.

"Oh I didn't realize . . ." he paused as if he was blindsided. "You would have to go to Vancouver for that." His voice became husky with sadness, "I have bad memories of Vancouver." He shook his head, "You'll become a sophisticated specialist and not be interested in a country doctor. I can feel the heaviness of losing you already."

Gently as possible she explained, "It's been my plan for years." She wondered if she was crazy. A good man like this didn't come along very often. Maybe only once in a life time. She did want to have at least two babies, and at thirty- four she needed to start her pregnancies now.

"Juli, I don't know what to say."

She could sense the depression and loss creeping over him. What was going on? This was way out of proportion; she was not dying. "Rich what's happening? I feel like you're shutting down."

He grunted and turned over to face the wall.

"Rich believe it or not I'm committed to this relationship. I'm not leaving you. I want to work it out."

He didn't respond. His shoulders were stiff.

Juli persisted, "Rich I'm not dying." It was then she realized he was sobbing quietly. She took him in her arms and cuddled his head and shoulders and smoothed his forehead. "Rich talk to me. Rich talk to me."

After a long silence he whispered hoarsely, "Sylvia left me. She died."

So that was her name. "Rich tell me about Sylvia."

He buried his face in her chest and slowly painstakingly told her, "Sylvia and I met at UBC and had a hot romance." He shuddered. "After my mom died when I was twenty-one it seemed like a good idea for us to marry. We were so much in love that we did everything together. I continued on at med school and Sylvia continued in her Commerce program. We decided to wait to have children because we were students." His voice broke and he shuddered as he relived those days. "Then when I was working at St. Paul's Hospital and she was articling, we decided to wait again. Life was complete with the two of us. She was so beautiful and so much fun; we laughed a lot. When we both turned twenty-seven we decided we could handle a child. She went for a Pap smear and bango, the world came crashing down. She had stage three cervical cancer; a very aggressive cancer that whipped through her body in spite of everything we tried. She died a week after her twenty-ninth birthday." He was silent so long Juli wanted to wrap her arms around him. "The cancer literally ate her up."

"Oh Rich I'm so sorry. I had no idea." That was traumatic. No wonder he had issues. She hoped talking about it would be like lancing a boil, terrible pain followed by release and hopefully, healing. Tears of sympathy dripped from her eyes. She held him close and gently rubbed his back.

He continued like a runaway train, now that he had started he couldn't stop. He had to get the poison out. "I watched her die inch by inch and I died with her." He sobbed for many minutes as Juli continued to hold him lovingly. "A year after she died I couldn't stand Vancouver, so when this position on Cortes came up, I applied. I bought this property and here I am. Living with the ocean and the rhythm of nature has been good for me until lately with the BP problem." Head in his hands he continued to sob.

"Rich no one can ever replace Sylvia."

"I know that but I also know I have to let her go." He blew his nose. "Juli thank you, this is the first time I have cried for Sylvia. I loved her so much that I froze up when she died."

"From what you have told me, I don't think she would have wanted you to suffer. She would have wanted you to live life to the full." Juli gently caressed his forehead.

"That's easier said than done," his voice was hoarse as he turned on his back staring at the ceiling.

"True. But at least now I know why you reacted so strongly to my leaving." She had caused him pain. How could that be when she wanted to protect him?

"You're the first person I have trusted." The crease between his eyebrows smoothed and he seemed to relax slightly.

"Thank you Rich." She kissed his forehead and nose.

His eyes opened and he gazed at her with the tender vulnerability of a newborn. He turned his head toward her and their lips met in a slow loving kiss. Rich looked at her exploring every inch of her face, then he relaxed back on the pillow saying, "Maybe we should start this discussion again. I feel so much more hopeful."

She decided to be completely open. "Okay hear this. I want a baby and I want to specialize. You want to live and practice on Cortes Island, but your vascular system is sending you messages that a solo practice on a remote island is not good for your body."

"I hear you. Go on," his voice sound puzzled.

"Here's what we could do: you could impregnate me now and that would be very easy as I'm twelve days into my cycle and very fertile."

"That would be easy and pleasurable," he smiled. "But what then? This sounds more complicated, not less."

"Nine months would be circa May twelfth. I could work at the treatment center until end of December and then move to Cortes. You'll be back at work by then and I could work two days a week, thus taking some of the load off you, and having time to enjoy my ever-expanding body . . . until end of April. Then if Junior is on schedule, I could have the summer to breast feed and start the UBC program in September." She couldn't believe that she had said all that, couldn't believe how organized she sounded.

"Wow, and I thought our biggest problem was driving on the Island highway. Suddenly I'm the father of a baby probably called Junior and my wife is a resident in Vancouver." He stood up and paced in the cramped bedroom.

"Rich, you could take two years and be a house husband or work part time."

He shook his head. "Juli it wouldn't work. Once you're a specialist you'll have to live in a city to have enough patients, maybe . . . maybe Campbell River. But long term I don't want to live there. Look at me. I have a house so remote it's off the grid and only accessible by boat. Do I look like a city slicker?"

"Good point. Why don't we go back to step one?" She desperately wanted this to work.

"I've forgotten what that was," he said as he sat down heavily.

"You could come home with me for a while. Please, please do it Rich. I want you in my life. I know we can work it out." She shouldn't have blurted everything in her mind. It had frightened him. She knew from fishing that once she had a big one hooked she had to reel it in slowly and have her net ready so it couldn't get away. Good thing Rich wasn't a fish. He was a man and he liked her a lot; she liked him a lot, too. Their pheromones were good together. Did she really want to be an internist? She could always do that in ten years if she still wanted to, but having a family, no, that had to be soon. Her biological clock was running out. "That was where I started. I meant it."

"That might be possible . . . I'd like to spend the next two months getting to know you. You'd be a good life-partner . . . we have similar education and interests. But more than that, it's as though the universe brought you into my life right when I needed you: kismet, karma, predestined partner. I need to listen to that."

297

"Right. It's a good idea." Take it slowly. Don't frighten him again. Besides it would be good to find out where his health was going. Two months would buy her time to see how he was healing. Be positive, she thought.

"How's this? I'll put you on the ferry Saturday and then I'll follow when I'm sure the Health Center is managing." His eyes met hers as if to say he would do everything in his power to make this work.

"My first choice would be to keep you with me. But I know you feel responsible for the residents of the island." She moved into his arms saying, "Come as soon as you can."

"Don't worry sweet woman, I will." They kissed long and deep, clinging to each other as if they were on a life raft in a stormy sea. He scooped her up in his arms and tenderly laid her on the bed. He was suddenly agonizingly impatient and nothing would stop him. Juli was panting and ready. Their union was swift and desperate, expressing their mutual need to stay together.

CHAPTER SEVENTEEN

Juli woke in the grey of early dawn and listened to the trill of a squirrel searching for its mate. She smiled, *I'm not searching anymore. I've found my soulmate, a man I consider my equal. I want to spend the rest of my life with him.* She turned on her side so she could watch Rich and send him healing energy. No wonder he was so tentative, losing Sylvia like that after she had helped him with his mother's death. Juli had to ask him more about that. She bet he was still hanging on to his parents, too. Right now he was totally relaxed in a deep sleep. His hair was curly and standing on end in places like the top of his head reminding her of a cuddly toddler. His five o'clock shadow now was a two week shadow and on its way to being a beard. His long lashes curled on his cheeks. *Maybe,* she thought, Junior would have lashes like that. *Oops, no baby, yet.* They had only committed to two months together in Victoria. She was looking forward to that. She was sure it was going to be fun.

Just then Rich opened his cobalt eyes, looked confused, then he smiled a broad welcoming smile filled with love. "Good morning love."

"Good morning Rich, the wonder man, giver of pleasure."

He laughed. "Juli you're nuts. You're supposed to think I'm taking advantage of you."

"And are you?"

"Not likely. A robust woman like you could do me serious damage." he trailed his finger down her cheek. He looked refreshed as though a burden of grief had been lifted from his heart.

"Not a chance," giggled Juli. "You've got the pleasure wand in your control."

He laughed again. They lay there for a long time basking in the glory that each was beaming to the other. Finally Rich rolled to the side of bed saying, "I'm going out to gather oysters for breakfast."

"Wait a minute Rich I want to ask you about something. Why did your mom die so young?"

At first he shrugged as if he was going to avoid the question, then he said quietly, "CVA."

"A stroke! Hypertension?" Juli's mind raced, *No it can't be.* That made his hypertension even more serious.

"Yes, her family doctor was changing her hypertension meds, he had discontinued one. She got up in the morning, went to the bathroom and collapsed. By the time the ambulance got there, she was dead." Rich's voice was a monotone, without feeling like a robot reciting instructions. "But I think it was a grief reaction from dad's death."

"That must have been a huge shock to you." Juli kept prodding gently. She had to help him get in touch with those feelings a little bit at a time.

"I don't know . . . I sort of went blank." He sat on the side of the bed, head bowed not moving. "I don't remember the two weeks after her death. Then I was angry for a long time at dad for not saving her, which was insane as he was already dead, and at her doctor for not being more careful. Then I started to blame myself. I should have checked her meds myself. Sylvia helped me see it wasn't my fault. She brought love and light into my life. We married almost a year to the day after mom died."

Whoa, this is important. He replaced his mom with Sylvia, then Sylvia died, too. She decided to keep going. "Rich tell me about your mom."

"She had long golden hair that smelled of violets, blue eyes like mine, and a smile that never stopped." His voice was soft and a gentle smile pulled at his lips.

"She sounds beautiful."

301

"She was. She devoted her life to me. Well to dad too; he worshiped her. When she died it was like a tire burst, sending her energy into the universe." He wiped his eyes. Something inside him shifted, energy entered his forehead and floated through his body as though his mother was trying to communicate with him.

Juli could see he was experiencing something profound. "Rich, if your mother was here right now, what would you say?"

He cleared his throat, "I'd say, Mom I miss you every single day. Mom thank you so much for taking such good care of me."

"Come here Rich, let me hold you". Rich sunk his head on her chest and she held him tightly. "And what would your mother say?" She could feel moisture running down her chest as Rich silently grieved for his mother.

"She would say. 'It was a great joy to take care of you. I love you and I always will.'" After a long time, Rich raised his head, "Juli I love you. Thank you for your gift of listening. You are good for me. I feel truly blessed."

"Rich I have known you only eleven days, but it seems like a lifetime. I love you and want to be with you always."

"That's my plan, too . . . Now let's get some breakfast. Maybe some of the bacon and eggs we picked up yesterday. I don't want to go out for oysters, now." he rolled off the bed and pulled her with him.

"Sounds good to me. I'll put the bacon on, and boil some water for tea. Next I'll go out and get some wood. The cabin feels a little chilly."

"Don't bother. The sun'll warm us up soon."

Several hours later Rich kissed her gently saying, "We need some fun . . . let's do a picnic. The sun seems warm enough now and the breeze light."

As she sniffed the air and pushed gently on his chest she grinned like a kid on school holiday, "Right, it's a wonderful day." Then she hesitated, "Are there any wolves there?"

"Not likely. There's not much of anything on Marina Island . . . except trees and oysters."

"Excellent. I'll make some cheese sandwiches and I'll be ready."

He took a quick suck at her ear as if he was considering if they should return to bed, then reluctantly he drew back. "I'll check on the boat and make sure we have an anchor."

As though they were in a continuing dance they glided out of the kitchen, had a refreshing shower, and dressed in shorts and t-shirts. They climbed into the runabout and set off to the west away from Manson's Landing. The shoreline was grey rock with granite cliffs fringed with emerald forest. Tiny wavelets glistened and sparkled in the afternoon sun. The bow of the boat sliced through them easily, leaving flat water and a spreading wake behind. "There it is," called Juli over the motor as she pointed at the now familiar sand spit jutting off Marina Island pointing at Cortes. She was delighted that she had recognized it so easily. She scanned the sky, noting a smoke haze to the east. Princess Louisa must still be burning, she thought.

"There's a narrow passage to get around this on the Cortes side," shouted Rich over the motor.

"Hey remember we paddled through Uganda Pass when we arrived." That seemed long ago. Could it only have been a few days ago? Her life was so rich and full of sensation that every day was a lifetime. She must have been a walking zombie before she came on this trip.

Rich steered the runabout on to the pure white sand, climbed out and threw the anchor up on the beach. "The boat'll be fine, we have an ebbing tide. You choose a spot and I'll bring the food basket."

Juli picked up their blanket, eased herself carefully over the gunwale of the metal boat, and felt cold ocean on her knees and soft sand under her bare feet. Unexpectedly a wave washed icy cold water up to her thighs so she scrambled quickly up the steep slope, across the sand to the waiting logs of driftwood. The center of the spit was filled with a bird's nest of silvery logs washed up and weathered over many years. Like everything else on Cortes the logs were bigger than life, giant Douglas fir that had broken loose from a log pile or maybe tumbled with old age into the ocean to begin a second life floating freely on the tides. A boater's worst nightmare was to hit one of these granddaddies and hole their boat. The unforgiving ocean would make a certain and chilly grave. Juli shook herself, *I'm on dry land, the logs are on dry land, use them for shelter.* She knew part of the thrill of living on Cortes was the excitement and inherent danger of living close to nature.

She spread the blanket against a log so that they would be protected from the wind, their faces shaded and their bodies warmed by the sun. "Good choice Juli," said Rich placing the food basket in the shade. "There's a light breeze off the ocean. It's cool."

Juli looked around. They were in the middle of the spit on the west side to catch the full afternoon sun. She could see a dark green conifer forest about one-quarter of a mile to the south and the rest of the sand spit jutting into the ocean about one-quarter mile to the north. Not another human was in sight. Rich spread his arms, stood and ran down the beach. Juli jumped to her feet following him like a kid let out at recess. The tempo quickened, they ran faster and faster like healthy young puppies let out to play, toes digging into the soft sand, calves straining. Rich ran right to the tip, stopping suddenly. Juli crashed into him. They clung together and fell into the shallow water. Rich pulled her on top of him, so that she was in the warm sunshine, and kissed her lips, tugging and nipping. Juli pushed away, shouting back over her shoulder, "C'mon lazy old man, catch me if you can." They raced up the east shore, hooting and laughing. Rich caught her and led her, over the logs piled in the middle of the spit, to the blanket, stripping off his shorts as he walked.

"Rich, that's scandalous." Nonetheless she wanted to stand there and look at him forever.

"Juli there's no one but us and the seagulls." His voice husky and eyes glazing with passion, he kissed her again, this time more deeply. Juli giggled her response. She felt free of all conventions, all inhibitions. Quickly she wiggled out of her shorts and soon they were joined in the eternal mating dance. A brief thought that there was no protection crossed her mind, but her hormones ruled her intellect and she urged him on.

CHAPTER EIGHTEEN

Juli woke slowly. Seagulls cried. Wind hummed against the rock the cabin used for support. The sun shone through the window, lighting the room with gold and happiness, for now the smoke had cleared. Pictures of sailboats under full sail and Rich smiling with a large salmon dangling beside him plastered the walls so that little of the white walls showed. On the bed a duvet cover of cobalt blue t-shirt cotton covered a warm fluffy duvet, wonderful for snuggling under, which she did.

Rich was deeply asleep beside her. She moved carefully to lay on her back as an aching tenderness filled her to overflowing, like pure clear water bubbling from as artesian well. He was such a part of her now that she couldn't visualize life without him. She had never had a close relationship like this, ever. She was close to her mother, who listened to her, and helped her, but that wasn't the same. Juli had been close to her brother and sister as a caregiver not an equal. Then there was Reggie who had taken Juli to school dances and house parties; they kissed and made out in his father's car, but in the end their interests were quite different as he went to trade school and she went to university; she was sad to break up with him as he was easy and comfortable to be with. At university in her twenties she dated Ted, of course, and lost her virginity. When she was thirty she had been a loner. But now, now she saw how it could be, much like someone who had been seeing in black and white and suddenly has color vision. So it was like that for her; being with Rich 24/7 was colorful. She saw and heard and felt everything around her in color, startling and vivid. They worked as a team, things happened easily. She didn't want to go back to her black and white world. But she had to. That was how she earned her living. That was how she contributed to society.

She turned over on her stomach slowly and carefully, so as to not wake Rich who was snoring softly. She needed to think outside the box. Rethink her goals. She could specialize in family medicine, then her skills would be useful on Cortes. Or maybe she didn't need to specialize. Rich was happy as a GP. Well that was not quite right, his hypertension showed something was wrong. She wanted to specialize as medicine was so complicated, and she would like more time to think about each patient. Her head began to ache from puzzling over all the variables. She shut her eyes sniffing in the comforting male smells. All this thinking and yesterday's adventure with the picnic on the beach had tired her. She pulled the covers over her head and slipped into a sound sleep.

Much, much later something tickled the back of her neck. She rolled her head away. Something tickled her neck. She turned back and opened her eyes to find herself staring into bright blue eyes filled with beauty and love. "Rich, hi," she stretched and edged closer, pressing against his warm body. "What time is it?"

"Its high noon and high time you got up to keep me company." His voice was so beautiful it made her heart ache.

Yawning, she said "I was so tired."

"How bout we hop in the boat and go to the Gorge for lunch?" As he talked he kissed her ear and breathed in her seductive scent.

"What's there?"

"Oh, ho, wait till you see," he whispered sexily into her ear.

"Tell me, please, please," she begged, pushing him gently away.

"Can't you wait?"

"No way. I'm not moving till I'm sure it's a better world out there." She pulled the covers over her head again.

"It is. I promise. We have this modern marina with a fabulous restaurant." He tugged playfully at the blanket.

309

She heard him but she didn't believe him at first. "No way. Two wonderful restaurants on this little island. Not possible." While she protested teasingly she remembered Dave had said something about a good restaurant at the Gorge.

"Yup and we're going there for lunch." He gently pulled her out of bed and steered her toward the shower. "Now make yourself even more beautiful and we're off."

Juli smiled and stretched; she felt wonderful and beautiful and loved. The hot water woke her up fully; she dried herself quickly and jumped into her shorts, which had been drying in the sun. She glanced out the window. The ocean was calm, and in spite of the smoky sky it was hot, but eerie. She was hoping the fires on the mainland would be controlled soon so the sun would shine brightly again.

"How's the tide? I'm not as tide naive as I was; that narrow enrance'll be tricky. I remember the cliffs." Juli stretched like the satisfied animal she was.

"It's slack now." He tugged the covers off her as his eyes ran over her body, not as a clinician but as a lover enjoying her beautiful body. "Besides we'll be in the runabout with a motor."

Juli enjoyed his caressing eyes for a few luxurious moments. Then she slid out of bed carefully brushing against him, knowing it would stimulate him further. Laughing with a sultry sexy tone she disappeared into the bathroom calling over her shoulder, "I love being close to Nature. I love how you work with the tides. It really makes the expression 'go with the flow meaningful.'" As she talked she grabbed her hoodie.

"Dress warmly. Wear a hat."

"Ha, I already have my hoodie." He was right again, she needed to be sensible. "I'm leaving my shorts on but I'll put sweats over them. And I have my kayak hat."

"Sounds good," came Rich's smiling voice as he rubbed lotion on his face and tossed the bottle to her. "Here's the sunscreen."

"Okay I'm ready," said Juli after rubbing the lotion on her face. Together they went to the dock and loaded the runabout. Juli tossed in her hoodie and her life jacket, and then eased onto the cold metal seat at the bow. "I felt safer and more protected in Yak," she announced as she looked around. A light breeze ruffled the clear blue ocean, and gulls called, broadcasting the presence of herring,

Rich stepped aboard and began immediately to check the motor and the fuel. "I know what you mean, but we need the motor. We don't have time to paddle there and back. Besides this boat is beamy and can handle most anything. We won't test it this time as there is a high pressure area building, so it will be a hot day with little wind." While he talked he started the motor and steered the boat away from his dock and turned west toward the entrance of the Gorge harbor.

Juli smiled as she remembered their first night on Read. She had been so sure Rich was a bossy male out to make her life miserable. Nonetheless, even then her body was totally aware of him.

They chugged part-way toward the now familiar Shark spit, turning north through the gorge, which was a dramatic bottle-neck channel carved by Nature through towering rocks. The current was fairly slack so the passage was easy.

Rich pointed ahead, "Look Juli, this opens up to a huge inland harbor. It's about two miles long by a mile wide."

"It's another whole world." Juli gazed around.

"Right, the water is so protected that it's calm and safe for boats," he shouted. "Plus, it's an excellent place for shellfish farming. Over there," he pointed to the right, "are oyster beds and deeper in the bay are scallops."

All she could see were grey weathered wooden rafts clinging together. "Wow that's a lot of them. Don't the yacht owners mind?"

"Yes, of course there are always pros and cons. Like everything in life, my life, your life." He didn't say more but from the huskiness in his voice Juli knew he included their relationship and their health and career plans. Shrugging as if to say we'll deal with that later he pointed, "We're going the other way."

Juli could see they were coming to a marina.

As he slowed the engine he said, "The docks are fully modern, constructed with concrete and able to handle the largest of the cruising yachts . . . like that one." Juli could hardly believe what she was seeing. "It's a bit over the top." Rich shrugged as they passed a sparkling white yacht that must have been one hundred feet in length with a helicopter on the upper deck. "Desolation Sound is a destination for yachties from all over the world."

Juli nodded in agreement while she tried to take in this magnificent many-fingered wharf with a grassy hillside leading to a large one-story wooden building framed with flowering bushes. She could have been in Vancouver it was so deluxe. Was she camping on a beach only three days ago?

"That's the restaurant." Rich pointed up the steep hill. "It was a floating house at one time. They brought it down from Kingcome Inlet."

"Rich, I feel like Alice in Wonderland and I have just shot down the rabbit hole. Everything's nature centered and then suddenly this blast of modernity. I'm in shock, culture shock."

Rich grinned, "You're amazing. I thought you might like to experience the soft side of life on Cortes, especially after that

313

wolf encounter." They pulled into the dinghy dock and tied up. Then hand in hand they walked up the steep hill to the restaurant. "We're not total barbarians here. I wanted you to know that."

"Juli, Juli," came a voice from behind her. "It's me Marigold." There stood Marigold with her expensive hair-cut and designer all-weather jacket, looking the antithesis of Juli in her sweats and over-sized, t-shirt borrowed from Rich. But she was a dear friend. Conflicting emotions shot through Juli; she wanted to keep Rich all to herself on one hand, and on the other she wanted to share him with her friend.

As Juli turned and smiled she felt Rich tense. "Marigold, hi."

Marigold laughed and glided toward them. "Isn't this fun. Running into you again." She winked at Juli as if to say, looks like my intention came true.

"Good to see you Marigold." Juli gave her friend a hug. "We were coming for lunch."

"Great!" she gushed. "Dave's up there getting a table. You must join us." Her eyes examined Rich with love and welcoming.

"You sure?" asked Juli leaning back to feel Rich's warmth and to check if this would be okay for him.

"Positive. And who is this gorgeous man?" Marigold asked, beaming a bright smile on Rich.

Suddenly Juli didn't like Marigold's questioning eyes inspecting Rich, although Juli knew she was dedicated to Dave and was teasing. She took Rich's hand pulling him toward the restaurant and effectively putting space between him and Marigold. Then she felt comfortable enough to introduce them. "Marigold this is Richard Thompson."

"Pleased to meet you Richard. Any friend of Juli's is a friend of ours." She gave him a welcoming hug "You're the local doc. I saw you when we were at Manson's."

"On leave." Rich smiled his brightest, "I'm glad to meet you."

Marigold slid her left arm into Rich's right and her right arm into Juli's left and steered them toward the restaurant, up the steep ramp. Finally Juli relaxed and let her friend show them the way and it felt comforting.

The restaurant had an expansive view of the marina and the boats at dock, and beyond that to a dozen yachts anchored in the sheltered bay. The brick path to the house was steep and lined with beautiful flowering shrubs and flowers: fuchsia, blush pink, scarlet red, gold, and purple colors twirled together into a sensational delight while delicate perfumes danced around them. A large well-maintained wooden deck, filled with colorful sun umbrellas and round tables, was inviting, but Marigold pointed at three wooden stairs leading to a rustic wooden door which she held open for them. As they entered the restaurant Dave smiled, stood, and greeted Juli enthusiastically, "Wow small world."

"On Cortes for sure," smiled Juli genuinely glad to see her boss and colleague.

Dave hugged Juli saying, "Sit down, sit down, and tell us what's been happening."

Juli liked his friendly greeting and thought that this was going to go well. "This is Richard Thompson. He's the local doc."

Dave stared, "Of course I saw him on Manson's dock the other day." He snorted. "Sorry I couldn't help you out."

"No problem. It worked out." Rich smiled and they shook hands.

"I'm glad you're here," interjected his wife drawing, attention away from her husband. "Now what are we going to eat?" Juli noted Marigold's maneuver and wondered what was going on.

"Everything's good," said Rich. "I come here often." Then he turned back to Dave. "I'm on leave." As he talked Rich picked up the menu and shared it with Juli, pointing out his favorites.

The waitress who had been watching him since he arrived came over to say, "Doctor Thompson, you're welcome. Thanks for helping Pete yesterday."

Rich beamed at her, "Hi Violet. I was glad to help. Dr. Armstrong, here," he pointed proudly at Juli, "helped out too." Marigold watched Rich's care and concern for Juli, happy for Juli but sad that she and Dave had lost it.

"Well we'll have to find something very special for you and your guests." Violet kept smiling and touching Rich's shoulder. "We have ginger butternut squash soup, all but the ginger grown on the island. And a mixed greens salad from Eagle's Nest organic farm, with a light vinaigrette."

"So far so good," nodded Rich.

"Me too," agreed Juli, noticing Dave picking at his napkin.

Marigold nodded, "That's for us too." Dave didn't notice.

"Great," said Violet. "Then for the Main I have a sockeye salmon burger. With ciabatta buns." She paused and added to Rich, "The salmon are running. Sam Wills caught these off the reef on Marina Island."

"That's for me," said Rich and Juli together. Dave shrugged. Marigold nodded agreement.

"Coming right up, four soups, salads, and salmon burgers."

After Violet left Juli asked, "How come you guys are still here? I thought you'd be over at Desolation by now."

317

"The fire at Princess Louisa changed our plans," said Marigold. "It was smoky at Squirrel Cove that day I saw you at the store. Dave thought it might be better on this side. We stayed at Manson's a night, you saw us there, too, and then came here. We had heard about this marina and wanted to see it for ourselves." She looked at Dave seeming to be asking him to agree with her.

"Yup, with all the smoke I decided the smartest thing would be to come to this side of the island," said Dave quietly, emphasizing what his wife had said and seeming to agree with her.

"Good decision. It's fine here, except for the dusky sky," nodded Juli. Rich drank his ice water and lounged back, letting Juli take the lead while he watched her with her friends.

"I thought I'd head north from here. But the smoke. . ." Dave shrugged helplessly.

What's going on? He was saying I, I, I. What about Marigold? Her eyes met Marigold's and her head did an almost imperceptible shake to say, 'no'.

Dave continued loudly, "So I'm thinking of leaving Dream Seeker here and taking a float plane to Victoria. That way we can come back when things are better."

Marigold's mouth dropped open in surprise, her eyes flickered over Dave then she changed the subject, "Dave, enough about us." She emphasized the 'us'. Dave glanced at her with an annoyed look. Blithely Marigold looked at Rich and continued, "You were kayaking in Von Donop. Was the fire up there? Were you in danger?"

"No fire up there," shrugged Rich.

Juli added, "Just lots of ocean and oysters." She paused. "And wolves."

"Wolves?" Marigold's eyes widened.

Dave nodded, "I warned you about them."

"You did . . . I thought we would never see them. However, we met three of them. They got a little too friendly. We packed up and left in the middle of the night."

"Juli that's terrible," said Marigold her voice husky with concern. "You could have been eaten alive."

Juli grinned a grin of triumph, "But we weren't. It was scary. We got out because Rich saw the animals lurking around. He woke me and we fled with Yak and our paddles. Fortunately Rich," Juli smiled at him, "ever the efficient guide, had stowed all supplies and our life jackets in Yak."

"That sounds like a close call," said Marigold looking concerned. Without a word Dave stood up and disappeared to the washroom.

Juli was on a roll, "We paddled Yak like the hounds of hell were after us." Her face flushed as she relived the drama of the flight.

"They were," interjected Rich lounging back in his chair looking very casual. "One wolf was swimming behind us. Two others were following us on the shore as we paddled out the narrow inlet. Fortunately they didn't catch us. But they might have."

"Rich warned me they might try to ambush us at the narrow neck of the inlet. Well that pumped up my adrenalin. The tide was ebbing into the inlet that helped us." Her voice was rapid and her hands animated.

"It wasn't a strong ebb," minimized Rich.

"I kept my head down. And paddled, and paddled." Juli demonstrated.

"I wouldn't have liked that," said Marigold. "Juli you're so brave." Out of the corner of her eye Juli could see Dave pacing on the outside deck.

"It wasn't bravery. It was fear that drove us." Juli's voice rose as her body remembered the terror.

"People on this island sure are hardy," said Marigold.

Juli giggled, "You don't know the half of it."

"C'mon spill the beans," coaxed Marigold. Dave leaned on the railing watching yachts leaving the marina, seeming to have forgotten them.

Rich smiled as he enjoyed hearing her version of events.

Dave, having finally returned to his seat to retrieve his coffee from the table, continued to watch the marina activity.

"My God, vicious wolves. This really is a wild island. I like Victoria. It's much tamer," declared Marigold smoothing her clothes.

At that point Dave turned and stared at Juli, "Speaking of Victoria, when are you heading back Juli?"

"Saturday or Sunday. I only booked off two weeks. I wish I had more time now."

Marigold listened then asked her own questions. "What about you Rich? Are you able to come to Victoria? We'd love to see you anytime."

Rich glanced at Juli as if to say it depends on Juli. "I'm hoping to get down in the near future."

Marigold looked at Rich and then Juli, "So how did you two meet?" She leaned eagerly forward to hear the details.

Juli spoke up, "We met twelve days ago when I arrived at Herriot Bay for the kayak trip. As I was a novice the tour leader assigned Rich to paddle with me." She was not going to tell them they had been alone for eleven days and nights.

321

"That was lucky Rich was on the trip," interjected Marigold, her voice coaxing for more information as she examined their faces.

"Yes," said Dave, leaning back in his chair. "I heard you might be kayaking from someone at the office. Marigold and I left Oak Bay Marina about the same time you went on holiday, so I didn't know the details." Right then the soup arrived: rich, creamy orange, piping hot, and fragrant. All was quiet as they devoured it, and Dave didn't press for details.

Marigold continued, "You're going back in two or three days, and we've got to be back Monday, too."

Dave chimed in, "I'm looking into the planes early tomorrow." *What about Marigold?* thought Juli. As he spoke, Violet quietly removed the bowls and delivered the fresh crisp salad. Once again quiet, except for a few *yums*.

Rich finished first, asked, "Dave, plane's a good way to go. Especially in the summer when there's no fog."

"It's fast and we'll get home quickly." Dave tapped unconsciously on the table. "What about you two?"

Juli smiled side-stepping the returning-home question, "This island's very civilized, with two world class restaurants. This is definitely the best island for eating north of Nanaimo and South of Prince Rupert." They all laughed, almost relaxed with one another. The empty salad plates disappeared and the Salmon burgers appeared: the buns crisp and fresh, the grilled salmon moist and colorful, with a light touch of aioli and a fresh leaf of lettuce.

As they settled back over drinks Dave, suddenly leaned toward Rich and asked, "So how is it being a doctor on an island?"

"Right now I'm on leave. I didn't look after myself and I'm a little burned out. But to answer your question, basically it's great."

Dave nodded.

Juli added, "Definitely a younger and healthier clientele than ours."

"Interesting," said Dave. Juli didn't know if he meant the practice or her relationship with Rich. Whichever, she chose to ignore it. But she did notice his fingers tapping and twirling his fork; it was as though he had an excess of energy. She thought he would be mellow after being on his boat with Marigold, but he wasn't. As well there was tension between him and Marigold. Juli made a mental note to ask her friend if she was okay.

"Are you guys going to talk doctor for very long?" asked Marigold.

"Shh honey, this is important to me." Dave roughly covered her hand. Juli saw the gesture and thought maybe she was mistaken. They had always seemed good together. A doubt crossed her mind as Juli remembered the rumors at work about Dave's behavior.

Dave continued, "Rich I'm restless lately. I'd be interested in getting out of Victoria sometimes."

What was that about? Wondered Juli.

"I've had a tough time finding locums this past two years. Unfortunately, I can't really say anything as I'm on sick leave."

"It's okay I'm not seriously looking for work . . . just want you to know Marigold and I like this island." Marigold eyes opened wide in surprise. He continued, "But what about you Rich? Any chance of you coming to Victoria?"

Rich looked at Juli, "I'm sure thinking about it."

"We can always use extra help at the treatment centers. There's no end of people with problems." Dave seemed sincere.

"Thanks Dave. I'll keep it in mind. And, hope to see you there." Rich smiled at Dave as though he felt welcomed.

"Marigold we need to get back to the boat," Dave stood with a jerk and headed for the door. So much for lunch conversation, thought Juli. He had been pacing or fidgeting most of the time. "Why don't you come and see our boat?" Dave pointed out the door toward the dock, "Right down there."

"Why not? I'd like that," said Rich as he rose and walked out of the café, joining Dave on his swift journey toward the docks.

Juli and Marigold, arm in arm, leisurely followed them. "I like him Juli. He's exactly what I envisioned for you. He'd be a great guy anywhere in the world: rural or urban." Marigold started to ask Juli about Dave's behavior, "Juli I want to. . ."

Juli, caught up in her thoughts about Rich didn't hear Marigold's plea for help. "Thanks Marigold. I like him . . . this is the beginning . . . we're still negotiating." As they neared the water Juli put a hand on the metal rail of the ramp leading to the more solid cement docks as it was extremely steep now. The tide had ebbed at least three feet while they were eating. That would be a good thing for the harbor as the ocean would flush out and then race back in with the flood, bringing fresh nutrients to the wild clams and oysters, and as importantly to the local shellfish farms.

Marigold laughed, "Negotiate away. But if the pheromones are right, and they sure seem to be, go for it. Compromise is the name of the game."

When they reached the men they were both on deck examining the roller-furling. Dave invited Juli aboard to have a look around. She agreed and then followed Marigold below to view the cabin details while the men intensely discussed wind and sails and sat-coms and GPSs, and inboard versus outboard engines.

Much later Juli and Rich motored sedately back to his cabin at Manson's, each deep in their own thoughts. Juli was glad they had run into Dave and Marigold again. It gave her a chance to see Rich with her friends. Surprisingly, now she was more concerned about Marigold and Dave's relationship than her's with Rich.

Right before Manson's Landing Rich turned the runabout toward his dock. It felt like coming home as the familiar dock and cabin welcomed them. Juli crawled on to the dock, fastened the line, dragged her gear out of the boat and collapsed on the dock. "What's up? asked Rich concern showing in his voice.

"Nothing really . . . too tired to move."

"That's something." Rich sat on the dock beside her, his feet dangling in the boat. "You've experienced a lot of new things in the past two weeks: kayaking . . . camping out . . . fleeing from wolves . . . helping at the health center . . . discovering my life." When he said the last, he smiled and searched her face for a reaction.

"Rich you're right. I came straight from work and I was exhausted when I got to Quadra. Certainly not in any shape for the adventure we've been having." When she saw the disappointed look in his eyes she added, "Rich I've been having the best time of my life. I'm rethinking much of it. That's what's taking energy. I'm trying to figure out how I can have it all: you and a career and babies."

She waited expectantly for him to say, 'I want you to have my babies.' When he didn't her green eyes probed him, looking for reassurance; instead, his eyes seemed to melt as he seemed to be contemplating how serious she was and how radically his life might be changing. He cleared his throat, "Juli we'll work on it together. You're not alone. Now come," he said as he got to his feet and gently taking her hand he helped her to her feet, treating her like a sister as if he needed distance.

Juli sensed a change and reacted to it by becoming hyper-independent. "You go first, I'll follow. I've got to carry my coat and lifejacket."

"I could come back for it." Rich looked confused by her tone.

"Thanks but I've got it." Juli, seeing his confusion, weakened and let him lead her along the unsteady dock, being careful not to trip on the uneven wood. The cabin was warm and filled with a soft glow from the late afternoon sunshine.

Inside the cabin Rich casually said, "I need a nap after all that food." His eyes pleaded with her for comfort.

"MMM, me too," whispered Juli feeling her body respond: swelling breasts, tingling nipples, moisture wetting her thighs. *So much for independence*; she could not refuse this man

327

anything. She swallowed and stood still, savoring the moment. Rich's soft lips and tickling beard brushed her neck, acting like the bang of a starting gun. Articles of clothing dropped off them like petals off a flower, revealing their soft hungry bodies. Rich picked her up as easily as if she was a piece of fluff, a delicious irresistible morsel. He carried her swiftly to the bed, laying her gently across it, knees bent, feet on the floor, and then he eased on top of her holding his weight off her with his extended arms. "Juli I can't get enough of you." He kissed the top of her head, sparks flashed through her fine hair increasing her stimulation and desire; he seemed to feel it too as he almost collapsed on her. His arms wavered. Juli thought he would fall on her, and she welcomed that, as she knew she could hold his weight. Plus, it would bring his throbbing engorged hardness closer, hopefully to ease the ache she felt deep in her pelvis. Surprising her, Rich flipped on his back pulling her on top of him, flesh to flesh. Her nipples swept his chest electrifying them further, waves of energy encircled them, making them one. Juli sighed with bliss; then as the sexual tension built, their mating dance began and all thought, except for pleasure, disappeared.

CHAPTER NINETEEN

Juli woke to peace and quiet. Her eyes roved around the room; it was small like the rest of the house. Rich had designed it as if it was a boat with very clever built-ins. The head of the bed nestled against a shelf with a drawer at each side. In one corner was a triangle-shaped shelf built to hold a computer or serve as a desk. A room, really a closet, which led to the bathroom, held shelves with baskets for clothing and extra linens and a small stacking washer and dryer. Generous sliding windows had been positioned to encourage a cross draft of healthy ocean air. She gazed out of the window on the water-side of the little cabin to see the dock swaying gently, nudged by the ocean.

It was so peaceful she felt like she had dreamed the wolves. She knew she hadn't. If she was going to live here she would have to learn a new skill set; most of what she needed for city survival didn't apply. She needed time to think. She had one more day and night with Rich, then she had to head back.

Rich must have heard her stir as he appeared in the doorway, smiling with two steaming hot chocolates. She smiled at him, struggled to a sitting position, patted the bed beside her for him to sit, and held out her hands to take a cup. He eased on the bed, "Hi beautiful," and kissed her cheek. They chatted about their adventures and sipped the sweet hot drinks.

Much, much later, after passionate sex followed by a deep nap, Juli woke to dusk. What had woken her? The cabin was ominously quiet. Rich should be breathing beside her. Where was he? Then she heard a choking sound. Her heart fluttered weakly and then pounded. She threw back the covers and raced to the door like a sprinter at the starting gun.

Rich was on the floor, on his back, unconscious. She hurried to him, flipping on the light switch as she passed it," Rich, Rich," she probed his mouth and rolled him on his side to clear his airway, while checking his carotid pulse. The pulse was weak, but palpable. His breathing was shallow. She grabbed a blanket off the bed and raced back to him, covering his chest and abdomen. Then he started to come to, moaning, "What happened?"

"Take it easy Rich you had a fall." He felt cold as a corpse and clammy. She slid her legs under his shoulders and cradled him in her lap feeling his scalp for lumps. "You have a bump on the back of your head."

"It hurts, too," came his harsh voice.

"You fainted." Her adrenalin was pumping so hard she could barely think. What made a healthy man faint? Her mind raced, seeking possible causes.

"More than a faint. It was so fast. My ears started ringing, that's the last I remember."

Stroke? Myocardial Infarction? Dehydration? Juli sifted diagnoses through her doctor brain, which had started to work. "Vagal Inhibition! That's what it was. Your blood pressure must have been way too low, causing the vagus nerve to shut everything down on you."

"Whatever it was I hope it never happens again. I don't remember hitting the floor."

His head was in her warm lap. "You could have been killed. Oh Rich I have just found you. I don't want to lose you. If you had hit your head on something hard . . ." Juli's hands shook as she rocked Rich's head and shoulders. She tucked the blanket around his shoulders. He tried to struggle up. "Let's stay still until you feel stronger." Juli sat on the floor with him gazing at his face lovingly. His pulse was stronger. His skin felt warmer. As she held him she eliminated diagnoses, one by one, and focused on his meds.

Gradually Rich got up to sit in a chair. Juli checked his blood pressure which was low, as they suspected. "Rich we have to get these meds sorted out."

Head in his hands, elbows on the table his quiet voice said, "I think I'm so relaxed off work and around you that the meds are over kill."

"Let's monitor you for the next twenty-four hours. And see if we can figure out what's going on. What meds did you take today?"

"This morning twenty-five mgs of hydrochlorothiazide and ten mgs of ACE inhibitor."

"How long have you been on that routine?"

"About a month, except for a few days on our kayak trip. I kept thinking the BP was stress and would go away with a good night's sleep . . . but of course it didn't. Finally last month I went to see Bill Holland in Campbell River. He's an internist. He told me to take the drugs regularly for three months and then see if the BP was controlled. Well he and I didn't reckon with the *Juli Effect.*"

"I think he's right considering how you spiked right up with three hours of work. And then there's your family history." Juli thought for a few minutes reviewing data in her grey cells. "But maybe the dose is too high. Why don't we phone Bill and get his opinion?"

"Good idea." He glanced at the clock on the stove, "It's eight pm so he'll be home. I have his number. It's on my desk." Rich waved vaguely. "He won't mind the late hour. But we shouldn't do this very often."

Juli got the number and dialed it. A man answered, "Bill Holland speaking."

"Hi, sorry to bother you but we have a bit of a problem. I'm Juli Armstrong. I'm with Rich Thompson and we need your opinion." She sounded breathless and nervous.

She handed the phone to Rich and he described what happened to Bill and told him Juli was a doctor too. After a number of answers Rich handed the phone back to Juli. He sagged in the chair and closed his eyes.

"Hi, it's Juli again." She listened and then responded, "Yes he was definitely unconscious, slow heart rate. The lump is like a goose egg. He landed on a wooden floor so I think he has a little concussion but no subdural bleeding." She paused to listen, "Yes, yes. Can we call you tomorrow?" Pause, "Thanks. Sorry about the late call. Yes, thank you. Talk to you again soon."

Juli hung up and looked at Rich; he was sleeping with his head on the table. "Rich, Rich wake up." He stirred and groaned. "I'm going to help you back to bed." Gently she helped him to his feet, and shoulder in his arm pit, arm around his waist, she slowly guided him back to bed, almost carrying him to the bedroom. He was only wearing his boxer shorts, so she covered him lightly with a blanket. He opened his eyes and gazed at her lovingly, "Thanks."

She decided to wake him every hour or so all night to be sure this wasn't a subdural. She was well rested and glad to do that for him. She hadn't eaten since lunch, so she went to the small kitchen and made herself a cheese sandwich and a glass of milk. Then she pulled on her stretch pants and a t-shirt and went back to Rich. He looked so vulnerable, so pale. Tears dripped from her eyes; she didn't want to lose this man. Juli sat in the chair staring out at the water for a long time. Finally, her decision made, she tumbled into bed next to Rich and slept, knowing she would wake soon to check on the man she felt so close to she could not conceive of life without hm.

CHAPTER TWENTY

As they sat at the table enjoying their morning hot chocolate the bright summer sun sparkled on the wavelets in the bay. Juli said, "I am not leaving without you. We have to work together to sort these meds out." Fleetingly she asked herself if she wanted that responsibility. Was she kidding, she got way more out of this relationship than she put in. Well that was not quite right. It had been quite equal, until now. The BP incident was a small blip in what she thought was going to be a life-long commitment. She loved this man, everything about him, how he smiled, the color of his hair, the ripple of his muscles, the way he looked at her with sincerity, his wit, his intelligence, his snoring at night. "I'll stay today and we can travel Sunday together."

"Juli you don't have to do that. I'll be okay." He smiled weakly.

"Rich I've been searching for you all my life. I'm not taking any chances now. Please let me do this."

335

"I think its overkill. My BP is stable. I'll be fine here."

"Rich, come with me," she begged. She had to go back but she also wanted to keep an eye on him and help to get this BP sorted out.

"I'd get restless in the city."

Rich you might like Victoria. It's not like Vancouver." Her mind raced. It would be the second phase of their relationship. They knew the sexual attraction was better than good, so now they could try the early-living-together phase. Once they reached the one-hundred-percent-commitment phase they could consider the time-to-start-a-family phase. There she went again, over-thinking everything.

"I might be willing to try it. Unfortunately right now I feel over loaded and confused by my work and health problems. I need more time." He smiled at her sadly, "I'm not ready to leave Cortes."

"You don't have to, come for a visit."

"No I don't think so. I need to stay here." He stared at his hands.

She leaned against him, burying her face in his chest, sucking in the male smells. "Rich please come," she begged again. She wanted him desperately, wanted to be with him 24/7, wanted to be there if he collapsed again.

He held her gently as if he was comforting a child, "Not this time. I need to think. To sort out my life. Come up on your next four days off."

Juli had sensed this coming. It had been too perfect. She had felt him pulling back several times, but she ignored it as she desperately wanted to be with him, more than with any other human being. She felt whole with him. A voice inside her whispered, *let him go Juli. Remember if you hold grains of sand in your hand, the tighter you squeeze the more they spill out.* She was positive that deep down he wanted to be with her. They would find a way for both of them to be happy. "Rich I understand. I don't like it but I understand. I love you and I always will. I'll be back as soon as possible."

He smiled and kissed the top of her head as though thanking her. She felt the change, no passion, and knew their relationship needed time, like a peach growing and plumping on a branch needed time to gain color and flavor and tenderness. She would, albeit reluctantly, return to Victoria alone.

Rich sipped his hot chocolate and leaned back in his chair. Emotions flitted across his eyes, fear of losing Juli, and worry about his own health. Then the wrinkles around his eyes relaxed, as though her reaction had reassured him and convinced him even more strongly that she was the woman for him. Rich squinted to the East, "I hope that rain cloud hangs over our island and dumps its load."

"It was there when we woke. I saw it right away." Juli heard the warmth in his voice and felt love welling up from deep inside her. Rich was a good man, trying his best, which was very, very good. She loved him even more for taking a stand against her; she didn't want to share her life with someone who wasn't honest.

He turned to look deep into her eyes and though he said "It's summer and usually we go for weeks without rain. I hope the fires at Princess Louisa are under control," he really was saying *I love you very much Juli.*

"You love this island," she stated as her eyes caressed him.

He continued to peer deeply into her eyes, "I do . . . and the people that live here. They're real."

She had only met the bunch at the clinic and if they were a sample of the people of this island she liked them too. Juli leaned across the table and he bent forward so that their lips touched. Suddenly, the sexual spark was there again, in full overwhelming force. Warm waves of sensation poured through her body. Giggling and trying to keep their lips connected, they wiggled free of the table into a full body hug. Rich murmured, "So that means we have a whole day in front of us with no plans." Juli giggled again feeling like the lid to a candy box had opened, "I wondered when you would figure that out." They easily slipped out of their night clothes and, lips still clinging, they glided to the bedroom and, as the kiss deepened, fell onto the bed in a jumbled heap of limbs. Each time was fresh. It surprised Juli that her body was so finely tuned to his. She was like a violin and he was the master who could make her sing.

Later that day Juli organized what she would take with her, leaving her foul weather gear hanging by Rich's door. Her backpack was half full.

"Good idea to leave that gear here. I'll keep it safe. Better than that I'll cherish it and each time I pass it I'll know you're coming back." His eyes caressed her lovingly. "Now that I've found you I don't want to lose you." He pulled her close, wrapping his arms around her, cradling her, breathing in her fresh scent, and lowered his lips to brush hers. Prickles of delight spread through her lips to her throat. In a voice husky with passion he forced himself to continue, "I can take you to the ferry in the runabout in the morning. That's the easiest way."

His words were like gentle puffs of warm air delivering sensation and alerting her to his masculinity, "Most scenic too."

"Sure." His eyes were glued to the long fringe of eyelashes fluttering against her lush cheeks like a butterfly seeking honey. His tongue darted out to search for the sweetness.

Her hand against his strong chest she pushed back, feeling the solidness of his hands on her butt, and looked into his eyes glazed with sexual desire. She teased him by plodding on with the details. "Good, I'll walk on the ferry and then at Quadra I can pick up my car from the Herriot Bay Inn."

Rich kissed her neck and keeping his lips against her he murmured in a husky voice, "I phoned Tom and he'll arrange to pick up his double kayak."

"I thought it was yours, Rich."

Now he nibbled and sucked on her ear, "No, but I plan to buy one. I enjoyed that trip a lot."

Juli could barely think as her body was so charged by his ministrations. Raggedly she continued, "We could buy one together and use it in the Victoria area too." Rich nodded but said nothing. He lifted her easily into his arms and, lips still locked in an intense exchange of hormonal messages, growling deep in his throat he carried her to the bedroom.

After lunch the day passed slowly with Juli savoring every second. She lay on the dock watching the ocean swirl as it bounced off the rocks. Rich had chosen a beautiful protected spot for his home. It was an oasis, a safe and quiet retreat from the world. She was rested and renewed and ready to return. She was in far better shape than when she arrived.

Rich appeared behind her, "How bout we go for a swim at the lagoon. The ebb is pulling the warm water out right now."

"Over beside Manson's?"

"Yah."

Juli rolled over, "You seem to have recovered from your fall."

"My headache is gone and I feel fine," he smiled his reassurance.

"Guess we need swim suits, lucky thing I happen to have one."

He offered her a hand and pulled her upright, then gave her a quick kiss and slapped her bum as she pranced off to get ready. When she reappeared in her spandex black one piece racing suit he declared, "Wow, that suit looks like it was painted on you."

"It's a little thin isn't it, but that's what's in the stores."

"I'm not complaining." He swept her in his arms and kissed her thoroughly.

"Rich remember we're on our way for a swim."

"It's not compulsory." He teased the strap off her shoulder.

"Rich, c'mon the exercise will do us both good." She took his hand and pulled him toward the door.

Rich followed her to the runabout, put in the oars, and rowed the short distance to the lagoon. As predicted the water poured out the narrow neck bringing warm crystal clear water from Manson's lagoon into the Bay. As the sun-warmed water washed over them, they swam right at the opening enjoying the challenge of swimming against the current. Seagulls squawked as silvery minnows slithered back to the sea. "Are there any big fish in the ocean behind us, waiting to gobble us up?"

"Probably, stay here in the shallows."

"You bet I will." Juli rolled over on her back. The sun beamed heat on her face and harmless white puffy clouds hovered overhead; the breeze had cleared away the smoke haze from Princess Louisa. "Rich this is like Hawaii."

"Not quite, but I know what you mean. It's pretty special."

When they were exhausted they headed back to his home. Juli flopped on the couch and was instantly asleep. Rich stood in the doorway for a long time soaking in her beauty.

CHAPTER TWENTY-ONE

Juli woke to the patter of rain on the roof, a firefighter's dream come true. She peered out the window to see grey, the sky and ocean blended together to give the illusion of great depth and no depth at the same time. She peered harder, circular ripples appeared on the mirror-still ocean with each drop blending and flattening as it joined its neighbor. Juli felt the cool air on her bare shoulders and sliding slowly under the covers she rolled closer to Rich. The heat of his body encouraged her. So she stretched full length beside him, feeling his welcoming response.

Out of the corner of her eye she noted it was seven am, the ferry left at nine fifty. They had lots of time. She snuggled in beside Rich. He was cozily warm and smelled good. She nibbled on his chest and throat. He groaned. Suddenly like a whale bursting out of the ocean he jerked up and grasped her with his strong arms. "Got you."

Juli laughed. "Rich stop. I'm goin' to Victoria today. C'mon don't tickle me." She rolled off the bed and in one smooth motion stood and pulled him upright. He smiled, "You started this; I'll finish it."

She giggled like a teenage girl caught admiring a handsome man, "Rich I teased you and I'm truly sorry. We have to go. The ferry waits for no one."

He groaned like a beached whale, "Too bad. I'll take a rain check."

Then, as a smooth team they dressed, ate breakfast, packed her lunch, and loaded the runabout. As Rich skillfully guided the runabout past the Gorge, through Uganda Pass and into Whaletown the sun broke through the clouds; the brief rain had disappeared. There was no dock near the ferry so he ran the boat up on to the beach. Sand and rocks grated against the metal hull as they ground to a stop. Juli flung her arms around him clutching him as if she never wanted to let go. He set her back on the seat, "Juli I'll phone and text, time will fly. You have to go now." His voice was calm but filled with regret and longing.

Tears blurred her vision as she shrugged on her backpack, smiled a weak good bye. Reluctantly she climbed out of the boat and stumbled up the beach and on to the bush-lined path. He didn't go with her but his eyes did, absorbing everything about her – lithe figure, bouncing curls, and a last wave from the top of the hill. From the boat he could see her running the last few yards to make it on the ferry. Rich waved at the various crew members who all smiled at him calling, "Hi doc."

The ferry was small and utilitarian. The open car deck held about thirty cars, which would be exposed in the winter storms as the waves washed over the open deck. Now the sky was lightening with great patches of pale blue among the rain-filled clouds. The cars clanked on the metal ramp behind her, filling the car deck orderly and quickly. The mighty engine throbbed, churning white water as it held the ferry tightly to the dock.

Juli struggled with the heavy metal door to the upper levels, the ships first defense against water. The steep narrow stairs ended at another heavy door, which she pulled open. The smell of coffee and scrambled eggs hit her as she passed the crew's lunch room. Passing part way down the length of the ship, through another heavy door, identical steep stairs, another heavy door and she was on the passenger deck. Plastic benches and a rose-colored brown lino floor provided a nondescript background for the view out the large windows on three sides. On a sunny day it was possible to stand outside near the stern railing, but today she stayed inside. If Rich had been here he would be greeting and being greeted by everyone. Juli sat facing the bow, sadness blurring her vision, while the sapphire ocean stretched all round.

At Heriot Bay on Quadra Island she walked off the ferry and turned down the dusty side road to the hotel. Tom waved to her from pub entrance; she waved back and walked right to him. "Hi Juli. Good to see you." He gave her a bear hug, warm and supportive. "Sorry we had to leave you."

"Don't give it another thought. Rich was a great guide." Juli blushed and Tom raised his eyebrows but said nothing. "Yak is okay. Rich has it at his place." She knew this was high season for him.

"Thanks, I got the phone message. I'll take the ferry over tomorrow and paddle back. I've got another group coming through on the weekend. So I'll need it by then."

"Rich might be able to tow it over, but you and he can work that out."

"Thanks for your concern Juli. Rich told me a bit about what happened with the wolves. Are you still shaken up?"

She wondered how much he knew and blushed "I never was very afraid. Rich loaded our supplies in the kayak before he went to sleep. I guess he had a premonition."

"He's used to reading nature's warnings."

"So when the wolves woke him, he hustled me right into Yak and we paddled like the devil was chasing us, for indeed he was. The big black wolf was swimming behind us. And growling."

He hugged her again. "I'm so glad you're safe." In a voice husky with emotion he said, "Come along and have a coffee and tell me about your adventures. The wolves were beyond scary." So they sat on the deck in the warm sunshine overlooking the marina. Juli had tea and a crunchy clubhouse sandwich to fortify her for the long drive ahead of her. Finally after thanking Tom for the delicious food caches and the great kayak, she made her goodbyes.

The tears stayed away as she drove across Quadra and waited at Quathiaski cove for the ferry heading for Campbell River. However, as the ferry pulled out she slumped in the driver's seat and sobbed as though her heart was breaking and it was. She felt abandoned and alone. Nothing consoled her, not the gentle rocking of the boat, not the golden sunshine which seemed dim without Rich, not the thought of returning to her own home in Victoria. It was as though a piece had been torn out of her heart. It would need time to heal; maybe it would be one of those wounds that refused to heal. She hoped so for she believed that the missing piece was lodged in Rich's heart, waiting to return to her. She couldn't believe she was thinking in soppy metaphors, but she was.

Robot-like she drove home and unloaded the car. All joy and ability to notice things around her were gone. She entered her condo, no rush of peace and comfort to greet her. She wandered into the master suite thinking she could easily replace the queen-sized bed with a king. A dressing room which held all her clothes in layered wire baskets and full width clothes cupboards could be expanded and still leave the bedroom spacious without dressers and clutter. The dressing room was a walk-through to a luxurious bathroom with a white rectangular tub and separate shower, which were joined as one unit and set against the right wall; a small linen closet stored towels and extra bedding, and on the left wall a vanity with two smoky granite sinks and a full-width mirror provided ample room for two. All was brightened by a tall narrow window through which, if she leaned out, she could glimpse the ocean, and when it was open and she was in the tub, she could smell the salt air. A large skylight over the window allowed her to see the sky in the day and twinkling stars at night and the occasion seagull on its way to the marina. She could easily share this space with Rich.

Still aching for him she unpacked, did a load of wash and settled into a hot tub. Still unable to relax she aimlessly scrubbed her skin and then admired her tanned legs. The phone rang. She jerked out of the tub, wrapped herself in a towel, and grabbed her phone, "Hello"

"Juli." It was his voice, deep, reassuring, a piece of her heart healed and throbbed with joy.

"Rich." She listened to his breathing as she knew he would be listening to hers. She carried the phone to her bedroom and lay on the bed wrapping the soft comforter around her nude wet body.

"You're safe."

"Sure, I took it easy. The drive was slow; I got in the right hand lane in the parade of cars. There were campers and trucks, lots of cars filling the double-lane highway. Nanaimo was slow as molasses in January but then it was easy going until after Duncan. The Malahat, as you know, is always slow and dangerous, as it winds through that small range of mountains separating the south island." She knew she was babbling and he didn't interrupt her. He, she hoped, was as hungry for her voice as she was for his. "How's it going up there?"

"Fine," his voice was low and sexy. "No wolves. And all our car accident victims are back home. "

"Good to hear that." She hated to bring him back to everyday but she had to know. "Your BP?"

"That's staying steady too." He cleared his throat as if he was shifting gears, "I'm taking it easy and puttering around here. My garden was a shambles so I spent two hours weeding and fixing the bird netting over the blueberries."

"Poor birds, they're hungry."

"You're a softy." Then his voice changed again this time to a serious tone, "Juli I miss you. I see your face everywhere. Smell your scent in the house, on the sheets. I may not wash them . . . ever."

She hugged the phone tightly. If she could, she would shoot down the line and land with a smack in his arms. "Whoa. . . I'm coming back in three weeks . . . they better be clean."

"Can you really make it in three weeks?" His voice sounded so grateful that she wanted to reassure him.

"I'll put in four or so extra shifts. They're flexible." To a point, she could be replaced. She didn't like that thought, as she counted on it for her income and didn't want to disturb that.

"When can you come?" he asked eagerly.

"How about Saturday the 28th?"

"Perfect."

"Great that's settled. I had a call on my answering machine from Marigold; she wants to do lunch. She's worried about Dave."

"What's that about?"

"I'm not sure and I'm not saying anything to anyone but you. Before my holiday I noticed that he was flitting in and out of the center, and rumor had it that he was weird – apparently not seeing patients and checking and rechecking everyone's time sheets. The office manager was glad he was going on holiday. She hoped the rest would settle him down."

"And did it?" His voice sounded concerned.

"You saw him at the restaurant . . . fidgeting and being inattentive."

"Well sort of, I thought he was an obsessive kind of guy."

"More obsessive recently. Something's going on. He's back tomorrow. I'll see what he's like."

"Good idea."

"I'll have to check on him before I see Marigold. I'm going in tomorrow for an afternoon shift. Dave will be back in the morning. I'll see what he's like. Thinking back I realize Marigold kept trying to get me alone, so I guess she was concerned then. I'm sorry now that I didn't take more time with her, but I was so buzzed from our relationship I couldn't think about her. I'll see her soon."

"Good luck. It's tricky at any time to wonder about a fellow professional, but doubly so when he is your boss and friend." His voice was like a massage, relaxing and soothing all the cells in her body.

"Yah. I'll be careful." They talked for a while longer, both reluctant to end the call.

CHAPTER TWENTY-TWO

August 12th Juli slid into the high-backed booth in a secluded area at an Oak Bay pub. It was clear that Marigold wanted extra privacy. Even though it was noon, the ambiance was dark with brown paneled walls, dark wood floors, low flickering fireplace flames, and muted lighting and sound. Marigold, wearing a black fleece jacket with a powder pink t-shirt showing at the unzipped neck, stood to welcome her and gave her a desperate hug that was so tight Juli gasped for air. Juli's antennae shot up: Marigold wanted to discuss Dave, and as she was her best friend this was fraught with problems.

Marigold smiled as they chatted about Juli's trip down island and Rich's health. "We left Dream Seeker at the marina."

"You left your boat up there."

"Certainly, it's a safe place and close to Desolation Sound."

"Did you take the float plane?" Juli leaned closer eager to hear the answer.

"Affirmative. It was dead simple: the plane landed in Gorge Harbor, picked us up on the dock close to Dream Seeker, and dropped us in the Inner Harbor here in Victoria. We took a cab home. Totally beautiful . . . effortless." She touched Juli's arm, "That's what you should do."

"What a good idea. I'll check into it." Was this a solution to her commuting problem? Just then the waitress in a short plaid skirt arrived for drinks orders. Tea for Juli; coffee for Marigold. Finally Marigold could hold back no longer. "Juli I feel I know you and can trust you." Then she blurted, "I'm worried about Dave." Tears welled up in her eyes.

"What seems to be the trouble? Juli asked cautiously.

Marigold leaned forward and in a confidential whisper said, "I'm not sure. I thought our holiday would make everything right, but it didn't."

Juli shifted into her professional persona, "Whoa, please start from the beginning."

"Juli it started about three months ago now." A tear ran down her cheek and plopped on her t-shirt. "We've been married twenty years and we had a wonderful loving relationship. But now," she sobbed, "everything has changed."

"So you were happy in the relationship until a few months ago." Juli decided to use her counselling techniques and stay as objective as she could.

Sob, "Yes. He's away from morning till late. At first I thought he had a lover. But now I don't think so. He says he's working. All I know is he seems muddled, can't make simple decisions like which restaurant to go to or whether to take the car for servicing or not. He worries about everything, obsessing over little things. And after years of great sex now our sex life is pitiful – actually, nonexistent."

Lack of sex, indecisive, obsessive thinking. What else? "Is he sleeping okay?"

"Most night only three to four hours, but if he drinks and passes out then maybe six hours."

Juli couldn't tell her about the complaints from work but she could help her try to sort this out. "So he's changed in the past few months and you notice he's not sleeping normally."

"Oh Juli," Marigold put her hand over her mouth as though she was trying to keep from screaming "I'm so afraid," she leaned across the table and whispered. "I found a bottle of diazepam in his pocket before we went on holidays."

Juli's eyes widened. This could be serious; he's anxious and treating it himself with diazepam. "You think he's taking them?"

"I don't want to, but I do because of the way he is calm for short periods." Marigold nodded and sniffed. The waitress appeared with their tea and coffee and asked for their meal order. Juli responded easily, "fish and chips and a large Caesar salad to share." Smiling, the waitress disappeared again to do their bidding.

Juli continued in a hushed voice, "That would explain some of his behavior. But why would he do that, risk his health?" She was thankful at least that Marigold hadn't said he was suicidal, but she had to ask, "Do you think he might harm himself or someone else?"

"No, nothing like that. I'm so worried. I don't know what's going on." Marigold's face looked stricken as though there had been a death of a loved one.

Juli took her hands in hers and look directly into her eyes. "Marigold this isn't the end of the world. I'm not sure . . . it sounds like he's anxious and trying to treat it with the diazepam. But we need to ask him. My theory is that he has low serotonin levels, which probably means a clinical depression, with the symptom of anxiety and obsessive behavior. Also we have to consider an addiction to tranquillizers. Both can be treated."

"He won't go for treatment." Marigold leaned away squeezing her eyes shut.

"If you and I team up and approach him he'll capitulate." Juli squeezed her friend's hands. Marigold sighed with relief. "How do we do this?"

"You and I will meet with him and get his agreement."

She wrung her hands, "I don't want him to hate me."

"I can't guarantee anything, but you two have been deeply in love for years. I'm sure that's still there, hidden by the depression." There the word was out again: depression. Dave needed treatment.

Marigold smiled hopefully. She and Juli would make a strong team.

That weekend, away from the office and in the privacy of their home, the two woman met with Dave and explained their concerns. At first he was defensive and claimed they were over reacting. But Juli and Marigold stood strong and united. Finally Dave softened saying, "I don't think I have a problem but if it'll keep the two off my case, I'll go to Paul Banks. In fact I'll phone him at home and go to see him today." Marigold looked at Juli and nodded; Juli nodded back, knowing Paul as a careful and knowledgeable psychiatrist.

For Juli the days settled into a pattern with long hours of work and wonderful long talks on the phone before bedtime with

Rich. His bass voice alone was enough to stimulate her hormones; she knew because her voice got husky, and tingling blood raced through her body. She lived for those phone calls. Usually she called him as he was always home unless of course he was out sailing or fishing. If she hadn't phoned him by ten PM her smart phone would vibrate letting her know he was impatient to hear about her day. She was glad to share the burden of her work and get a second opinion about some of her patients. The joy of sharing with a loving partner made her glow. Everyone commented on her appearance.

CHAPTER TWENTY-THREE

On the 24th of August Juli had her first visit with Marigold since Dave had seen the psychiatrist. Marigold welcomed her with open arms into her beautiful waterfront home: The whole house was various shades of grey with splashes of color. Juli liked it as she was into grey and minimalism lately. *Keep it simple* was her mantra. She gazed out the floor-to-ceiling window at the sun glistening on the wavelets. In a storm the ocean would roar and splash beneath the cantilevered rooms; Juli wondered if living in a house perched over the ocean was a good idea; Dave and Marigold liked living here; Juli much preferred Rich's cabin and rickety dock in the relative calm of Manson's Bay.

Juli knew that on the lowest level Marigold had a studio with north windows so she could paint in pure light. The east part of the studio was used for clay work with benches and storage and a kiln. Marigold spent some part of each day there sculpting. She loved the terracotta color of the Vashon red clay, which when fired brought her figures alive.

But now Marigold, still concerned about Dave, hugged Juli gratefully. "Juli thanks so much for helping me. Dave's started on antidepressants and seems calmer. I worried the first few days, he seemed desperate. He even cried and begged me to let him have the diazepam . . . he begged me. You would have been proud of me: I was sympathetic . . . but firm that he had to do what Paul recommended."

"Good for you Marigold. That's the kind of support he needs." Juli hugged her friend. "Once he gets over the initial problems with the antidepressant the main effects will settle in. It's a serotonin uptake inhibitor; however, he'll still have to have counselling to work through some of his anxieties and why he succumbed to the temptation of tranquillizers. As physicians we have ready access to many drugs and we are duty and morally bound to handle them judiciously." Juli sounded moralistic and hated that; so she softened toward her friend, "Marigold he's going to be okay. We helped him in time. And you're going to get your husband back."

Marigold's eyes filled and she sniffed. "I hope you're right. I don't know what the future holds but I do know we're on the right track." Suddenly her voice sounded stronger, "Last weekend he stayed home for the first time in months and we actually cuddled before bedtime. Juli I love him so much I want to protect him from all pain. But I can't." She dabbed her eyes, "Now that it's out in the open it seems so much better. So enough about Dave and me. Come sit down and tell me all about your life. I have appreciated your support; I couldn't have gotten this far without you."

Juli plopped onto the comfortable couch glad to be off her feet. It was seven pm and the end of a long day at the clinic. It had been a weird day with a flood of sore throats and leisure-time injuries. "Rich is fine. . . wonderful. I'll tell you all the details but first can I have a cup of tea and let's order some take-out food. I'm starving."

"What do you feel like? Thai? Chinese? Italian?"

"No hot noodles. I've been off spicy foods lately." She yawned and sagged back on the couch, "Maybe a pizza, no pepperoni." Her eyes closed and her face sagged with fatigue.

"Pizza it is, no pepperoni," Marigold dialed as she watched Julia and placed their order. As she hung up the phone Juli jumped up to make the tea. She staggered and flopped back on the couch in a faint. Marigold hovered over her, "Juli, Juli are you alright?"

Juli opened her eyes, "That was strange It happened at the clinic yesterday, too. My blood pressure must be too low."

"You fainted," soothed her voice. "Stay there. I'll make the tea. You must be dehydrated and maybe starved."

"Yes, yes, that's it. I'll help." Juli struggled to a sitting position.

"I insist . . . lie down." Juli allowed herself to be eased back on the couch. Marigold checked her pulse, the rate was fast. Marigold, tutting her concern, disappeared to boil the water. She called from the kitchen, "Juli did you eat today?"

"I didn't have time. Just nibbled. I felt a little nauseated, like a touch of the flu." She rested back on the couch noticing that she felt slightly nauseated again.

Sticking her head outside the kitchen Marigold asked softly, "Now don't get mad at me . . . but is your period late?"

Juli shook her head. "I don't think so." She blushed. "No way . . . not that . . . not possible." Then she went silent. Swiftly calculating: her last period started on the 20th of July, this was the 24th of August; therefore as she was usually twenty-eight days, she was due for a period August 17th or 18th. Out loud, "Marigold, I'm six or seven days late . . . that's nothing to worry about. You know that."

"I know nothing. You fainted that's enough for me." She called over her shoulder as she headed for the bathroom, "I have a pregnancy test kit that I used last year for my niece who was visiting. Luckily it came up negative; she was only seventeen and not at all prepared to support a baby." As she calmly sauntered back she said, "I can see by your face you're not surprised - so something did happen on the trip."

Juli nodded slowly and blushed.

"Okay, okay don't tell me yet." Marigold eased to Juli's side holding out a plastic cup. "Let's check first. Pee in this container; young women faint for one main reason."

Juli laughed, then seeing Marigold's face she said, "You're serious. I'll pee; you'll see." *Please God don't let there be any HCG in my urine.*

Marigold nodded. "You still haven't told me about the trip."

"I will, I will," promised Juli on her way to the bathroom.

Marigold called after her, "My intention worked, didn't it? Rich seemed healthy to me, obviously he was sexy, and as a doctor potentially wealthy. Those were the three things I asked the universe for."

Juli grunted from the bathroom.

Together they tested the sample. Juli held the cup of urine with shaking hands while Marigold held the pregnancy strip vertically so that arrows were pointing down and carefully dipped the test strip into the urine sample for three seconds. Juli held her breath as Marigold laid the test strip on a flat surface to wait for the color band to appear. Juli slipped into her doctor mode: "The time taken for display of results directly depends upon the concentration of HCG - human chorionic gonadotrophin hormone . . . the developing embryo uses it to maintain fetal viability by preventing the disintegration of the corpus luteum of the ovary and thereby maintaining progesterone production."

"Yes Juli. Take a deep breath and watch with me."

Juli sucked in a deep breath. Time stood still. Was this really her life? Was this really possible? She flashed back to the lake and knew if she was, that was when it happened; or, maybe that wonderful picnic at Shark Spit. Otherwise they had been very careful about using condoms, well pretty careful. How careful can you be when you're having sex many times a day for days on end? On one hand she felt excited about possibly having a baby, as she wanted one before she got any older. On the other hand, she wasn't married, not living with Rich, and not sure about her own body. As a doctor she knew how many things had to go right to achieve a healthy mother and baby.

"Look at that," whispered Marigold her voice in total awe, "two faint bands in the control and test areas."

Juli stared. It couldn't be right. "Test it again."

The next strip looked positive too. Marigold stared at her, mouth open.

"This can't be true," protested Juli. "This can't be true. I'll follow it up with a blood test."

"Sure looks like you're good and pregnant."

"It can't be. Let's test it again."

"Sorry kid, it's been positive twice." Marigold patted her shoulder to comfort her as if she was a baby herself.

"There's no way it could be that easy. Some couples try for years before conceiving." Remembering Rich she smiled and felt the warmth of hormones spreading through her body. *No it can't be. I'm not ready. What will Rich say?* If it was true it must be because her egg was so eager to join with his sperm that it somehow assisted. Rabbits ovulate every time they have intercourse; maybe there was a bit of rabbit in her.

"Do a blood test," ordered Marigold sitting down and rubbing her forehead as if she was confused, "Well my friend I think you better tell me everything. What were you doing three weeks ago?"

She was a good friend and deserved to know some of the details, thought Juli. It would be a relief to tell someone. "Marigold I almost don't know where to start."

"Start at the beginning." She saw Juli look at the door. "Don't worry it's the pizza. I'll get it . . . and the tea. You put your feet up."

Juli sighed and slumped on the couch. Reality was beginning to sink in. Her life was changing and she had little control. Suddenly she felt like she was at the end of a whip traveling near the speed of sound. She shook her head trying to regain control and heard her own voice sounding strained and weak, "The kayak trip . . . I needed a holiday badly." She watched Marigold enter the room carrying a large pizza box. "You know most of it. You want the gory details?"

"You did need a holiday," agreed Marigold setting down the pizza boxes. The odor of cheese and tomato sauce enveloped Juli, making bile rise in her throat. "My god it might be right. I always used to love pizza." Marigold looked at her friend's pale face and suddenly the reality hit her: "Wow, Juli you're pregnant; you're going to be a mother. I'll be an aunt." She giggled, "Maybe Auntie Mame style."

Juli gulped, words flowed out of her mouth, "The guide and the other couple left the first morning. At first I thought the guide would come back, but he didn't. I should have insisted on returning, but you know how tired I was. I thought it would be a harmless little trip. I didn't like Rich; we argued about everything. I don't know what happened. It must have been the solitude, the wilderness. . ." her voice trailed off and she blushed remembering the nights.

Marigold smiled gleefully, "Or your hormones were exactly right."

"That too."

"One should never underestimate hormones." Marigold smiled broadly, "Once upon a time Dave and I were joined by hormones; I hope it'll happen again." Right now he didn't even smell right. Nonetheless she would remain steadfast, supportive, and hopeful that their relationship would come back.

"I know. I know. I walked or should I say paddled right into that." Juli nibbled at the pizza knowing she needed food, but still felt repulsed by the odor.

Marigold put her feet up and relaxed back on the sofa, suddenly confident Juli would handle her life and that Dave and she would work it out too. "So you spent two weeks with him. He knows about ovulation and pregnancy; he's not naive."

"We used a condom every time. .   . except once . . . maybe twice . .   . maybe three times."

Marigold laughed with joy for her friend. "That's all it takes for some people. Not for Dave and me, of course." And maybe that was a good thing, she thought considering how screwed up their life was now.

"We were really careful." They had used condoms, a lot of condoms. No one could have sex continuously and not expect Mother Nature to take advantage of that.

"Obviously. Sorry I didn't mean to be sarcastic." Marigold touched her friend's arm. "What will Rich say?" Marigold leaned forward biting into the hot pizza enthusiastically.

"I don't know. We never got much past the heavy breathing." Juli hesitated a long moment, "I think I can count on him."

"Sure you can. If he's a doctor, he's a responsible person. The little I saw of him over lunch at The Gorge he seemed super responsible to me. . . and handsome. You're fortunate to have found this wonderful man."

Juli shook her head and clamped her lips together. "Nonetheless . . . I don't plan to put this on him. . . I'll get a nanny."

Marigold shook her head, "She can't replace the blond curly hair, or the 6'4" with broad shoulders." She stood up abruptly, "You're not going to eat this pizza. I'm going to get you some plain old soda crackers."

"He is handsome." Juli giggled and smiled as she thought of Rich.

Marigold settled down beside Juli again offering her the crackers. "Yummy. This is sooo romantic . . . you and the handsome doctor in the wilderness."

Juli smiled at her friend's excitement. She was in a fantasy world, Juli was in the real one. "Yes he looks great, but that doesn't mean he wants to be a father. He's on leave because his health is bad; his BP ricochets up and down. I have to be prepared to do this on my own." Juli nibbled on a cracker.

"That's too bad. I'll help all I can," offered Marigold as she devoured the pizza. "You'll be okay working at the clinic until about eight months."

"Yes, for sure I'll keep working, and, and hire the nanny once the baby is born."

"Don't jump too far ahead. Send your energy to your babe; he's developing his nervous system now."

"My baby . . . ooh I like the sound of that." And she did. Mother Nature and her own natural tendencies made her feel warm and compassionate toward the babe. But she realized she didn't want Rich in her life if he wasn't fully committed to her and the babe. "I won't tell Rich until I see him. Maybe I won't tell him at all."

"Ah," she said gently. "Better rethink that."

Juli replied quickly, as though she was testing her friend, "Maybe I'll have a D&C and then there would be no baby."

"That's crazy think. Forget it. That's not an option." Marigold sat close to her, encircled her with her arms, and pulled her close. "I hate to tell you but you're getting old. This babe is right on time. This babe is precious."

Juli's breath caught in her throat as she realized Marigold was right. She leaned into Marigold's warmth. "Marigold," she cried as if her heart would break. "You're right and I want this baby one way or another, with Rich or without him. It's my decision." She felt her confusion disappearing. Deep inside, her confidence was increasing like a tiny stream growing into a mighty river.

"Here . . . eat a bit of pizza and here's your tea. Sip it and relax. You need some time to think about everything."

Juli chewed slowly, deep in thought. This was the 24th, and in four days she would be in Rich's arms again, feeling the heat of his lips. He would be delighted, he would move to Victoria and help raise their child or, she shuddered, he would refuse to become a parent and insist on an abortion. She would hate him for that. He wasn't like that. But he was having his struggles with his health. He might not feel able to assist her.

Marigold sat silently sipping her tea and watching the play of emotions across her friend's face. She offered her friend some pizza, "C'mon Juli try this. A little food is what you need."

"Maybe you're right." Juli nibbled on the crust again. No wave of nausea. She bit into the pizza which was feta cheese and tomatoes and something that looked like eggplant, she picked that off. However, the crust was crisp, the tomatoes full of flavor and the cheese salty. She ate with more interest than she had for several days.

Marigold smiled. "Tell me more about the trip. We saw you at Squirrel cove and the Gorge but we really didn't talk much. Tell me from the beginning please." She hoped if she got Juli to talk about the trip again it would help her work through her feelings about the babe and its father.

"It was incredible. I shared a double kayak with Rich. I hated him at first. He was so controlling . . . insisted on packing the kayak . . . and in being in the stern steering seat. Before the end of the first day I was glad he was doing everything, though I didn't let him know. I was tired and sore from paddling and the dripping salt water was eating into my skin." She rubbed her hands as though remembering the beating they took. "My hands were numb. We paddled from Harriot Bay to Read Island. The last hour or so we were fighting the tide, which was heavy going. I doubt I could have made it alone."

"So maybe the universe was taking care of you," soothed Marigold.

"We had to share a tent."

"You and, and him?" Marigold giggled, "Wow, is that when it started?" She leaned forward, eager to hear all the details.

"No, I was in pain and mad at him. The next morning when I struggled out of my drugged sleep, as he had given me analgesics in the night, everyone was gone but Rich."

"One night of pain and Richard becomes Rich."

"That's what he wanted to be called," Juli said trying to sound innocent. "As I was saying they were gone. The others were real novices, especially the wife, and they decided to call it quits, and since the ebb was early, that's when they left. I was pretty shocked."

"I can imagine. Why didn't you demand to go back?" Marigold had kicked off her shoes and was curled up in a comfortable chair near Juli.

"I thought of that but he looked so pathetic and he assured me he was a capable guide. And he needed a holiday . . . so did I."

Marigold laughed out loud. "Methinks the lady doth protest too much. C'mon tell me what happened next."

"Nothing happened and I didn't tell him I was a doctor and that I was as burned out as he. At that moment he was so understanding and he had been so caring in the night that I decided to take a risk and continue on. So that's what happened."

"More detail please," begged Marigold.

Juli giggled. "At every stop there was a cache of gourmet food - bacon, eggs, biscuit mix . . . and he caught a salmon. You would have laughed your head off - I did - if you had seen it flipping about in his lap in the kayak."

"My god you had fresh salmon and other great food." Marigold gathered up the remnants of the pizza and moved it to the kitchen. She returned quickly not wanting to miss a word. This trip was worth hearing about and she hoped Juli would get to the sexy part soon.

"And fresh oysters off the beach." Juli lounged back putting her feet up on the table.

"Yum, who cooked?" Marigold tucked a soft blanket around Juli's legs.

"He did. I did stuff . . . like help put up tents and start fires."

"Ah ha, when did the sparks fly, the hormones juice up?"

Juli laughed, "It took wolves to drive me into his bed . . . rather sleeping bag." Juli pulled the soft blanket Marigold had put over her up to her chin as she thought about those lean wolves.

"Wolves?"

"Yes coastal wolves, the kind that can swim thirteen kilometers in the ocean."

"Stop stalling," prodded her friend. "There's only one wolf I'm interested in. . .walks on his hind legs."

"Okay. Okay." Juli smiled, "We were sleeping under the stars on a small island when I heard a pack of wolves howling. I jumped into the sack with him and that was it. I had no thought but to survive."

"And survive you did."

"Marigold he's a great lover and considerate. But it was more than that, the trip was the most wonderful time of my life, watching shooting stars, swimming in fresh water lakes, watching herons and eagles, listening to the wind in the tree tops."

"And lots of good sex. Don't forget that."

"Yes for sure," Juli closed her eyes smiling with joy as she remembered their unions. Then her eyes popped open, "The most harrowing too."

"You mean the wolves?"

"Yah. I know I told you about it when we had lunch at the Gorge but I need to tell it again. When we were way down in Von Donlop Inlet wolves were prowling around. And finally, seconds before they attacked, we escaped in the kayak."

"That's awful. From ecstasy to hell."

"You got it."

"I would have been paralyzed with fear."

"My adrenalin hit and I moved like lightning. We paddled for hours, out Von Don, down Sutil channel, past Whaletown, and through Uganda Passage right to his cabin near Manson's Landing."

"So he took you to the safety of his cave."

"That's one way of looking at it. It's right on the water, tiny but comfortable. We stayed there to recover. By then he knew I was a doctor, I can't remember exactly when I told him . . . It was the car accident; that's when I told him. On our way to the health center I saw Dream Seeker at Manson's dock. Then you know what happened: I asked Dave to come."

"Yah . . . That was the first time I really saw his fear. I would have had to push him off the boat to get him to go with you."

"I was surprised he wouldn't come with Rich and me." She shrugged. "But I didn't really have   time to worry about it."

"It doesn't matter. He's getting back on track now. But you, you're a marvel. What a tale of adventure and romance! You've done so much in only weeks."

"I know. It seems like I've come alive. My life used to be like I was running under water, and now I'm swimming swiftly on the surface with the current." All the time they were talking Juli was relaxing on the couch. "I'm so tired and I have to work tomorrow. Help me up. I've got to go home."

Marigold assisted her friend to her feet and kept her arm around her waist as they walked to the door. "Now don't you worry Juli; everything's going to be alright for you and for me."

"I sure hope so."

CHAPTER TWENTY-FOUR

August 28th the morning of the day of her trip back to Cortes and Rich, Juli woke early and nibbled one of the soda crackers that she now always kept with her, and languidly rose from bed. Caressing her abdomen she whispered: "Dear baby, how are you today. Did you have a good sleep? I think so, you were so quiet you didn't bother me. But then you still are pretty tiny. What would you like for breakfast besides soda crackers? They settle me down but will never grow strong bones for you. How about a poached egg on toast? I can manage that surely but no coffee for me or you. Coffee makes me retch and I'm sure stirs up your little life. First we brush our teeth; you don't have teeth so really it's my teeth." Humming to herself Juli dressed in well-worn jeans and t-shirt and headed to the kitchen to nibble at toast and an egg. She knew not to gobble but to give her digestive system time to cooperate. Once she was sure the food would stay down, and as she had packed the night before, she grabbed her lunch from the fridge and her duffel bag from the floor, and she headed out the door. The drive up island was broken by several bathroom stops and one short nap in the car at Ladysmith.

The Campbell River ferry and the drive across Quadra were easy. Then as the ferry pulled away from Herriot bay she looked at the expanse of shimmering blue water and felt a deep relaxation fill her body as though she had settled into a tub of warm water. Her heart thumped slowly and strongly as she anticipated Rich's loving welcome. Sure enough he was waiting at the dock at Whaletown, pointing at the side parking and smiling, and waving. After she parked her car and retrieved her bag he grabbed her and lifted her off her feet and twirled her around. "Juli, Juli, Juli." Waves of love swept over her, enclosing her in a soft warm cloud surrounding and supporting her and Rich. It felt so right, as though her whole life had been leading to this point of warmth and comfort and safety.

Arm in arm they walked to his runabout pulled up on the beach. Juli tossed her knapsack into the boat and carefully followed it to the mid-ship seat, noticing the sun-warmed aluminum sides, while Rich pushed the boat off the beach and climbed carefully in over the bow, caressing her shoulder as he passed on his way to the outboard engine. The ocean was calm, clear and cold but swimmable if she so desired, which she didn't as she was intent on being with Rich. The motor started instantly with the first pull of the starter rope and they waved goodbye to the crew on deck of the ferry and headed out of Whaletown to Uganda Pass and Manson's. Seagulls squawked; an eagle perched at the top of a dead fir, watching for her opportunity to sweep in for a morsel. Juli breathed deeply, sucking in the energy of Mother Earth. The extremely low tide made Shark Spit lunge out from Marina Island seeming to block the pass. Rich carefully navigated between the red and green buoys, and as they passed the tip of the spit Juli watched the white sand bottom through the crystal clear water slide under them. On the Cortes side a regal blue heron stood in the shallow waters patiently waiting for a fish. The still ocean glistened like a small pond. Sun reflected off the surface and she was glad she was wearing her sunglasses. Rich smiled, leaned forward and put his hand comfortingly on her knee. In this fashion they skimmed along in his small boat heading for home. *Home*, she smiled with relief and happiness.

The dock and cabin were exactly as she remembered. As she opened the cabin door she breathed deeply infusing her body with the smell of cedar. Every muscle, every cell in her body relaxed and she collapsed on a kitchen chair smiling. "You look like the Cheshire Cat. What's going on?" asked Rich as he took the kettle off the wood fire stove and made tea.

"I'm happy; no, delighted; no, ecstatic to be here." She jumped up and flung her arms around him.

Much, much later as they lay side by side on the bed Juli said, "Rich I want to go back to Von Don. I loved it there and I think that by now the wolves have moved on."

"Yes I expect so. Good idea. We need to clear up that tent we left for the wolves. It would be the last trip of the year as the nights are getting cool. Yes, a great idea."

Juli didn't say, but that was where she wanted to tell Rich about the baby.

"We can be off first thing in the morning, however for the rest of this afternoon and evening I have plans for you." His blue eyes filled with emotion as he murmured deep in his throat, "I have plans." And grabbed her, pulling her toward him. She responded with a cooing sound and gentle nips on his chest.

CHAPTER TWENTY-FIVE

"This is Sutil Channel," shouted Rich, invigorated to be on their way. Once again he was in the stern steering the small motor and she was sitting amid-ships, with her back to the bow so she could watch him and be close to him. Juli sucked in a deep breath of fresh ocean air, knowing it was healthy and the life she wanted to lead. Rich grinned at her like a boy on a school holiday, totally at home in the runabout; she completely trusted his judgment on the water. She was beginning to depend on him.

"I know Sutil Channel, we paddled across here in daylight and down the middle in the dark," Juli shouted back. He was taking care of her again; she liked that feeling.

"Right," he shouted over the steady drone of the motor. "Once again we'll stay in the middle of the channel, the flow is north and will be strongest there."

Juli nodded and pointed above the forest, "Do I see rain clouds over there?"

"Maybe. But it hasn't rained more than a few drops all summer that was when you were here. Rain sure would be a blessing. The forests are dry," he shouted over the motor.

"I hope it holds off for two more days."

Rich shrugged as if it didn't matter to him.

As they arrived at the entrance to Von Donop Inlet the wind died and Rich turned their boat into the inlet, once again the quiet beauty filled her with peace. The rough rocks where the wolves had perched reminded her of their narrow escape; that seemed more like an adventure now not a nightmare. The water birds, a few cormorants and mergansers, splashed unconcerned.

"Oh no," cried Juli as they approached their camp: the tent they had to leave behind had collapsed and was in a pile looking like a garbage dump. They pulled up on shore, climbed out of the boat, and slowly made their way to their abandoned camp site. The desperate animals had torn the walls of the tent in their search for food, bits of fabric were strewn over the rocks.

Rich sighed, "I thought this is what we would find. I've brought garbage bags . . . here." He handed a couple to Juli.

Without speaking they worked their way through the debris. Her hands, thankfully enclosed in latex gloves that Rich had provided, were covered with dirt particles clinging like frightened children. Juli carried her full bag to the water's edge and Rich followed with his; then he unloaded the tent and their supplies. Together they carried everything up the gentle bank to the grassy camp site and set the tent up, piling the supplies and sleeping bags inside.

They looked at the desolation for many minutes. Juli whispered, "If we had been asleep we would have been eaten."

Rich hugged her, "I stayed on watch. We escaped. And from the looks of our camp site they were ferociously hungry."

"Do you think they'll be back?"

"I doubt it. If their den was close-by and they passed here often, we would see scat. I think they're far away."

Tears ran down her cheeks. Juli covered her face with her hands and sobbed as if her heart would break. What was going on with her? Why was she so upset? It had been a close call but they had escaped. They hadn't died. But still she felt a deep sadness.

Rich looked up from checking the tent pegs. "Juli come to me," he coaxed, opening his arms. She moved into their protection and felt safe. "Juli tell me what's going on."

"I don't know. Suddenly I feel sad." She heaved a great sigh.

This was coming from somewhere else, thought Rich. She had been helping him with his losses of his mom and his wife, and he realized he hadn't asked about hers. "Juli sweetheart, when have you felt like this before? Come, tell me." He sat down on a flat rock near the beach carrying her with him.

Juli felt comforted and safe. She nuzzled into his sweatshirt. "I don't know. Probably when dad left. Mom and I sat on the couch together and cried. I remember feeling terrified . . . as though my whole world was collapsing."

"So when your dad left you were scared."

"Yah, I wasn't sure we could live without him. And Mom seemed frightened too. And Mikey and Shirley were crying. I don't remember much after that. The pain came in flashes, like when mom was working and Mikey had a tantrum. Or if I was home with the kids and one of them had a fever."

"You felt sad and afraid. You had way more responsibility than you should have had for your age." He gently, lovingly smoothed her hair.

"I suppose so." She had felt sad and afraid.

"And it was lonely, maybe even embarrassing when you had no parent at school functions."

"I was a pretty sorry lonely little girl."

"That's how you felt. So feel it now. I'm here. It's safe."

Juli felt blackness sink over her. She shuddered but didn't shut it out as she usually did. Waves of fear and desperateness washed through her. Wave after wave. With Rich holding her it was safe so she let the waves of pain roar through her body like water breaking through a dam. She sobbed, "Dad why did you leave me. I wanted you to love me." She doubled up, with physical pain joining the emotional. Rich continued to stroke her hair gently. She sobbed and sobbed as though the pain would never go away. Then much to her surprise she felt warmth, only a very small wave. Then the black cloud began to thin out, letting small rays of light into her thoughts like a beautiful sunrise.

She became aware of Rich's warm chest and arms circling and supporting her. "Rich thanks for helping me through that. I knew it was sitting deep inside me and I have expended energy to keep it there. Thank you so much. I feel like a dam broke and released the sadness and fear. They just came gushing out of me. Now I feel vulnerable as though I'm a six year old starting again."

"Juli I'm grateful you shared this with me. I want you to know I think you were very brave and protected your siblings from a very lonely childhood."

"I did and I did it pretty darn well." She smiled tentatively still amazed at how light and whole she felt. She sniffed and sat back on her heels watching Rich gazing at her lovingly. "I'm okay now so we better get organized. C'mon let's fix our sleeping arrangements."

Once inside the tent Rich hugged her tightly saying, "Juli I missed you so much. Every day you were gone was like a week. I was bereaved." His hands ran over her body, his lips nuzzled her neck. She knew what he wanted. "You're even softer than I remembered."

"Rich let's talk a bit," she said as she gently pushed him away and settled on the open sleeping bag.

He straightened, "Oh what's up? Is this more about your dad?"

"Not exactly." How would she tell him? She didn't know how. She blurted out, "Rich I am softer."

"Of course you are. Juli cuddle up and tell me all about it." He pulled her close, smoothing her hair back gently. She put her face in his chest, sucking in the male smell of him.

He continued to smooth her hair. His fingers patient and loving, not intrusive or demanding.

"Rich I've made a mess of it." This was too soon. She had only known him a short time. She did know he was kind and competent and loved by the people of this island. Obviously he was glad to have her back, but he had his own health and work problems. She would tell him about the baby but she wouldn't expect him to do anything. *Wrong thinking.* This baby would be abandoned by its dad before it was born. She didn't want that. She wanted her child to have two parents.

"Tell me all."

"Rich I fainted at work." She held her breath waiting for his reaction.

"Fainted?" She felt his body tense. "Do you do that often?"

He sounded curious rather than concerned. That helped her feel calmer. "Never. . ." She gulped. "I told Marigold about it."

"Oh?"

"She made me . . . do a pregnancy test." She felt his breathing stop. What was he thinking?

His calm expression faltered and a muscle in his cheek twitched. His face went pale. His mouth opened and shut and she felt him stiffen as if he was afraid of what she might say.

"It was positive."

His eyes popped so wide open it was as if they would jump out of his head.

That took the wind out of his sails.

"Really." He continued to look at her as if she had turned blue right before his eyes. "Could be a false positive."

"Nope." She decided to continue with the reality lesson. "I followed up with a blood test to be sure. It's positive. I'm about four weeks pregnant."

He cleared his throat and croaked, "Four weeks."

She recognized his confusion and shock; she had been there. They were embarking on the greatest adventure of their lives without conscious planning. She didn't know about him, but she always planned everything, right down to her meal menu for the week and its grocery list. The universe had sent him to her; their pheromones had drawn them together; they were compatible and had fun together. Maybe this was written in the sand; maybe this was inevitable. She could feel him swallowing. She waited while he absorbed the news.

Suddenly he flushed. And then he started laughing so hard he flopped on the sleeping bag.

"What are you laughing about? This is serious." In her surprise and irritation Juli thought of turning away, dashing to the boat and leaving, but because of the gravity of the situation she could not. Instead she started to pound his chest.

Smiling like the cat who had eaten a bird he blurted, "Oh Juli my darling, it's wonderful." He jumped to his feet, grabbed her and twirled her around.

She blinked and pushed away. "I'm not so sure." His reaction had startled her. She thought he would be reserved and doubtful.

"Give me a kiss." He snuggled his lips against her soft neck.

She pushed him away again, albeit gently. "That's what got me in this mess in the first place."

"Don't worry. If you're pregnant, you can't get pregnant again. So no worries."

What was he talking about? Now her brain had gone numb. "Please be serious."

"I am serious." His smile had disappeared and he was peering into her eyes as if he was looking for something.

She couldn't stand it any longer and blurted her worst fear, "I don't want an abortion."

He pulled her tightly to his chest, his voice husky with emotion, "Don't even go there. There will be no abortion," he stated firmly. "This baby is too precious."

Juli started to sob, partly with relief that he wanted the baby and for joy that he thought it was precious too. "I was afraid you'd think I used you as a sperm bank."

"You did and it was a great idea." He watched her face intently.

"Of course not," she said out loud but a little voice in her head said, *Bingo*, that's exactly what happened. Juli admit it; you wanted a baby; Rich was an available male. She didn't like what she saw of herself even if that had been unconscious and hormone- driven. No that wasn't the whole story; there was more to their relationship. How much more? Enough to make a life together . . . to raise a child? She didn't know; there were no guarantees. The Zen of relationships, live in the now and the now was good. "Rich I didn't consciously plan this but I am glad I'm pregnant and I want this baby."

"This baby? My baby? Our baby!" He seemed relieved and was smiling broadly still.

"Yes our baby. I want you in my life but if this isn't your path say so." She had to give him an out; she wanted him to have a choice. Their relationship was important and they could work that out, right now the decision was about this baby.

"I couldn't be more pleased. I want a child and I want you to be his or her mother. I want us to be a family." He pulled her close, enfolding her in his warm strong arms. She sobbed for joy, wetting the front of his sweat-shirt. Carefully, as though she was a fragile vessel, he pulled her down beside him. The ocean stirred happily against the tiny beach and squirrels trilled, calling their mates. Soft murmurs came from the tent as they melded together into one and pledged their love.

Much later Rich looked thoughtfully at the dark clouds and then being extremely cautious he packed the runabout, which was pulled up above the tide line, with emergency supplies and their lifejackets, and covered everything with a tarp. Once it was dark it would be difficult to find anything. If they didn't need to leave in a hurry then he could take the supplies out in the morning. Satisfied, he entered their tent and fell deeply asleep. He wasn't aware of the wind building in the high canopy. Or that the birds had disappeared.

CHAPTER TWENTY-SIX

In the dark Juli woke to Rich shaking her, "Wake up! Wake up, we've got to leave. Right now."

Dazed from sleep Juli couldn't understand what was going on. "Rich I need to sleep." She snuggled back into their sleeping bag and was instantly asleep.

"Juli," he screamed as he backed out of the tent, pulling on her foot.

"Rich what is it?" She flipped over and crawled on her hands and knees, grabbing her clothes. Heart pounding. The last time he woke her, wolves were stalking them. "Is it the wolves?"

"No. . . . fire." He pulled roughly on her arm trying to hurry her out of the tent. "No rain this summer . . . forest is tinder."

Juli sniffed, noticing the smell of smoke for the first time. "What's happening?"

"Thunder woke me. Didn't you hear it?"

"No. I was exhausted. I slept." Was that her groggy voice?

Rich darted in and out of the tent grabbing their possessions like a squirrel trying to get her babies to safety. "Probably a lightning strike . . . I smell smoke, lots of smoke."

"No," she cried as she scrambled to her feet, fully awake now, pulse racing. "This can't be happening."

Rich was standing, staring toward the forest to the north. "The winds are in the canopy," he warned.

"What a nightmare." Juli's heart raced. She felt panic. She jerked upright, hitting her head on Rich's outstretched arm.

His voice struggled to be calm. Nonetheless she could hear the urgency he was unable to disguise. "Douglas fir are whipping back and forth. Propelling fire through the forest." He sounded breathless, "Hear the crackles?"

She could, much to her horror. She pulled on her jeans and hoodie but didn't bother with her shoes.

His staccato voice continued, "Animals racing past. No flames . . . yet." He struggled into his jacket.

"I'm moving," she gasped breathlessly as she started to pull up the tent pegs.

He shouted, "Leave the tent." Pulling on his hat he grabbed her hand screaming, "Boat . . . go to . . . boat." They raced toward the runabout propelled by fear. Three stags, eyes wide, nostrils flaring, bounced past. The harsh breathing egged them on. Slipping on the round beach rocks they each grabbed a gunwale and hauled the boat over the rough beach like super-humans. Juli didn't feel the skin on her feet bruising in her haste to reach safety.

She stumbled as she clutched the bow of the runabout, which was parallel to the beach. Rich stepped into the stern and pushed off, forcing the stern into deep water. Waves slapped at the hull as he started the engine. Adrenalin driving her muscles she jumped on the bow pushing away from shore with all her might. Simultaneously Rich slammed the motor into reverse. Swiftly swinging her legs over the gunwale she thumped onto the bow seat. The runabout rocketed backwards into the inlet. The engine coughed and died. Juli's heart skipped a beat, was she going to end her life like this? In a blaze of fire? Their baby hadn't had a chance yet. Smoked filled her nostrils. She covered her nose with the neck of her hoodie. The bow swung toward the entrance of the narrow inlet. Rich calmly went through the starting procedure again as though this was a routine event. The engine hiccoughed and caught, and roared as Rich fed it more fuel, driving the boat ahead. Wind whistled past her ears. "That's it Juli, we're doing it," shouted Rich. They weren't safe yet. They could die. Cold sweat ran between her shoulder blades unnoticed. A squirrel screamed behind them. A deer swam past heading to shore, toward their abandoned tent. She feared for its life, but could do nothing. Rich grunted behind her, "We have a chance. Stay calm and hang on. The tide is slack."

The wind is behind us and will drive the fire our way. She hunched down in the boat. "I'm hanging on . . . as hard . . . as I can." Her hands grasping the metal gunwale were starting to ache and burn. Would the wind blow the hungry fire on to them? Would the smoke destroy their lungs? Would the fire consume all the oxygen? Was this Armageddon?

"We have to get through to the open," he shouted. "This small inlet could boil from the heat."

"I'm praying," shouted Juli over the crack of tree tops breaking in the wind. Pulse racing. Sweat beading on her forehead. Trying not to panic. She could calmly manage catastrophic bleeding, heart attacks and broken accident victims, but a raging fire of this magnitude was way out of her comfort zone. Nonetheless she trusted Rich to make good decisions, his knowledge was far greater than hers. She would focus her energy on surviving, every cell in her body reached out to Rich to assist him to propel them to the safety of the open ocean.

"Love, soak your hair with water," ordered Rich as he dipped his hat in the ocean and plopped it on his head. He strained his eyes peering ahead through the darkness, which was lit in flickers from the raging inferno behind them. Forcing the boat to speed through the water now starting to flow into the inlet, they were in a slow motion movie, a horrible movie of death by fire.

Juli's heart pounded like a bird trapped in a cage as adrenalin rallied her body to flee. She forced her voice to be calm, "Flames. Over there," she pointed to the north and east.

"Soak your hair again. Pull your hood up and keep your head down," his voice was hoarse with effort.

Juli dipped her hand in the ocean, splashing water over her head and shoulders, grateful that they had a possible escape route. The sickening odor of burning wood and charring flesh assailed her nostrils; the final screams of scorching forest animals surrounded them and would echo through her memory forever. She scooped more water onto her head, pulled her hood up and wet it, too. For good measure she rubbed a handful of water on her tummy, thinking *here's for you baby. Don't worry you are safe deep in my tummy.* The water was still cool, that was a good sign. Maybe they had a chance.

They bent low, protecting their faces. The incoming current strengthened as they neared the mouth of the inlet. "We're doing it Juli. Just a little further." The straining engine moved them slowly, painfully forward, seeking safety. As they squeezed through the narrow entrance the sight of ocean ahead gave her hope. Gradually they crept forward past the wolf rocks and finally, painfully, into the safer water of Sutil Channel. Juli rested on the gunwale, laughing with relief. They would live; their baby was safe.

Once in the channel Rich turned the boat so they could watch the forest. The flames jumped the inlet, where they had been moments ago, leaping from swaying crowns on the north to their twins on the south. It was as if a torch bearer was holding a flame which ignited the tinder-dry firs as he leapt across the narrow inlet. Fire spewed; pine cones ruptured with bangs like rifle shots. Black smoke descended in waves. Trees exploded. Animals screamed. Fear. Death. Destruction.

Juli started to cry, tears ran in a torrent down her cheeks. "Those poor animals."

Rich was concerned for the wild life but his first priority was people. "A family lives on the inlet. I hope they evacuated." As if on command a small power boat and then a sailboat spurted out of the inlet, racing, fighting for their lives.

Juli flicked her light to announce their presence. The two boats drew close, converging slowly until the power boat was on their left and the sailboat on their right. "Rich it's Dream Seeker. I didn't know they were up here." Rich smiled a welcome as they came along side. Dave and Marigold greeted them from the deck of their sleek sailboat. Marigold waved gaily and shouted, "Hi Juli. What are you doing here? Stay close." Juli waved back. Dave was at the helm in shorts and wind jacket while Marigold looked very prepared and nautical in her yellow foul-weather gear. Their runabout seemed as small as a mouse next to an elephant as it bumped against the sleek yacht. Dave leaned over the railing, "Hi you two. That was a close call." Marigold bubbled, still on an adrenalin high, "Dave and I were having a little honeymoon weekend. Thought it would be the quietest night of our life." She laughed almost hysterically, "Something woke me. The whistling of the wind through the struts and the metallic clank of the halyard against the mast . . . the screaming of squirrels . . . the smell of smoke. I called Dave. He didn't move. Shrugged into my foul weather gear. Grabbed the flashlight and went up on deck. The wind whipped my hair into my face and tore at my clothes. I hung on to the safety line and felt my way to the bow." Marigold gestured dramatically with her hands as she leaned over the safety line to her audience below. "I had to check the anchor line as it might chafe through. I decided to feed another line. I took the extra line fastened to the top of the cabin and continued forward. It wasn't easy. Right then a stag plunged into the ocean screaming. I looked up and saw flames being tossed across the canopy. I roared back into the cabin and shook Dave and started the engine. By the time he was at the helm I was hauling in the anchor rode and the anchor. Dave gunned it and here we are." She clung to the lines and leaned further down toward the runabout. "I was scared."

Juli stood up to pat Marigold's outstretched hand to comforted her, "You're okay now Marigold."

Dave moved to put his arm around his wife. Juli heard her sigh with relief.

"Rich and I were here for a quiet weekend too."

On their other side in a large old wooden runabout was a family of four, Bob and Janice Rogers and their two children: Ocean and Sky. They basically babbled their fear and their greetings, then they all sat in silent horror watching the flames lighting the sky. They clung together for about an hour with Dave and Marigold serving hot steaming chocolate drinks and cheese sandwiches as they bobbed together on the now choppy sea. Gradually Juli became calmer.

Bob Rogers announced, "We haven't had a fire like this for at least ten years. It was inevitable."

His wife added, "The forest was as dry as tinder."

"Then you think lightning started it?"

"Yes, Mother Nature started it and Mother Nature will end it." Almost as Bob prophesied, the rain started. At first it was a sprinkling of tiny drops, then as though the heavens had opened giant drops splashed on them, warm wet blobs.

"If this keeps up and the wind continues to drop we'll be able to go back to our house," said Bob his voice hopeful. His children cried, "Daddy, we want to go home."

"Out of the mouth of babes," whispered Juli noticing the total trust the children had in their father and patted her tummy gently.

Janice added, "Our place is right on the water near the head of the inlet. We have a metal roof. Besides the fire was mainly across the upper part of the inlet. We had to duck under it on our way out. Bob will make sure we're safe."

Juli shivered with envy; she wanted what Janice had. *Juli, you fool, think about it; Rich does keep you safe.* Rich had kept her safe from the wolves and now the fire. Something melted deep within her as tears ran down her cheeks, tears of joy and thankfulness.

"So you and your family are heading back in. You could also come south with Juli and me," offered Rich generously, nodding at Bob. "We're going to my place near Manson's."

"Goin to Manson's? That's quite a distance in the dark," said Bob.

"Come along," Juli urged.

"We'll be okay. We can always anchor near the entrance for a few hours while it cools down." His wife nodded agreement. A little thing like a forest fire was not going to drive them off their property.

Rich turned to the sailboat asking, "And the Thorntons?"

"We're going to follow you back to the Gorge and make sure you're safe," Dave promised. Marigold nodded agreement.

"That would be welcome," said Rich appreciating Dave's support. Juli smiled with relief and thanks.

"We've decided to keep Dream Seeker at The Gorge Marina. It's easy to get a float plane to Victoria. That's how we got here and that's how we'll get home."

Marigold added, "This is going to be our home away from home. The plane makes commuting simple. We'll be neighbors."

"Great," smiled Rich. The wind continued to drop and the frequency of cracks from exploding wood was diminishing. And now that Marigold and Dave were accompanying them, they would be as safe as if they were secured to a dock, so Juli wasn't worried about their return trip.

"I thought your name was familiar and now I recognize your voice," said Bob. "You're the doctor. So I know you're sensible."

Juli could tell by their drift against the shore that they were being dragged south toward Rich's cabin, and if a moon came up and they had glimpses of it through the clouds it might be quite pleasant, particularly if the rain eased. She was grateful they had escaped and wanted to spend the rest of the weekend laying in his arms, breathing in his strength.

"When we get in cell phone or radio range we'll notify the coast guard where you are Bob. Good luck," called Dave as the flotilla broke up with Bob and his family moving toward the inlet, and the large sailboat and Rich's small runabout heading south together, looking like a whale with a baby at its side.

Black smoke and steam billowed above the forest and hovered like a menacing storm cloud. Juli was thankful she could no longer see flames licking toward the sky. As she peered forward she could vaguely see the dark edge of the shoreline. So here she was, for the second time in her life, in the middle of the night on a dark ocean in a tiny boat with Rich. This time not wolves but a raging wild fire had driven them off shore. Once again fear crept into her bones as swiftly as the crackling fire tearing through the forest, and she felt her hands tremble. Rich sensed her fear; he was concerned too but he felt confident on the water and knew they could safely navigate to his cabin. "Relax, Dave and Marigold will keep an eye on us. Their yacht can withstand anything."

"I know. I know," said Juli sliding to the mid-ship seat and leaning toward him. She liked the calm sound of his voice and knew this was not bragging or false reassurance, Rich knew what he was doing. He was calm under pressure, doctoring or captaining. Tonight when he woke her she had grasped the danger instantly and followed his directions without question. She trusted him. Completely. With her life and her baby's. She had known him only since July 24th and now she trusted him more than anyone else she knew. But it was more than that; she was solidly attracted to him, sexually attracted. She wanted to spend her life with him. She might even move to this island to be with him. He seemed to be as attracted to her as she to him. She felt his commitment, his willingness to work out differences. Her pulse slowed to normal and she looked around and saw he was right; they were smoothly proceeding down the center of the channel, the ocean helping them. She blinked her light at Dream Seeker, and Marigold flashed an answering light back. "That felt good . . . I like having them close by."

"Me too. The rain is getting lighter," said Rich. "Let's hope it continues until the fire is out."

"Yes."

Just then the moon peeked through the clouds and lit the water as it had the night they were fleeing from the wolves. Mother Nature was taking care of them, thought Juli. That was a sign, a good sign. On the other hand, two emergency middle of the night escapes from Von Donop Inlet certainly wouldn't encourage her to return there. They left Sutil Channel and turned southeast, keeping Marina Island on their right and Cortes on their left. The red and green buoy markers for Whaletown harbor were easily visible as they motored past. The ferry, which always overnighted on the island, was brightly lit; Juli wondered about that.

As they passed Shark Spit and entered Uganda passage, dawn, wearing a smoky pinkish pallor, gradually lit the dusky sky. A ginger-orange sun struggled to light their way. Juli wiped her eyes, blinking to wash the smoke out. The air still stank; smoke invaded her nose and tasted on her tongue. She would never forget this odor. An eerie quiet, broken only by the hum of their engine, closed around them like a cocoon. Sensing her unease, Rich leaned forward to whisper reassurances, "It's not much further. Hang in there Juli. It's going to be okay." She liked his concern. Near the entrance to Gorge Harbor Dave and Marigold waved as they passed them and turned into the harbor.

Rich leaned toward her, "Juli, we can follow them and stay at the marina."

"Rich that doesn't make sense. We're almost at your place."

"Right. But we could stay with your friends."

"Forget it. Let's keep going. I want to be in our bed tonight."

"You're a good sport."

"Not really, I need to be with you, alone." Juli sat straighter, forcing her eyes to stay open. Tears filled her eyes. She felt supported by Rich. Here was a man who would be a good friend and partner. "Do you think the fire has spread down here?"

"Before the rain the wind was out of the southeast," said Rich thoughtfully. "That would keep it up in the northern sector. Now I don't feel any wind, so that's in our favor. Except, of course, we have this haze hanging around." Suddenly then the sound of a large laboring plane attracted their attention. Rich looked up and waved. "There's the water bomber. It'll finish off anything that the rain doesn't get," shouted Rich as excited as a little boy who thinks Santa Claus has arrived at his house.

"That's good," said Juli, feeling safer than she had since Rich woke her. Suddenly, she wanted to put her head down as it was so heavy.

"Look." Rich pointed ahead at a motley collection of boats crowded together, "There's the public wharf at Manson's. We're almost home." The excitement in his voice fed energy to her adrenals.

We're almost home. We're almost home, Juli liked the sound of that. Over the glassy ocean Juli could see the public dock twinkling with fairy lights. The lights on the odd assortment of boats probably meant the residents were on the alert and uneasy because of the fires on the island.

They approached his dock slowly. Everything looked the same. How could it? She was so different. Steering them confidently Rich eased the boat next to the dock. They stayed still for a moment, then he said, "We're here. I'll steady us . . . you climb out."

"Thanks," said Juli softly. "This will be easier than when I had to get out of Yak."

He laughed, "You bet . . . maybe we can make it as much fun."

Juli eased onto the narrow dock, pulling the line with her, and wrapped it securely around a cleat.

Rich shut off the engine and scrambled out after her, wrapping his arms around her they clung together, grateful they were safe. His soft lips caressed her ear and he whispered huskily, "Welcome to my dock."

Juli whispered, "If you had been asleep we would have been trapped." He gently pulled her to her feet and led her off the dock and into the cabin.

Rich led her to the couch and sat beside her, "the animals warned us . . . they gave us our chance to escape."

The animals, that was another matter; of course they would be decimated with the youngest and oldest suffering the most. Tears ran down her cheeks. Juli covered her face with her hands and sobbed as if her heart would break. What was going on with her? Why was she so upset? It was a close call but they had escaped. No humans died. But still she felt a deep sadness . . . such devastation

"Juli come here," said Rich opening his arms. She moved into their protection and felt safe. "Juli tell me what's going on."

"I don't know. I'm full of grief. The animals. The forest." She heaved a great sigh. "Plus it's the work we do. I see people suffering every day. I can help some of them, but many I can't." The pain churned her gut and made her heart ache.

"Juli, love, we're part of a team; we play our part. We help as many as we can. The rest is up to our teammates. We're all working together."

"Rich you're so right. Thank you for reminding me. And of course, I'm not six years old anymore and living in fear."

"As for the animals only some of them died, many escaped." He gently smoothed her hair.

"I'm thankful for that," came her muffled voice as she snuggled into his arm reassured by his strength and calmness.

"Juli the animals will multiply and the forest will grow back. Animals are like that. Forests are like that. Some of the cones need intense heat to germinate. When we come back next year you won't know there was a fire . . . well except for a few standing burnt sentinels to remind us to be very careful with campfires."

Juli sniffed and pulled back from his chest. "We're so blessed." He watched her struggling to be brave as he gently wiped a tear off her cheek. "Juli I won't lie to you; the baby was a surprise, a good surprise. I wanted to have a child so badly with Sylvia that when she died I mourned for her and for the children we would never have. My work has been my life; I live day to day; I thought this would be my life forever. Then like a miracle from heaven you stepped into my kayak, fussing and fuming and challenging, and looking marvelously healthy and beautiful. At that moment something inside me shifted; a small kernel came alive again and kept expanding. I love you. I want to spend the rest of my life with you. Our child is icing on that cake."

Juli clung to him feeling love and relief pouring through her veins, igniting her with hope. She wanted to share this baby, share him or her with Rich.

Cutting into their thoughts his phone vibrated.

"Yikes." As he read the message Juli watched his face go pale so she knew it was something serious. Rich turned to her, holding her gently in his arms. "What is it Rich?"

"Fire caused havoc down here too . . . at Smelt Bay and Squirrel Cove. The health center is full of people with injuries. They want to treat as many as possible on the island . . . although the helicopter is on its way and the ferry is standing by."

"Oh my, that's terrible. We should go and help."

"Yup. But me, not we." He got up off the couch and patted a soft fleece blanket around her. "You stay here and rest with the baby."

"Don't be crazy. I'm coming." She pushed the blanket off. "You're my baby too and I have to keep an eye on you."

Rich smiled. "I was afraid you'd say that. Let's help out. . . I'll watch your back and you mine, then we'll know when it's time to leave. We'll both remember we're part of a team. We'll help but we'll stay healthy ourselves."

"Right. Speaking of teams, I'm phoning Dave. Maybe he'll help too. That would lighten the load." As she talked Juli dialed Marigold's cell which had reception at the Gorge. "Marigold, hi. Rich and I are heading to the health center at Manson's. Apparently it's been inundated with fire injuries." She listened. "Correct. Rich and I are going. The baby is fine." She listened again. "That would really help. Hope to see you there. Bye. For now." She turned to Rich, "Marigold's going to talk with Dave. I don't know if we can count on him or not. But let's go."

"I have our supplies ready." As he talked he headed for the door and down to the dock. Juli followed, grabbing their water bottles as she left.

As before, the runabout took them swiftly to Manson's Landing and their waiting truck. Within minutes they were at the health center. The parking lot was so crowded that they parked on the road and walked back, greeting people as they went.

They slipped in the back door through the ambulance entrance. All the stretcher-beds were full, plus other patients, arms in slings, heads bandaged, and IV drips running, sat around the perimeter. All smiled or nodded when they saw their beloved doctor. Rich went through, with Juli following like the tail of a comet, to the hall between the treatment rooms where they ran into Mary looking harassed and tired. "Thank God you're here. We're bursting at the seams."

"Give us a status report then we'll get to work. You remember Juli Armstrong? She'll work too."

This time Mary greeted Juli with a hug, "Thank you so much for coming. I didn't know how much longer we could keep up this pace."

Andy appeared from an examining room, stopped abruptly and smiled when he saw them. "Welcome. You are in time."

Rich smiled and shook his hand.

Then Andy was all business: "We shipped Ted T and John P off in the ambulance for smoke inhalation. The helicopter is coming in for Mike E who looks like a myocardial infarction. We'll send him to RJH's cardiac ICU."

Mary chimed in, "In the waiting room we have Sydney with chest pain, Muriel with burned fingers, and several asthma attacks, and a sore throat, and a baby with a fever. And the whole volunteer fire department needs to be checked over."

Andy said, "As before Mary can triage." They all nodded agreement. Mary added, "How do you guys want me to stream these patients?"

"I've had experience with burns lately," offered Juli.

Andy nodded approval and said, "I'll take the breathing problems."

Rich smiled and said, "I'll take anything."

Juli noted to talk to him later, as she knew it was more difficult to handle a large variety of patients, and Rich needed to think about ways he could lower his stress level and stay healthy and still practice medicine.

"Okay, let's get going." Rich rubbed his hands together, ready for the challenge.

A commotion at the front entrance drew their attention. Dave, carrying his medical bag, and Marigold burst into the hallway. "We're here. Don't know if we're any good, but we're here." Dave looked frazzled but willing and Marigold looked worried. Rich aware of Dave's struggle with depression and anxiety stepped forward and shook his hand. "We have the best job for you. We have fifteen or so volunteer firefighters who need to be checked over and any fire related injuries noted and treated. We can put you in treatment room three," he looked at Mary who nodded agreement, "and funnel them to you."

He turned to Marigold, "Glad you're here . . . can you be his assistant?"

"Gofer you mean. Sure, that's why I'm here, and if anyone needs a portrait sketched I can do that too."

They all smiled with the load lightened. Dave headed for the treatment room already containing a firefighter.

The next four hours flew by as they provided good care for all the patients. When the last patient left they finished their dictation and gathered in the coffee room. Rich was tired and he was flushed. Juli knew he was hypertensive. She handed him a cup of hot tea laced with sugar and milk." Marigold and Dave appeared hand in hand, "We're done. Every single firefighter checked over and sent home. . . except for five referred on to Comox: Rex R . . . headache and vomiting, possible carbon monoxide poisoning, Tom Z with red eyes possible corneal burn, three others with hoarseness and coughs and bronchial spasms going for chest x-rays.

"Good work Dave," smiled Rich clasping his hand. Dave smiled and put his arm around Marigold and pulled her close.

Andy and Mary were exhausted too, "Thanks to all of you. Without your help and expertise this would not be finishing so well. It'll calm down now, and Mary and I can handle the rest."

After handshakes all around and more thanks, Dave and Marigold, and Rich and Juli, walked out together smiling companionably. Juli could see by their loving glances Marigold and Dave were solid as a couple again. The foursome stopped in the parking lot, giving each other hugs, and Dave said, "We're flying back day after tomorrow. So we'll see you in Victoria." Their ride back to the marina was waiting so Dave and Marigold climbed in the car and waved goodbye.

Rich put his arm around Juli's waist and hugged her close, "Come Love, let's go home and give our baby a rest." Juli sunk into his arms realizing how tired she was and grateful for his strength. "Remember I love you and want to spend the rest of my life with you."

Juli let out her breath as tears filled her eyes. "Rich that's how I feel too." Juli knew there was a lot to sort out and that the road ahead would be full of exciting challenges, but Rich was a good match for her and she knew deep in her heart that they would be good parents and good lovers.

So our intentions came true: Marigold's intention to send me a sexy, healthy man, Rich if possible; and my intention for Marigold and Dave to be happy and smiling and supporting one another; and finally, my intention to have the best holiday of my life.

And now my intention is to live in

harmony, peace, and love

with

Rich and our baby.

****

Vanessa Mateland

makes her home in Victoria, British Columbia. When she and her husband cruised the Desolation Sound area in 2005, she fell in love with Cortes Island. With the loving support of her husband they built a small cabin. Since then they have spent many happy summers swimming and boating in the warm pristine waters. Vanessa weaves this tale with this stunning island as the backdrop.

43752367R00232

Made in the USA
Charleston, SC
05 July 2015